WITHD
D1092433

This volume contains INU-YASHA PART 3 #3 (second half) through INU-YASHA
PART 3 #7 in their entirety.

STORY AND ART BY
RUMIKO TAKAHASHI

ENGLISH ADAPTATION BY
GERARD JONES

Translation/Mari Morimoto
Touch-Up Art & Lettering/Wayne Truman & Bill Schuch

Director of Sales & Marketing/Dallas Middaugh
Marketing Manager/Renée Solberg
Sales Representative/Mike Roberson
Assistant Editor/Bill Flanagan
Cover Design/Hidemi Sahara
Graphics & Layout/Sean Lee
Editor/Julie Davis
Editor-in-Chief/Hyoe Narita
Publisher/Seiji Horibuchi

Printed in Canada

Published by Viz Communications, Inc.
P.O. Box 77010 • San Francisco, CA 94107
www.viz.com and www.j-pop.com

10 9 8 7 6 5 4 3 2
First printing, May 2000
Second printing, July 2001

INU-YASHA GRAPHIC NOVELS TO DATE:

INU-YASHA VOL. 1
INU-YASHA VOL. 2
INU-YASHA VOL. 3
INU-YASHA VOL. 4
INU-YASHA VOL. 5
INU-YASHA VOL. 6
INU-YASHA VOL. 7
INU-YASHA VOL. 8
INU-YASHA VOL. 9

VIZ GRAPHIC NOVEL

INU-YASHA
A FEUDAL FAIRY TALE™
VOL. 6

STORY AND ART BY
RUMIKO TAKAHASHI

CONTENTS

SCROLL ONE
HATRED UNSPENT
7

SCROLL TWO
A SOUL ASUNDER
27

SCROLL THREE
MONK ON THE MAKE
45

SCROLL FOUR
JEWEL THIEF
63

SCROLL FIVE
WIND TO NOWHERE
81

SCROLL SIX
THE CURSED HAND
99

SCROLL SEVEN
THE MONSTER WITHIN
117

SCROLL EIGHT
THE MASTER PAINTER
135

SCROLL NINE
THE ARTIST'S DREAM
153

SCROLL TEN
TAINTED INK
171

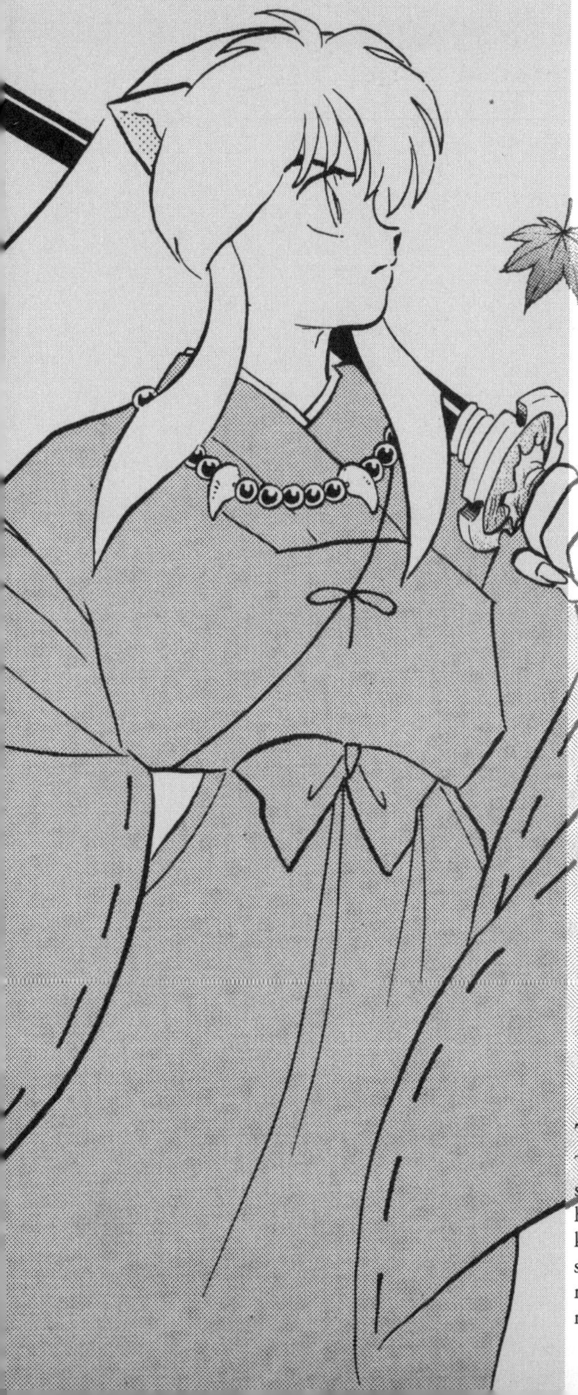

THE STORY THUS FAR

Long ago, in Japan's era of the "Warring States" era of Japan's Muromachi period (Sengoku-jidai, approximately 1467-1568 CE), a legendary doglike half-demon called "Inu-Yasha" attempted to steal the Shikon Jewel, or "Jewel of Four Souls," from a village, but was stopped by the enchanted arrow of the village priestess, Kikyo. Inu-Yasha fell into a deep sleep, pinned to a tree by Kikyo's arrow, while the mortally wounded Kikyo took the Shikon Jewel with her into the fires of her funeral pyre. Years passed.

Fast forward to the present day. Kagome, a Japanese high-school girl, is pulled into a well one day by mysterious centipede monster, and finds herself transported into the past, only to come face to face with the trapped Inu-Yasha. She frees him, and Inu-Yasha readily defeats the centipede monster.

The residents of the village, now fifty years older, readily accept Kagome as the reincarnation of their deceased priestess Kikyo, a claim supported by the fact that the Shikon Jewel emerges from a cut on Kagome's body. Unfortunately, the jewel's rediscovery means that the village is soon under attack by a variety of demons in search of this treasure. Then, the jewel is accidentally shattered into many shards, each of which may have the fearsome power of the entire jewel.

Although Inu-Yasha says he hates Kagome because of her resemblance to Kikyo, the woman who "killed" him, he is forced to team up with her when Kaede, the village leader, binds him to Kagome with a powerful spell. Now the two grudging companions must fight to reclaim and reassemble the shattered shards of the Shikon Jewel before they fall into the wrong hands.

THIS VOLUME

The resurrected body of Kikyo, now possessed by her vengeful spirit, cannot let go of her hatred for Inu-Yasha as the demon who killed her. And since Kagome's reincarnated soul was used by the orgress Urasue to animate Kikyo's corpse, Kagome herself is now no more than a soulless husk…or is she?

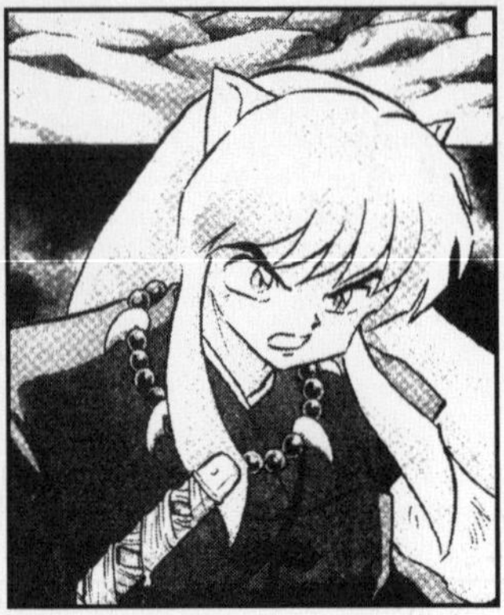

INU-YASHA
A half-human, half-demon hybrid son of a human mother and a demon father, Inu-Yasha resembles a human but has the claws of a demon, a thick mane of white hair, and ears rather like a dog's. The necklace he wears carries a powerful spell which allows Kagome to control him with a single word. Because of his human half, Inu-Yasha's powers are different from those of full-blooded monsters—a fact that the Shikon Jewel has the power to change.

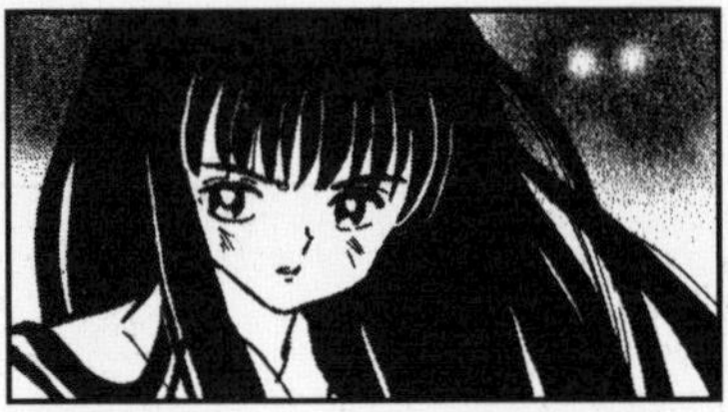

KIKYO
A powerful priestess, Kikyo was charged with the awesome responsibility of protecting the Shikon Jewel from demons and humans who coveted its power. She died after firing the enchanted arrow that kept Inu-Yasha imprisoned for fifty years.

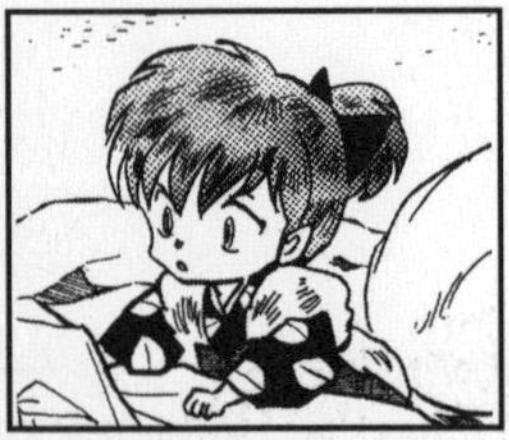

SHIPPÔ
A young fox-demon, orphaned by two other demons whose powers had been boosted by the Shikon Jewel, the mischievous Shippô enjoys goading Inu-Yasha and playing tricks with his shape-changing abilities.

KAGOME
Working with Inu-Yasha to recover the shattered shards of the Shikon Jewel, Kagome routinely travels into Japan's past through an old, magical well on her family's property. All this time travel means she's stuck with living two separate lives in two separate centuries, and she's beginning to worry that she'll never be able to catch up to her schoolwork.

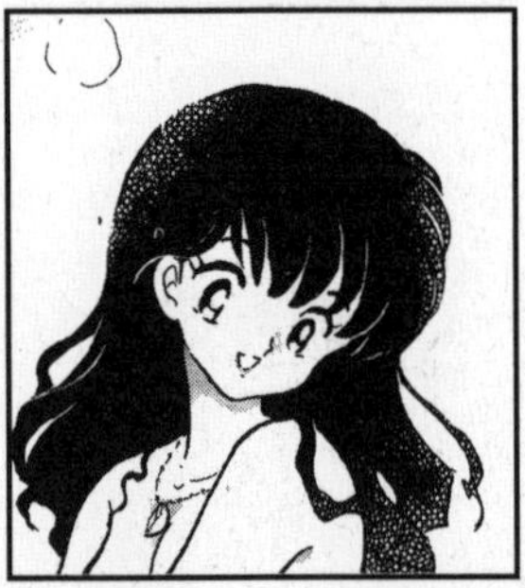

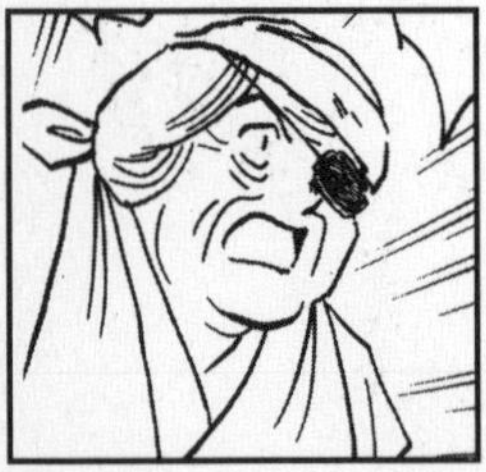

KAEDE
Kikyo's little sister, who carried out the priestess' wish that the Shikon Jewel should be burned with her remains. Now fifty years older, Kaede is head of the village. It is Kaede's spell that binds Inu-Yasha to Kagome by means of a string of prayer beads and Kagome's spoken word—"Sit!"

MIROKU
An easygoing Buddhist priest with questionable morals, Miroku is the carrier of a curse passed down from his grandfather. He is searching for the demon Naraku, who first inflicted the curse.

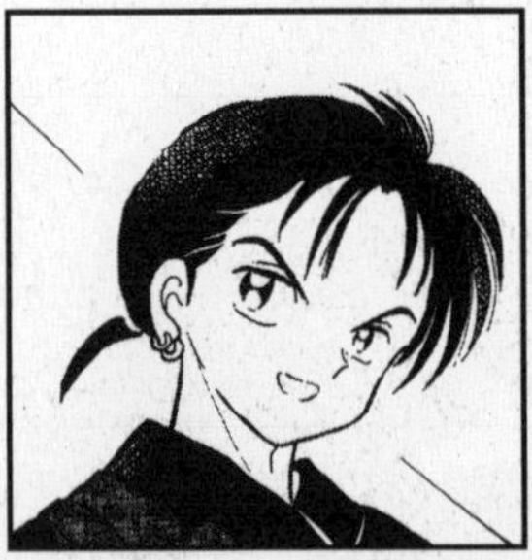

SCROLL ONE

HATRED UNSPENT

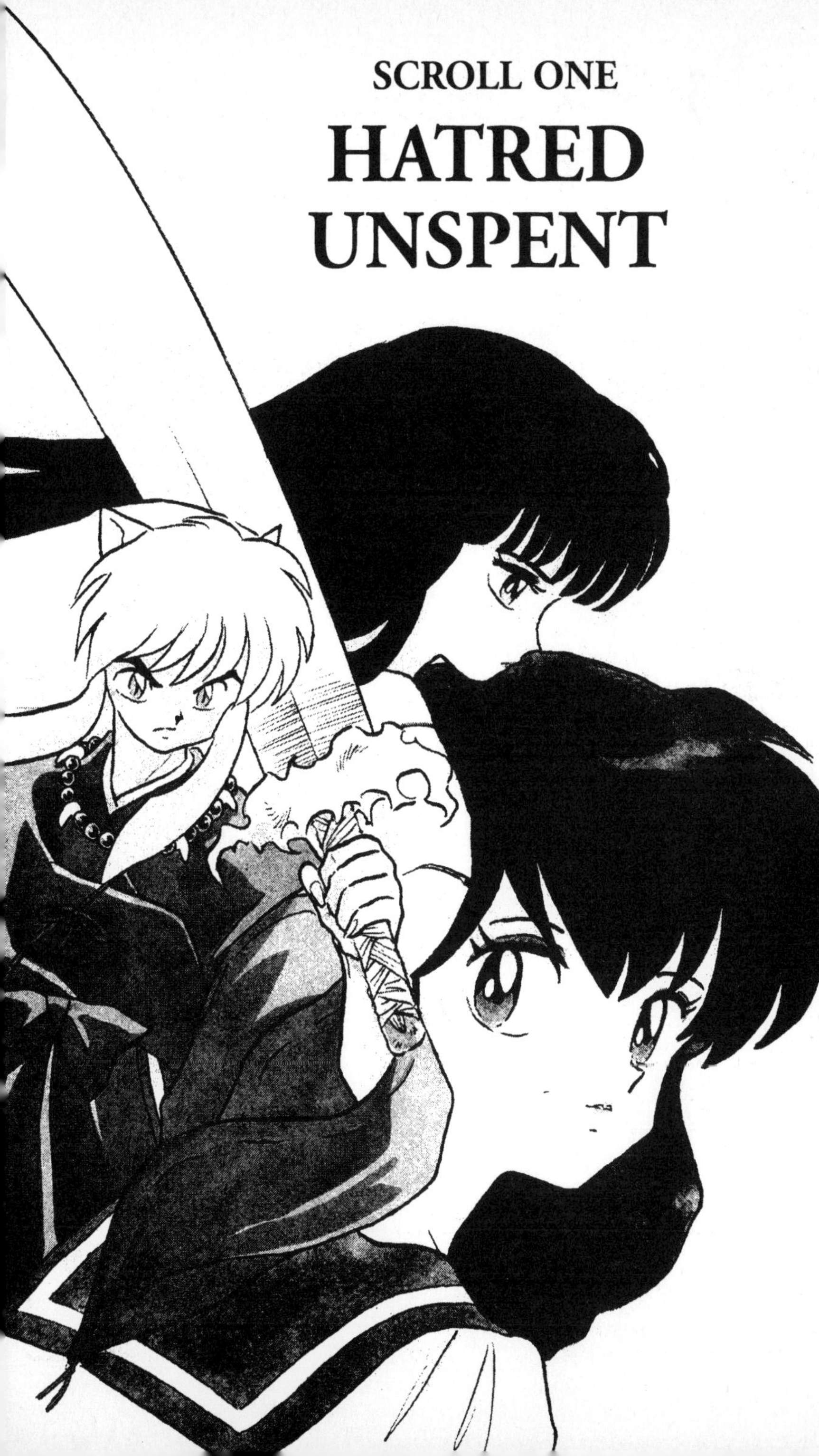

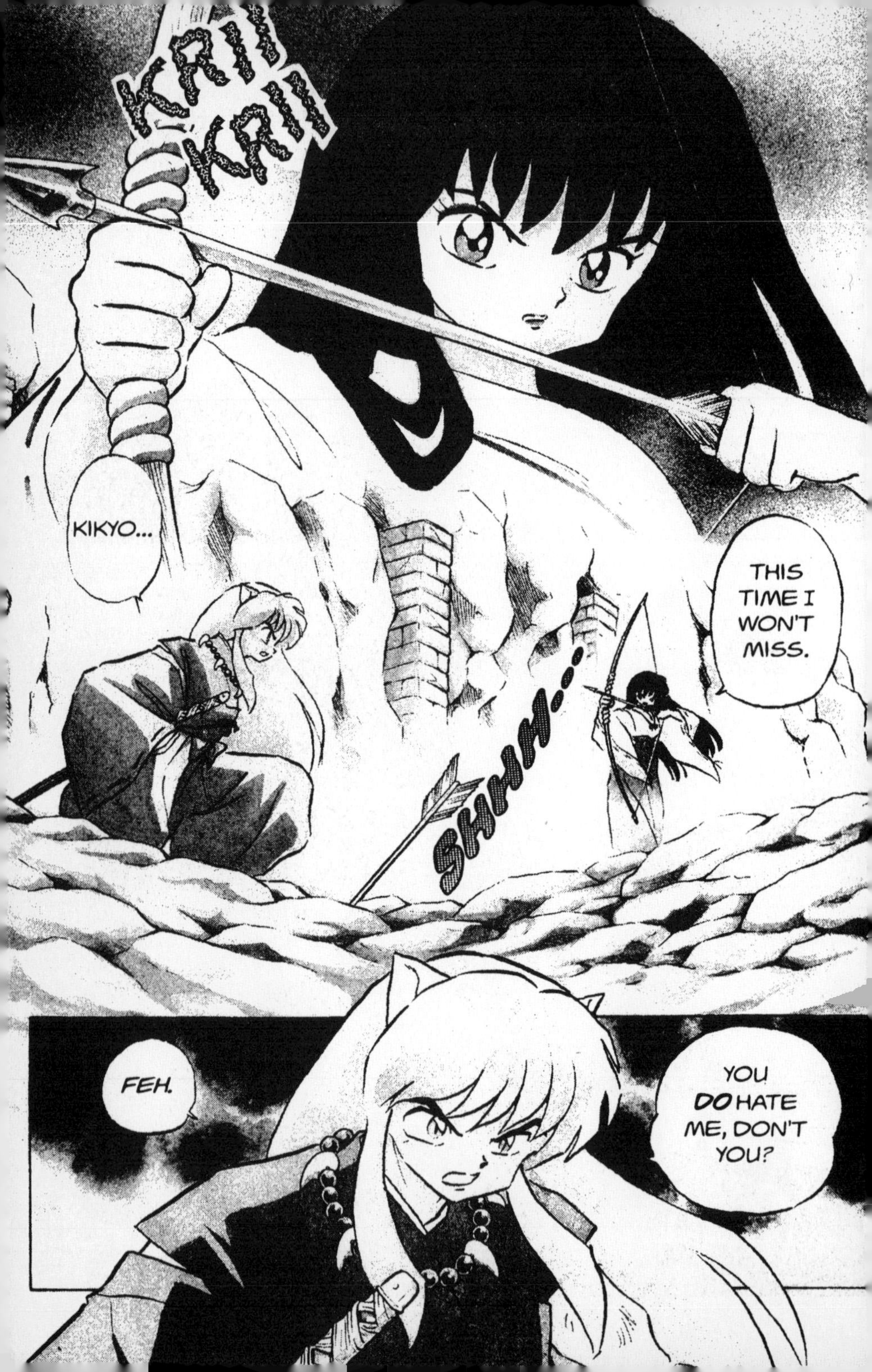
KRII KRII
KIKYO...
THIS TIME I WON'T MISS.
SHHH...
FEH.
YOU **DO** HATE ME, DON'T YOU?

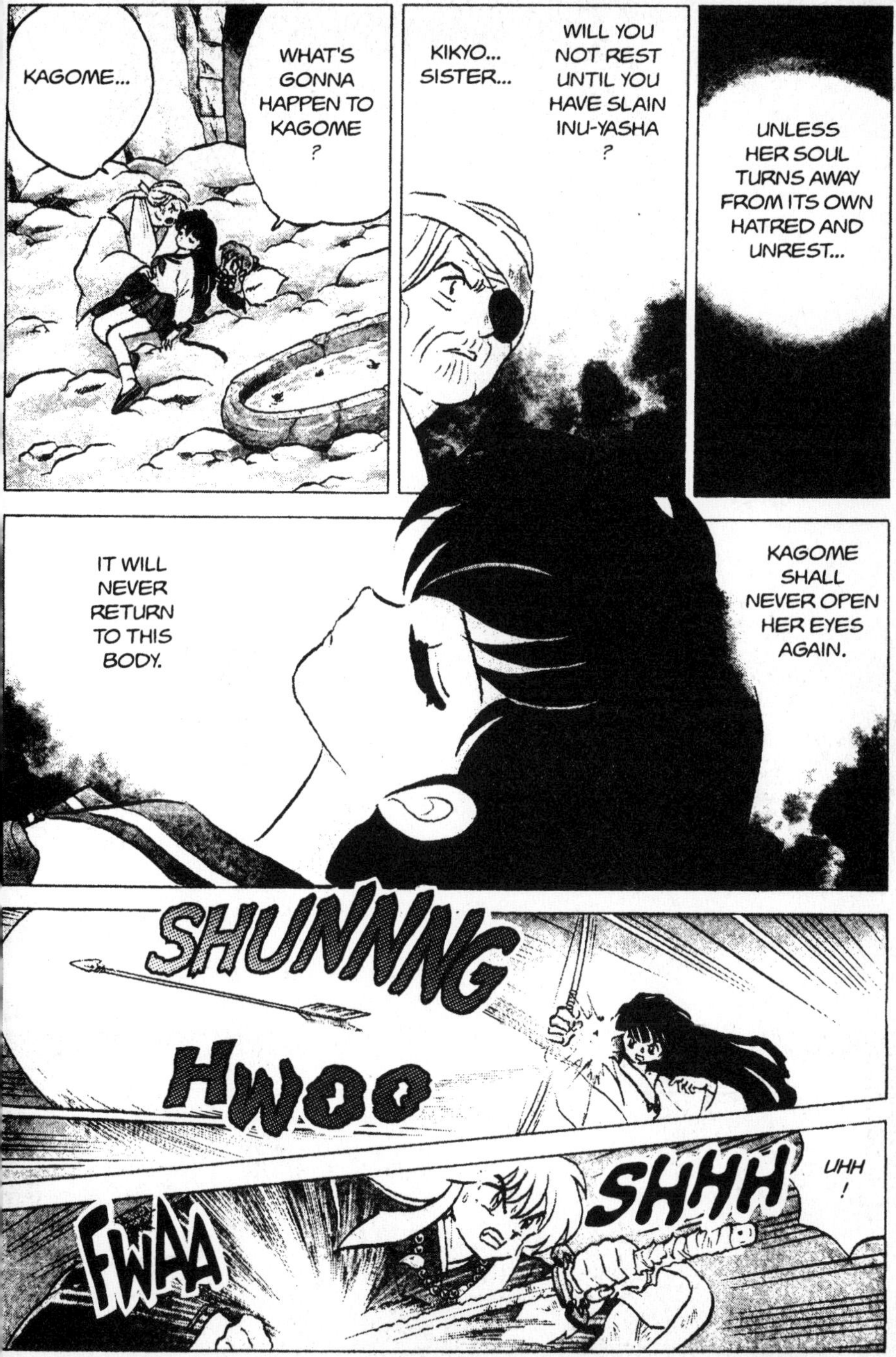
KAGOME...
WHAT'S GONNA HAPPEN TO KAGOME ?
KIKYO... SISTER...
WILL YOU NOT REST UNTIL YOU HAVE SLAIN INU-YASHA ?
UNLESS HER SOUL TURNS AWAY FROM ITS OWN HATRED AND UNREST...
IT WILL NEVER RETURN TO THIS BODY.
KAGOME SHALL NEVER OPEN HER EYES AGAIN.
SHUNNNG
HWOO
FWAA
SHHH
UHH !

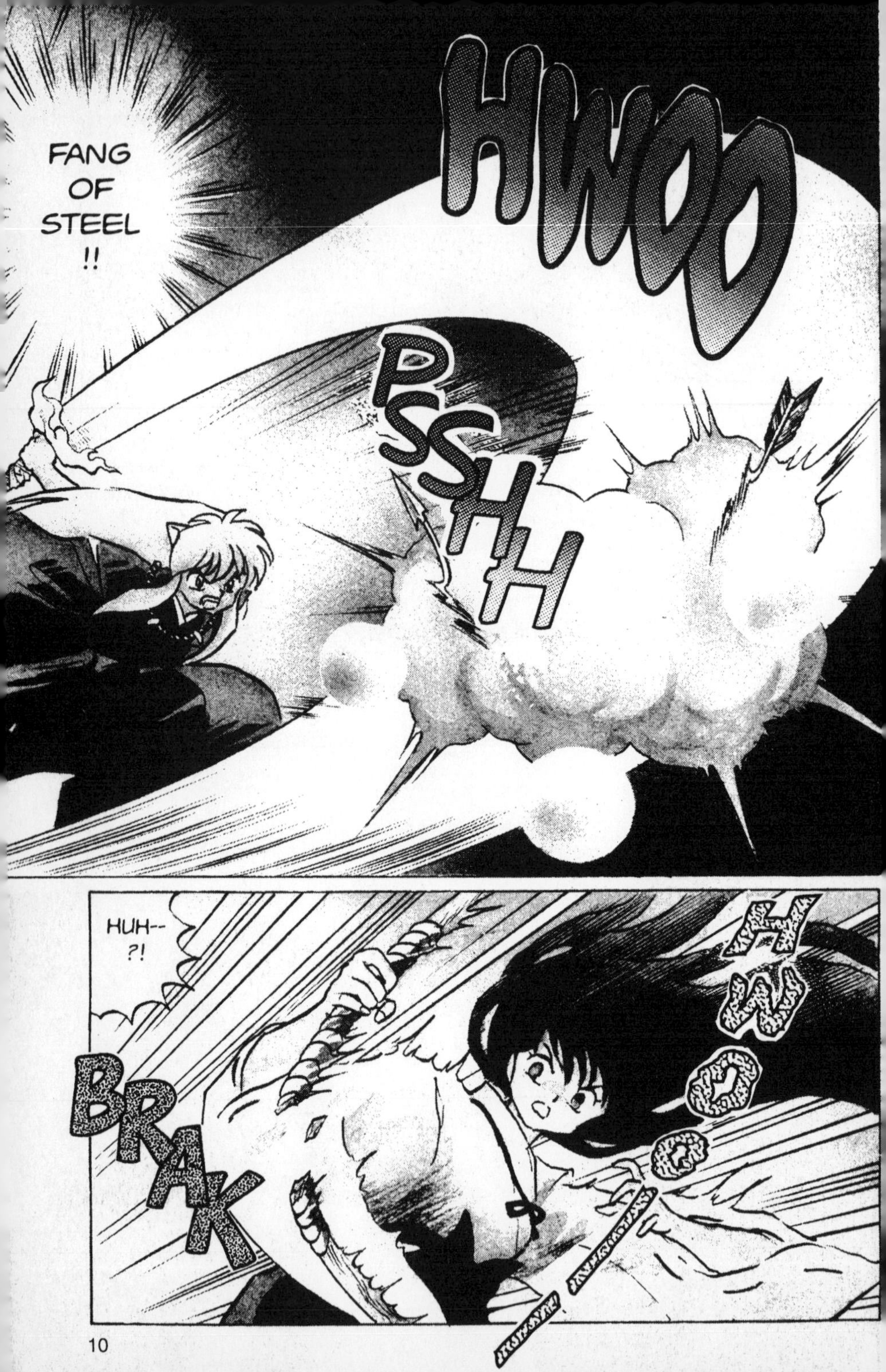
FANG OF STEEL !!
HWOO
PSSHH
HUH-- ?!
BRAK
HWOOO

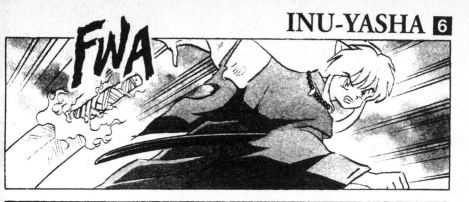

HE'S
THROWING
AWAY THE
TETSUSAIGA...
?!

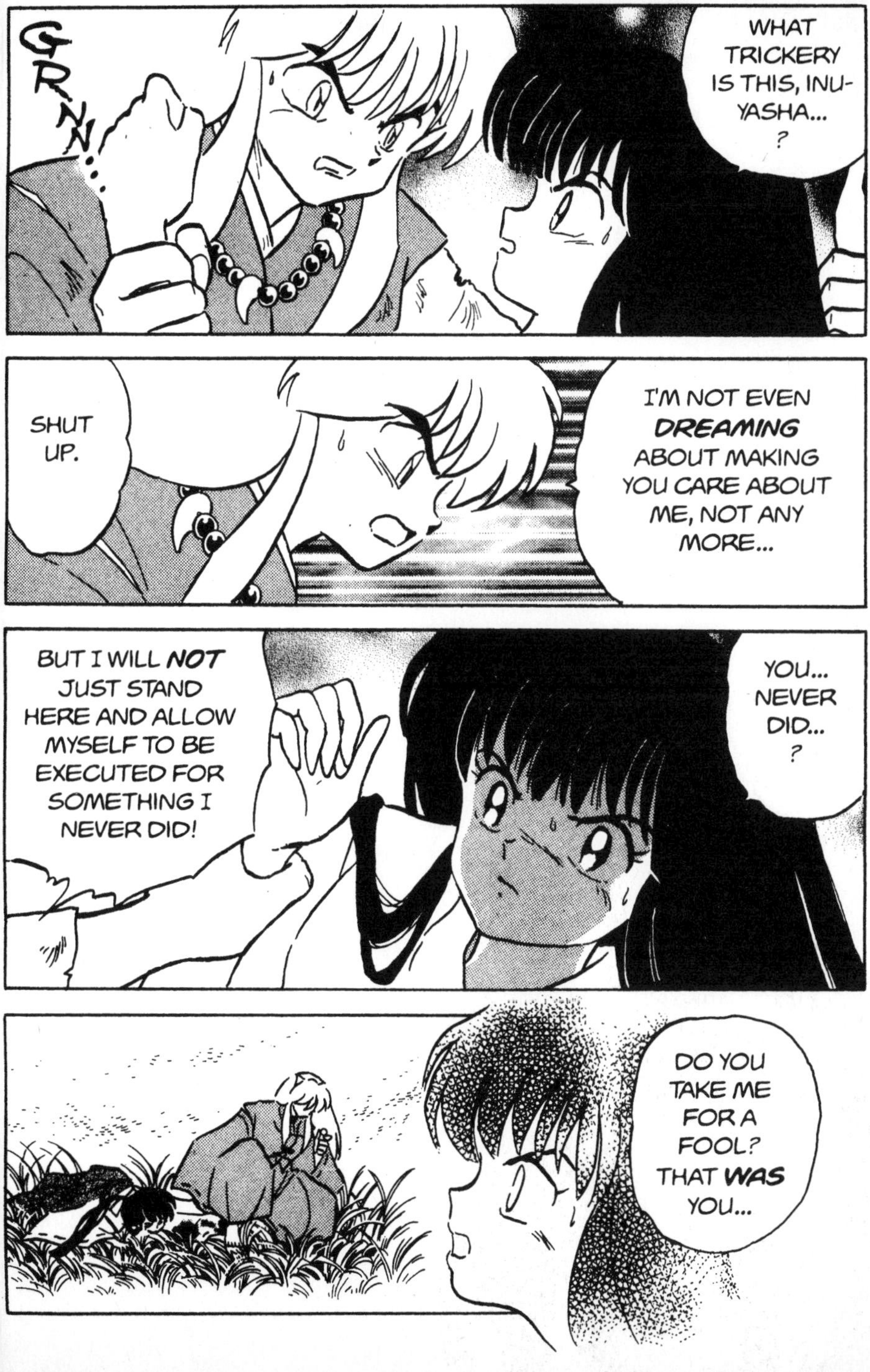
GRNN...
WHAT TRICKERY IS THIS, INU-YASHA... ?
SHUT UP.
I'M NOT EVEN DREAMING ABOUT MAKING YOU CARE ABOUT ME, NOT ANY MORE...
BUT I WILL NOT JUST STAND HERE AND ALLOW MYSELF TO BE EXECUTED FOR SOMETHING I NEVER DID!
YOU... NEVER DID... ?
DO YOU TAKE ME FOR A FOOL? THAT WAS YOU...

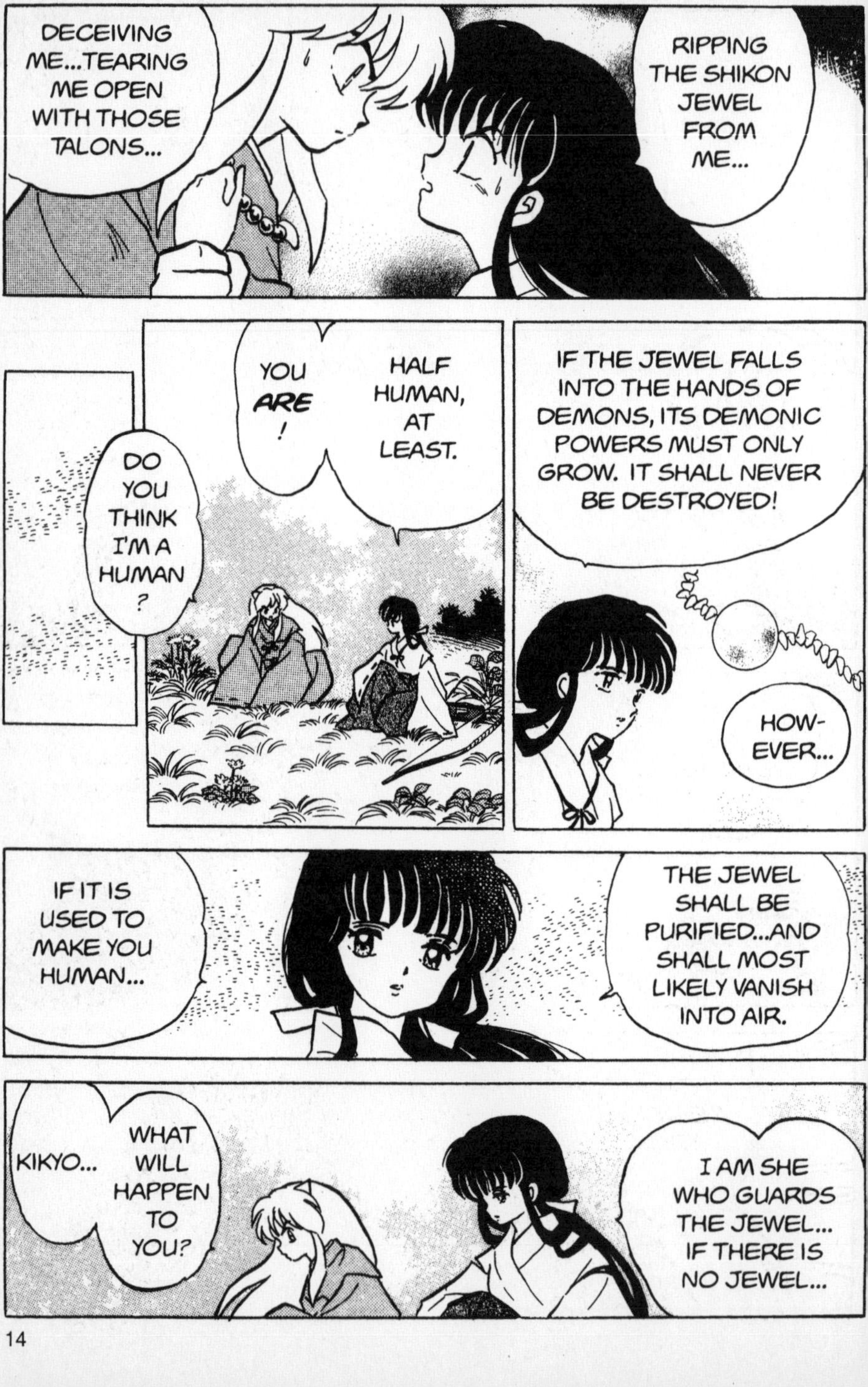
DECEIVING ME...TEARING ME OPEN WITH THOSE TALONS...
RIPPING THE SHIKON JEWEL FROM ME...
DO YOU THINK I'M A HUMAN?
YOU *ARE*!
HALF HUMAN, AT LEAST.
IF THE JEWEL FALLS INTO THE HANDS OF DEMONS, ITS DEMONIC POWERS MUST ONLY GROW. IT SHALL NEVER BE DESTROYED!
HOW-EVER...
IF IT IS USED TO MAKE YOU HUMAN...
THE JEWEL SHALL BE PURIFIED...AND SHALL MOST LIKELY VANISH INTO AIR.
KIKYO...
WHAT WILL HAPPEN TO YOU?
I AM SHE WHO GUARDS THE JEWEL... IF THERE IS NO JEWEL...

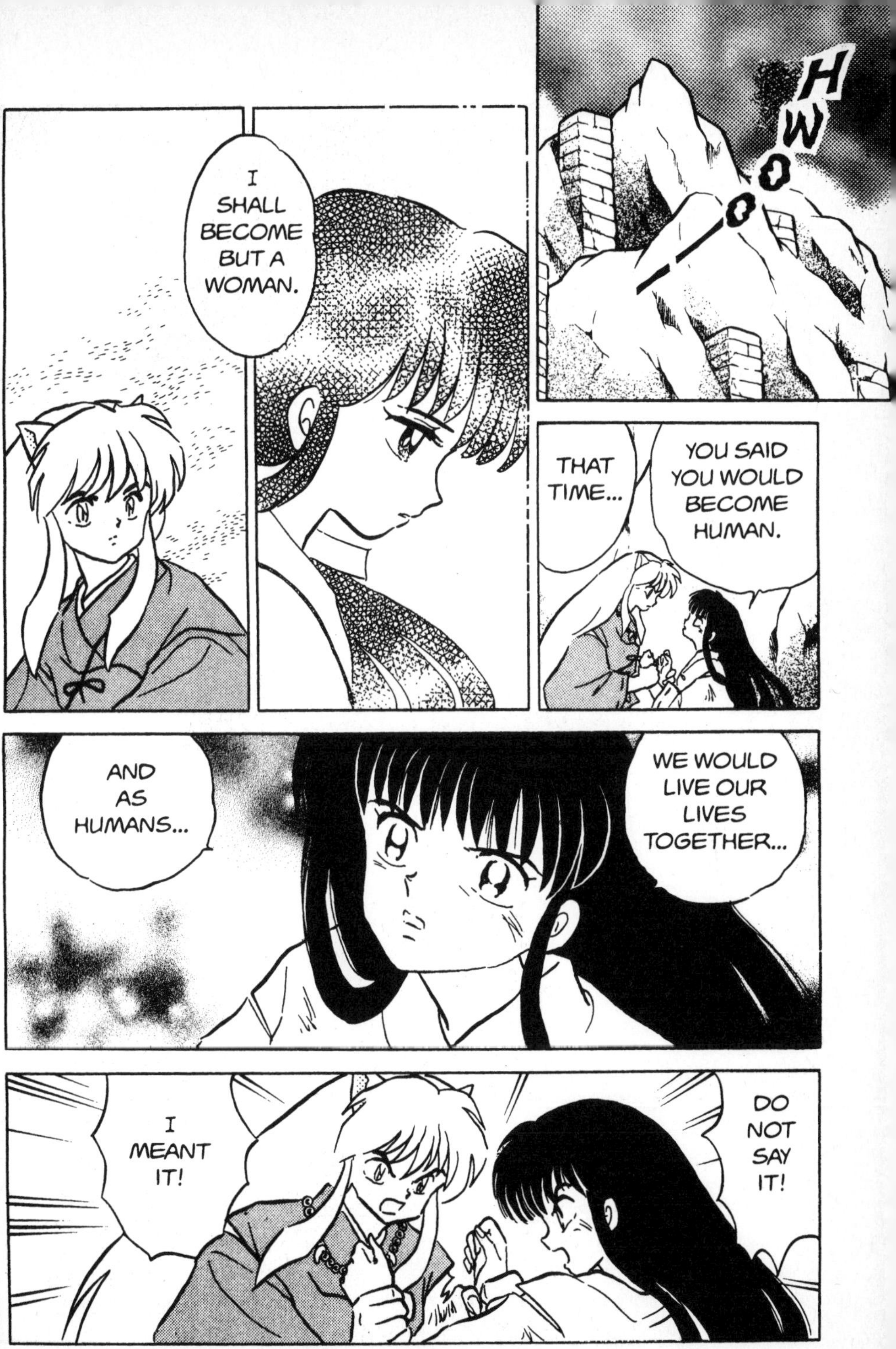
I SHALL BECOME BUT A WOMAN.
HWOOO
THAT TIME...
YOU SAID YOU WOULD BECOME HUMAN.
AND AS HUMANS...
WE WOULD LIVE OUR LIVES TOGETHER...
I MEANT IT!
DO NOT SAY IT!

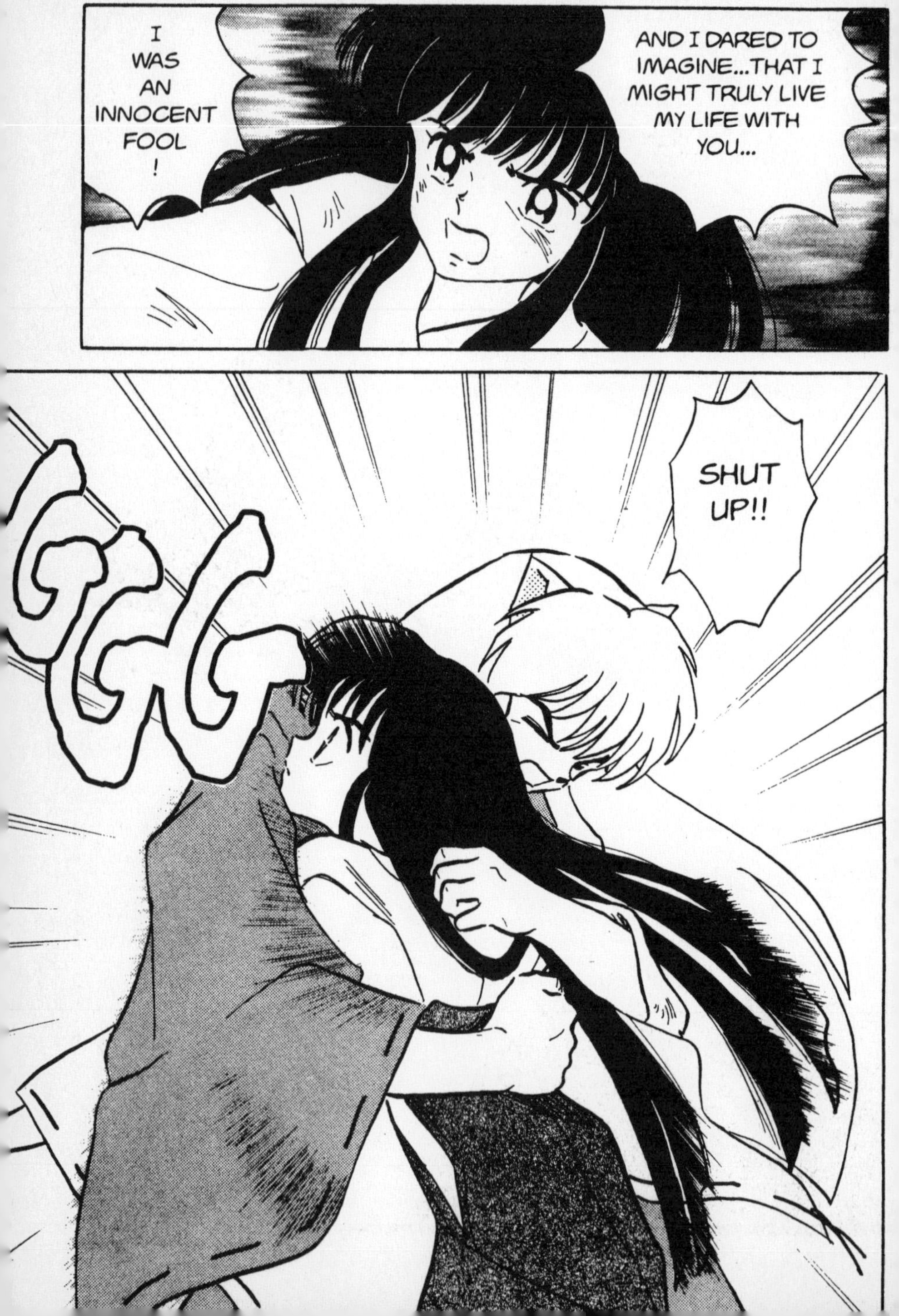
I WAS AN INNOCENT FOOL!
AND I DARED TO IMAGINE...THAT I MIGHT TRULY LIVE MY LIFE WITH YOU...
GGG
SHUT UP!!

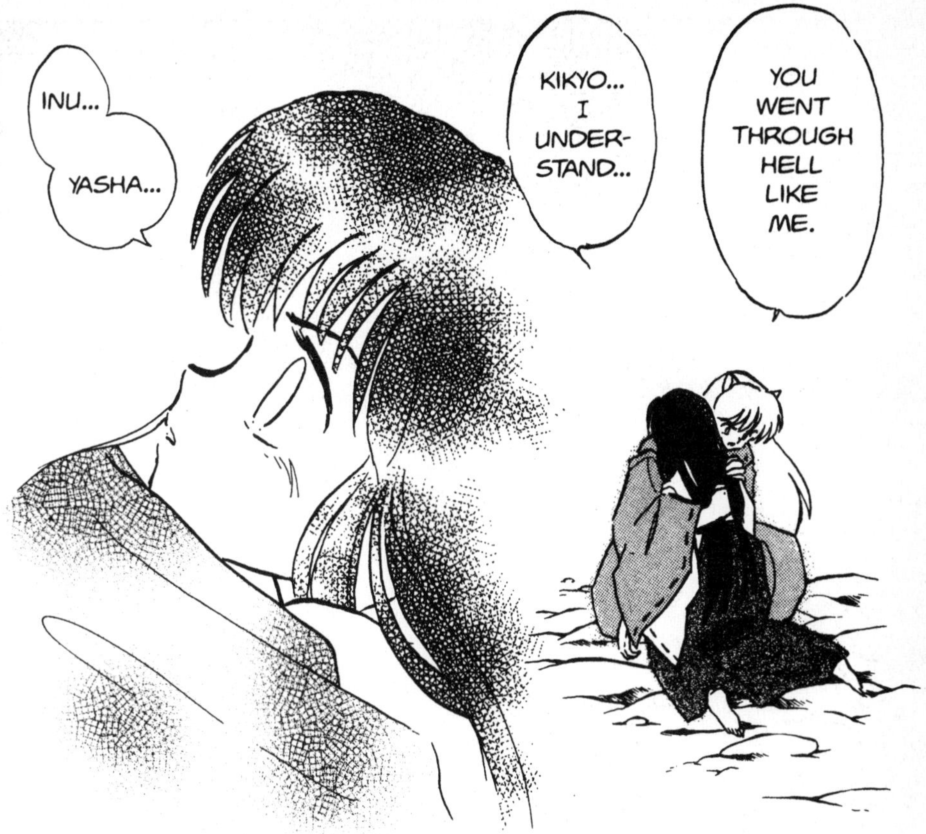
INU... YASHA...
KIKYO... I UNDER-STAND...
YOU WENT THROUGH HELL LIKE ME.

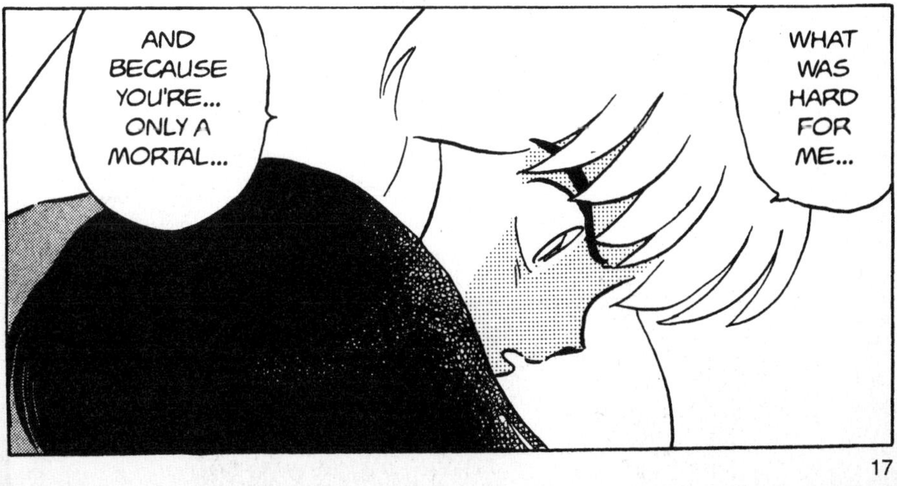
AND BECAUSE YOU'RE... ONLY A MORTAL...
WHAT WAS HARD FOR ME...

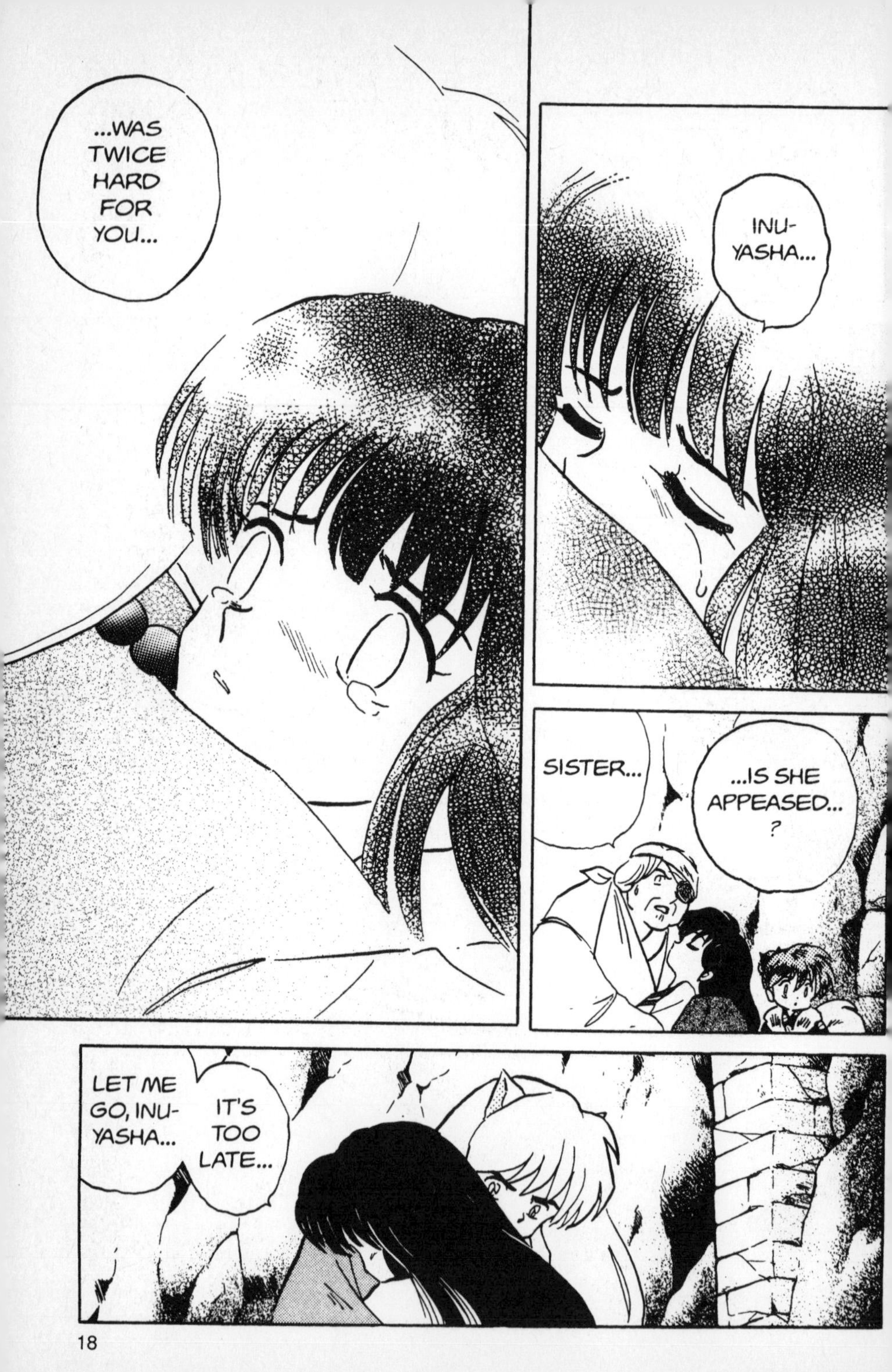
...WAS TWICE HARD FOR YOU...
INU-YASHA...
SISTER...
...IS SHE APPEASED...?
LET ME GO, INU-YASHA...
IT'S TOO LATE...

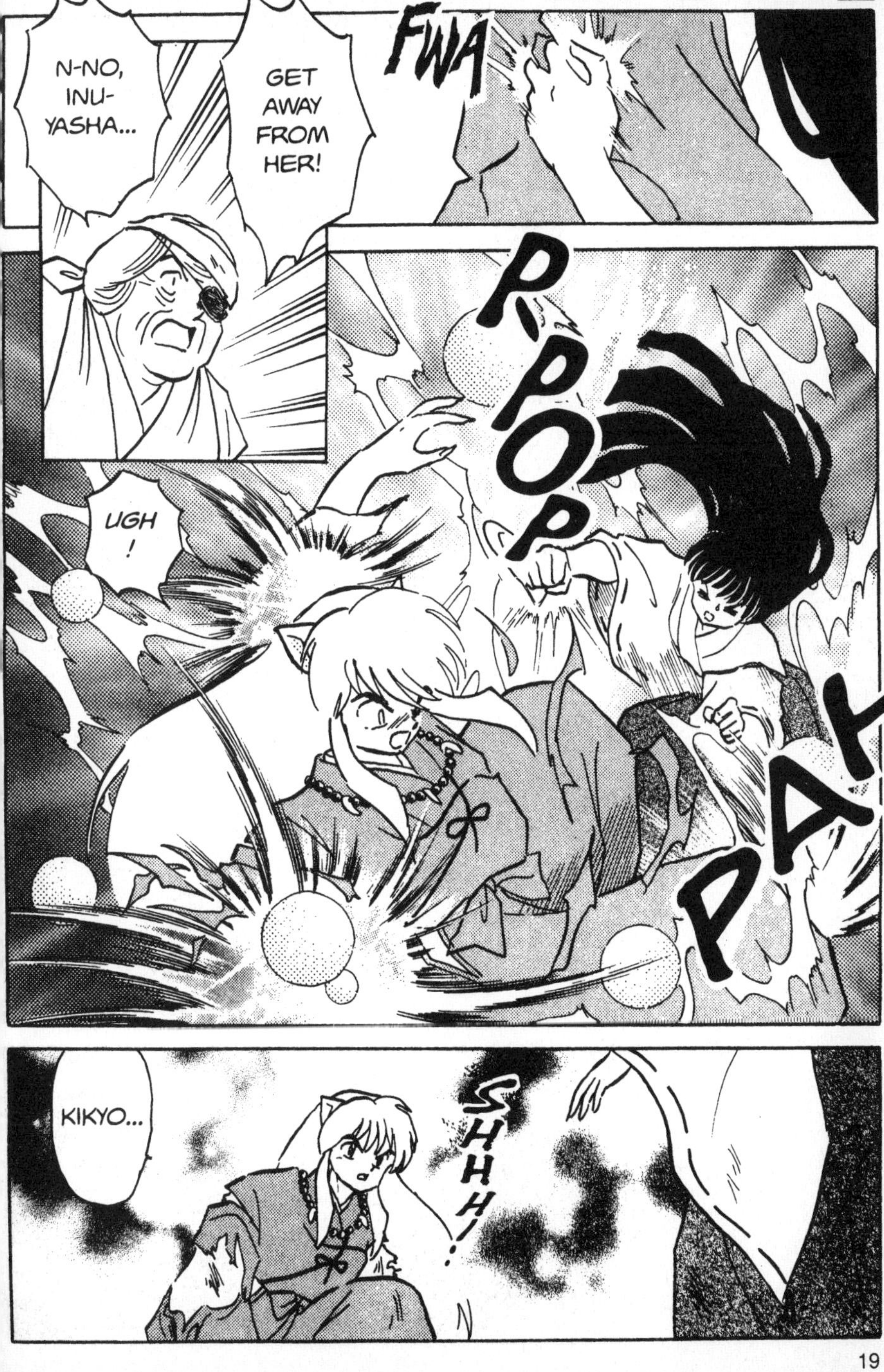
FWA
N-NO, INU-YASHA...
GET AWAY FROM HER!
RPPOP
UGH!
PAH
KIKYO...
SHHHH!

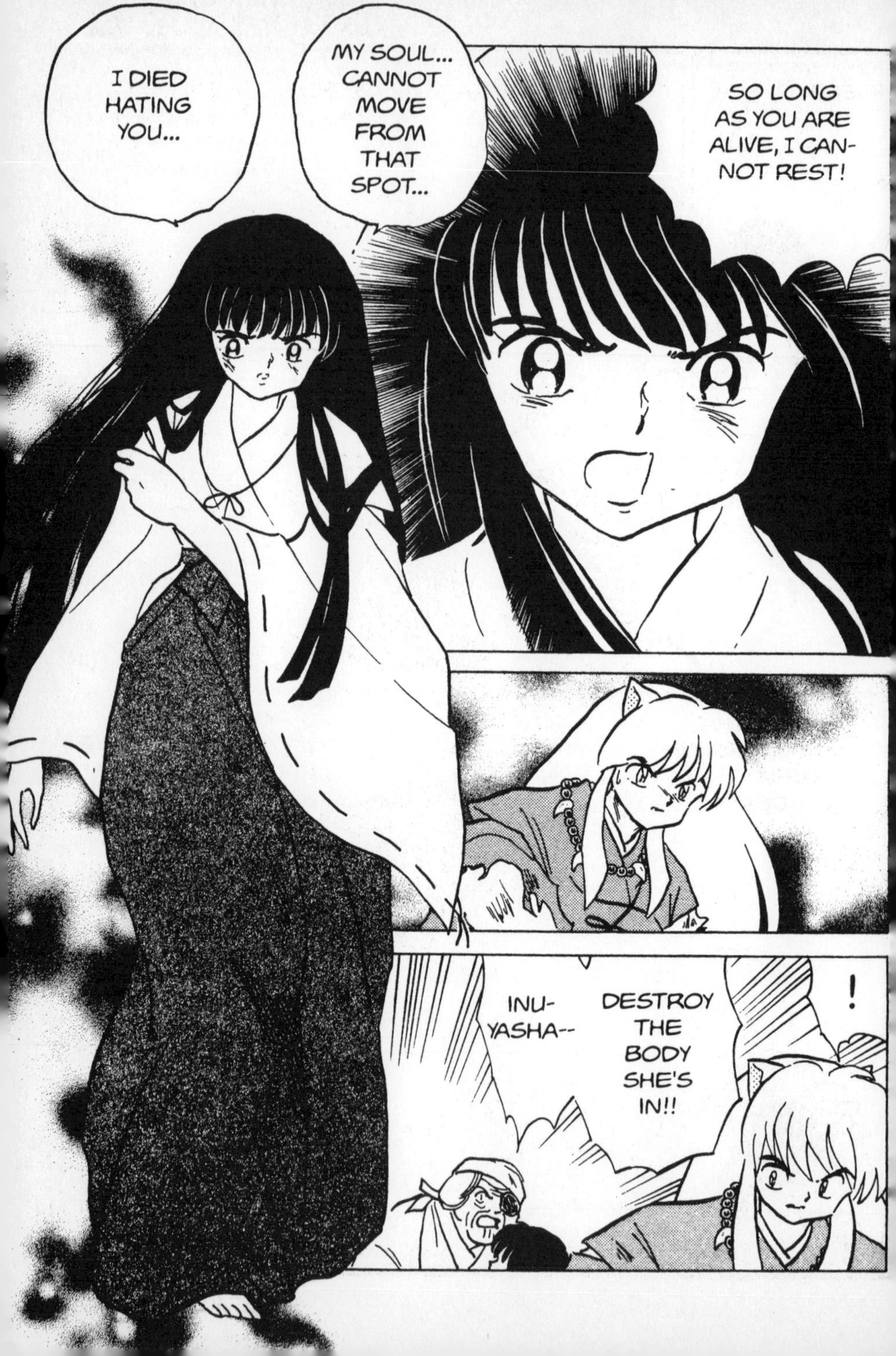
I DIED HATING YOU...
MY SOUL... CANNOT MOVE FROM THAT SPOT...
SO LONG AS YOU ARE ALIVE, I CAN-NOT REST!
INU-YASHA--
DESTROY THE BODY SHE'S IN!!
!

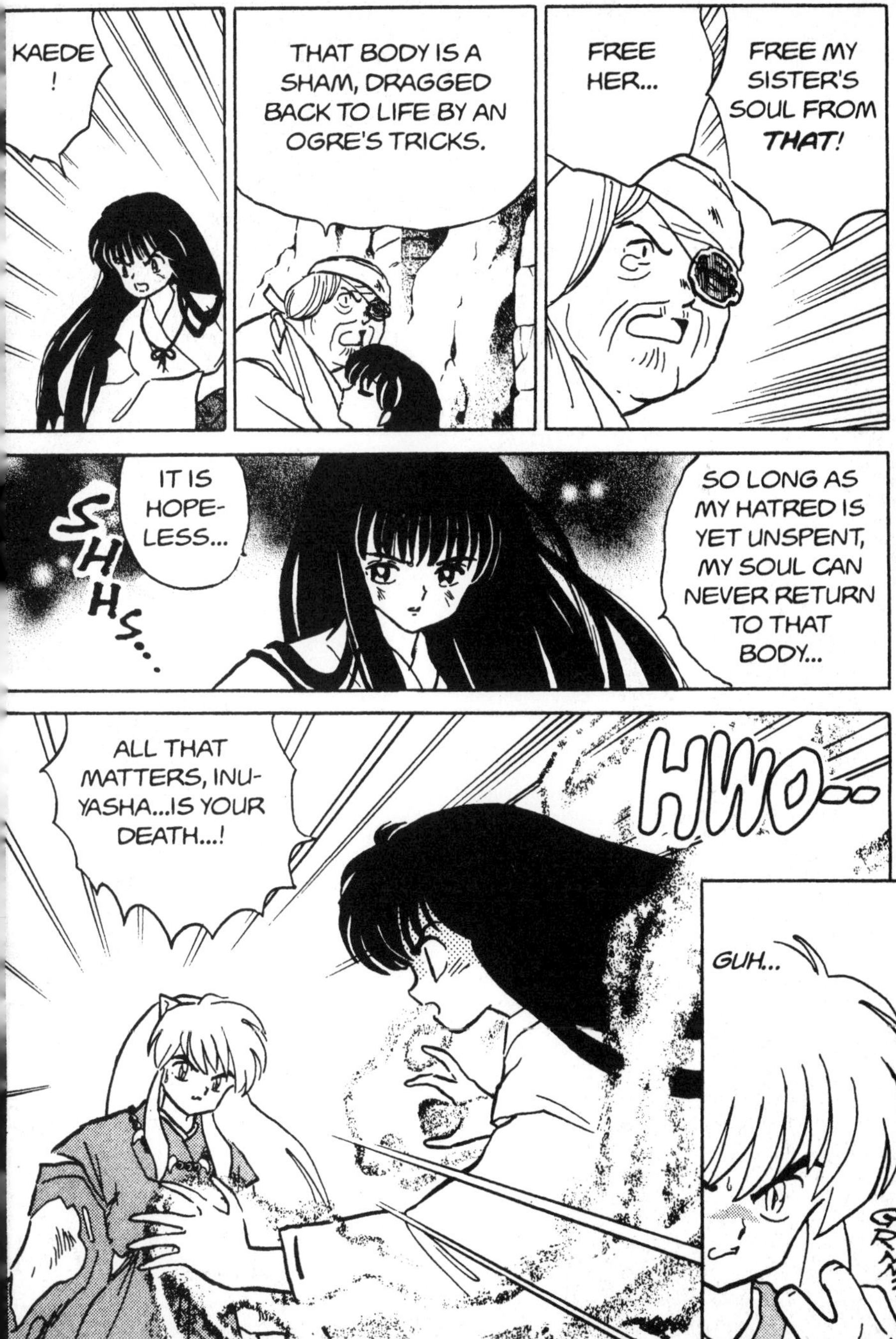
KAEDE
!
THAT BODY IS A SHAM, DRAGGED BACK TO LIFE BY AN OGRE'S TRICKS.
FREE HER...
FREE MY SISTER'S SOUL FROM *THAT*!
SHHS...
IT IS HOPE-LESS...
SO LONG AS MY HATRED IS YET UNSPENT, MY SOUL CAN NEVER RETURN TO THAT BODY...
ALL THAT MATTERS, INU-YASHA...IS YOUR DEATH...!
HWO...
GUH...
GRNN...

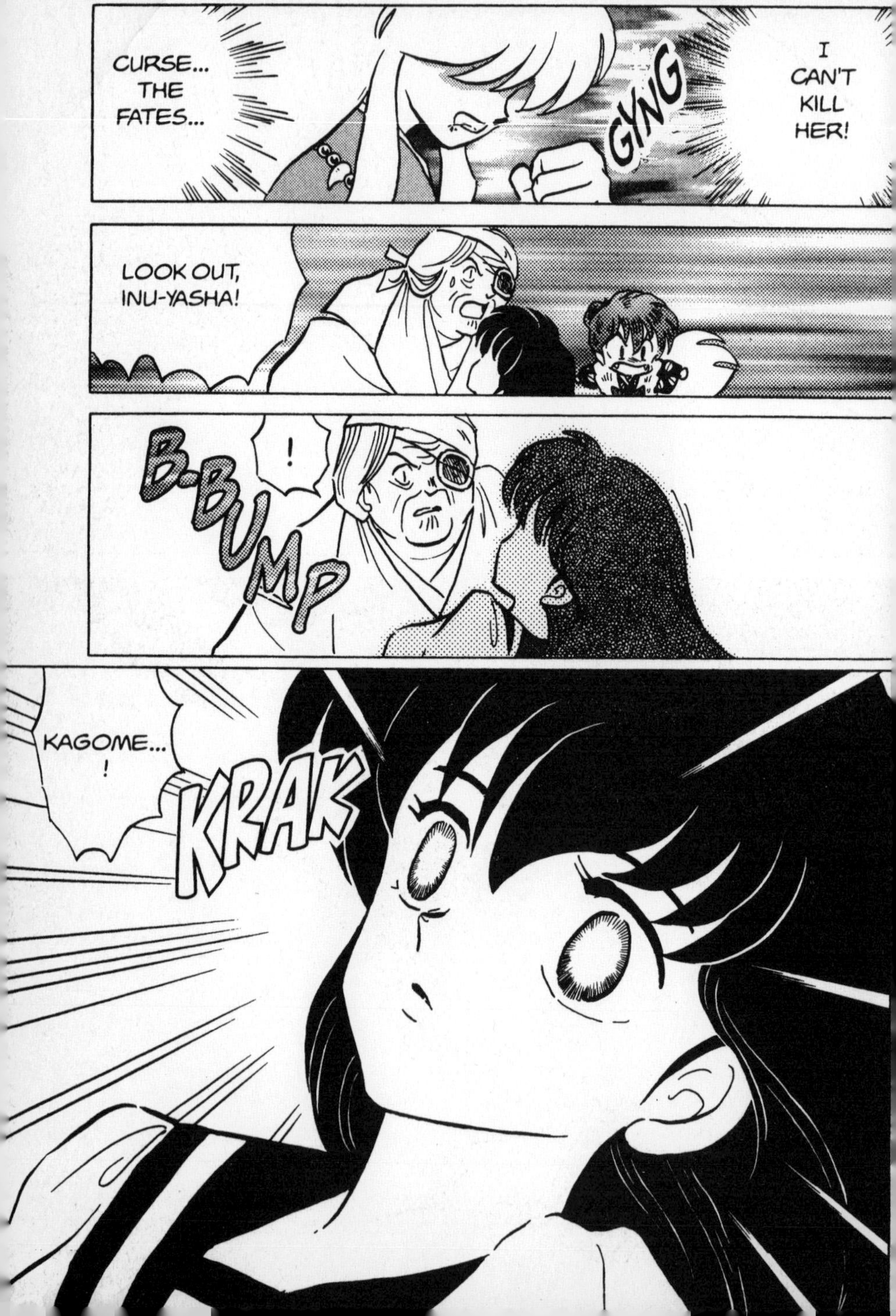
CURSE... THE FATES...
GYNG
I CAN'T KILL HER!
LOOK OUT, INU-YASHA!
B-BUMP
!
KAGOME... !
KRAK

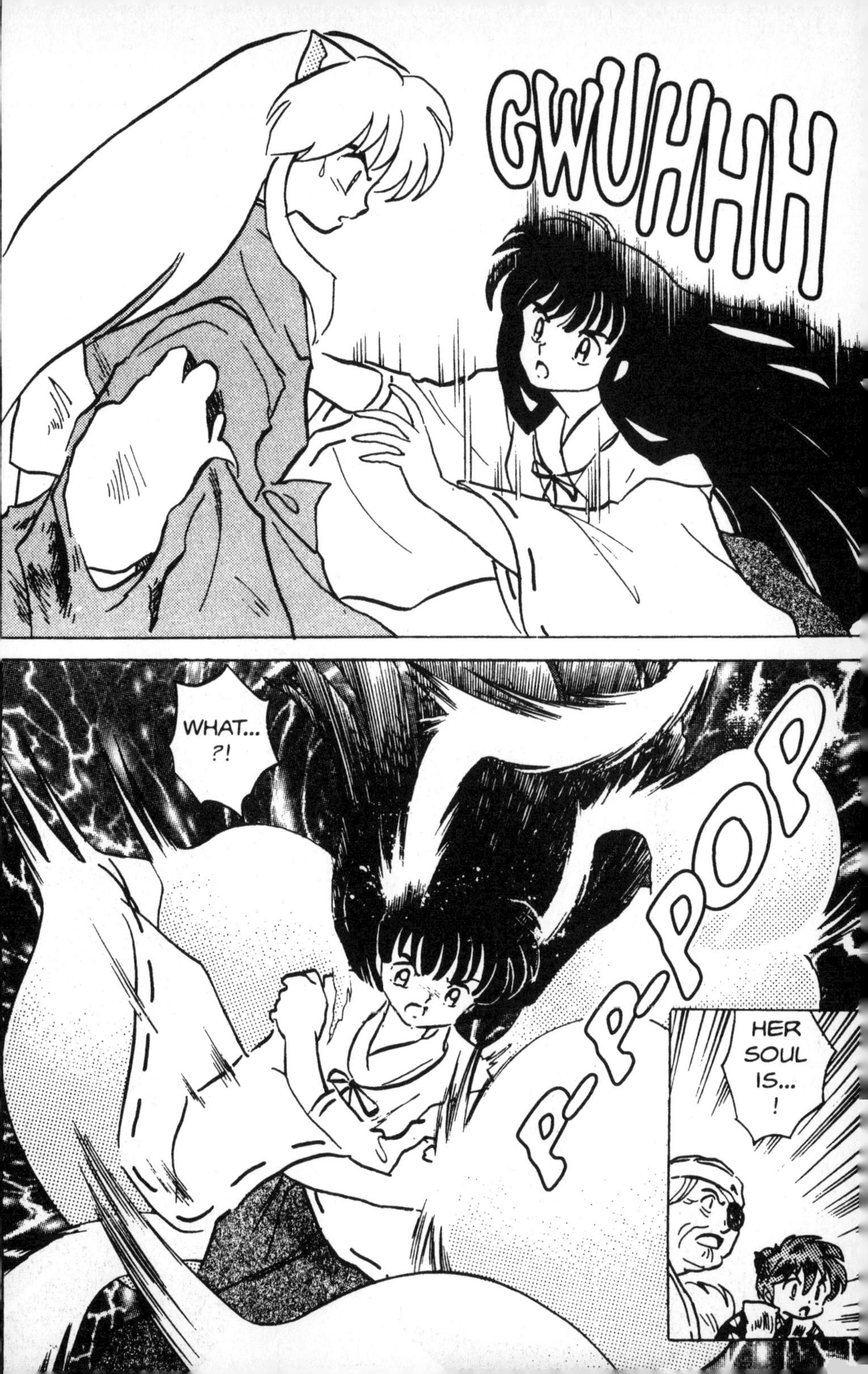
GWUHHH
WHAT... ?!
P-P-POP
HER SOUL IS... !

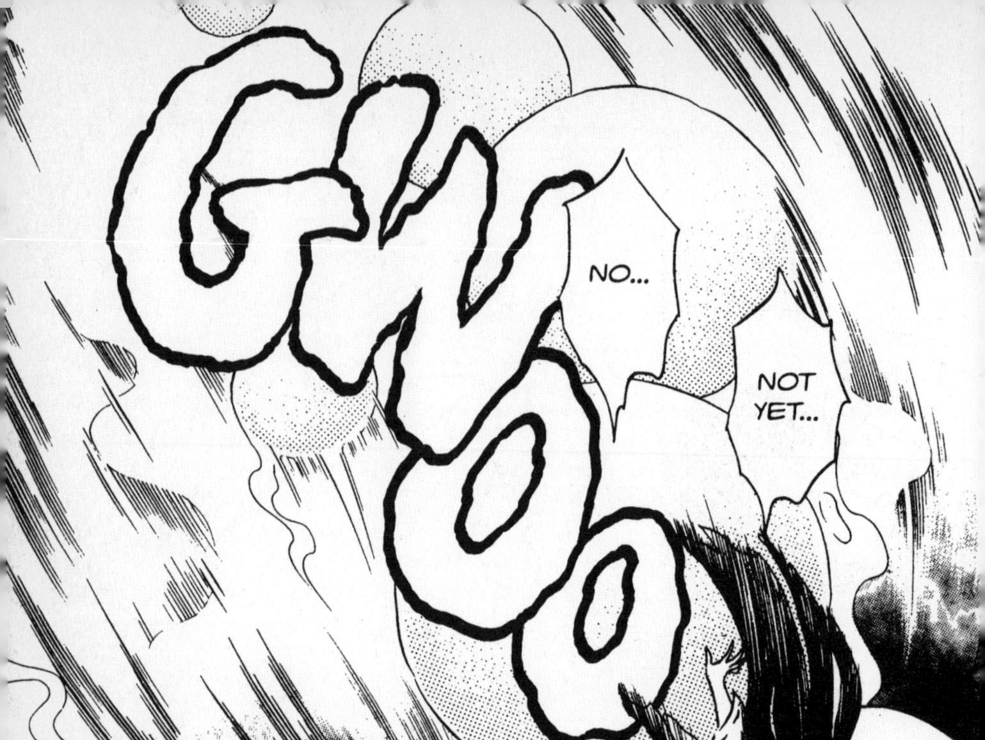
GYOOO...
NO...
NOT YET...

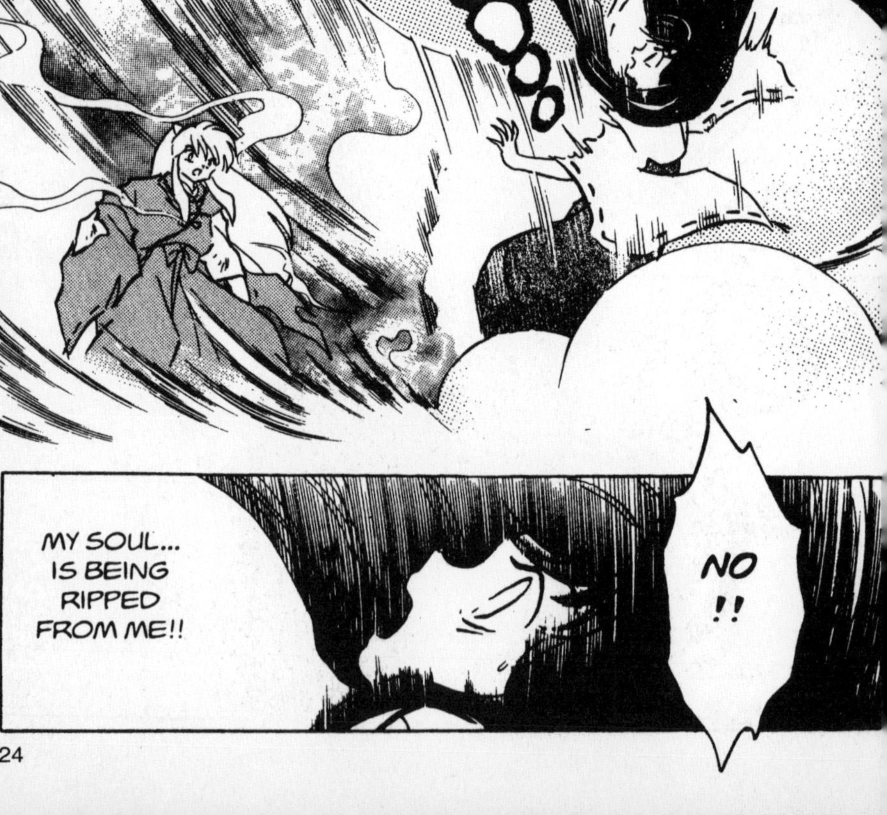
MY SOUL... IS BEING RIPPED FROM ME!!
NO !!

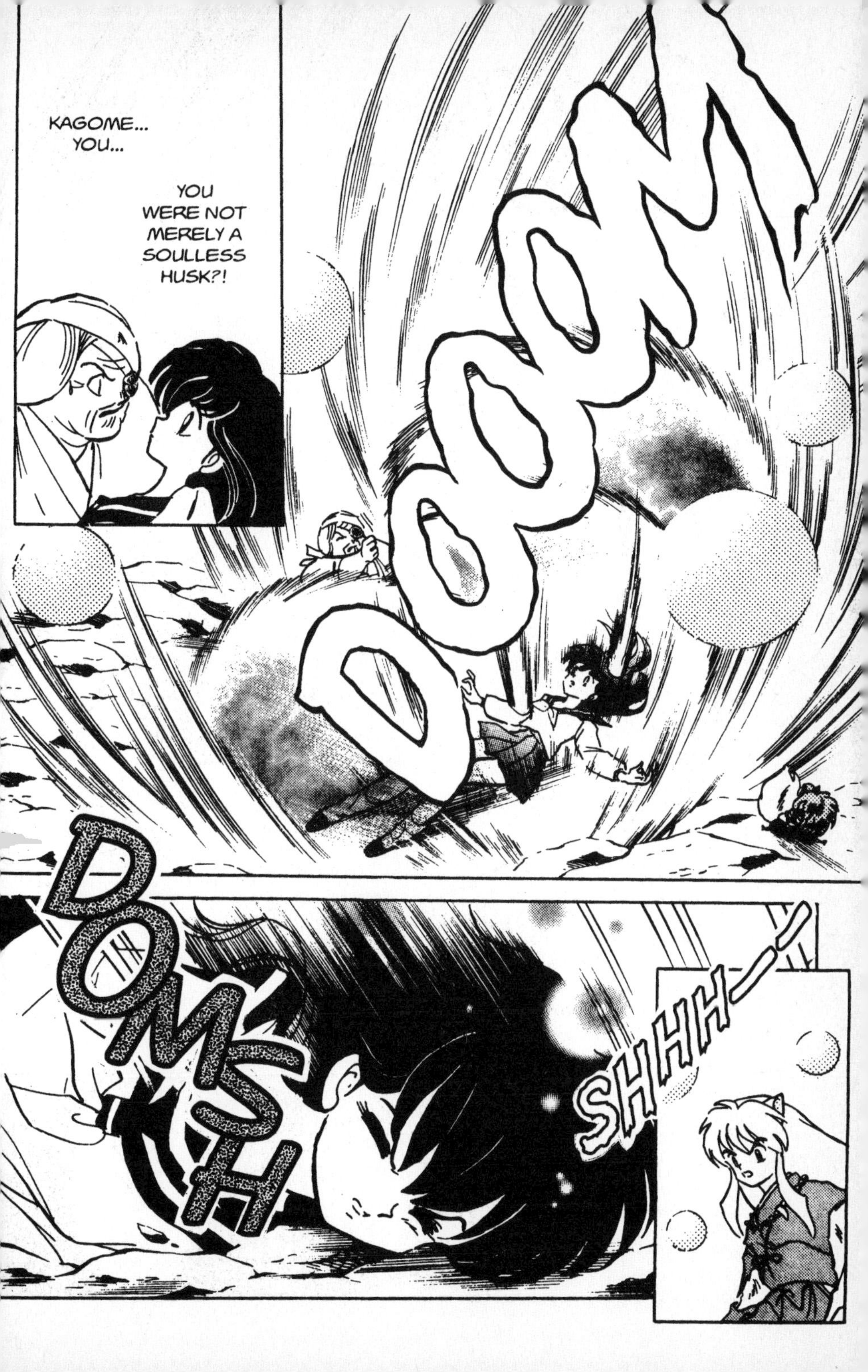
KAGOME... YOU...
YOU WERE NOT MERELY A SOULLESS HUSK?!
DOOOOM
DOMSH
SHHH—!

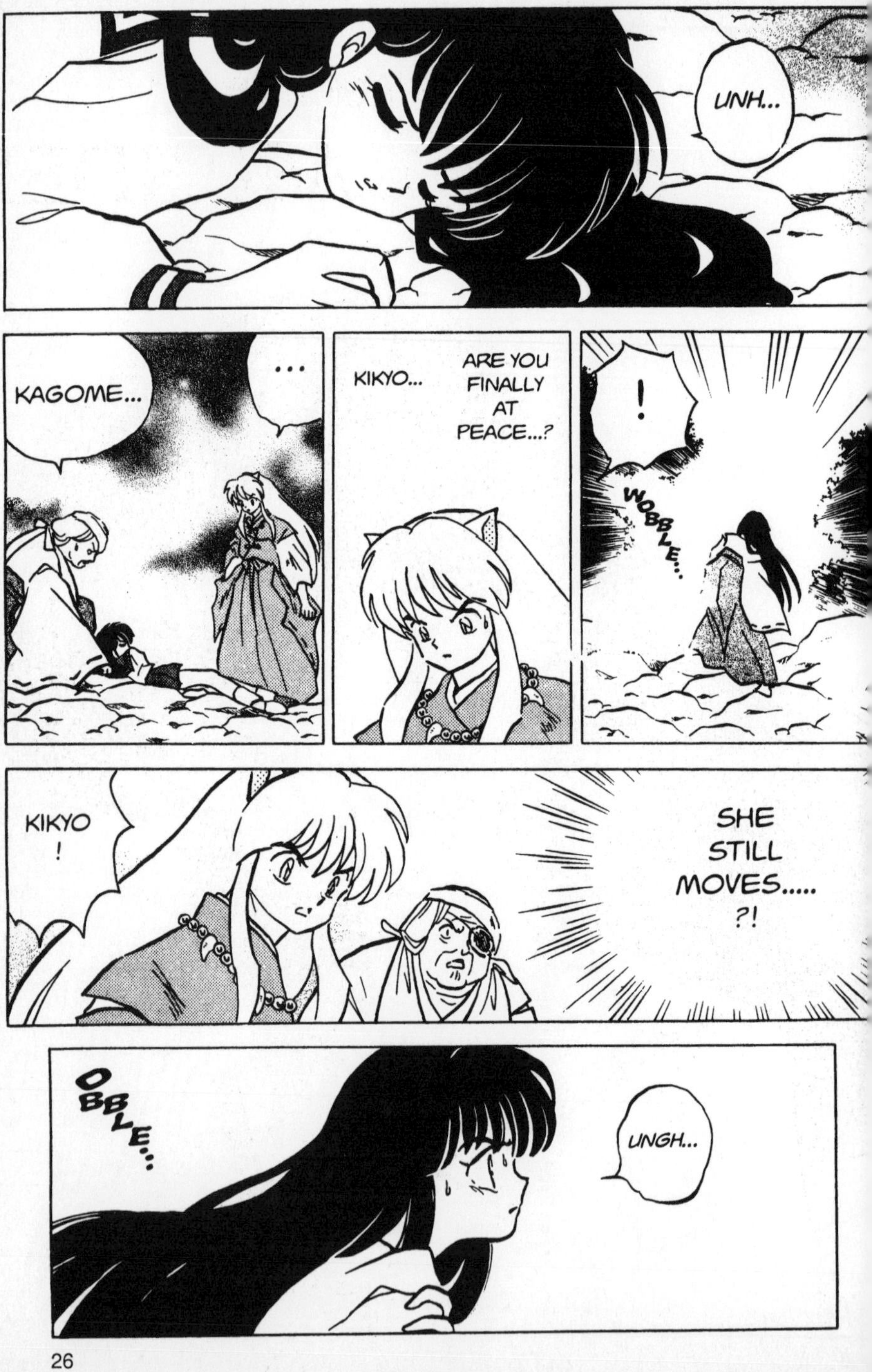
UNH...
KAGOME...
...
KIKYO...
ARE YOU FINALLY AT PEACE...?
!
WOBBLE...
KIKYO !
SHE STILL MOVES..... ?!
OBBLE...
UNGH...

SCROLL TWO

A SOUL ASUNDER

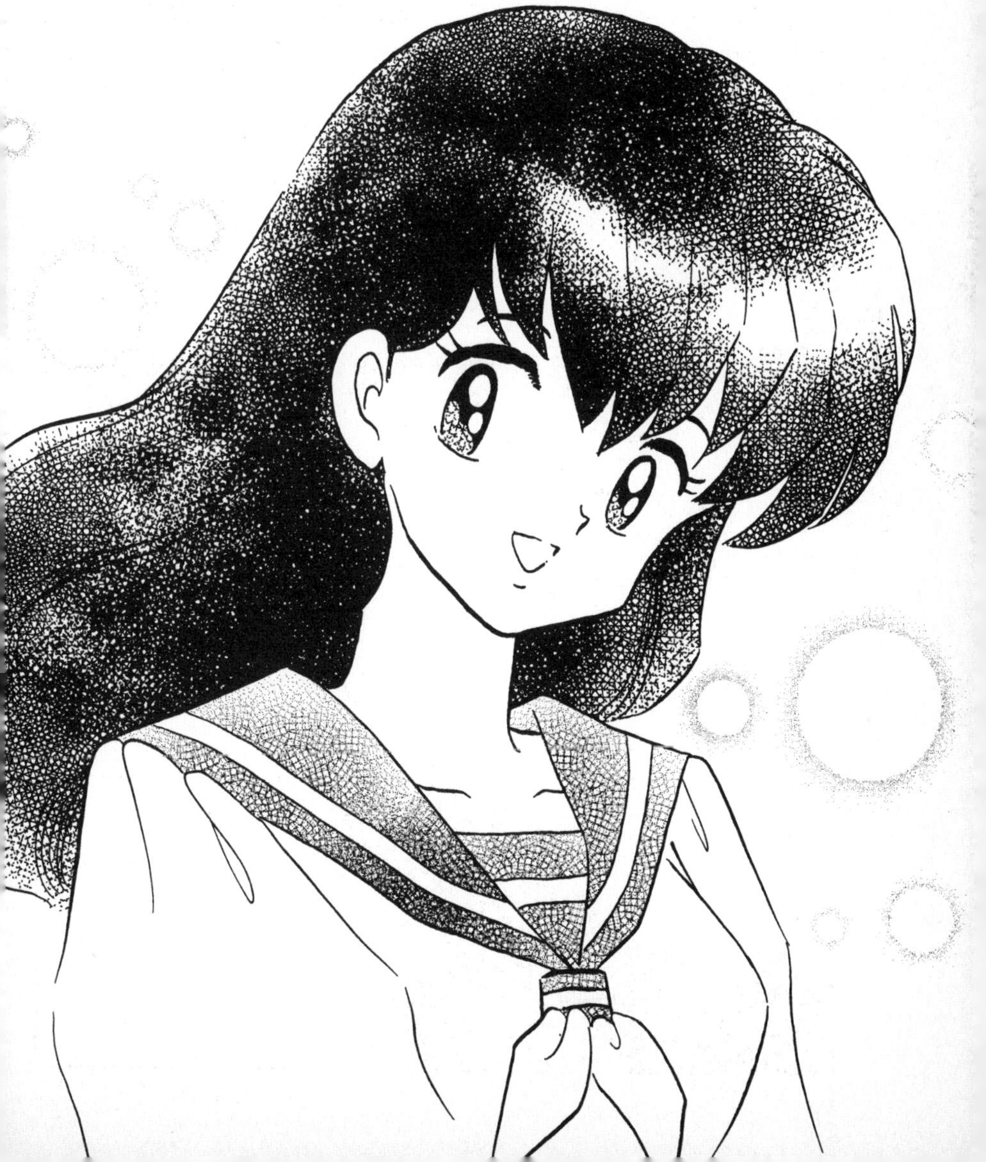

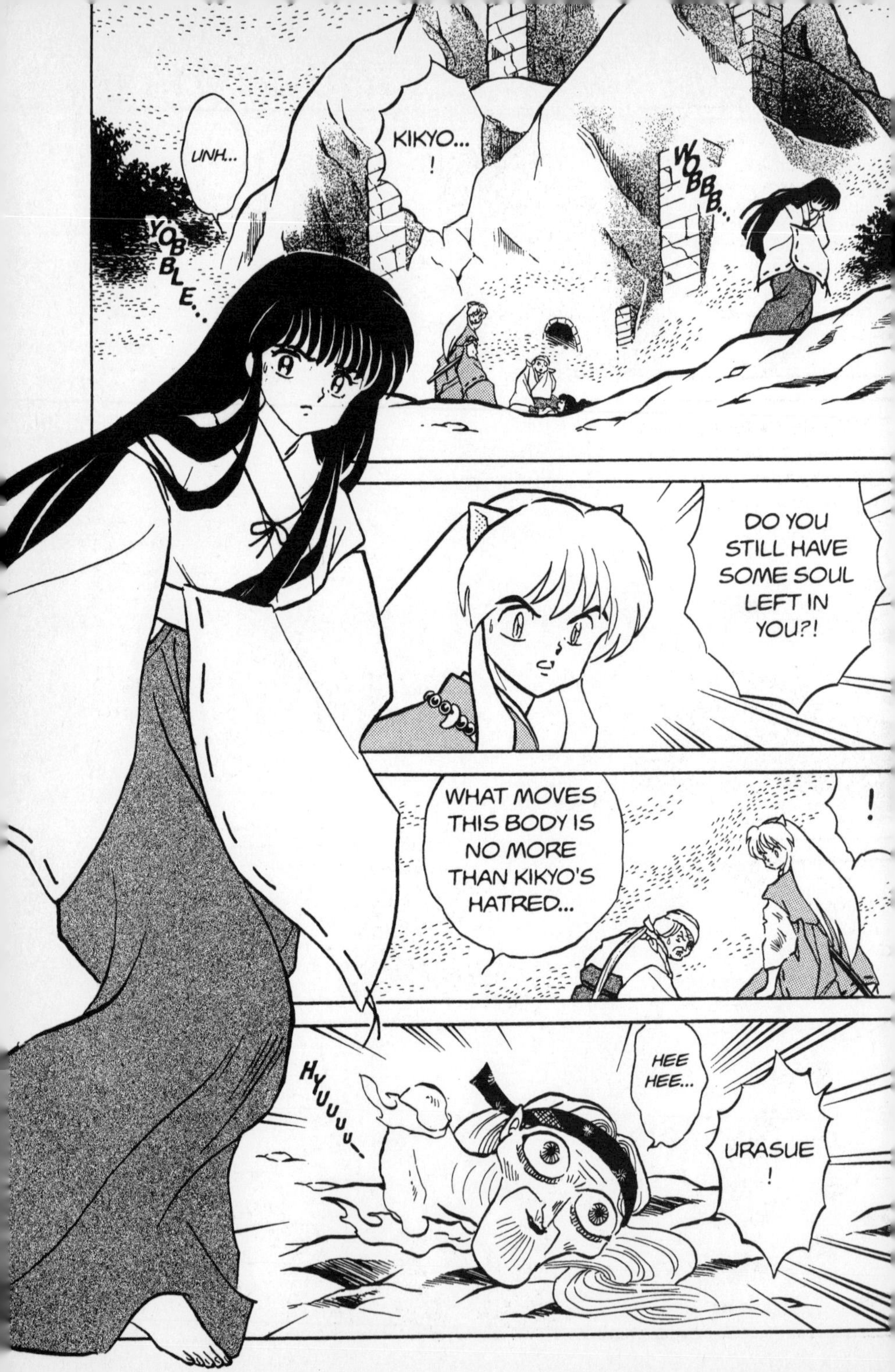
UNH...
YOBBLE...
KIKYO...!
WOBBB...
DO YOU STILL HAVE SOME SOUL LEFT IN YOU?!
WHAT MOVES THIS BODY IS NO MORE THAN KIKYO'S HATRED...
!
HYUUUU...
HEE HEE...
URASUE!

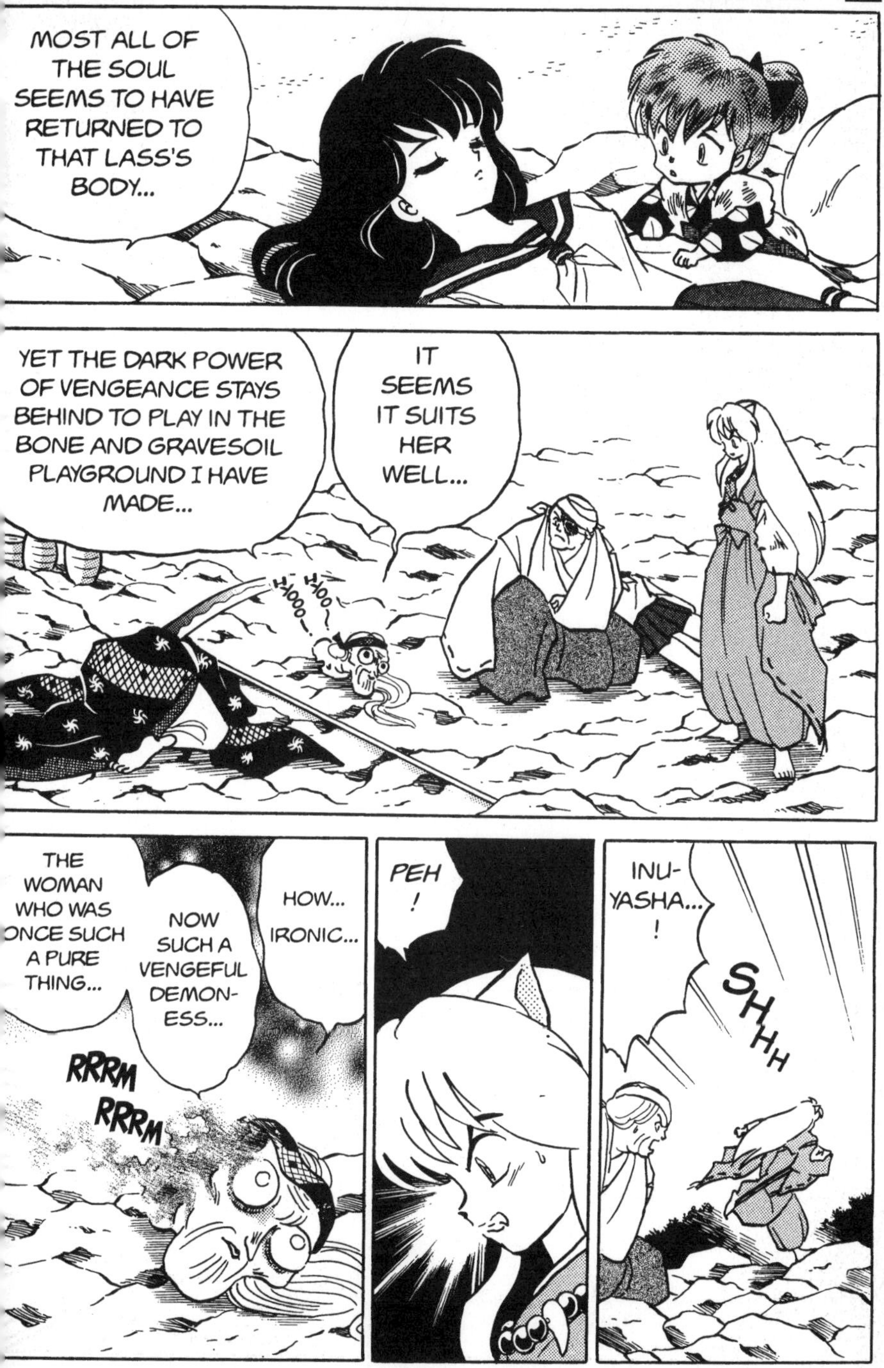
MOST ALL OF THE SOUL SEEMS TO HAVE RETURNED TO THAT LASS'S BODY...
YET THE DARK POWER OF VENGEANCE STAYS BEHIND TO PLAY IN THE BONE AND GRAVESOIL PLAYGROUND I HAVE MADE...
IT SEEMS IT SUITS HER WELL...
H-HOO~ H-HOO~
THE WOMAN WHO WAS ONCE SUCH A PURE THING...
NOW SUCH A VENGEFUL DEMON-ESS...
HOW... IRONIC...
RRRM RRRM
PEH!
INU-YASHA...!
SHHH

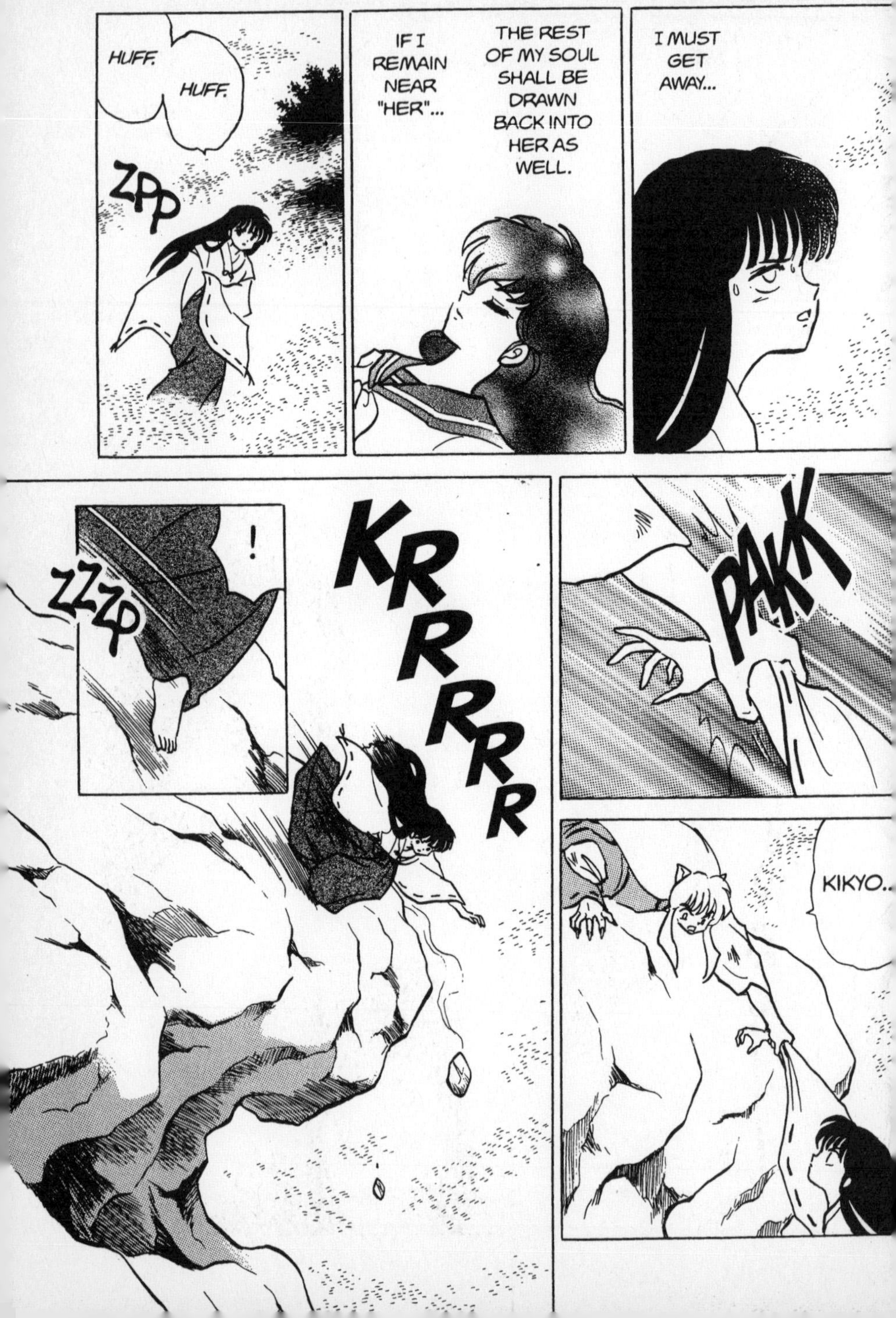
HUFF.
HUFF.
ZPP
IF I REMAIN NEAR "HER"...
THE REST OF MY SOUL SHALL BE DRAWN BACK INTO HER AS WELL.
I MUST GET AWAY...
ZZZP
!
KRRRRRR
PAKK
KIKYO...

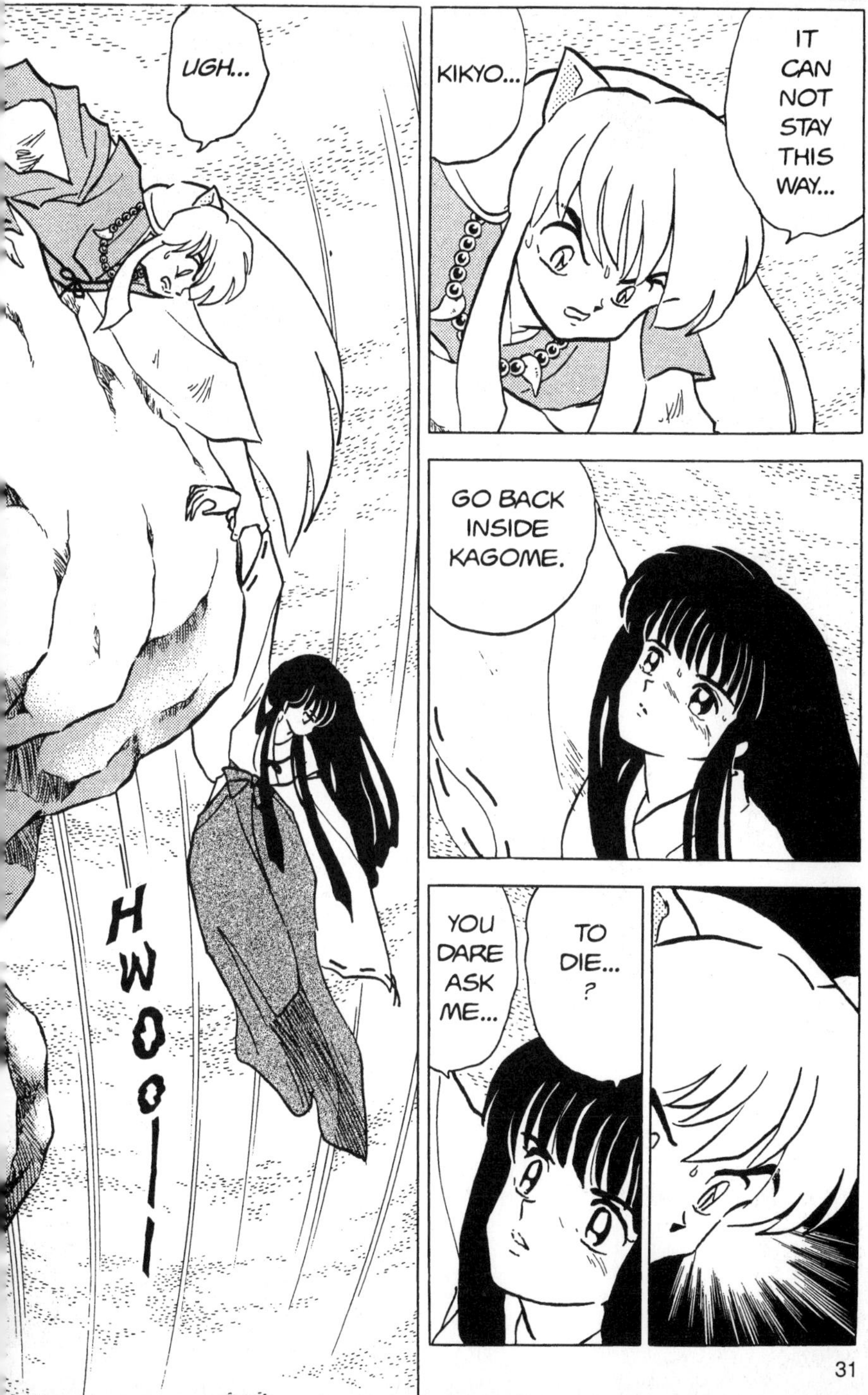
UGH...
HWOOII
KIKYO...
IT CAN NOT STAY THIS WAY...
GO BACK INSIDE KAGOME.
YOU DARE ASK ME...
TO DIE...?

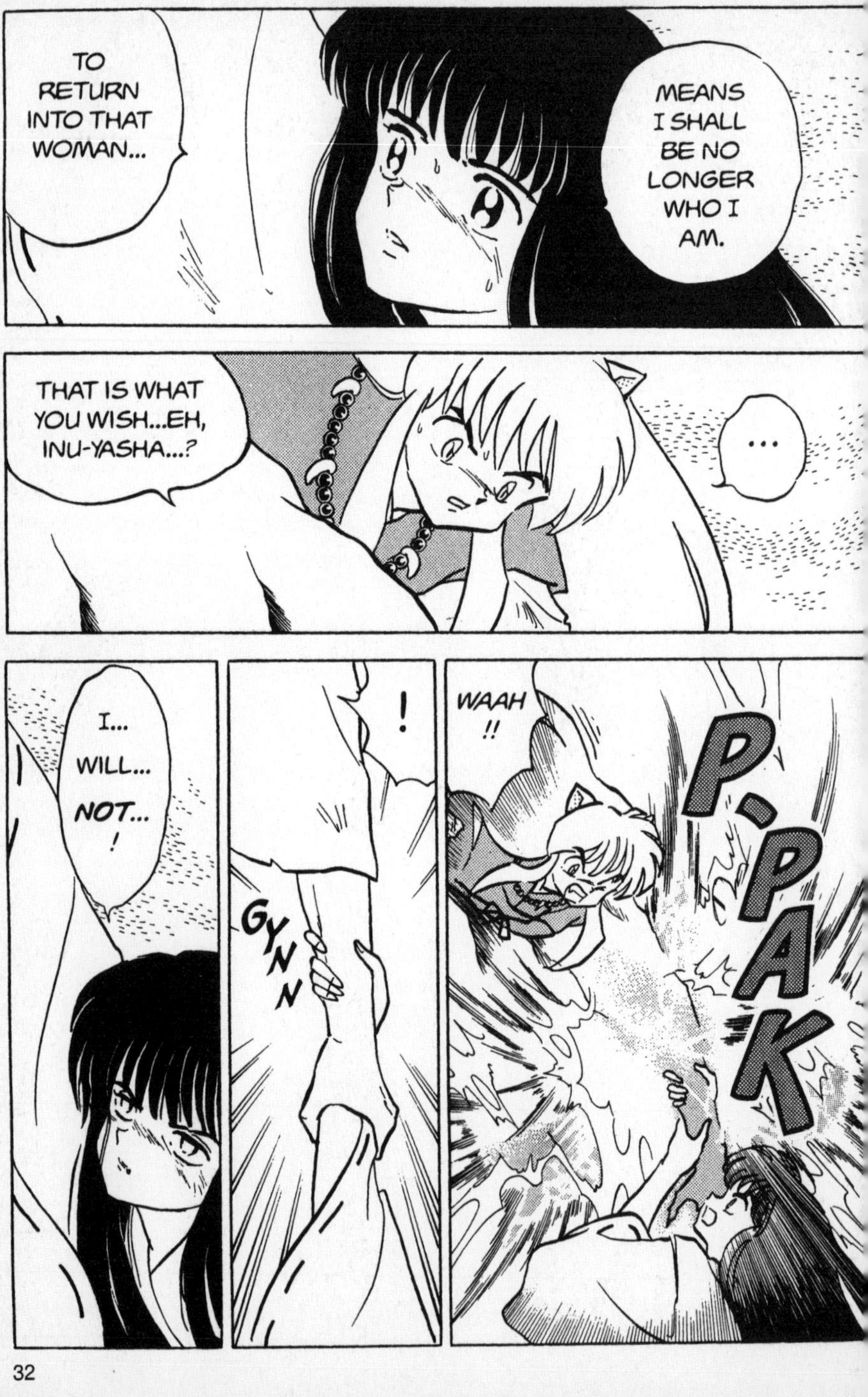
TO RETURN INTO THAT WOMAN...
MEANS I SHALL BE NO LONGER WHO I AM.
THAT IS WHAT YOU WISH...EH, INU-YASHA...?
...
I... WILL... NOT... !
!
GYNN
WAAH !!
P-PAK

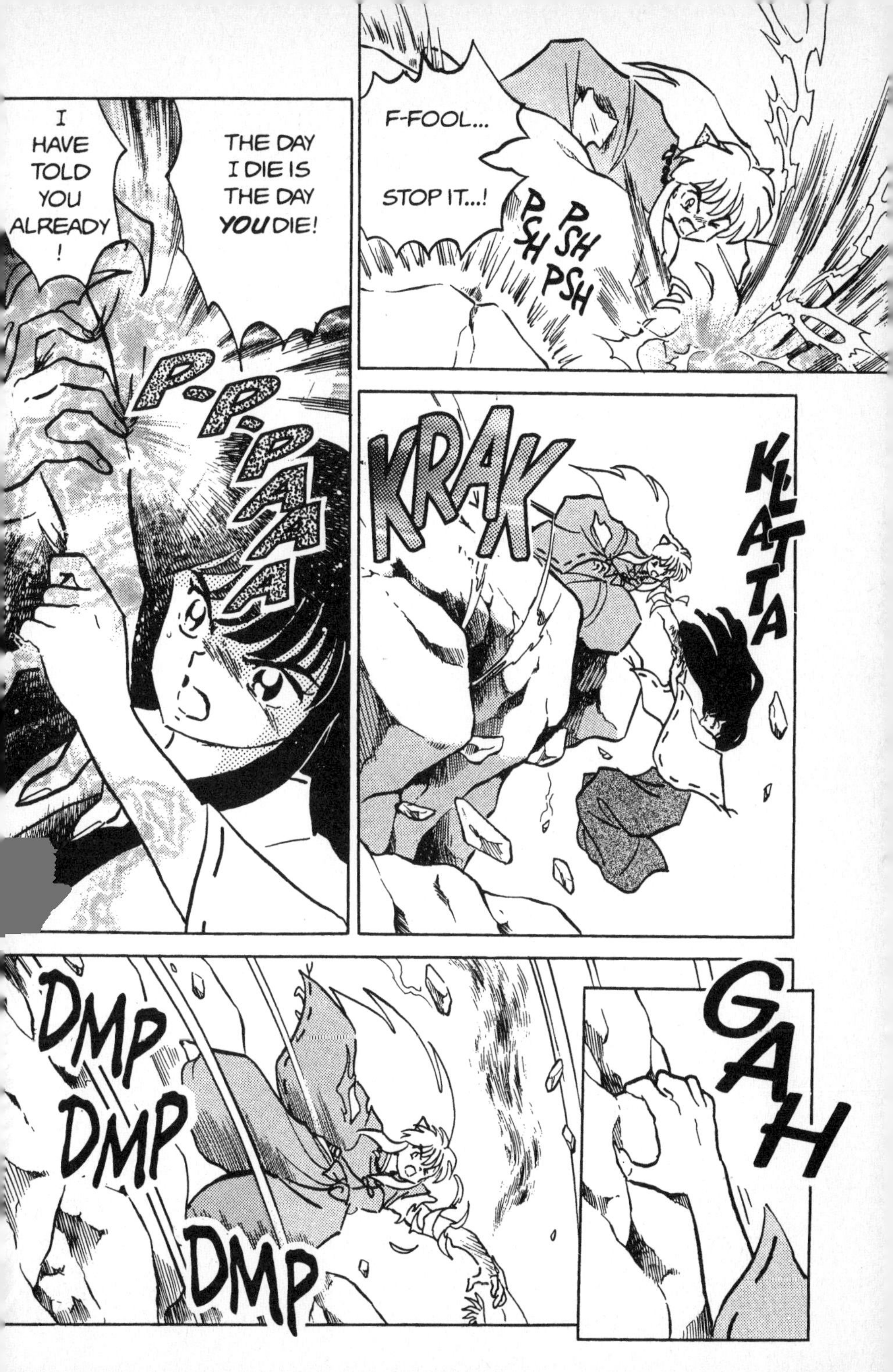
I HAVE TOLD YOU ALREADY!
THE DAY I DIE IS THE DAY YOU DIE!
P-P-PAAA
F-FOOL...
STOP IT...!
PSH PSH PSH PSH
KRAK
KLATTA
DMP DMP DMP
GAH

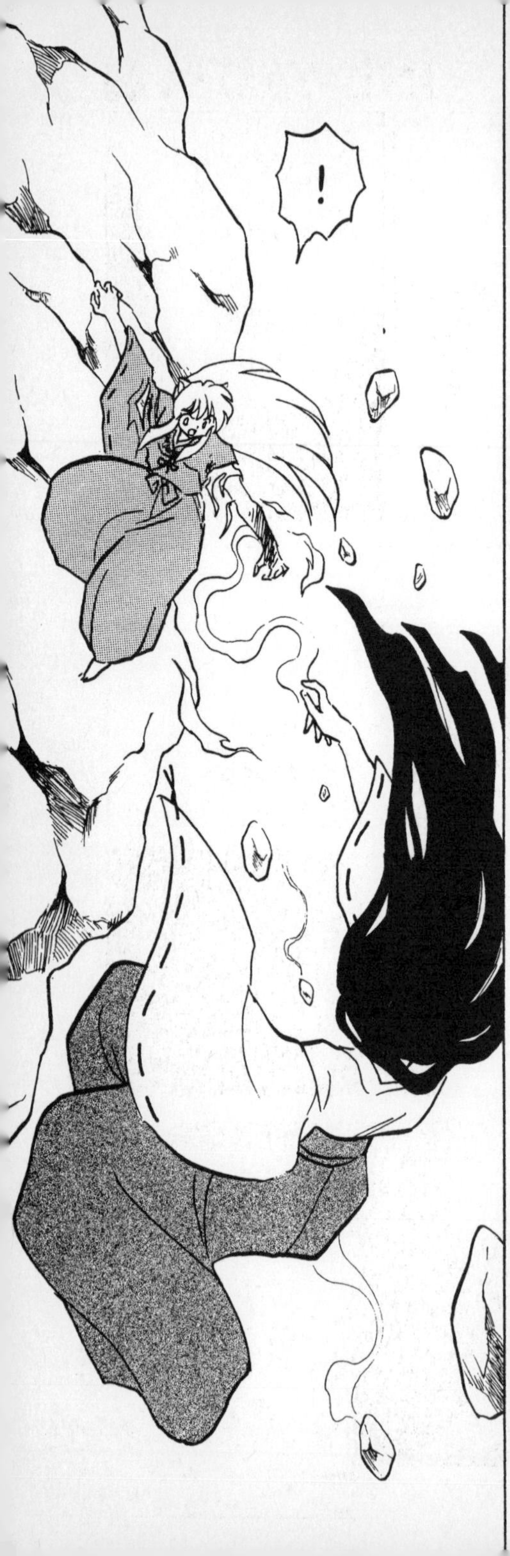
!

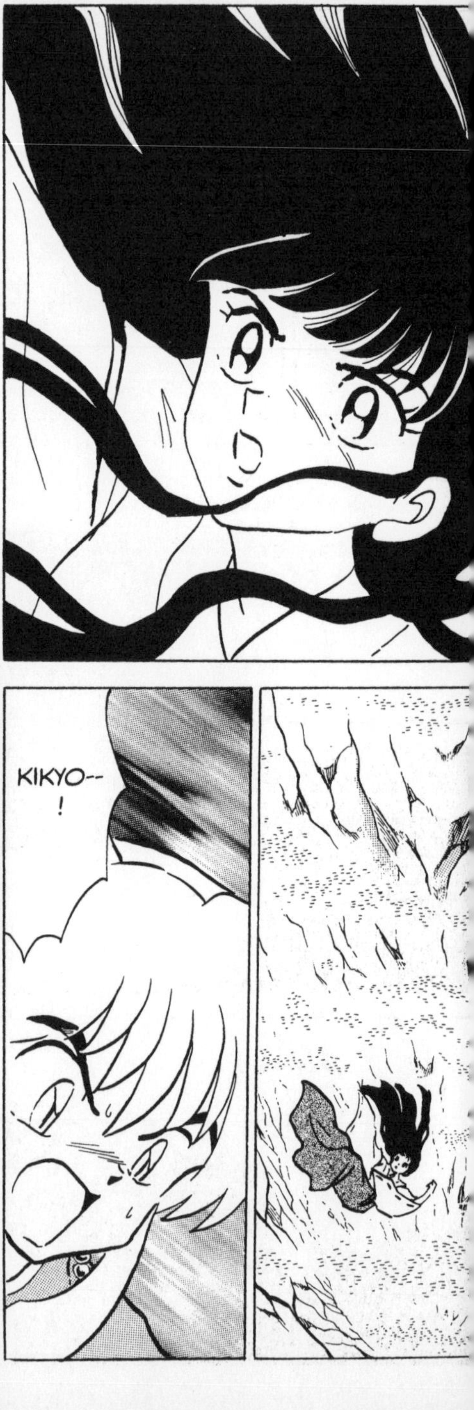
KIKYO--!

WHY,
CURSE
IT...

WHY
MUST IT
END LIKE
THIS...?!

KLATA

50 YEARS AGO...
A PRETENDER
IN KIKYO'S FORM
SHOT ME WITH
THAT ARROW...

THEN
BORROWED
MY FORM AND
ATTACKED
KIKYO...

SOMEONE...
HAD A GRUDGE
AGAINST US
BOTH...

BUT
WHO...

AND
FOR WHAT
FOUL
PURPOSE...

SHKK...

INU-
YASHA...

SH...

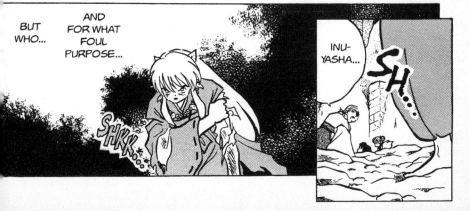

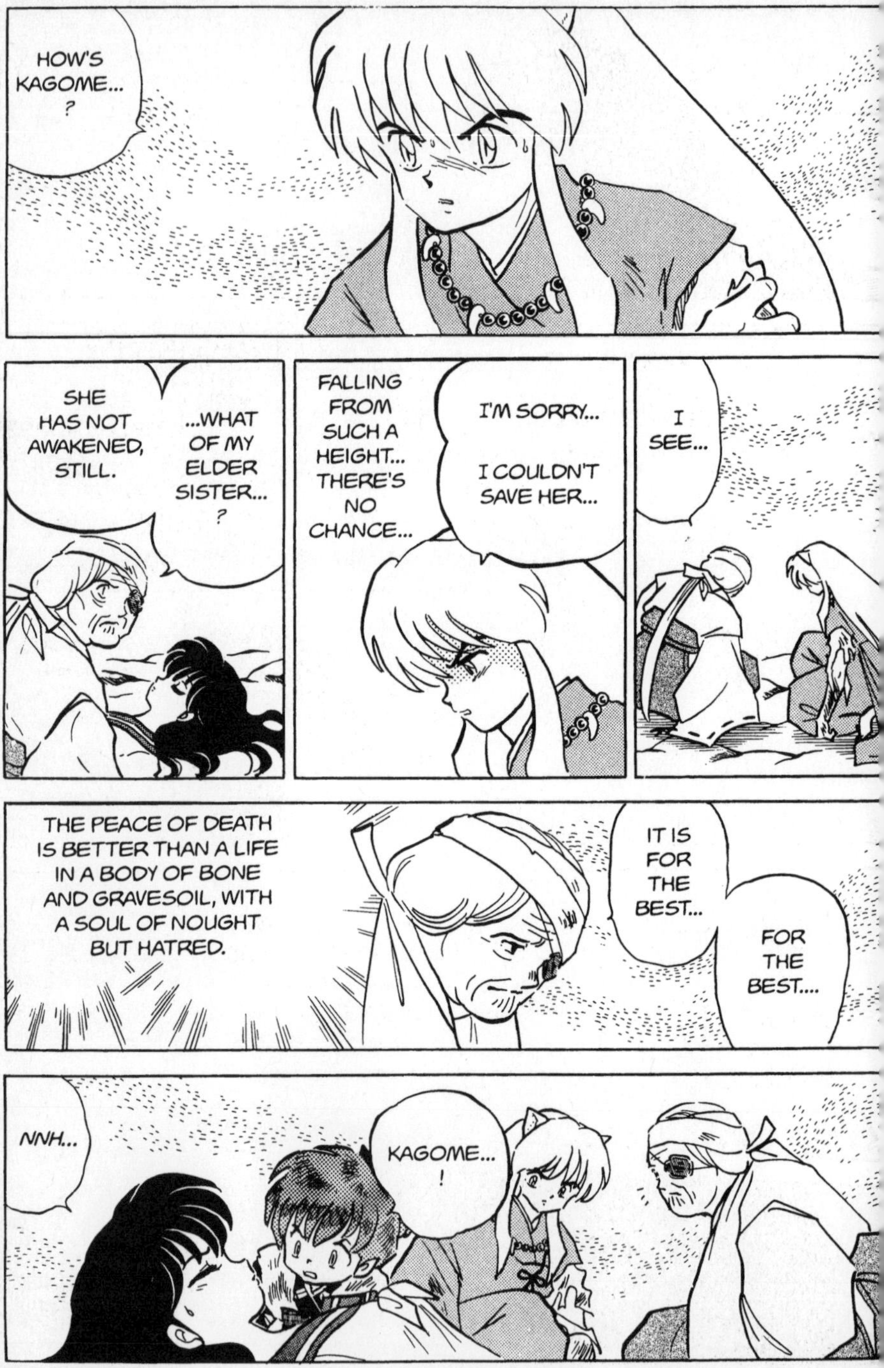
HOW'S KAGOME...?
SHE HAS NOT AWAKENED, STILL.
...WHAT OF MY ELDER SISTER...?
FALLING FROM SUCH A HEIGHT... THERE'S NO CHANCE...
I'M SORRY... I COULDN'T SAVE HER...
I SEE...
THE PEACE OF DEATH IS BETTER THAN A LIFE IN A BODY OF BONE AND GRAVESOIL, WITH A SOUL OF NOUGHT BUT HATRED.
IT IS FOR THE BEST...
FOR THE BEST....
NNH...
KAGOME...!

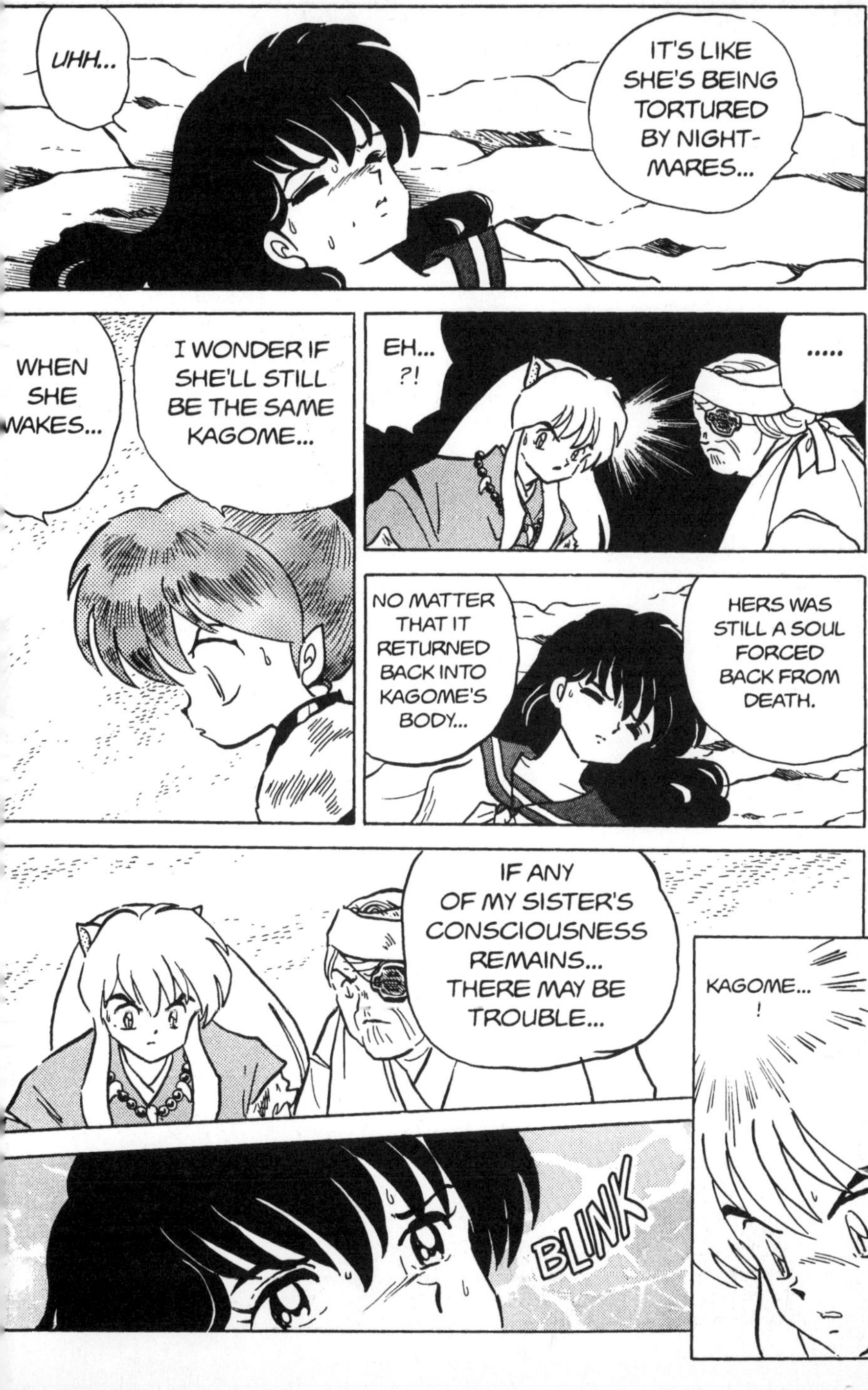
UHH...
IT'S LIKE SHE'S BEING TORTURED BY NIGHT-MARES...
WHEN SHE WAKES...
I WONDER IF SHE'LL STILL BE THE SAME KAGOME...
EH... ?!
.....
NO MATTER THAT IT RETURNED BACK INTO KAGOME'S BODY...
HERS WAS STILL A SOUL FORCED BACK FROM DEATH.
IF ANY OF MY SISTER'S CONSCIOUSNESS REMAINS... THERE MAY BE TROUBLE...
KAGOME... !
BLINK

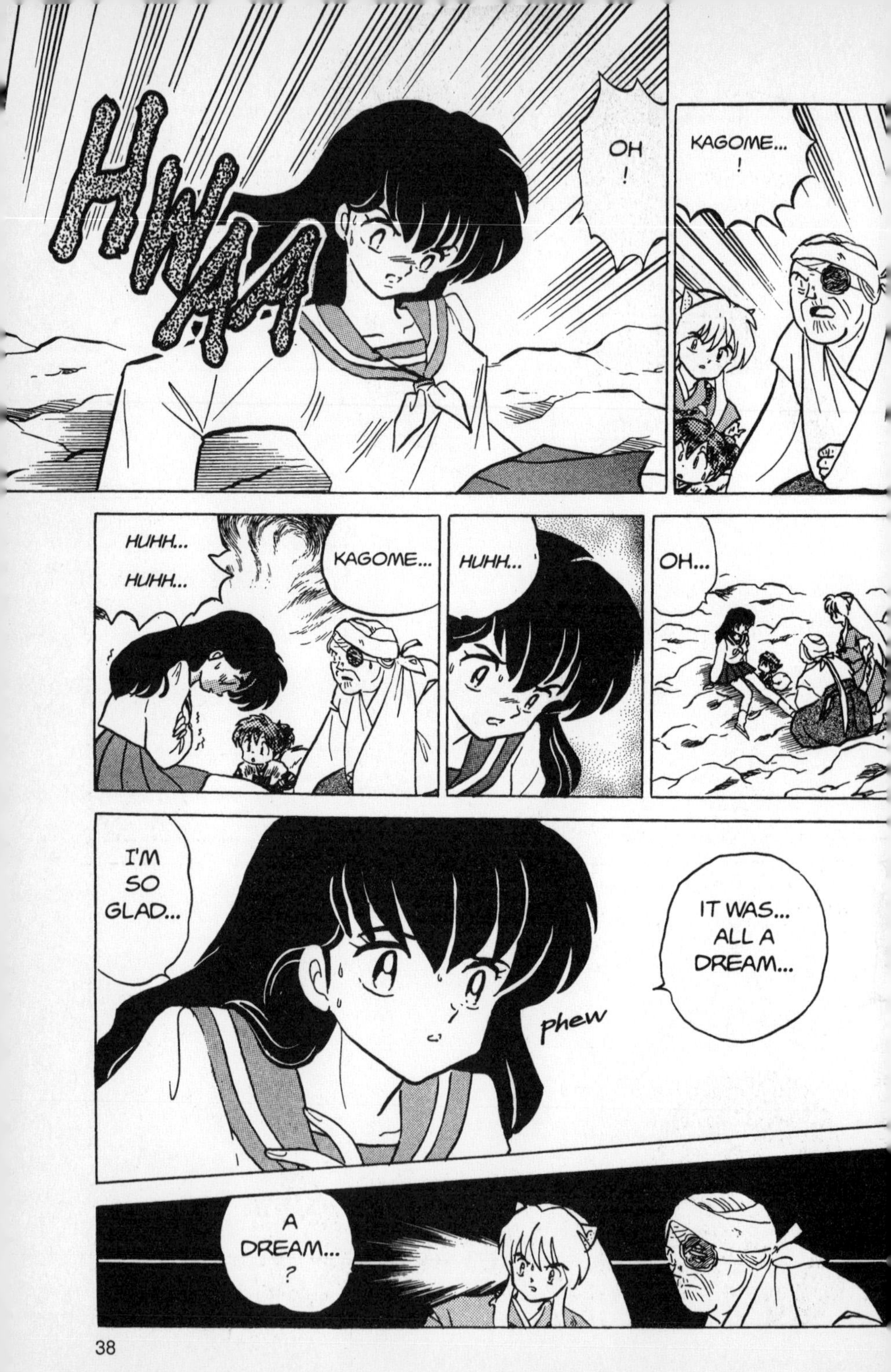
HWAA
OH !
KAGOME... !
HUHH... HUHH...
KAGOME...
HUHH...
OH...
I'M SO GLAD...
phew
IT WAS... ALL A DREAM...
A DREAM... ?

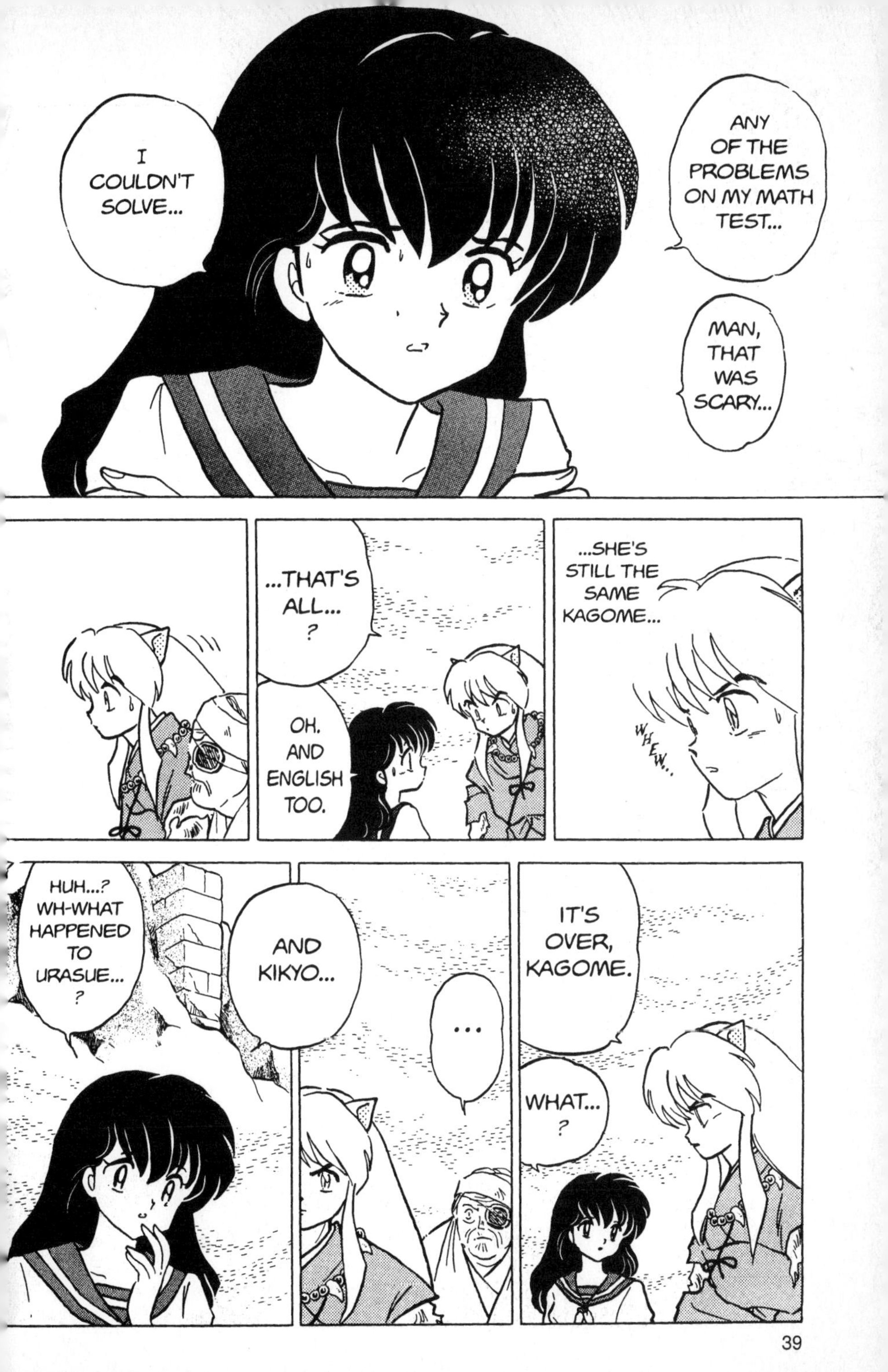
I COULDN'T SOLVE...
ANY OF THE PROBLEMS ON MY MATH TEST...
MAN, THAT WAS SCARY...
...THAT'S ALL...?
OH. AND ENGLISH TOO.
...SHE'S STILL THE SAME KAGOME...
WHEW..
HUH...? WH-WHAT HAPPENED TO URASUE...?
AND KIKYO...
...
IT'S OVER, KAGOME.
WHAT...?

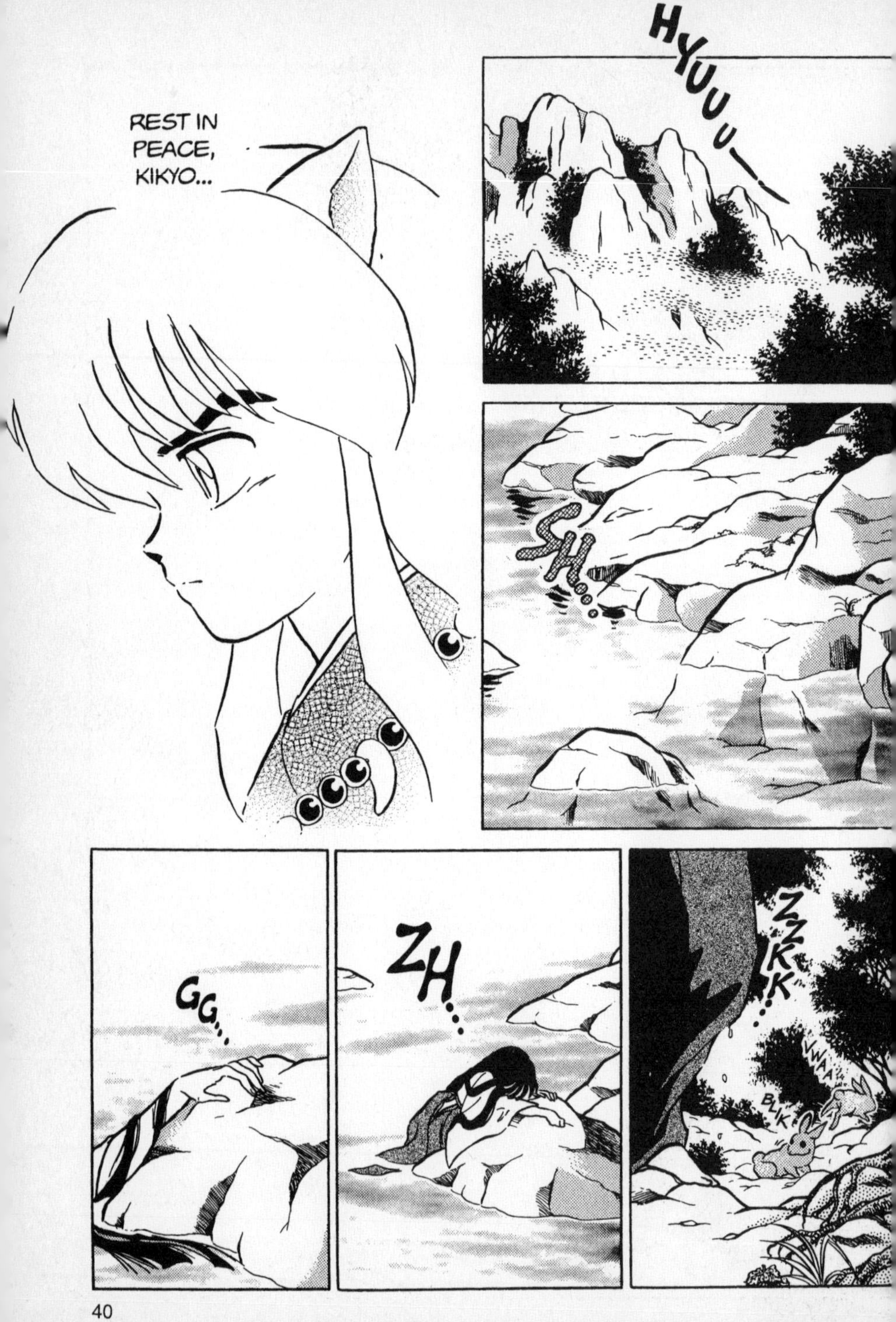
REST IN PEACE, KIKYO...
HYUUU...
SH...
GG...
ZH...
ZZKK...
VWAA
BLIK

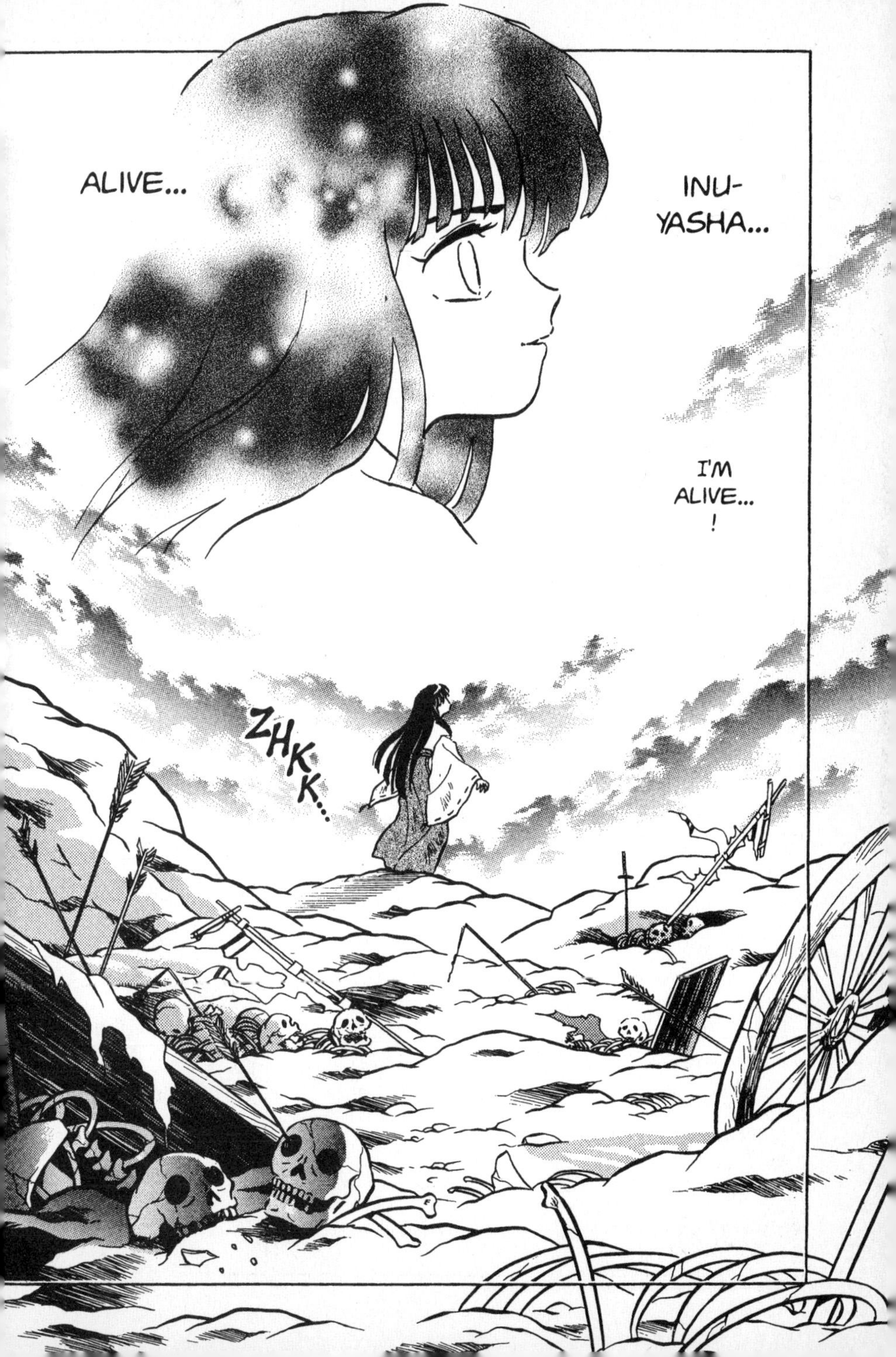
ALIVE...
INU-YASHA...
I'M ALIVE... !
ZHKK...

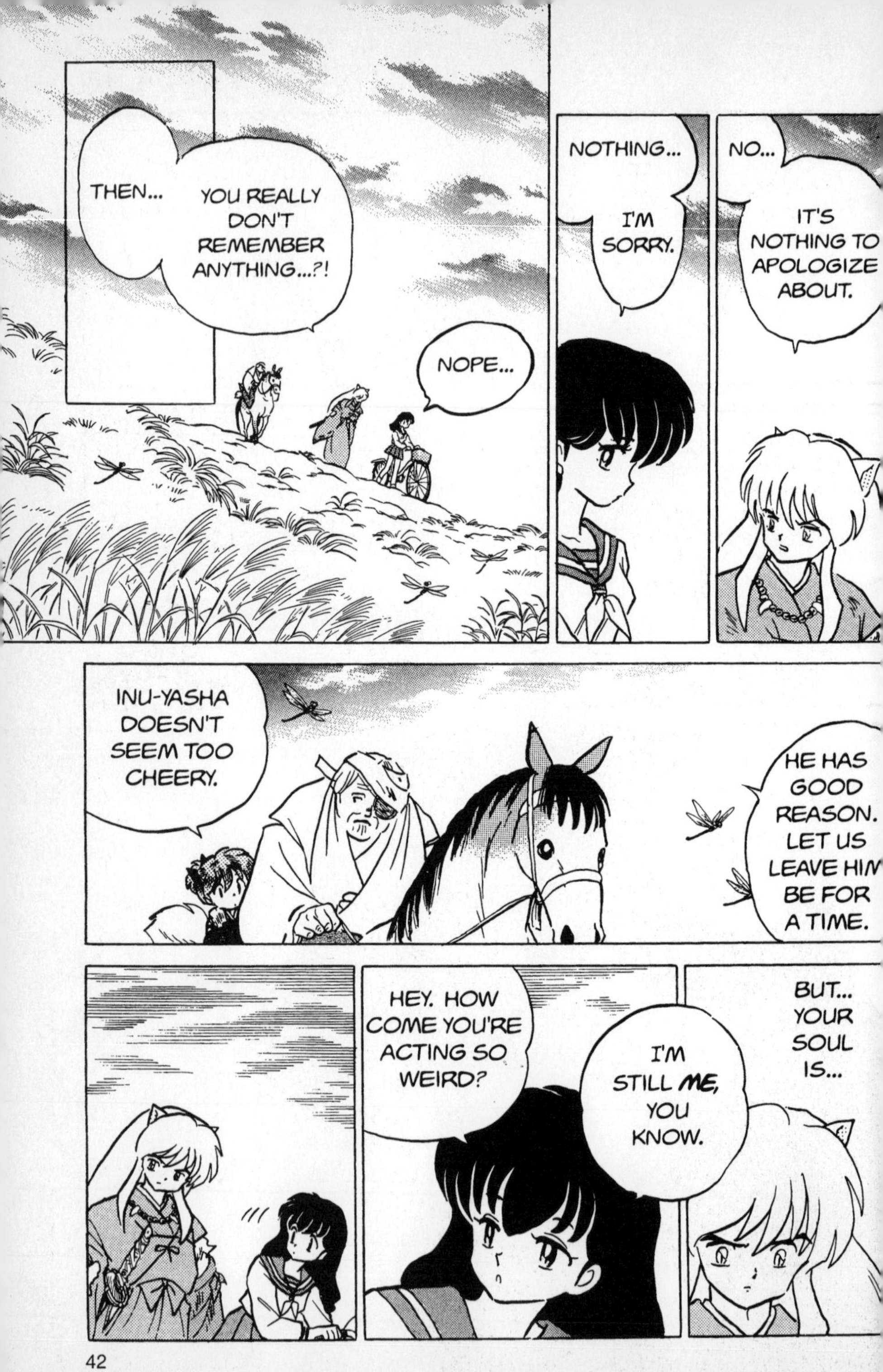
THEN...
YOU REALLY DON'T REMEMBER ANYTHING...?!
NOPE...
NOTHING...
I'M SORRY.
NO...
IT'S NOTHING TO APOLOGIZE ABOUT.
INU-YASHA DOESN'T SEEM TOO CHEERY.
HE HAS GOOD REASON. LET US LEAVE HIM BE FOR A TIME.
HEY. HOW COME YOU'RE ACTING SO WEIRD?
I'M STILL *ME*, YOU KNOW.
BUT... YOUR SOUL IS...

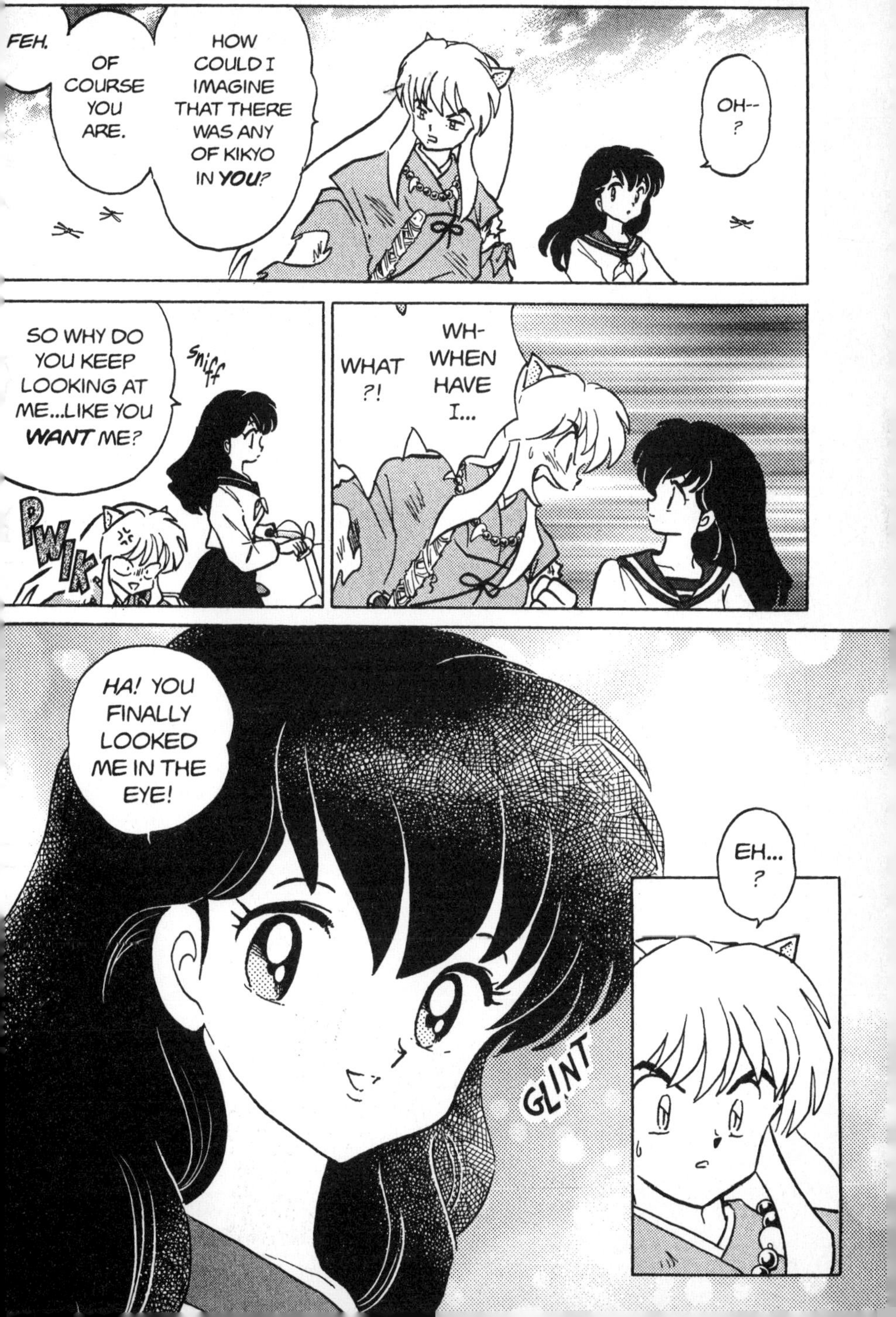
FEH.
OF COURSE YOU ARE.
HOW COULD I IMAGINE THAT THERE WAS ANY OF KIKYO IN *YOU*?
OH-- ?
SO WHY DO YOU KEEP LOOKING AT ME...LIKE YOU **WANT** ME?
sniff
PWIK
WHAT ?!
WH- WHEN HAVE I...
HA! YOU FINALLY LOOKED ME IN THE EYE!
EH... ?
GLINT

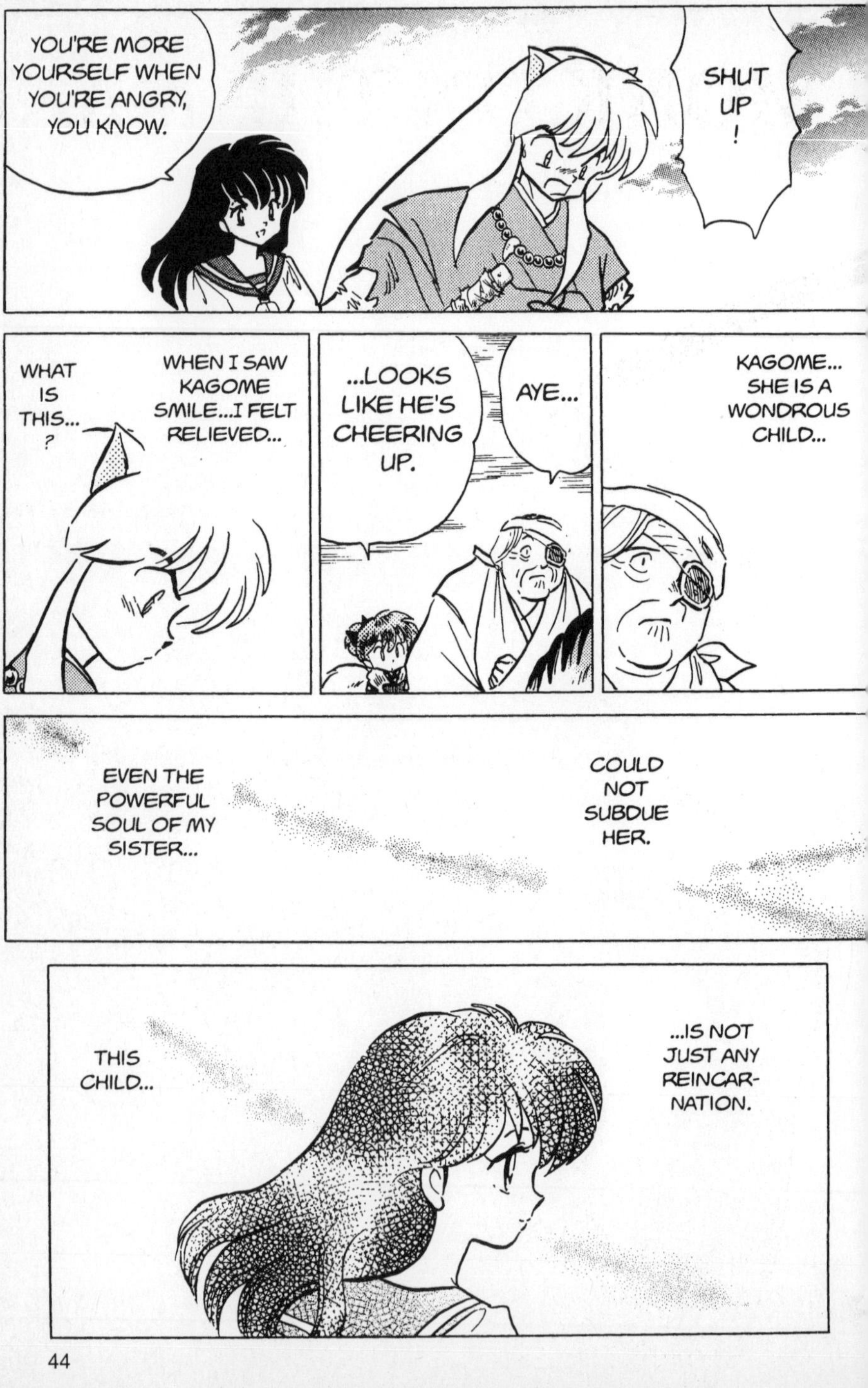
YOU'RE MORE YOURSELF WHEN YOU'RE ANGRY, YOU KNOW.
SHUT UP !
WHAT IS THIS... ?
WHEN I SAW KAGOME SMILE...I FELT RELIEVED...
...LOOKS LIKE HE'S CHEERING UP.
AYE...
KAGOME... SHE IS A WONDROUS CHILD...
EVEN THE POWERFUL SOUL OF MY SISTER...
COULD NOT SUBDUE HER.
THIS CHILD...
...IS NOT JUST ANY REINCAR-NATION.

SCROLL THREE

MONK ON THE MAKE

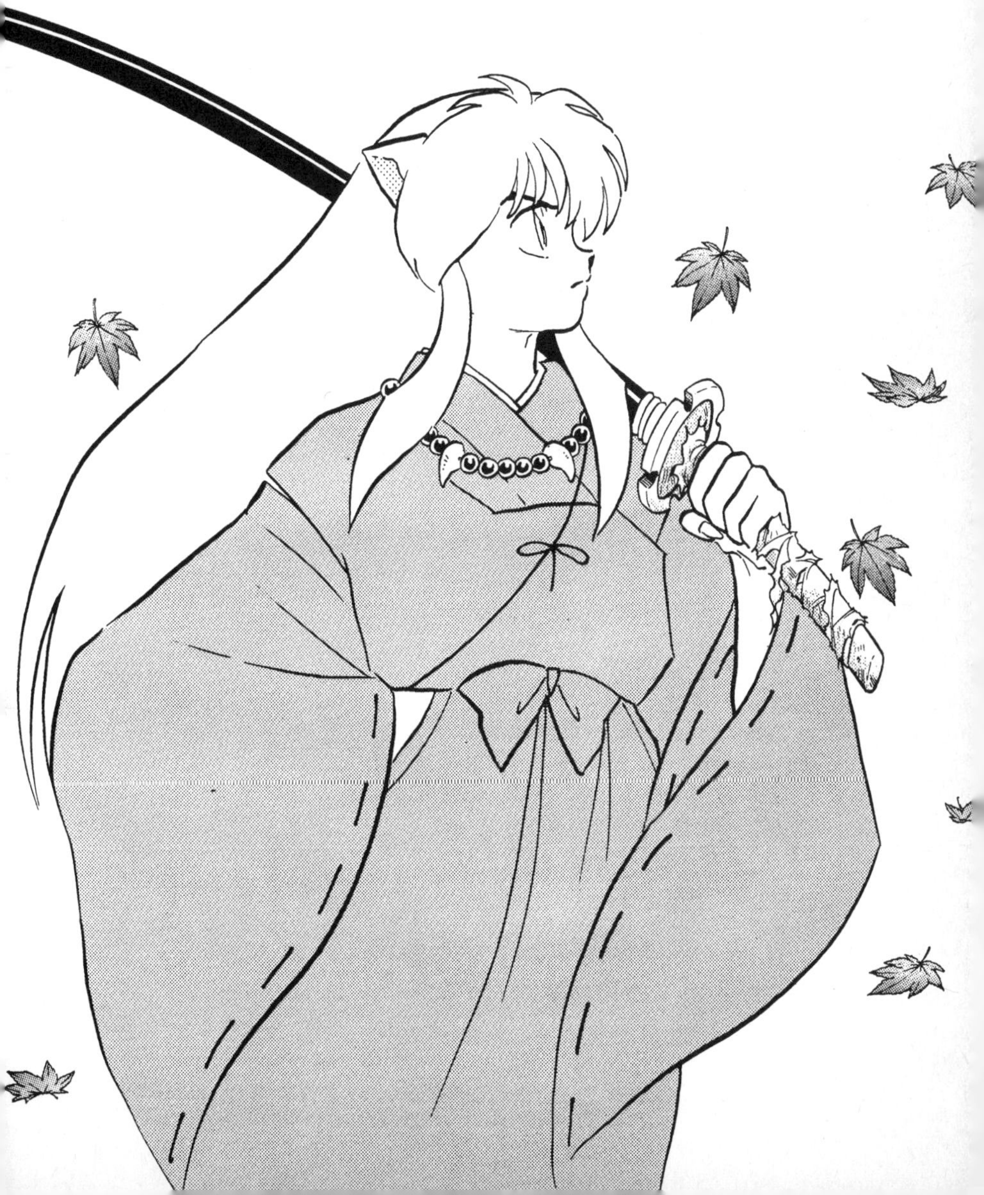

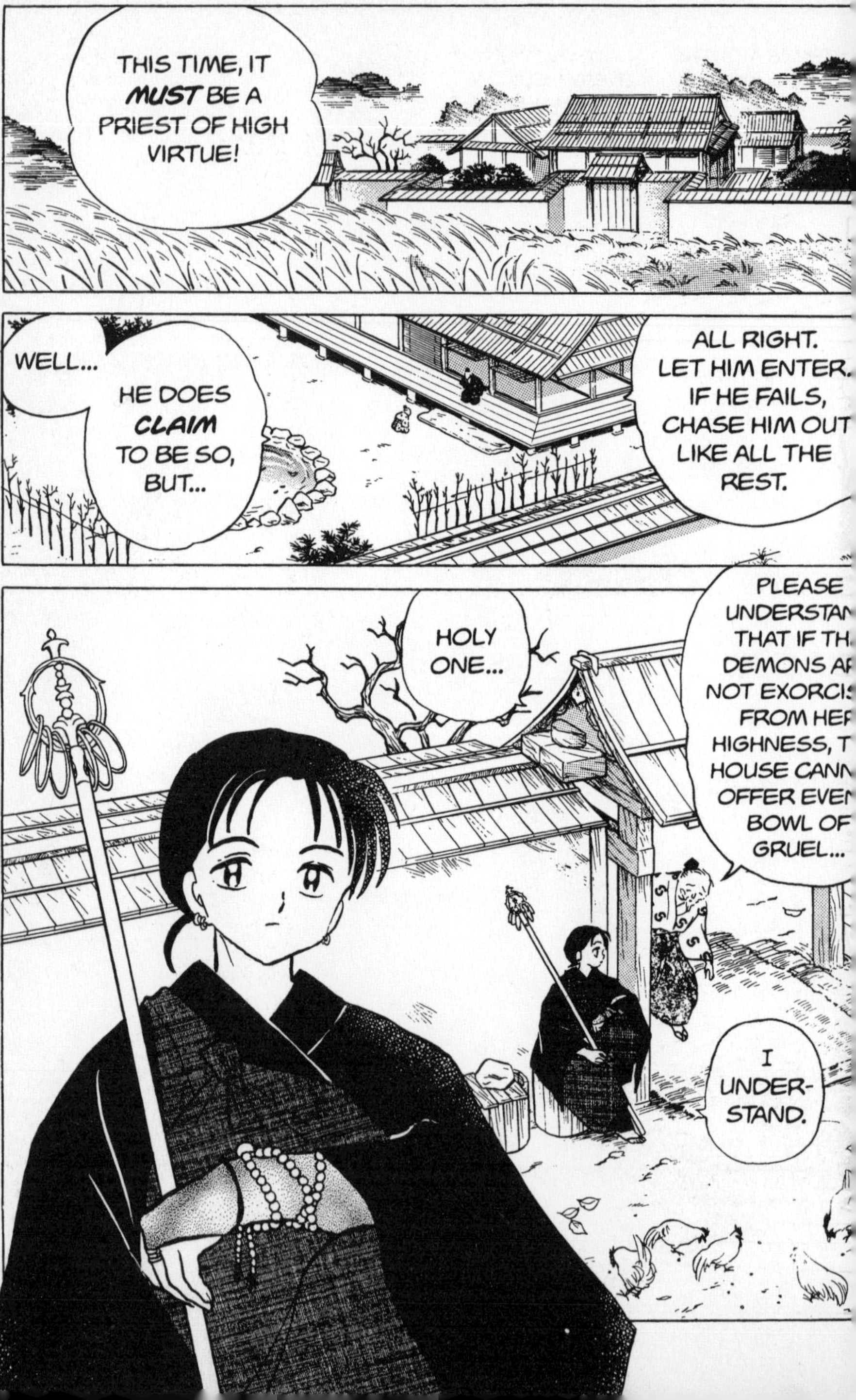
THIS TIME, IT MUST BE A PRIEST OF HIGH VIRTUE!
WELL...
HE DOES CLAIM TO BE SO, BUT...
ALL RIGHT. LET HIM ENTER. IF HE FAILS, CHASE HIM OUT LIKE ALL THE REST.
HOLY ONE...
PLEASE UNDERSTAN THAT IF TH DEMONS AR NOT EXORCIS FROM HEF HIGHNESS, T HOUSE CANN OFFER EVEN BOWL OF GRUEL...
I UNDER-STAND.

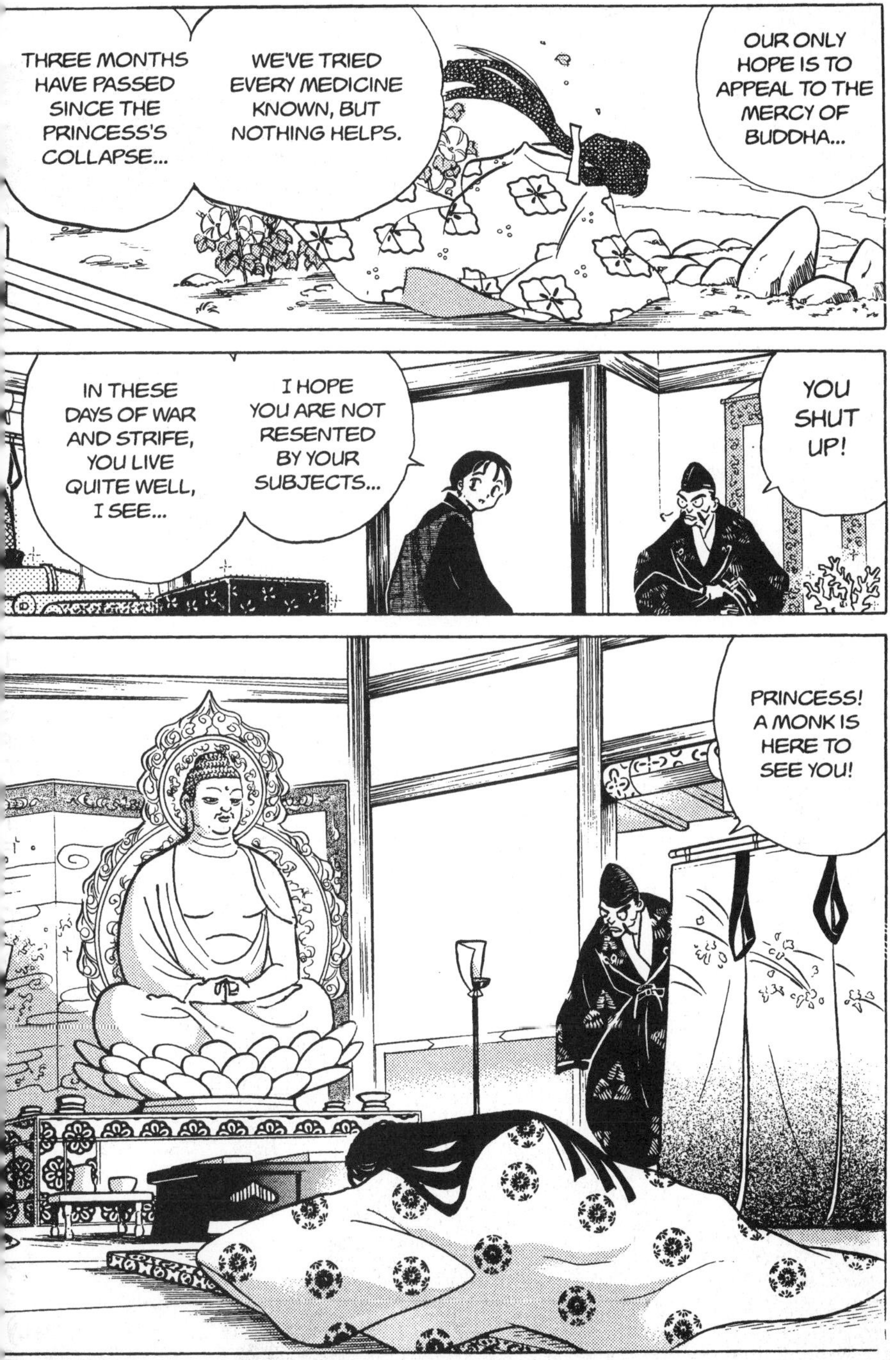
THREE MONTHS HAVE PASSED SINCE THE PRINCESS'S COLLAPSE...
WE'VE TRIED EVERY MEDICINE KNOWN, BUT NOTHING HELPS.
OUR ONLY HOPE IS TO APPEAL TO THE MERCY OF BUDDHA...
IN THESE DAYS OF WAR AND STRIFE, YOU LIVE QUITE WELL, I SEE...
I HOPE YOU ARE NOT RESENTED BY YOUR SUBJECTS...
YOU SHUT UP!
PRINCESS! A MONK IS HERE TO SEE YOU!

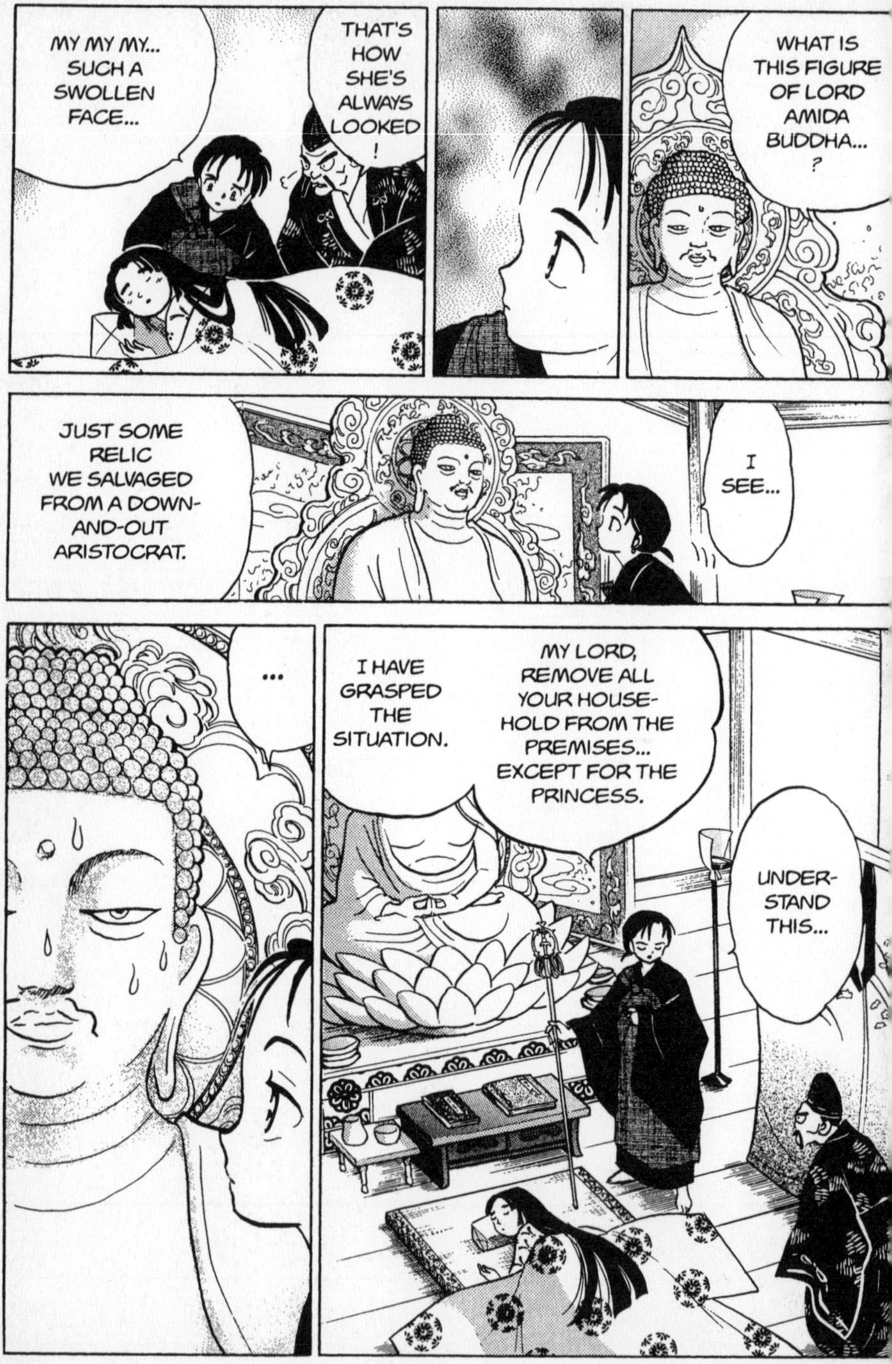
MY MY MY... SUCH A SWOLLEN FACE...
THAT'S HOW SHE'S ALWAYS LOOKED!
WHAT IS THIS FIGURE OF LORD AMIDA BUDDHA...?
JUST SOME RELIC WE SALVAGED FROM A DOWN-AND-OUT ARISTOCRAT.
I SEE...
...
I HAVE GRASPED THE SITUATION.
MY LORD, REMOVE ALL YOUR HOUSE-HOLD FROM THE PREMISES... EXCEPT FOR THE PRINCESS.
UNDER-STAND THIS...

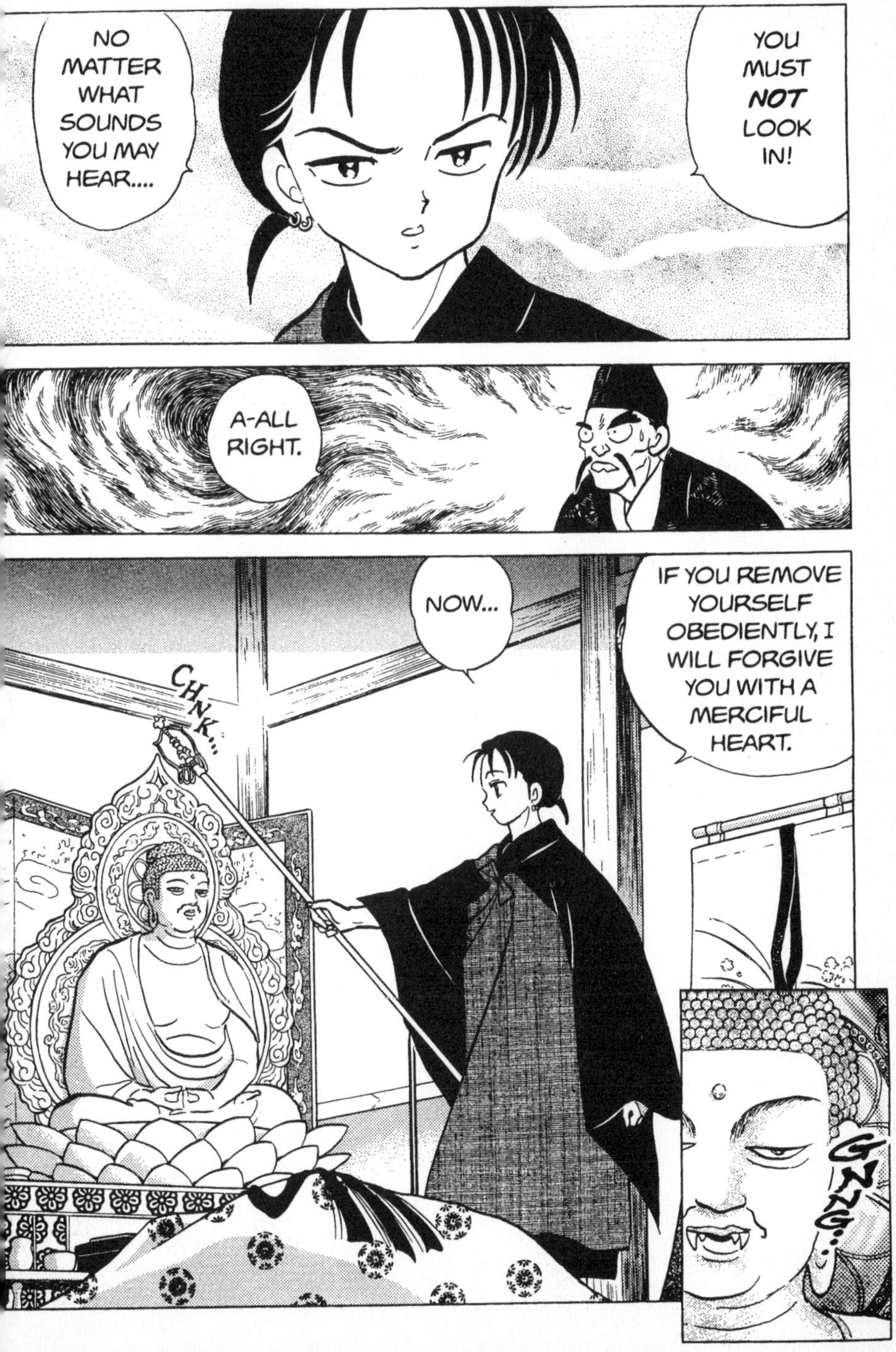
NO MATTER WHAT SOUNDS YOU MAY HEAR....
YOU MUST NOT LOOK IN!
A-ALL RIGHT.
CHNK...
NOW...
IF YOU REMOVE YOURSELF OBEDIENTLY, I WILL FORGIVE YOU WITH A MERCIFUL HEART.
GNNG...

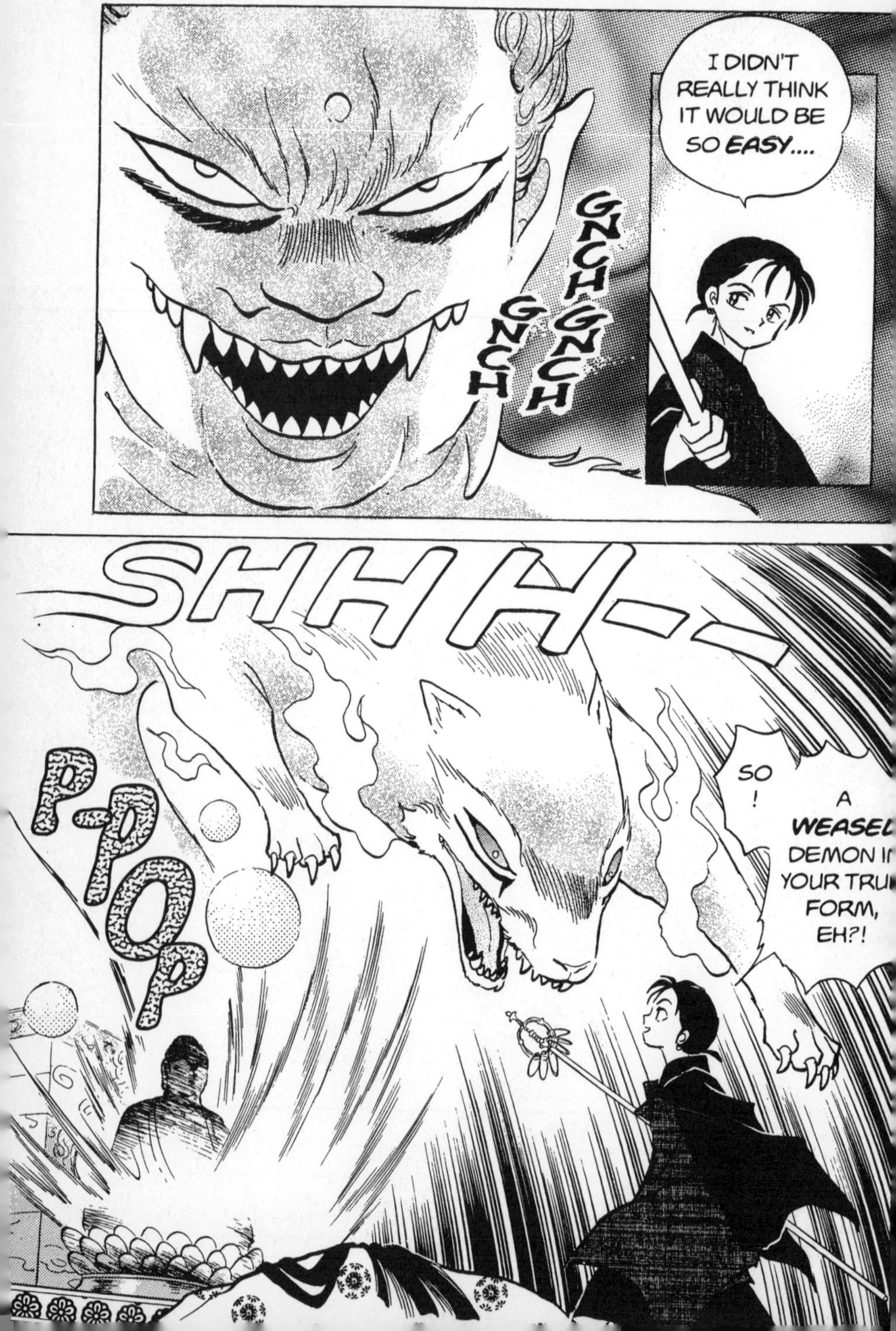
GNCH
GNCH GNCH
GNCH
I DIDN'T REALLY THINK IT WOULD BE SO *EASY*....
SHHH--
P-P-POP
SO! A *WEASEL* DEMON I YOUR TRU FORM, EH?!

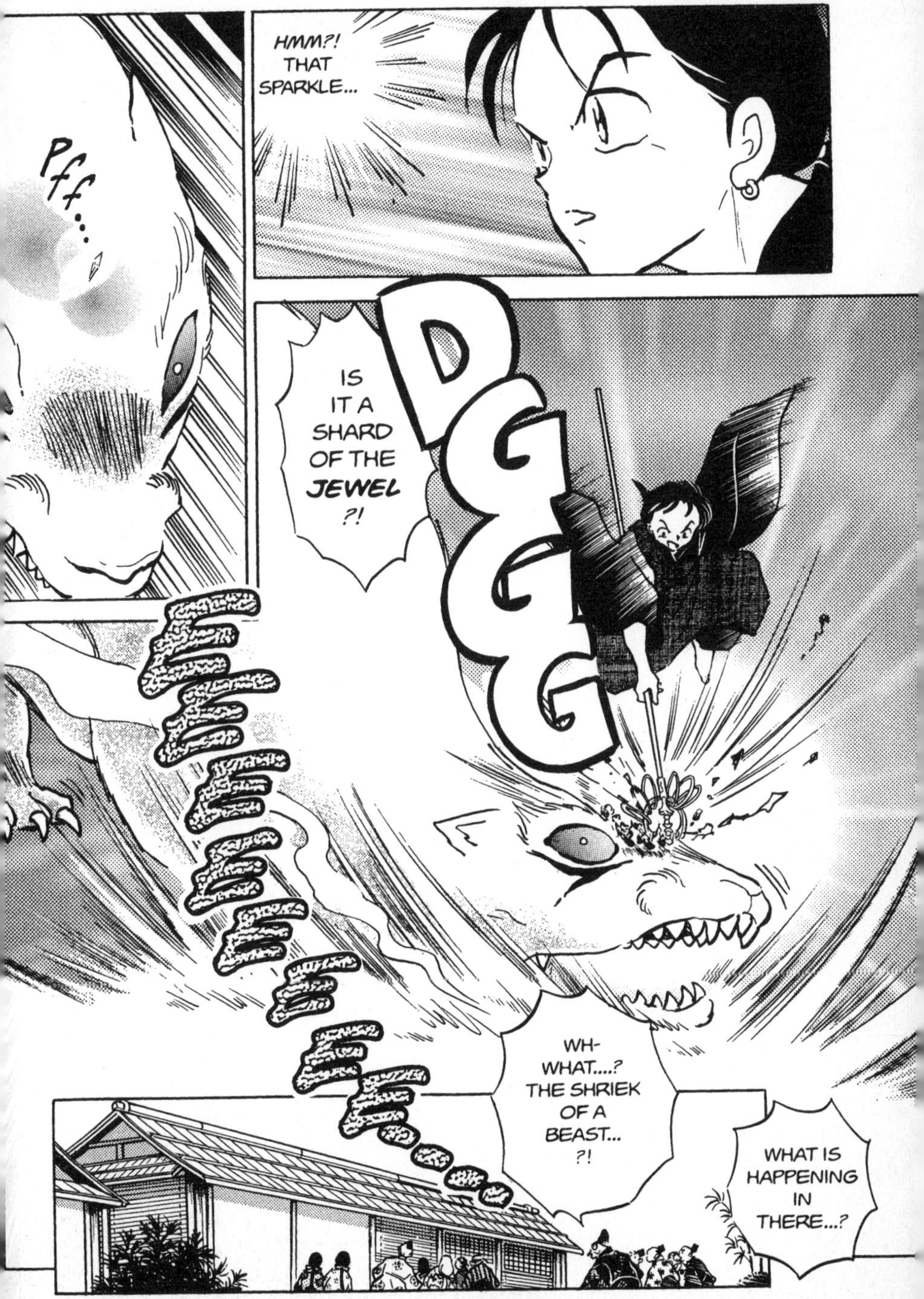
Pff...
HMM?! THAT SPARKLE...
IS IT A SHARD OF THE JEWEL ?!
DGGG
EEEEEEEEE.....
WH-WHAT....? THE SHRIEK OF A BEAST... ?!
WHAT IS HAPPENING IN THERE...?

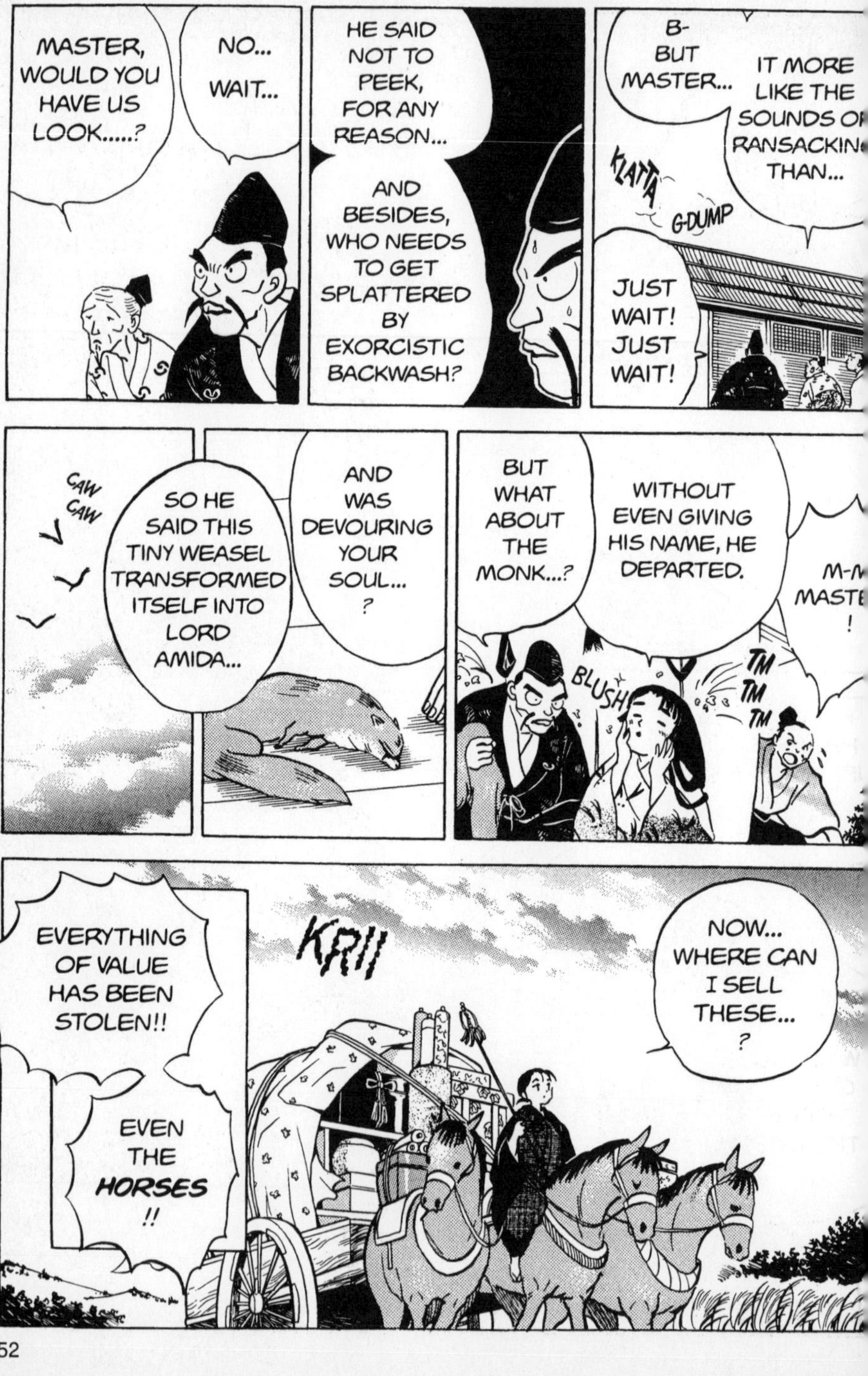
MASTER, WOULD YOU HAVE US LOOK.....?
NO... WAIT...
HE SAID NOT TO PEEK, FOR ANY REASON...
AND BESIDES, WHO NEEDS TO GET SPLATTERED BY EXORCISTIC BACKWASH?
B-BUT MASTER...
IT MORE LIKE THE SOUNDS O RANSACKIN THAN...
KLATTA
G-DUMP
JUST WAIT! JUST WAIT!
CAW CAW
SO HE SAID THIS TINY WEASEL TRANSFORMED ITSELF INTO LORD AMIDA...
AND WAS DEVOURING YOUR SOUL...?
BUT WHAT ABOUT THE MONK...?
WITHOUT EVEN GIVING HIS NAME, HE DEPARTED.
BLUSH
M-M MASTE !
TM TM TM
EVERYTHING OF VALUE HAS BEEN STOLEN!!
EVEN THE ***HORSES***!!
KRII
NOW... WHERE CAN I SELL THESE...?

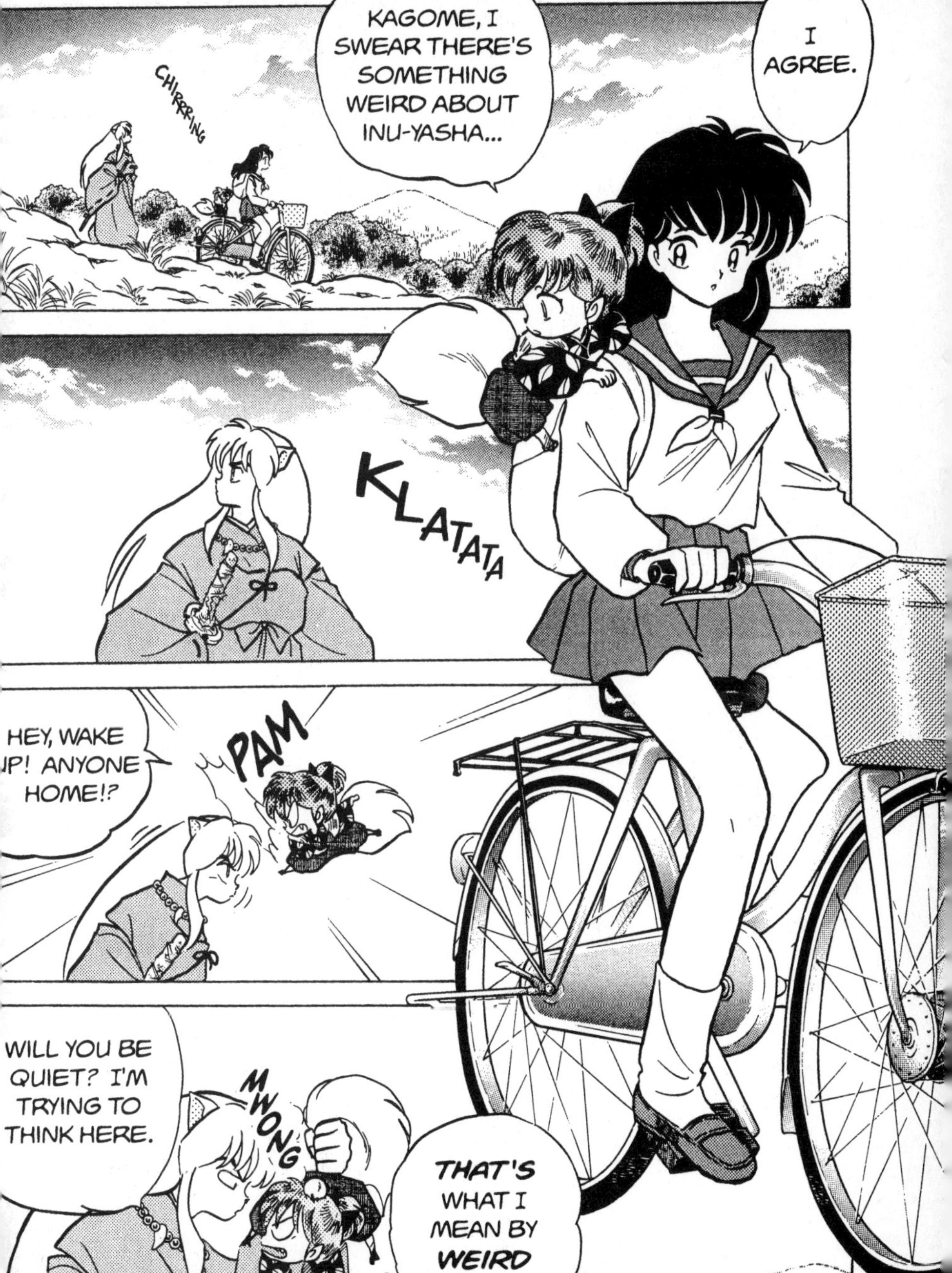
CHIRRRING
KAGOME, I SWEAR THERE'S SOMETHING WEIRD ABOUT INU-YASHA...
I AGREE.
KLATATA
HEY, WAKE UP! ANYONE HOME!?
PAM
WILL YOU BE QUIET? I'M TRYING TO THINK HERE.
MWONG
THAT'S WHAT I MEAN BY WEIRD!

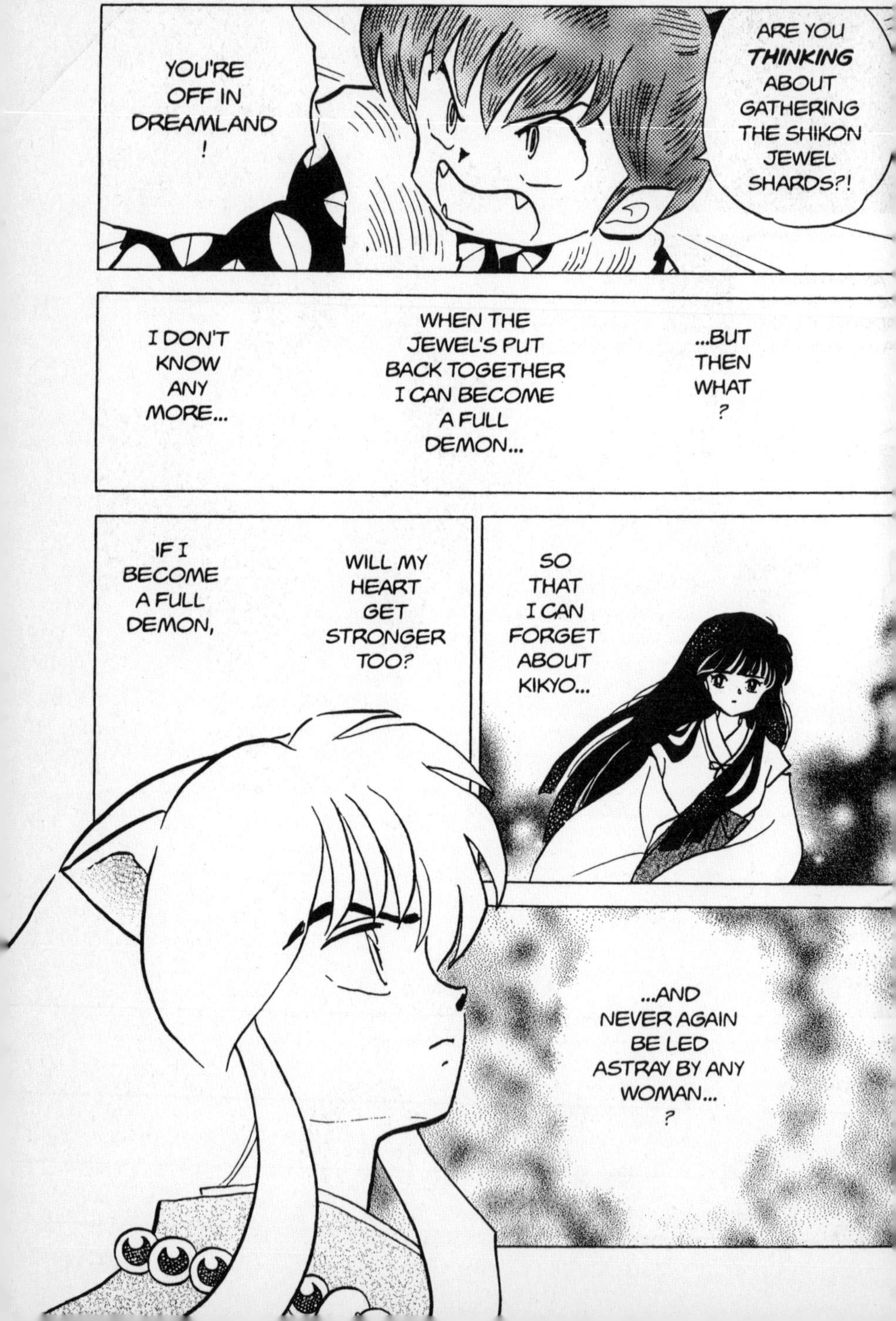
YOU'RE OFF IN DREAMLAND!
ARE YOU *THINKING* ABOUT GATHERING THE SHIKON JEWEL SHARDS?!
I DON'T KNOW ANY MORE...
WHEN THE JEWEL'S PUT BACK TOGETHER I CAN BECOME A FULL DEMON...
...BUT THEN WHAT?
IF I BECOME A FULL DEMON,
WILL MY HEART GET STRONGER TOO?
SO THAT I CAN FORGET ABOUT KIKYO...
...AND NEVER AGAIN BE LED ASTRAY BY ANY WOMAN...?

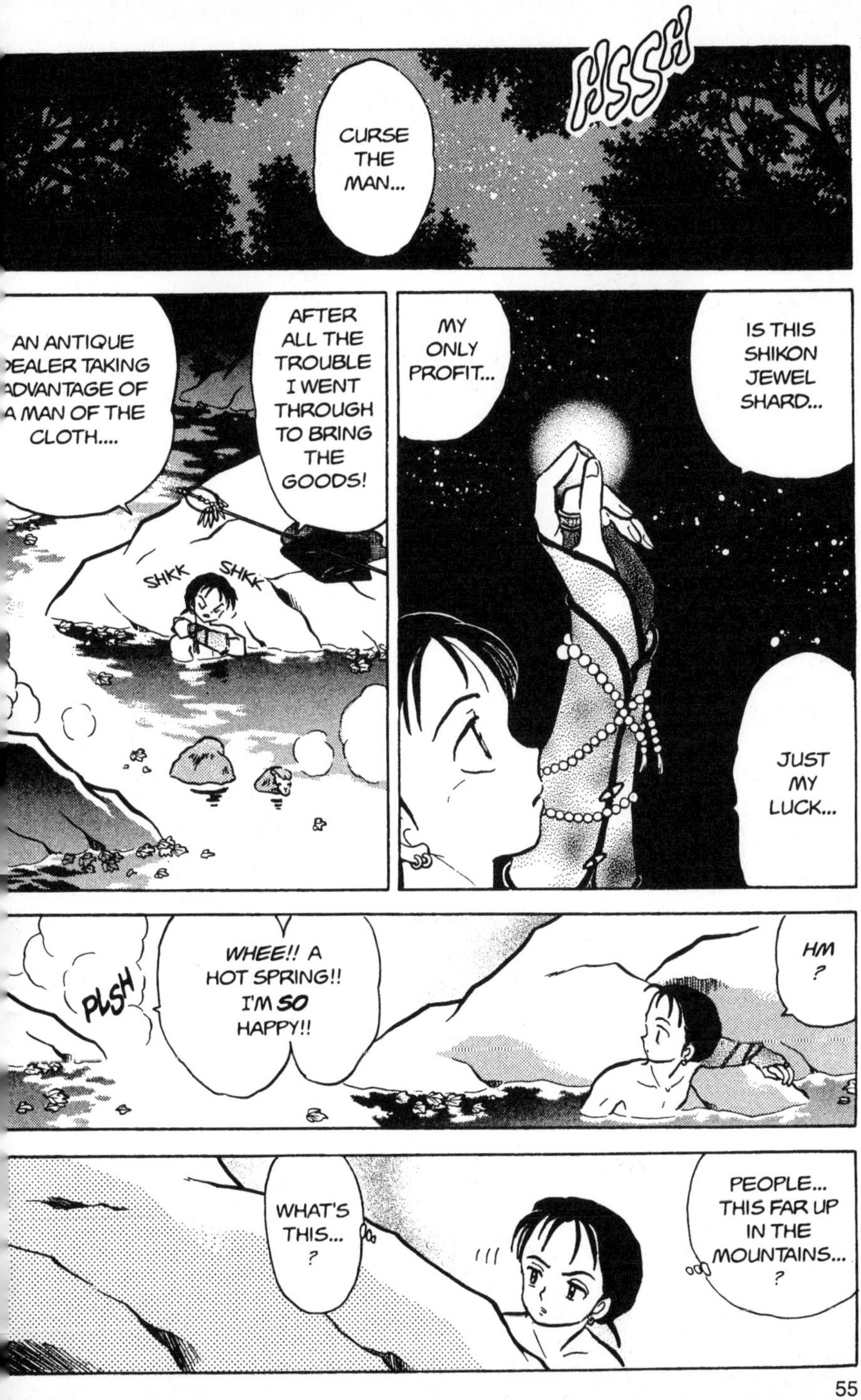
HSSH
CURSE THE MAN...
AN ANTIQUE DEALER TAKING ADVANTAGE OF A MAN OF THE CLOTH....
AFTER ALL THE TROUBLE I WENT THROUGH TO BRING THE GOODS!
SHKK SHKK
MY ONLY PROFIT...
IS THIS SHIKON JEWEL SHARD...
JUST MY LUCK...
PLSH
WHEE!! A HOT SPRING!! I'M *SO* HAPPY!!
HM ?
WHAT'S THIS... ?
PEOPLE... THIS FAR UP IN THE MOUNTAINS... ?

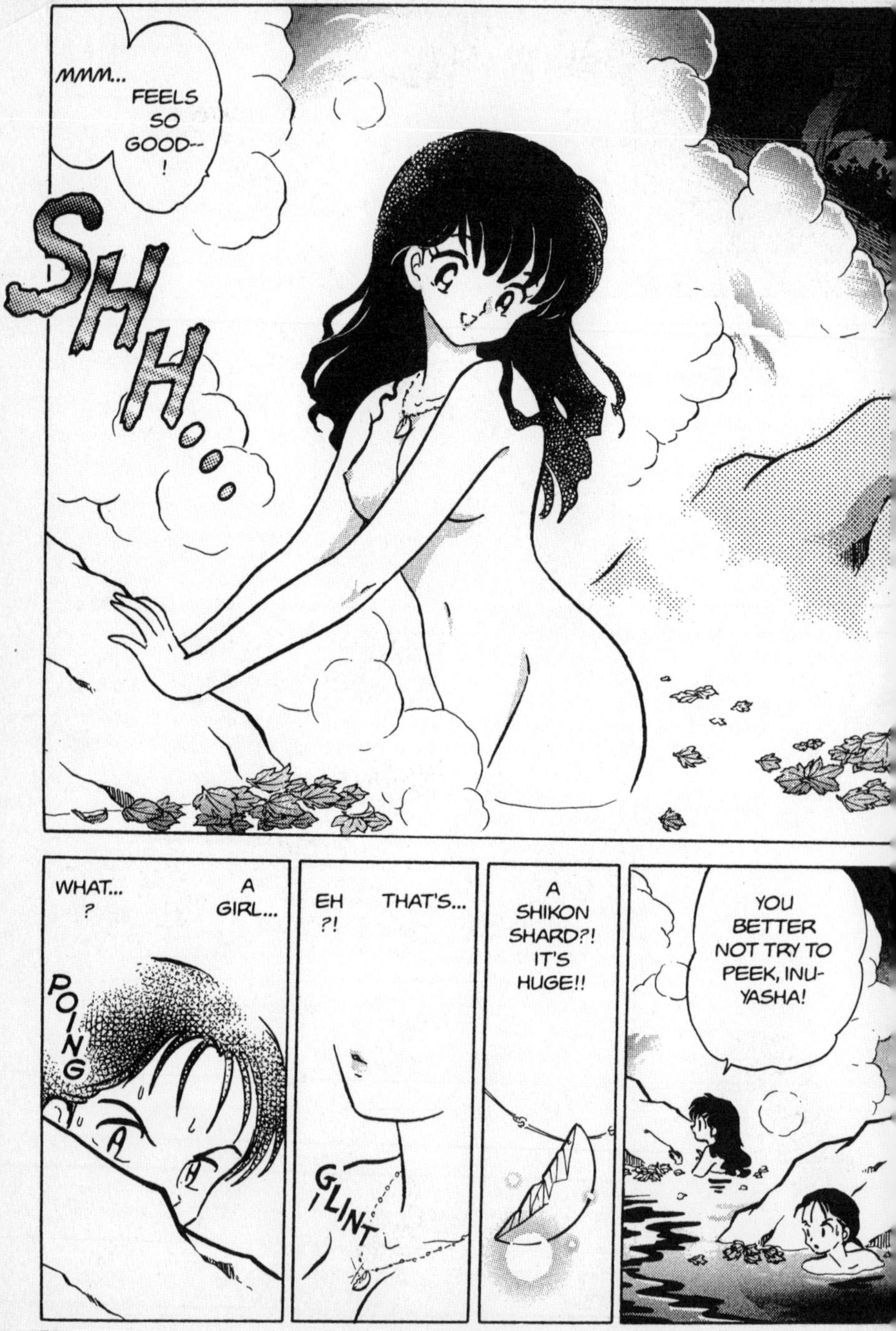
MMM... FEELS SO GOOD--!
SHHOOO...
WHAT...?
A GIRL...
POING
EH?!
THAT'S...
GLINT
A SHIKON SHARD?! IT'S HUGE!!
YOU BETTER NOT TRY TO PEEK, INU-YASHA!

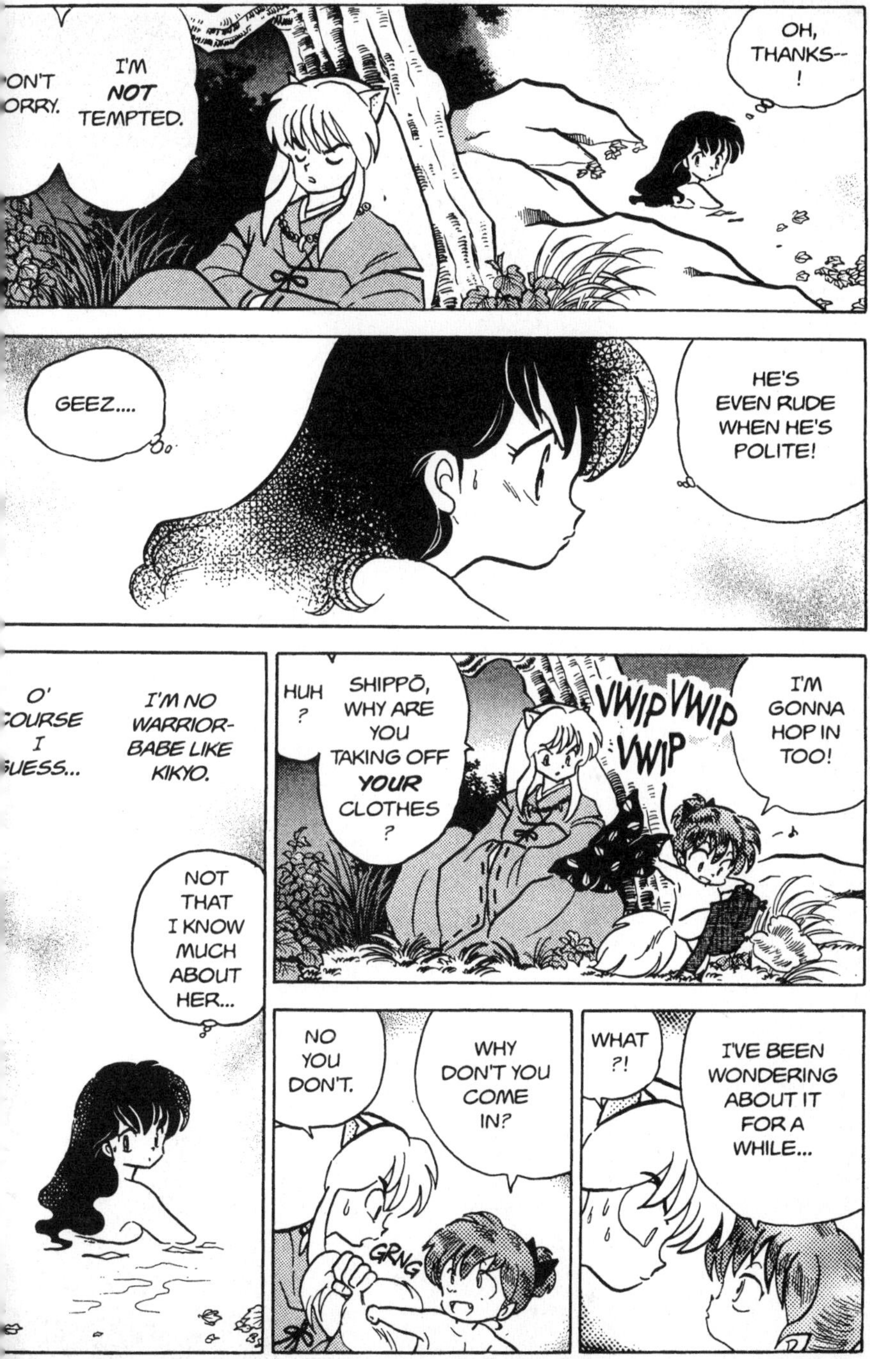
ON'T ORRY.
I'M NOT TEMPTED.
OH, THANKS--!
GEEZ....
HE'S EVEN RUDE WHEN HE'S POLITE!
O' OURSE I UESS...
I'M NO WARRIOR-BABE LIKE KIKYO.
NOT THAT I KNOW MUCH ABOUT HER...
HUH?
SHIPPŌ, WHY ARE YOU TAKING OFF YOUR CLOTHES?
VWIP VWIP VWIP
I'M GONNA HOP IN TOO!
NO YOU DON'T.
WHY DON'T YOU COME IN?
GRNG
WHAT?!
I'VE BEEN WONDERING ABOUT IT FOR A WHILE...

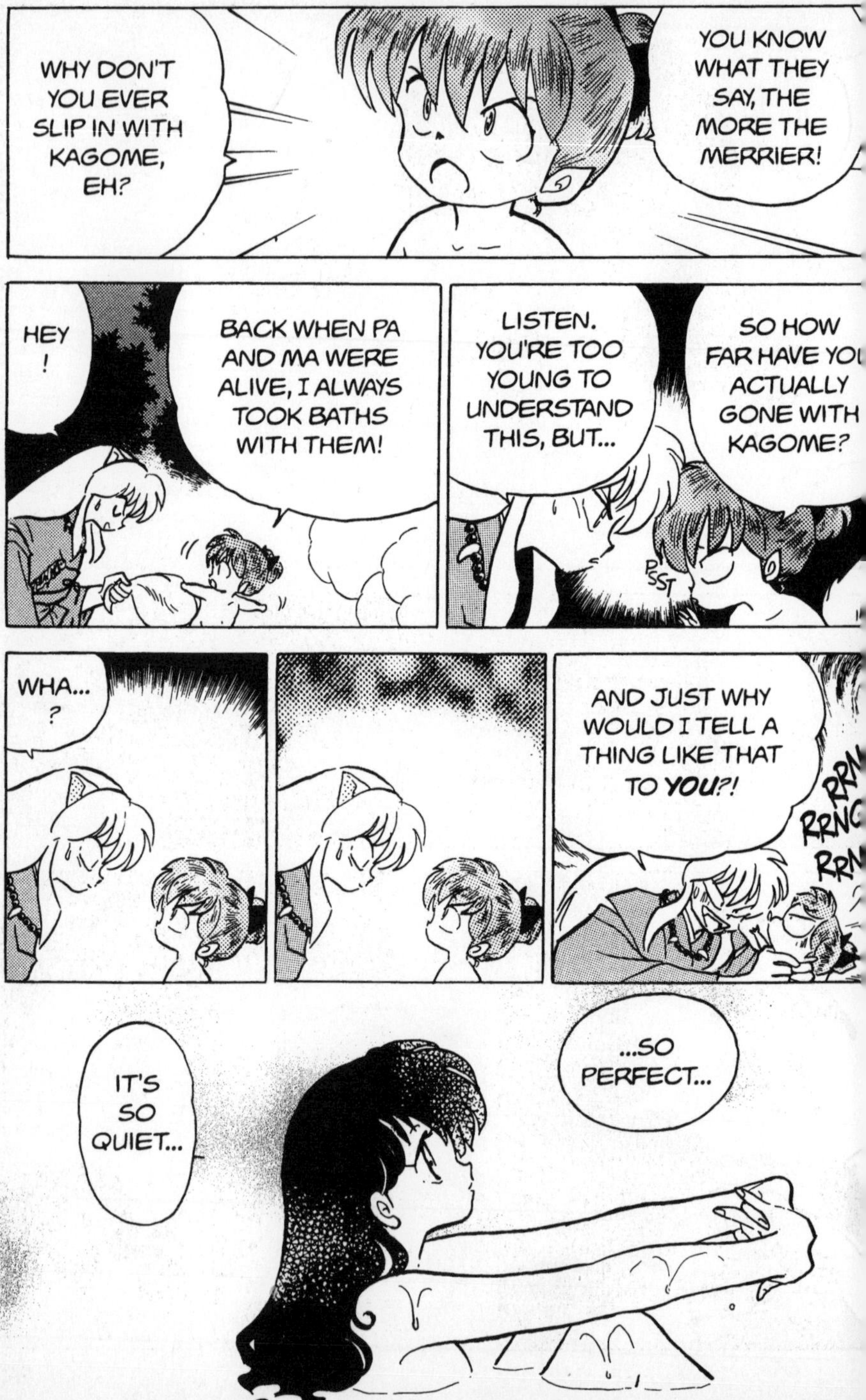
WHY DON'T YOU EVER SLIP IN WITH KAGOME, EH?
YOU KNOW WHAT THEY SAY, THE MORE THE MERRIER!
HEY!
BACK WHEN PA AND MA WERE ALIVE, I ALWAYS TOOK BATHS WITH THEM!
LISTEN. YOU'RE TOO YOUNG TO UNDERSTAND THIS, BUT...
SO HOW FAR HAVE YOU ACTUALLY GONE WITH KAGOME?
PSST
WHA...?
AND JUST WHY WOULD I TELL A THING LIKE THAT TO *YOU*?!
IT'S SO QUIET...
...SO PERFECT...

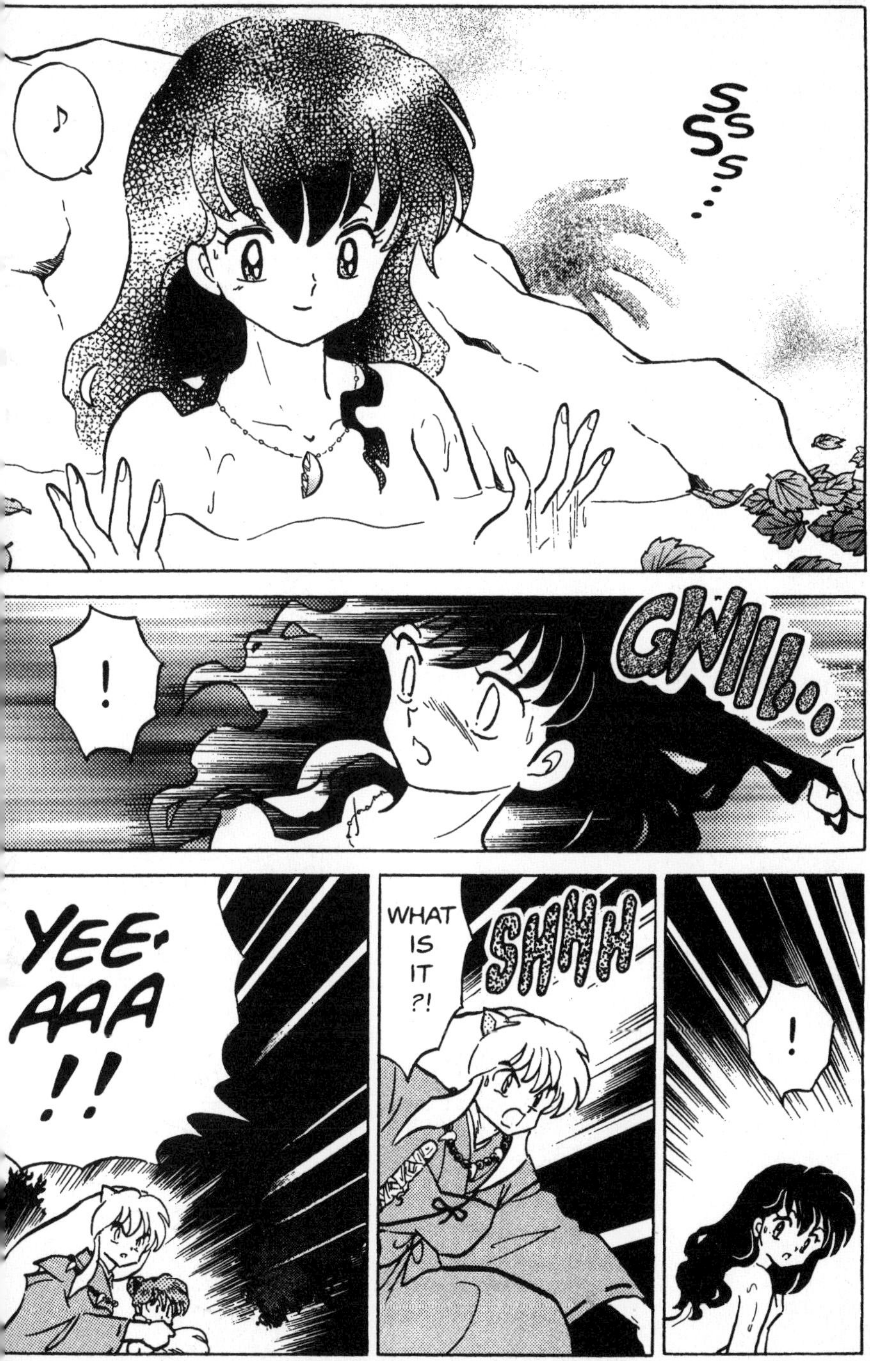
♪
SSSS...
!
GWIIL...
YEE-AAA!!
WHAT IS IT?!
SHHH
!

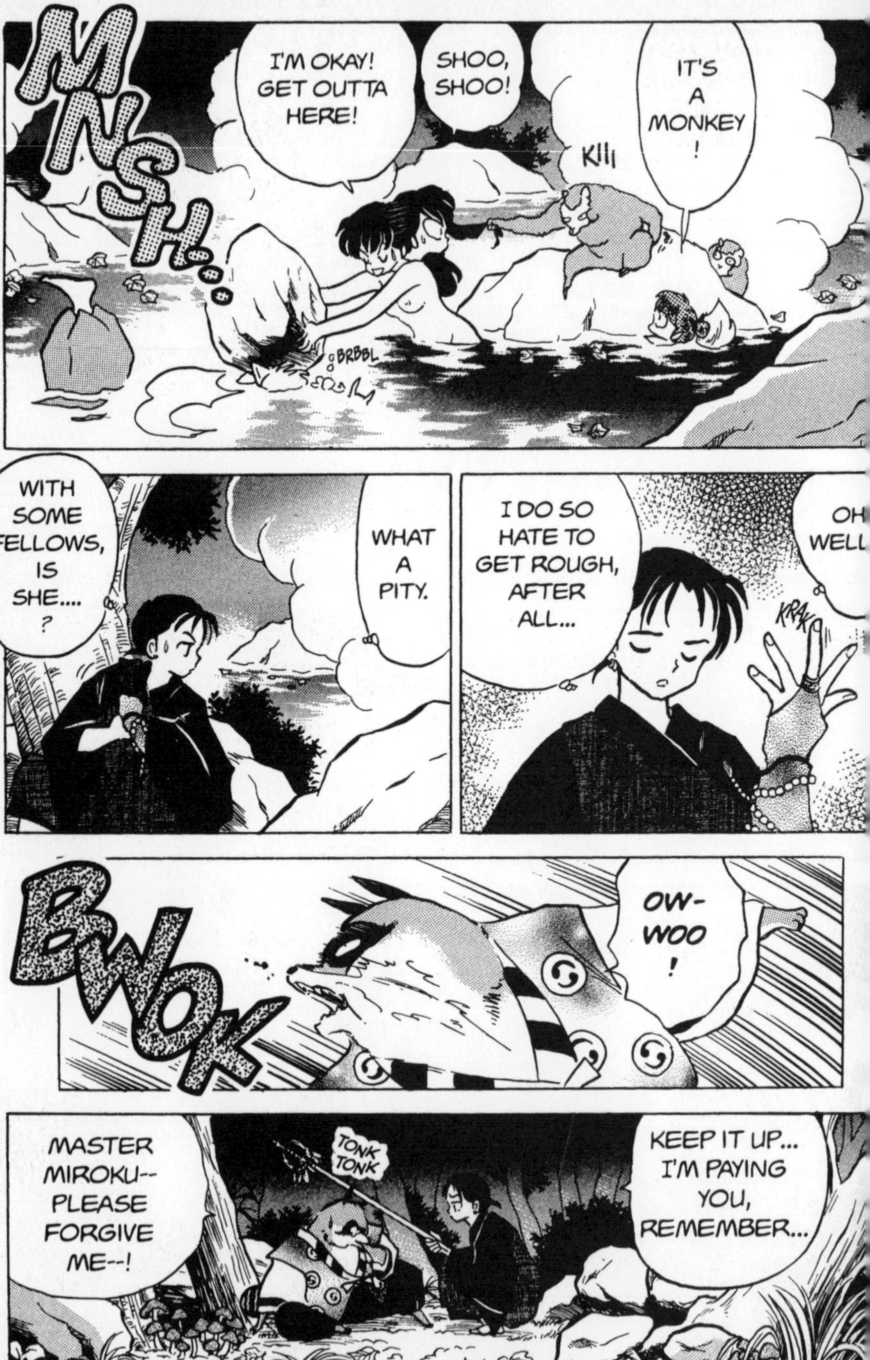
MNSH...
I'M OKAY! GET OUTTA HERE!
SHOO, SHOO!
KIII
IT'S A MONKEY !
BRBBL
WITH SOME FELLOWS, IS SHE.... ?
WHAT A PITY.
I DO SO HATE TO GET ROUGH, AFTER ALL...
KRAK
OH WELL
BWOK
OW-WOO !
MASTER MIROKU-- PLEASE FORGIVE ME--!
TONK TONK
KEEP IT UP... I'M PAYING YOU, REMEMBER...

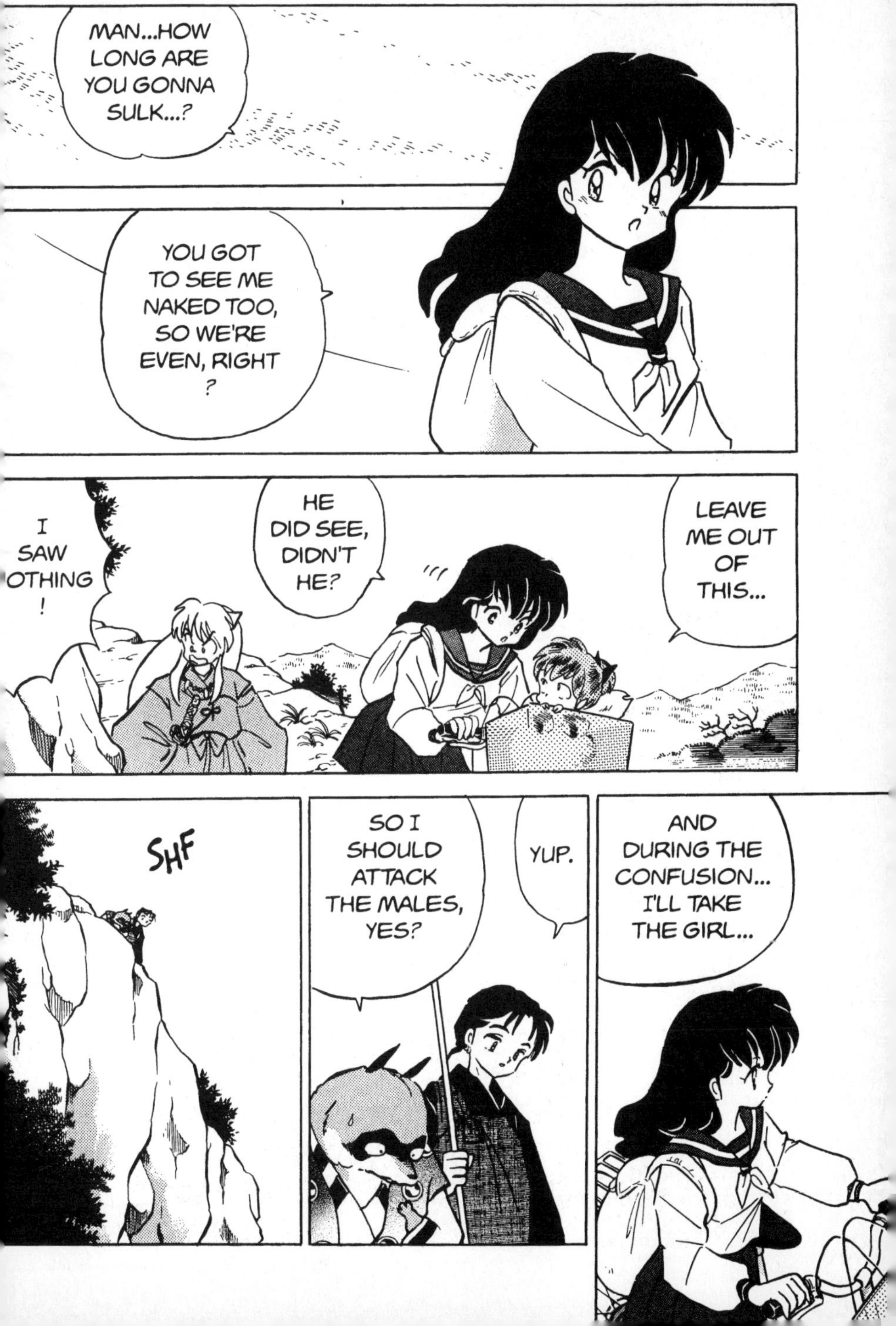
MAN...HOW LONG ARE YOU GONNA SULK...?
YOU GOT TO SEE ME NAKED TOO, SO WE'RE EVEN, RIGHT ?
I SAW OTHING !
HE DID SEE, DIDN'T HE?
LEAVE ME OUT OF THIS...
SHF
SO I SHOULD ATTACK THE MALES, YES?
YUP.
AND DURING THE CONFUSION... I'LL TAKE THE GIRL...

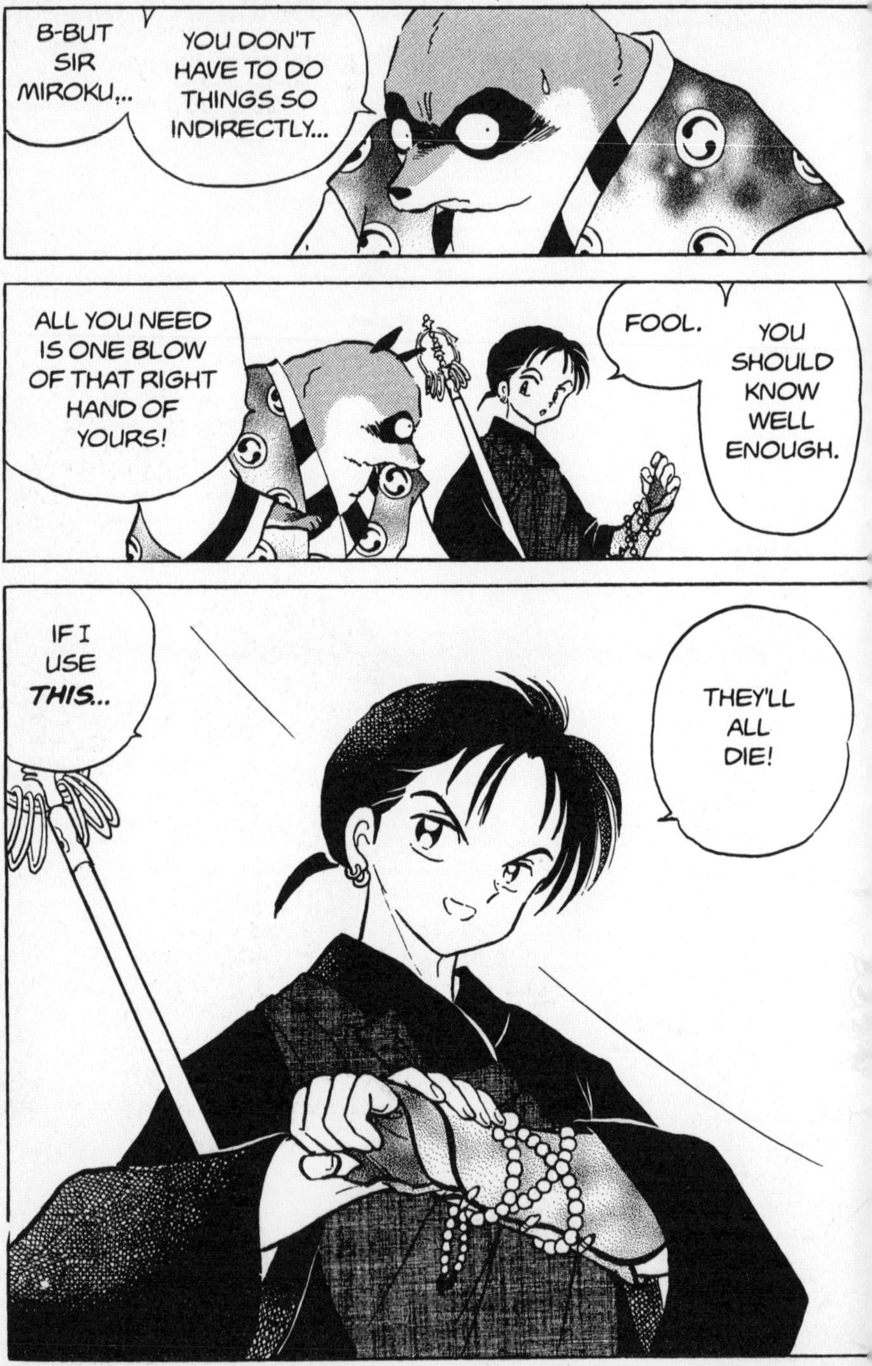
B-BUT SIR MIROKU...
YOU DON'T HAVE TO DO THINGS SO INDIRECTLY...
ALL YOU NEED IS ONE BLOW OF THAT RIGHT HAND OF YOURS!
FOOL.
YOU SHOULD KNOW WELL ENOUGH.
IF I USE *THIS*...
THEY'LL ALL DIE!

SCROLL FOUR

JEWEL THIEF

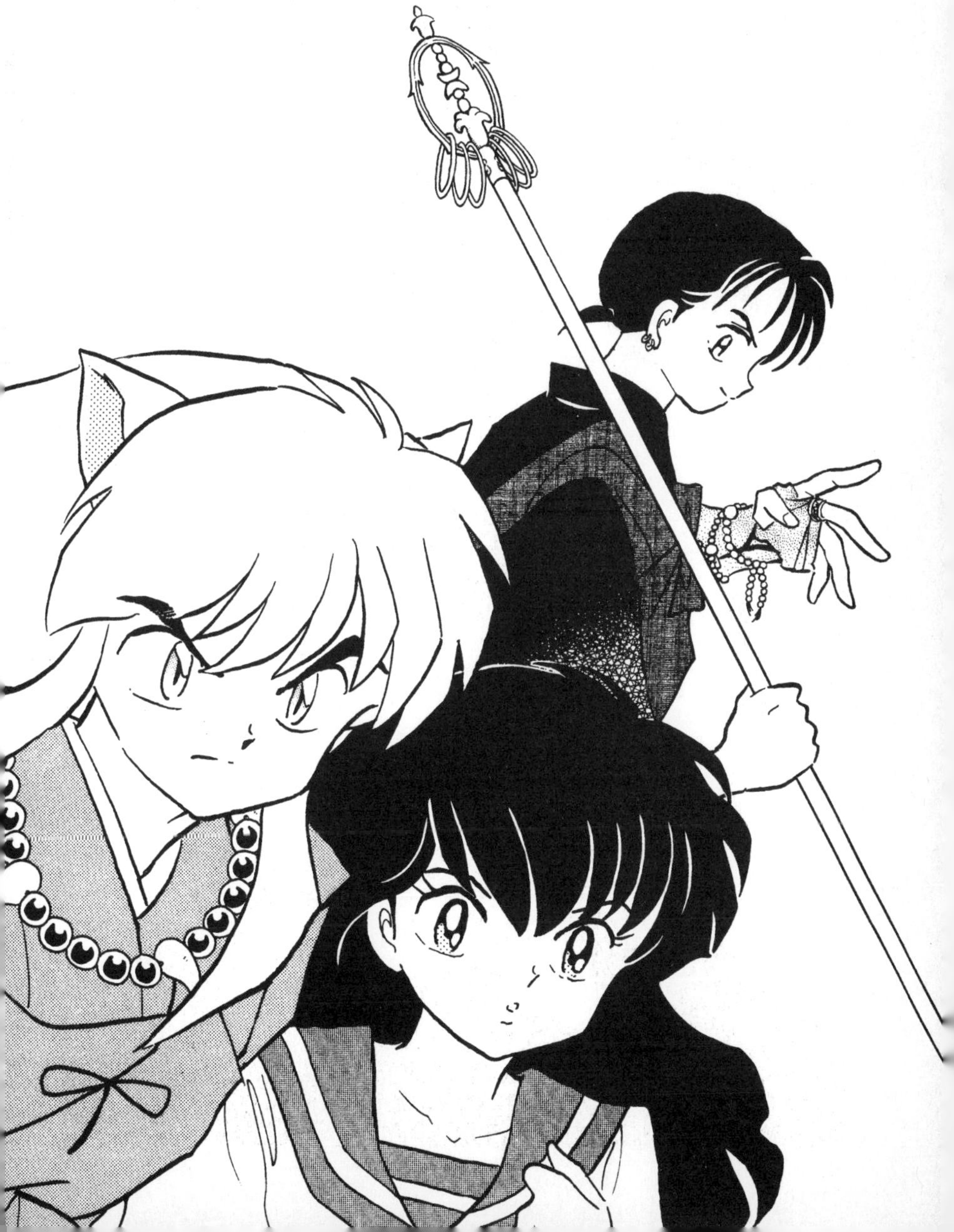

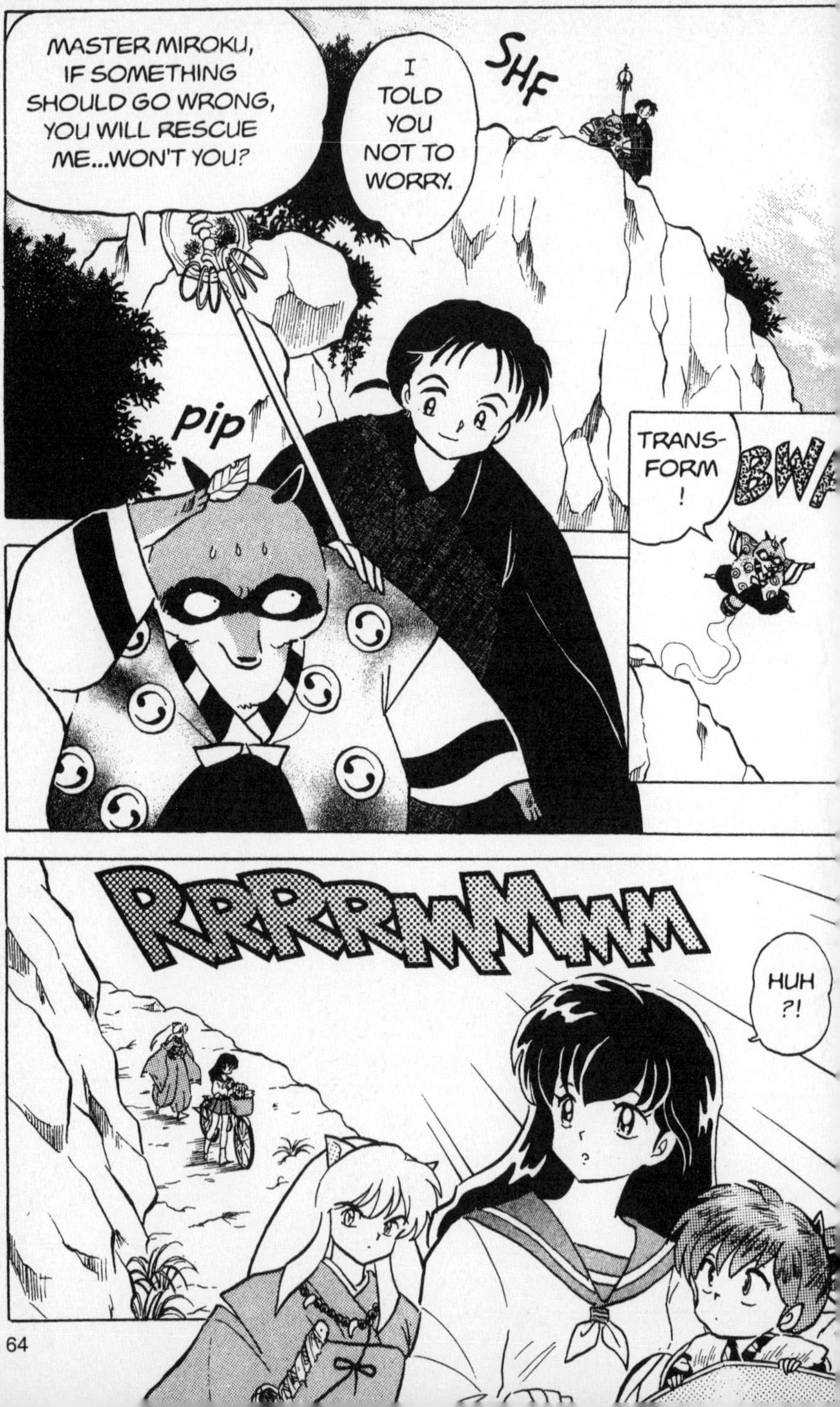
MASTER MIROKU, IF SOMETHING SHOULD GO WRONG, YOU WILL RESCUE ME...WON'T YOU?
I TOLD YOU NOT TO WORRY.
SHF
pip
TRANS-FORM!
BW
RRRRRMMMM
HUH?!

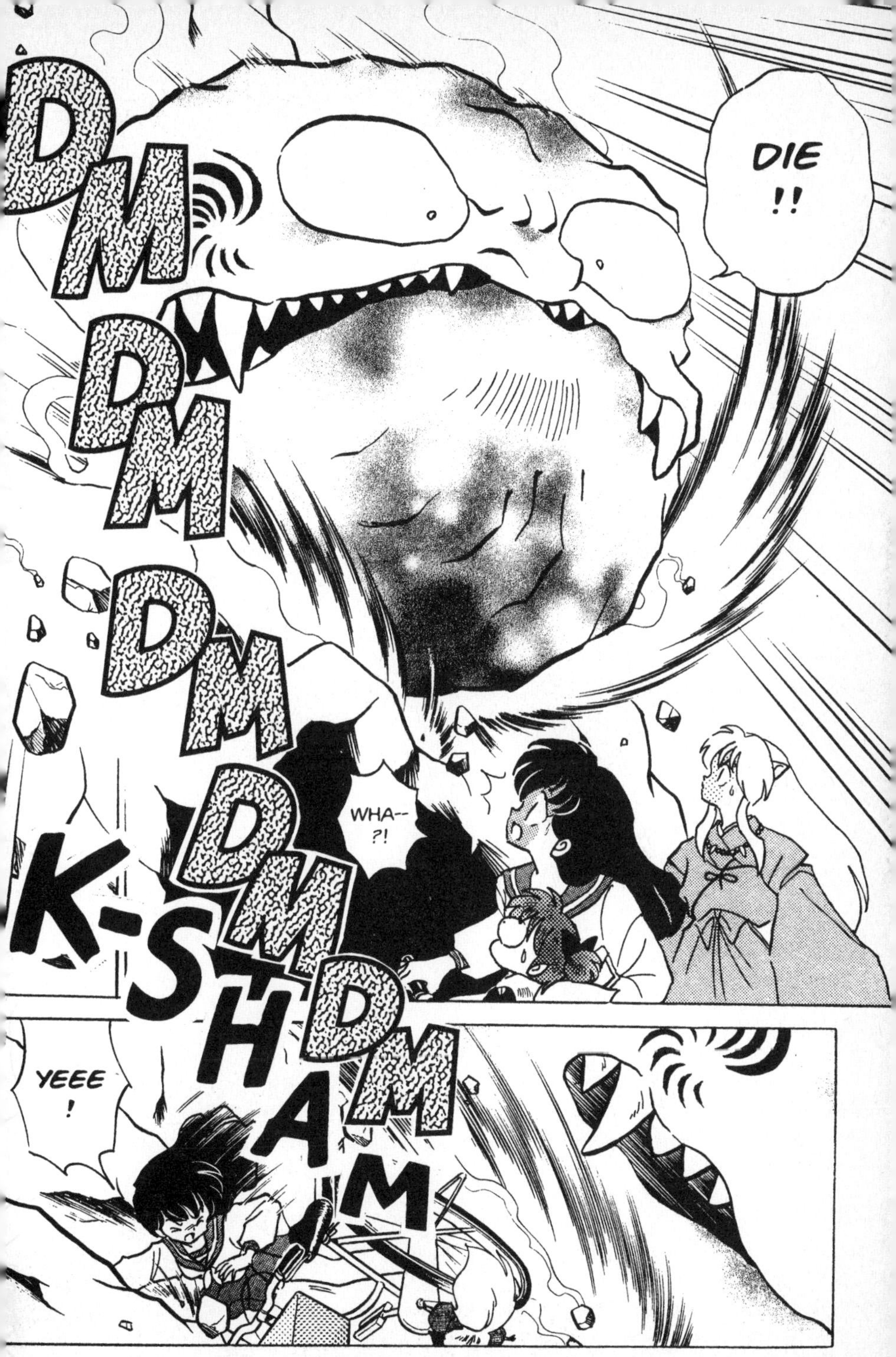
DMDMDMDMDMDMDMDM
DIE !!
WHA-- ?!
K-SHAM
YEEE !

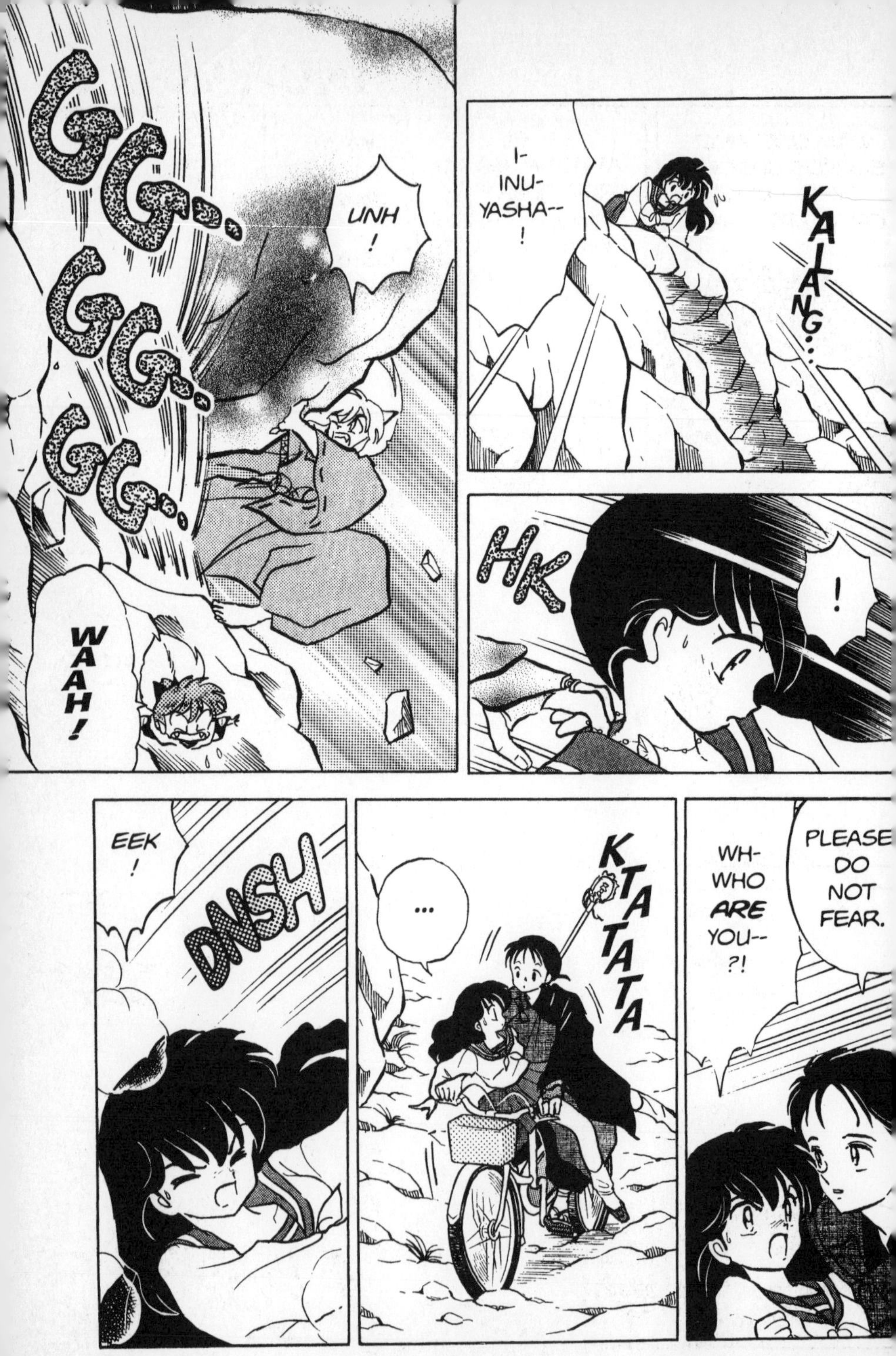
GG..
GGG..
GG...
UNH!
WAAH!
I- INU-YASHA--!
KALANG...
HK
!
EEK!
DNSH
...
KTATATA
WH- WHO ARE YOU--?!
PLEASE DO NOT FEAR.

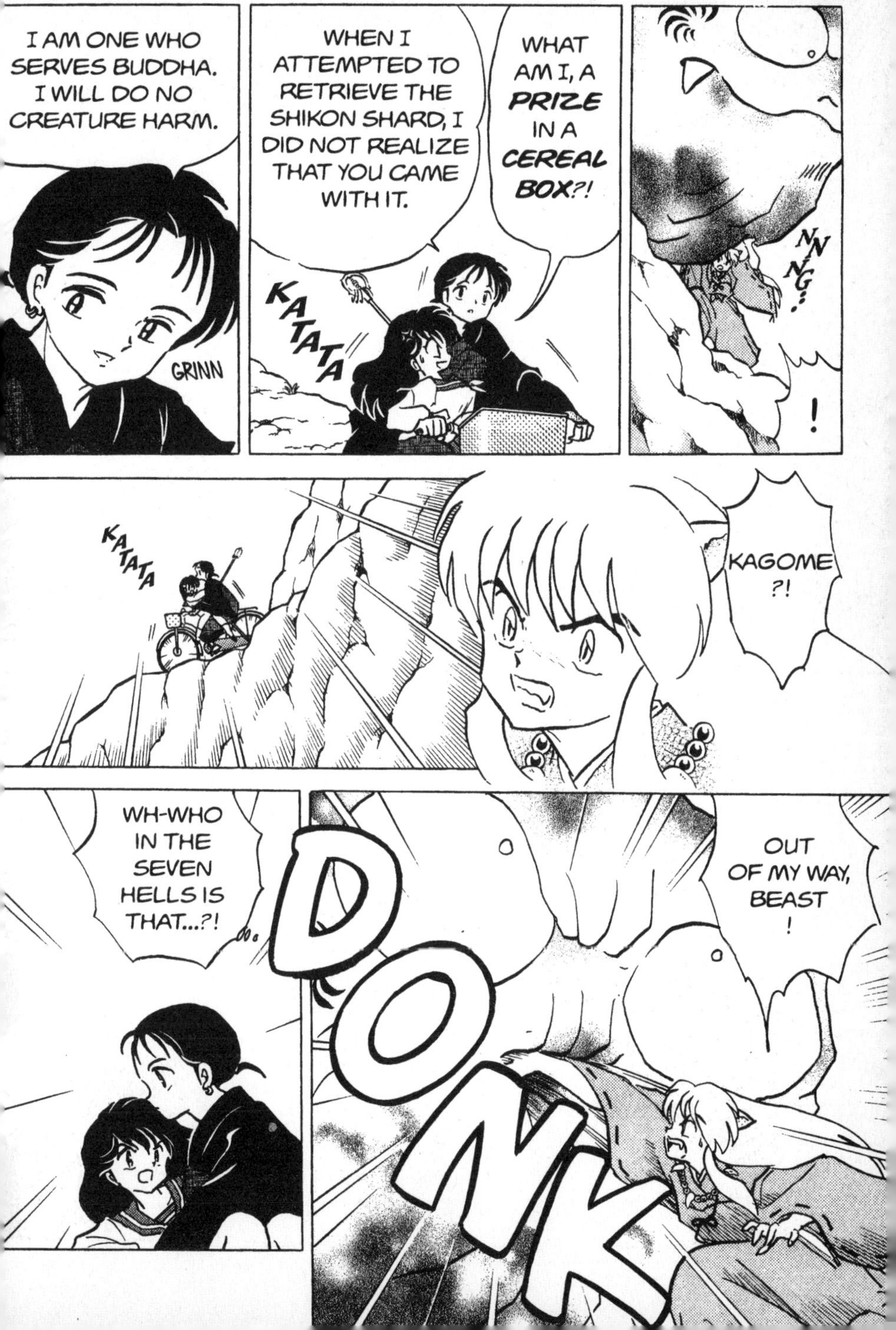
I AM ONE WHO SERVES BUDDHA. I WILL DO NO CREATURE HARM.
GRINN
WHEN I ATTEMPTED TO RETRIEVE THE SHIKON SHARD, I DID NOT REALIZE THAT YOU CAME WITH IT.
WHAT AM I, A PRIZE IN A CEREAL BOX?!
KATATA
NNNG..!
!
KATATA
KAGOME ?!
WH-WHO IN THE SEVEN HELLS IS THAT...?!
DONK
OUT OF MY WAY, BEAST !

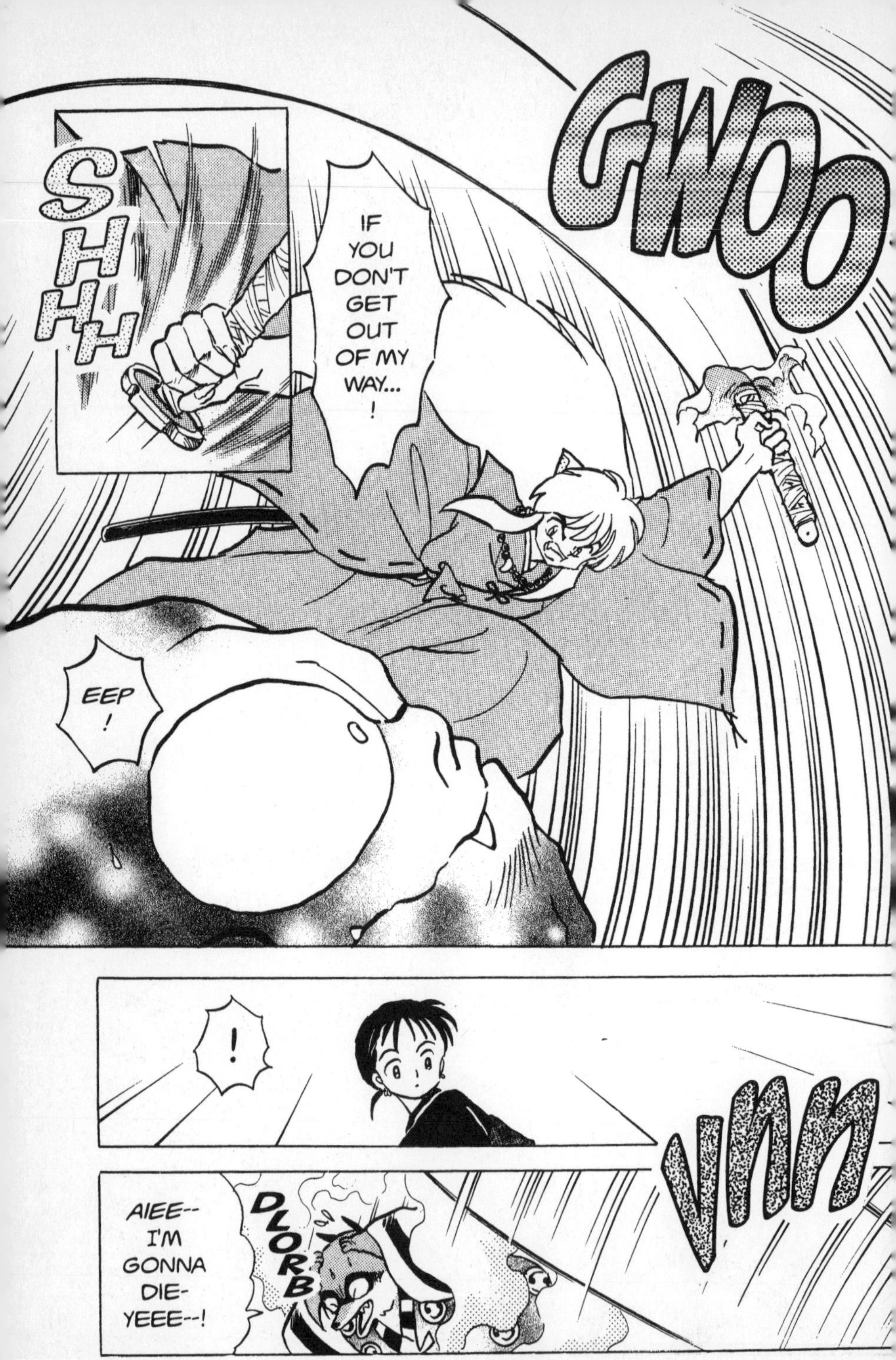
SHHHH
IF YOU DON'T GET OUT OF MY WAY...!
GWOO
EEP!
!
VNNN
AIEE-- I'M GONNA DIE-YEEE--!
DLORB

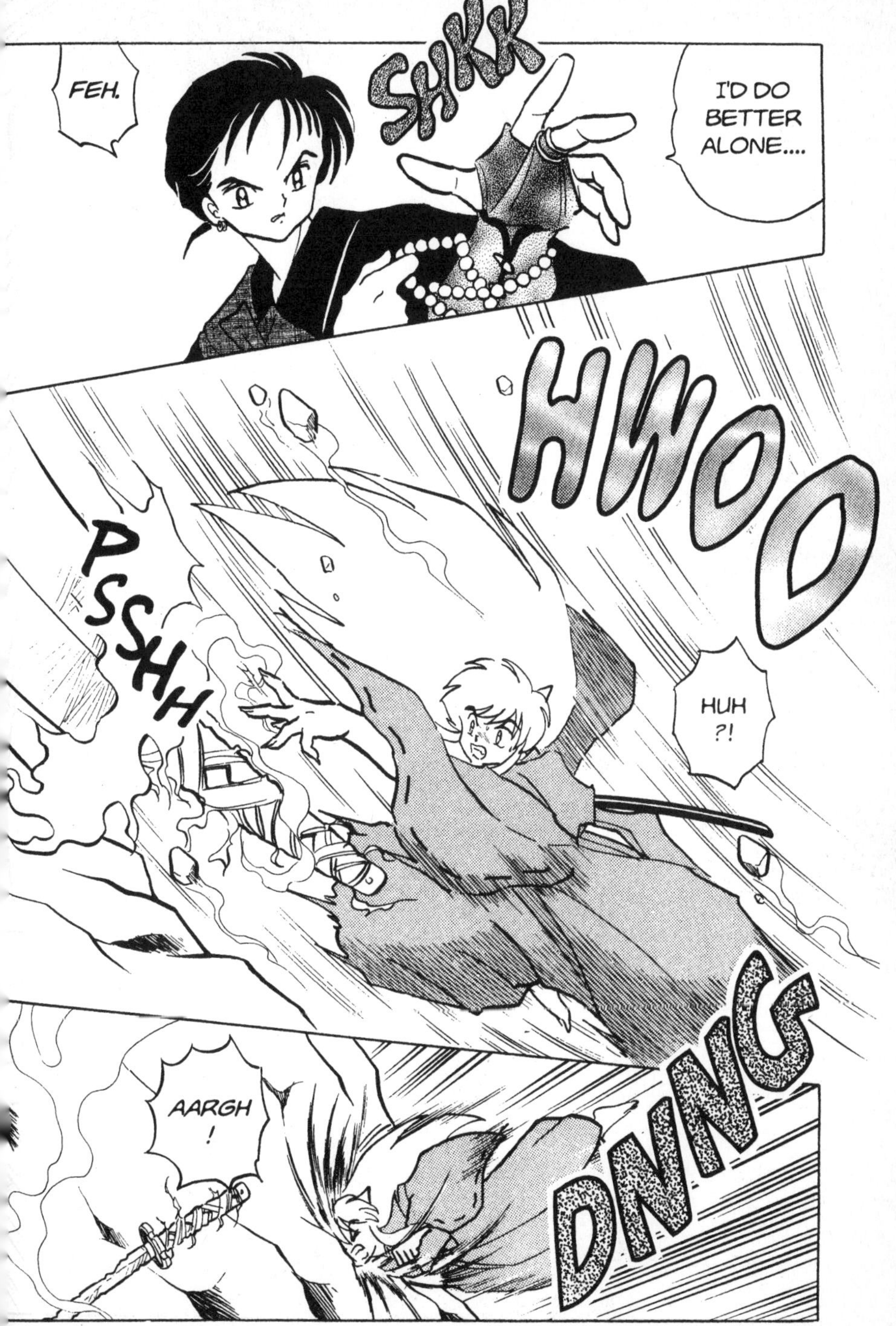
FEH.
SHKK
I'D DO BETTER ALONE....
HWOO
PSSHH
HUH ?!
AARGH !
DNNG

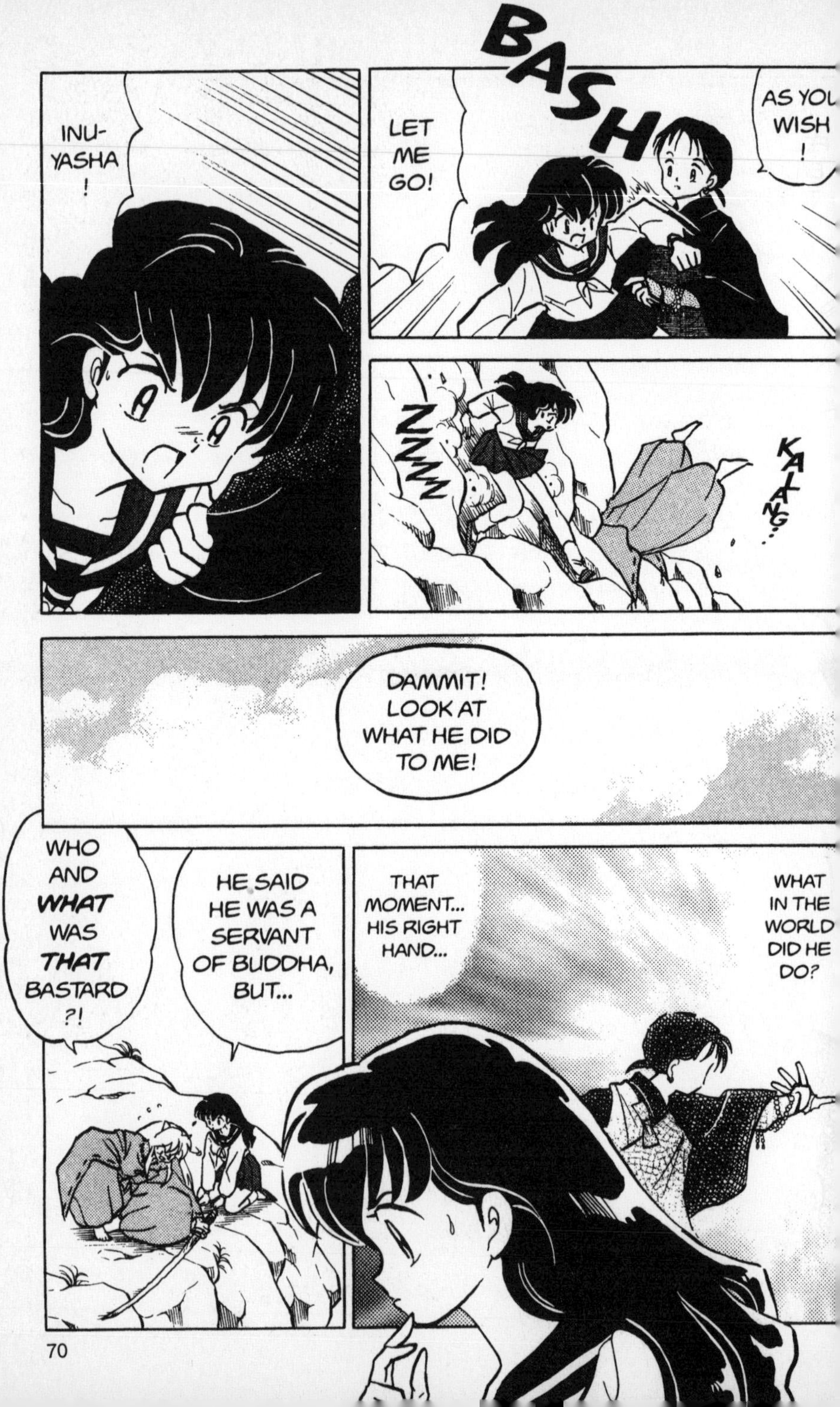

INU-YASHA!
BASH
LET ME GO!
AS YOU WISH!
ZZZZ
KALANG...
DAMMIT! LOOK AT WHAT HE DID TO ME!
WHO AND **WHAT** WAS **THAT** BASTARD?!
HE SAID HE WAS A SERVANT OF BUDDHA, BUT...
THAT MOMENT... HIS RIGHT HAND...
WHAT IN THE WORLD DID HE DO?

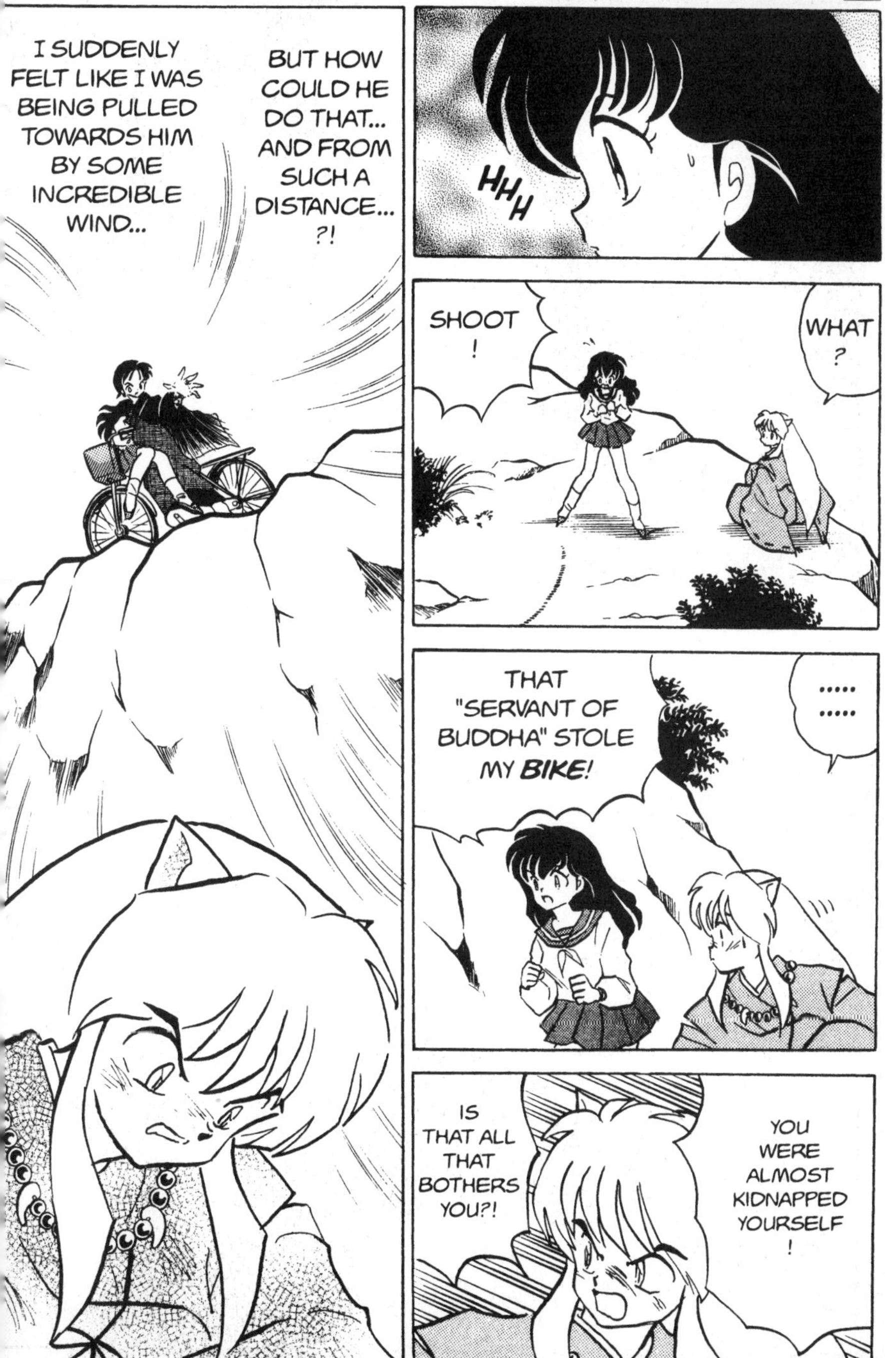
I SUDDENLY FELT LIKE I WAS BEING PULLED TOWARDS HIM BY SOME INCREDIBLE WIND...
BUT HOW COULD HE DO THAT... AND FROM SUCH A DISTANCE...?!
...
HHH
SHOOT!
WHAT?
THAT "SERVANT OF BUDDHA" STOLE MY **BIKE**!
....
IS THAT ALL THAT BOTHERS YOU?!
YOU WERE ALMOST KIDNAPPED YOURSELF!

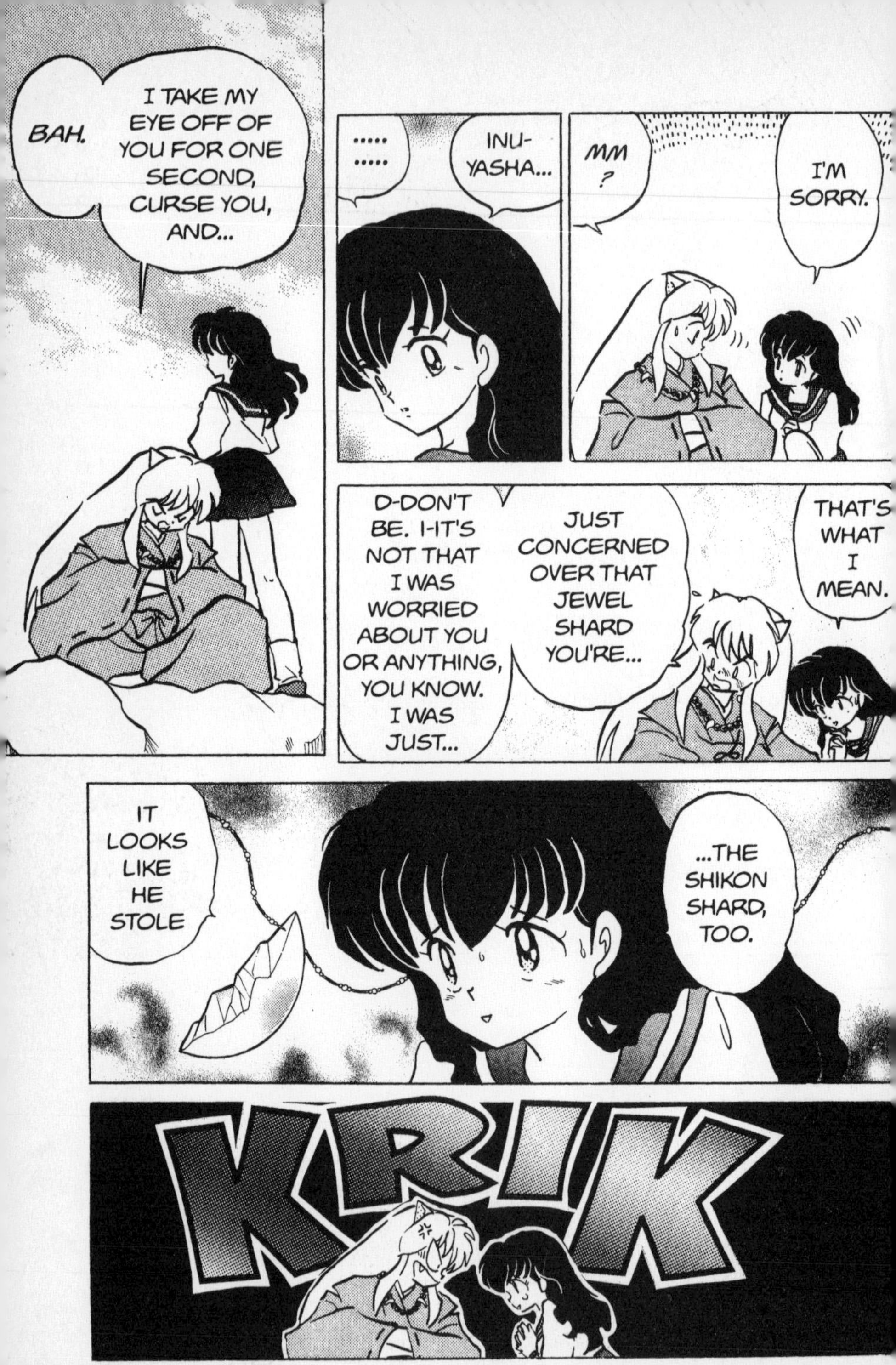
BAH.
I TAKE MY EYE OFF OF YOU FOR ONE SECOND, CURSE YOU, AND...
......
......
INU-YASHA...
MM ?
I'M SORRY.
D-DON'T BE. I-IT'S NOT THAT I WAS WORRIED ABOUT YOU OR ANYTHING, YOU KNOW. I WAS JUST...
JUST CONCERNED OVER THAT JEWEL SHARD YOU'RE...
THAT'S WHAT I MEAN.
IT LOOKS LIKE HE STOLE
...THE SHIKON SHARD, TOO.
KRIK

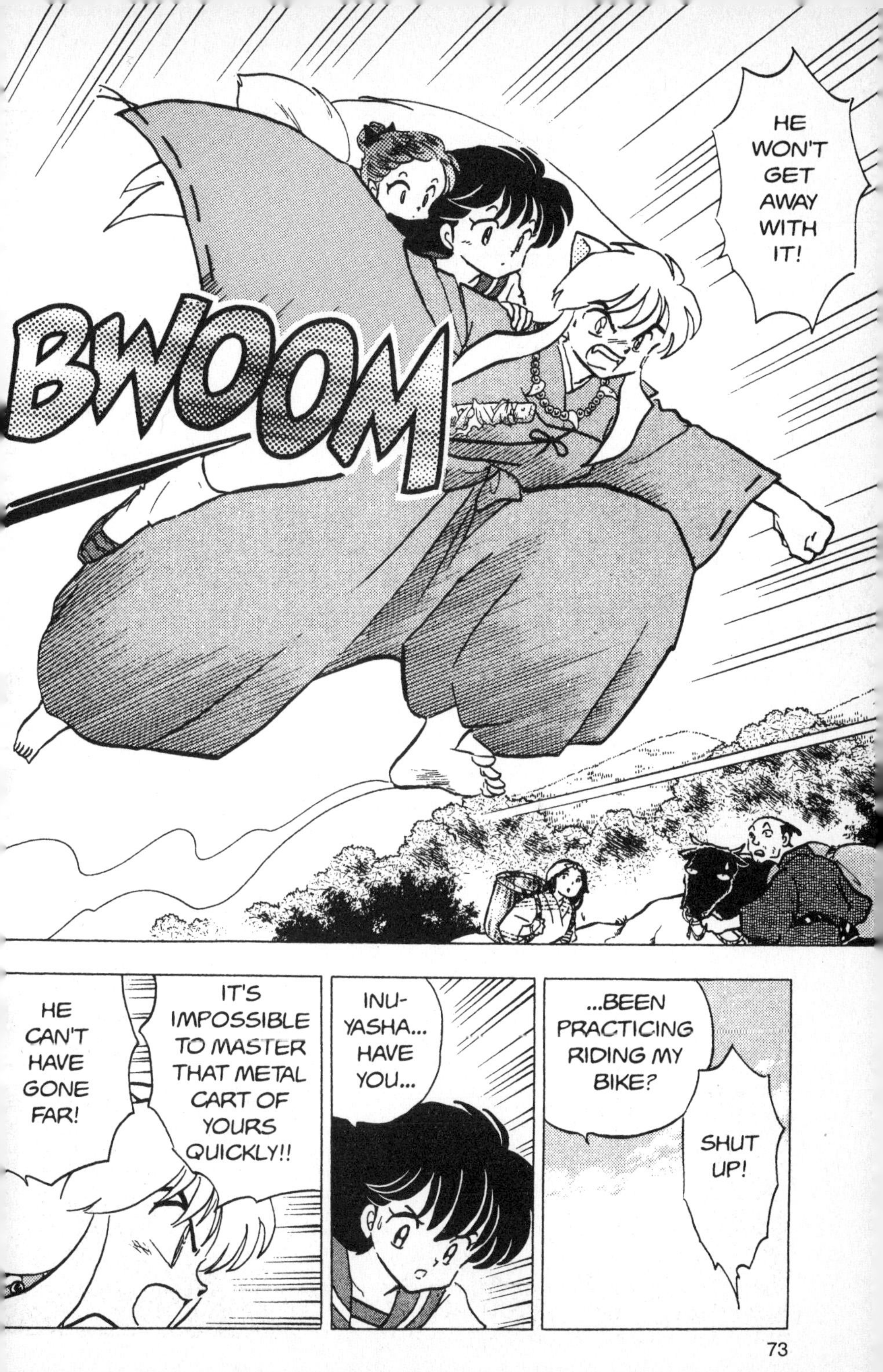

BWOOM
HE WON'T GET AWAY WITH IT!
HE CAN'T HAVE GONE FAR!
IT'S IMPOSSIBLE TO MASTER THAT METAL CART OF YOURS QUICKLY!!
INU-YASHA... HAVE YOU...
...BEEN PRACTICING RIDING MY BIKE?
SHUT UP!

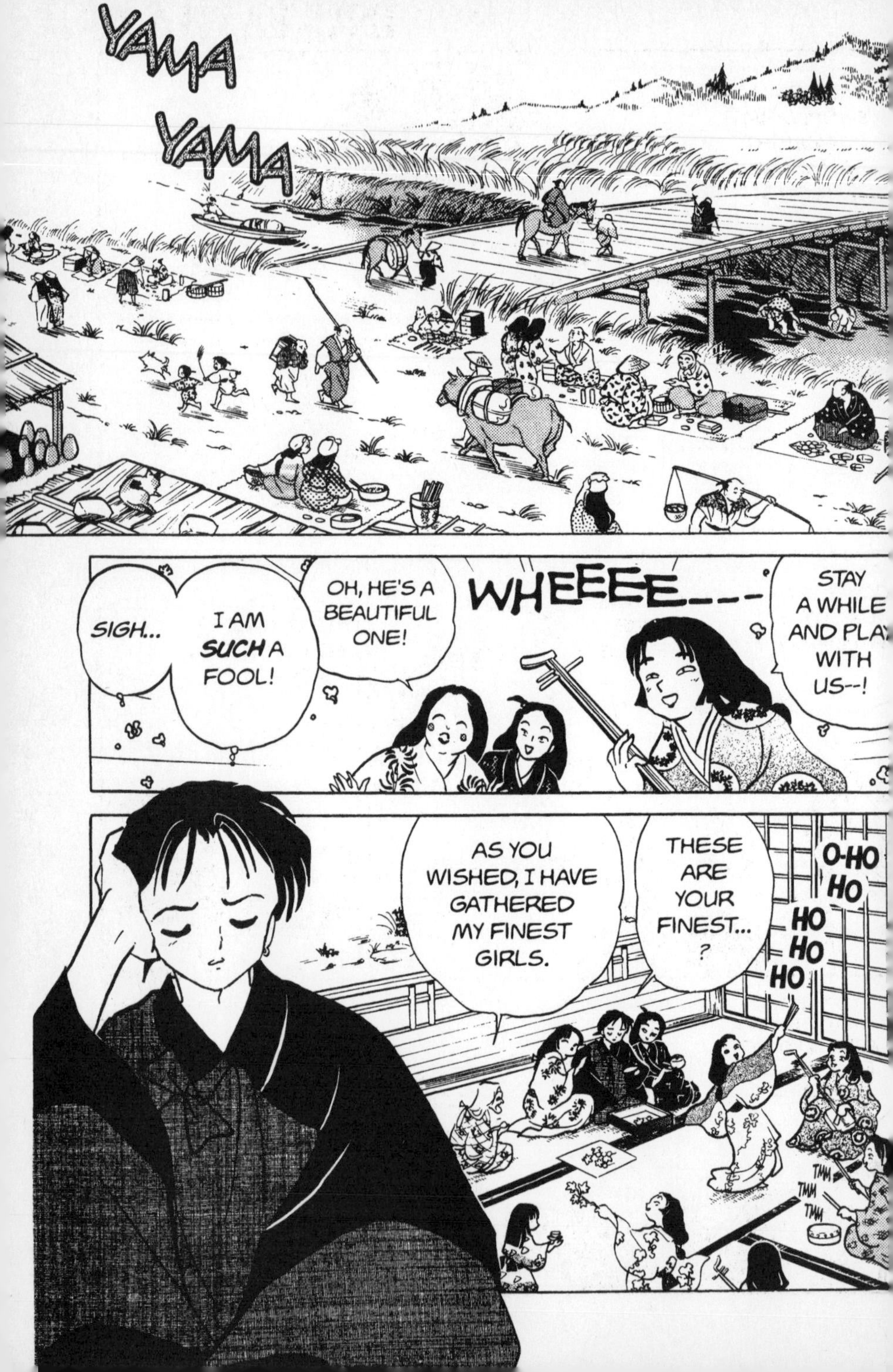
YAMA
YAMA
SIGH...
I AM SUCH A FOOL!
OH, HE'S A BEAUTIFUL ONE!
WHEEEEE---
STAY A WHILE AND PLAY WITH US--!
AS YOU WISHED, I HAVE GATHERED MY FINEST GIRLS.
THESE ARE YOUR FINEST...?
O-HO HO HO HO HO
TMM TMM TMM

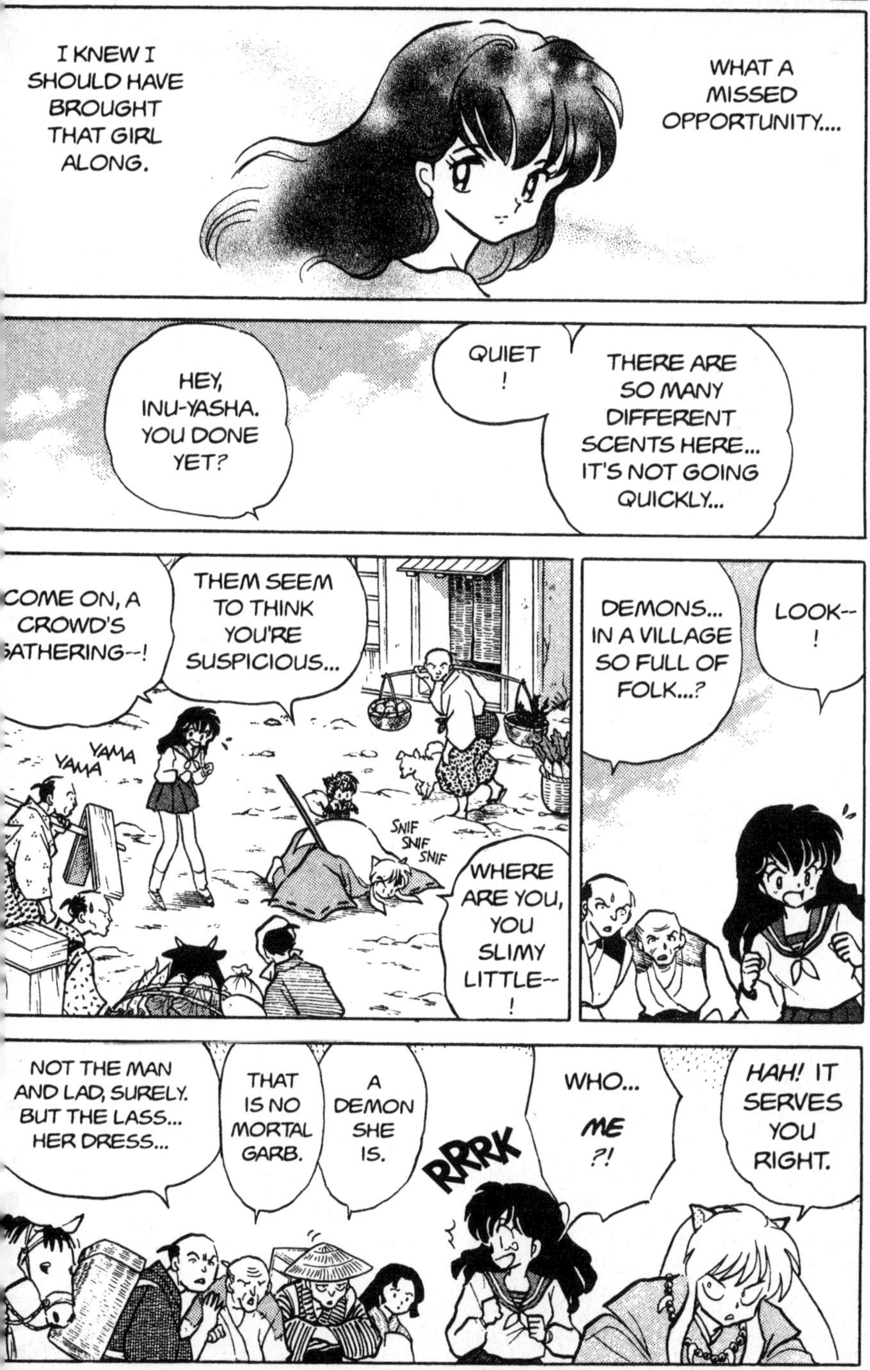
I KNEW I SHOULD HAVE BROUGHT THAT GIRL ALONG.
WHAT A MISSED OPPORTUNITY....
HEY, INU-YASHA. YOU DONE YET?
QUIET!
THERE ARE SO MANY DIFFERENT SCENTS HERE... IT'S NOT GOING QUICKLY...
COME ON, A CROWD'S GATHERING--!
THEM SEEM TO THINK YOU'RE SUSPICIOUS...
YAMA YAMA
SNIF SNIF SNIF
WHERE ARE YOU, YOU SLIMY LITTLE--!
DEMONS... IN A VILLAGE SO FULL OF FOLK...?
LOOK--!
NOT THE MAN AND LAD, SURELY. BUT THE LASS... HER DRESS...
THAT IS NO MORTAL GARB.
A DEMON SHE IS.
RRRK
WHO... ME?!
HAH! IT SERVES YOU RIGHT.

CAW CAW

HEY... MAYBE HE'S NOT HERE?

HE *MUST* BE--!

SNIF SNIF

BUT WHY WOULD A THIEF DILLY-DALLY AROUND A PLACE LIKE THIS...?

SNIF SNIF

OH!!

EH?

AIEE-- DEMONS--!!

DM DM DM

HEY, YOU!

GWRRR

BICYCLE THIEF!

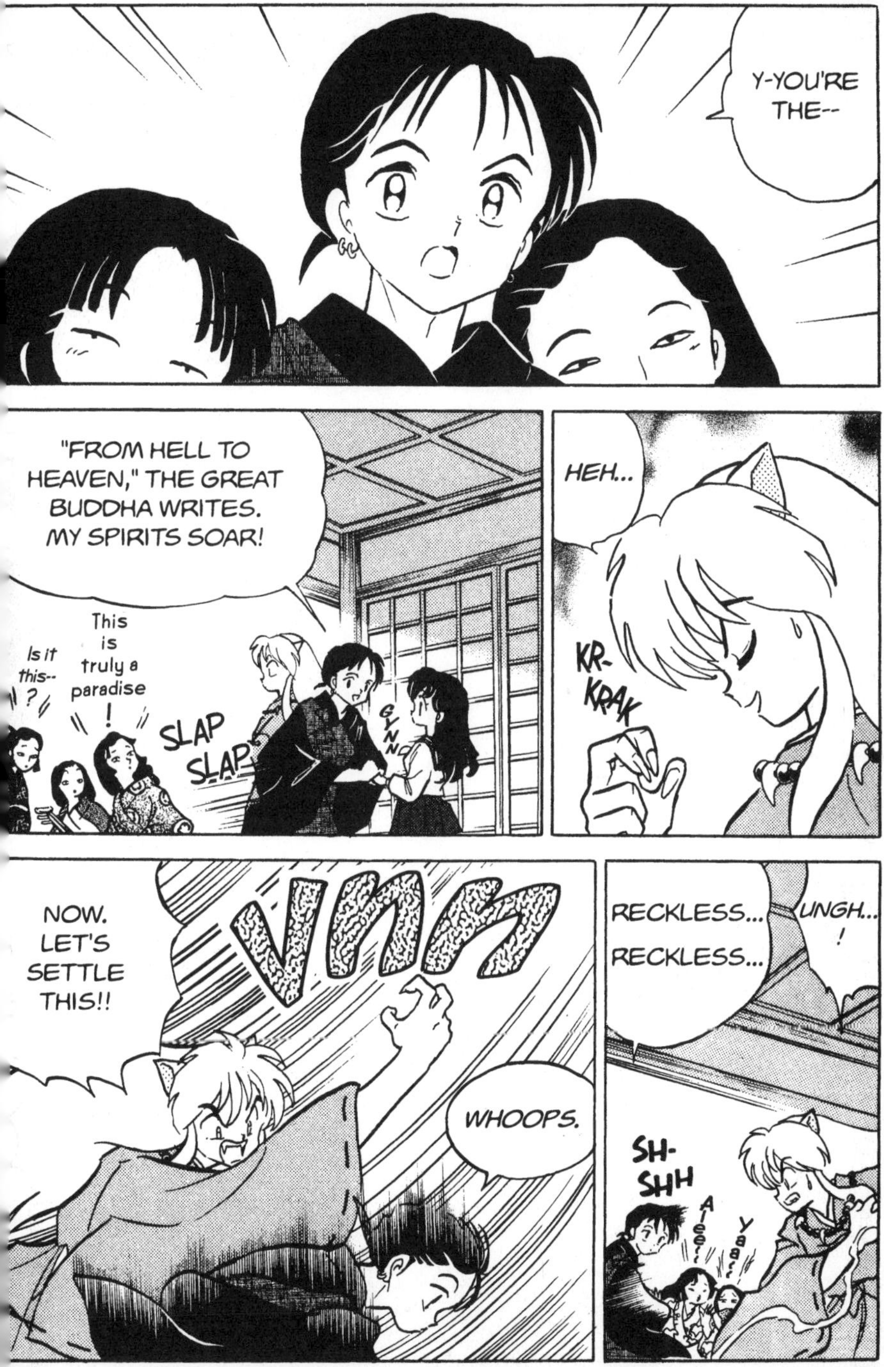
Y-YOU'RE THE--
"FROM HELL TO HEAVEN," THE GREAT BUDDHA WRITES. MY SPIRITS SOAR!
Is it this-- ?
This is truly a paradise !
SLAP SLAP
GYNN
HEH...
KR-KRAK
NOW. LET'S SETTLE THIS!!
VNN
WHOOPS.
RECKLESS... RECKLESS...
UNGH... !
SH-SHH
Aieee!
Yaa!

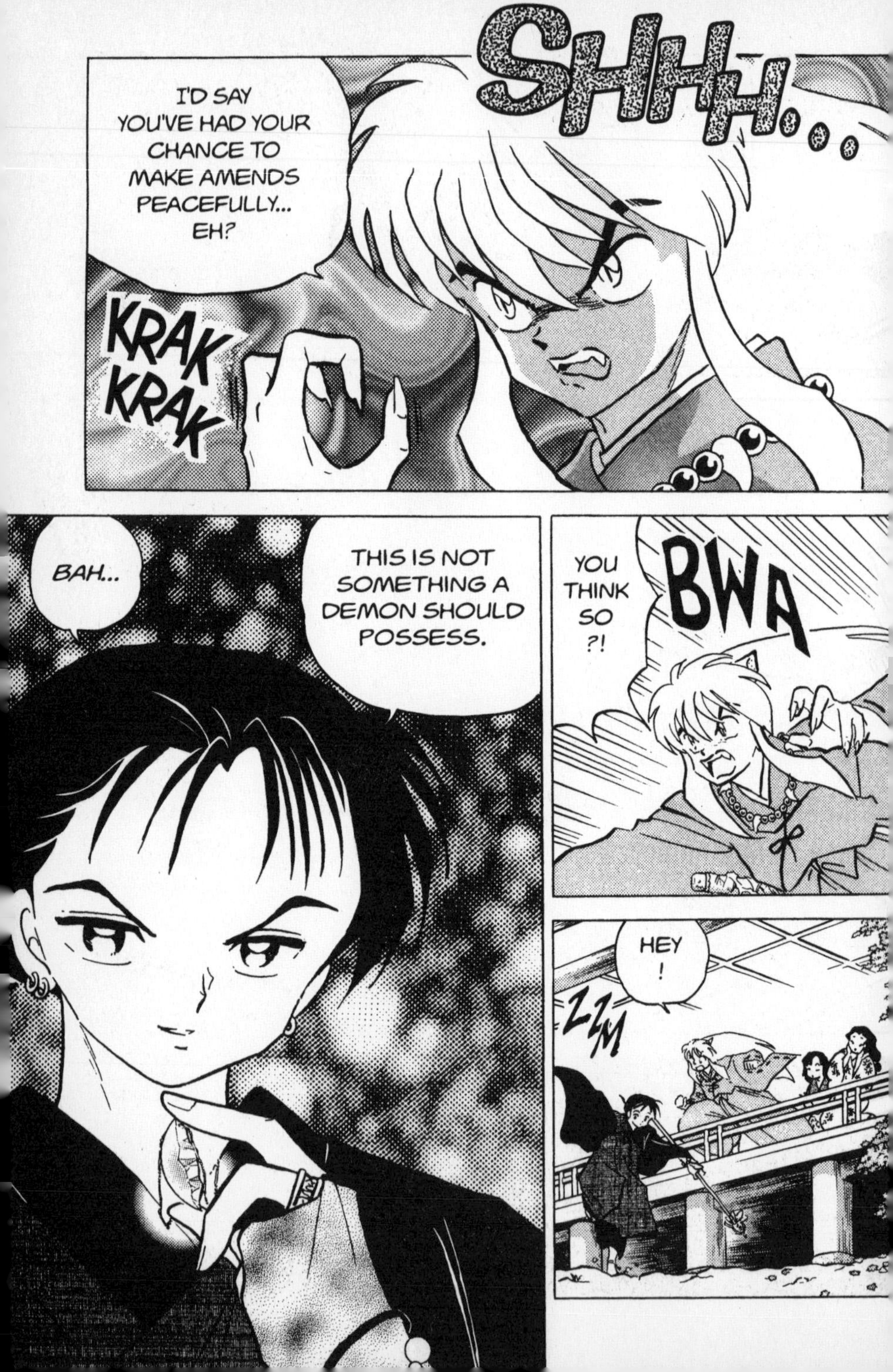
SHHH...
I'D SAY YOU'VE HAD YOUR CHANCE TO MAKE AMENDS PEACEFULLY... EH?
KRAK KRAK
BAH...
THIS IS NOT SOMETHING A DEMON SHOULD POSSESS.
YOU THINK SO ?!
BWA
HEY !
ZZM

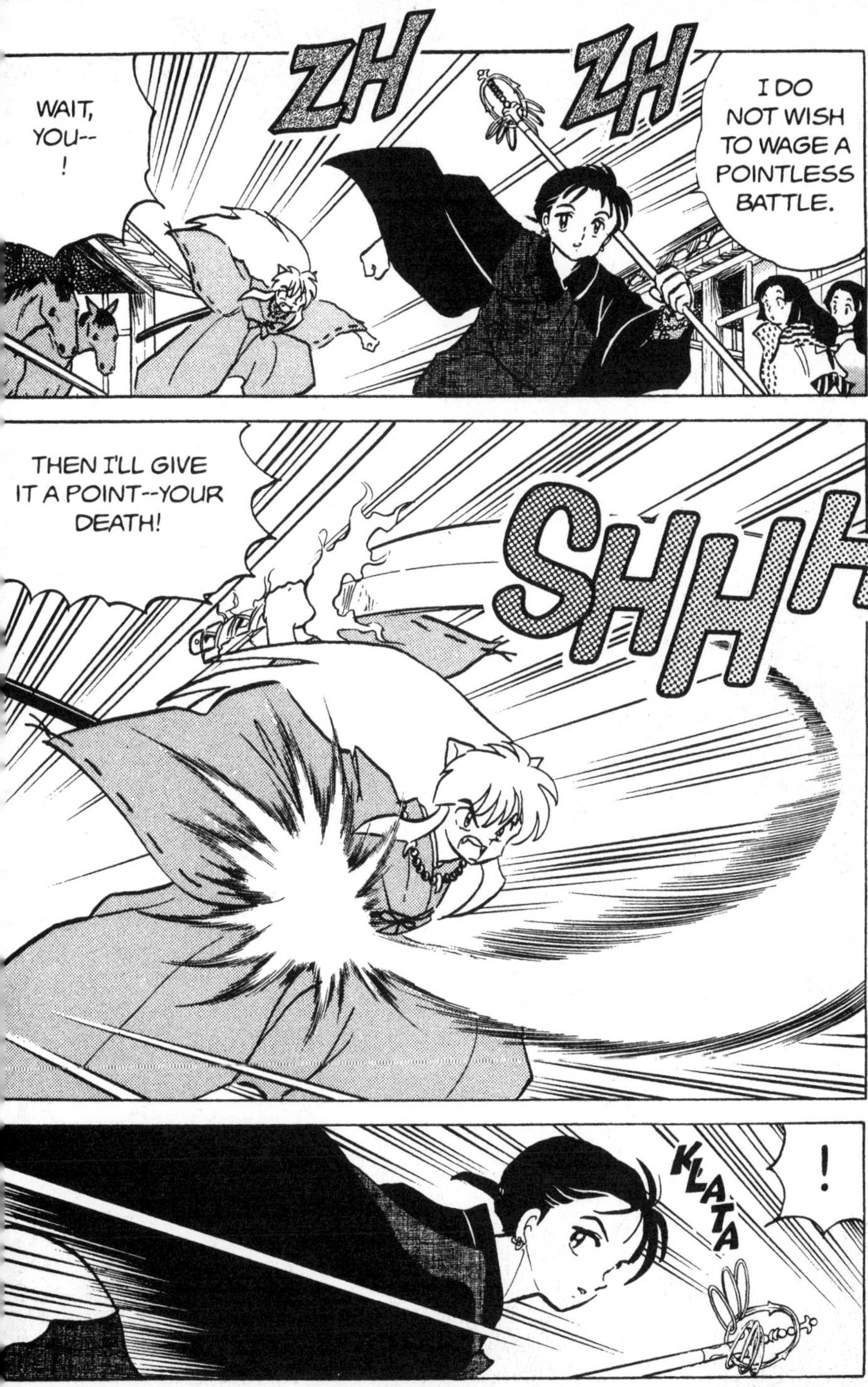
WAIT, YOU-- !
ZH ZH
I DO NOT WISH TO WAGE A POINTLESS BATTLE.
THEN I'LL GIVE IT A POINT--YOUR DEATH!
SHHH
KLATA
!

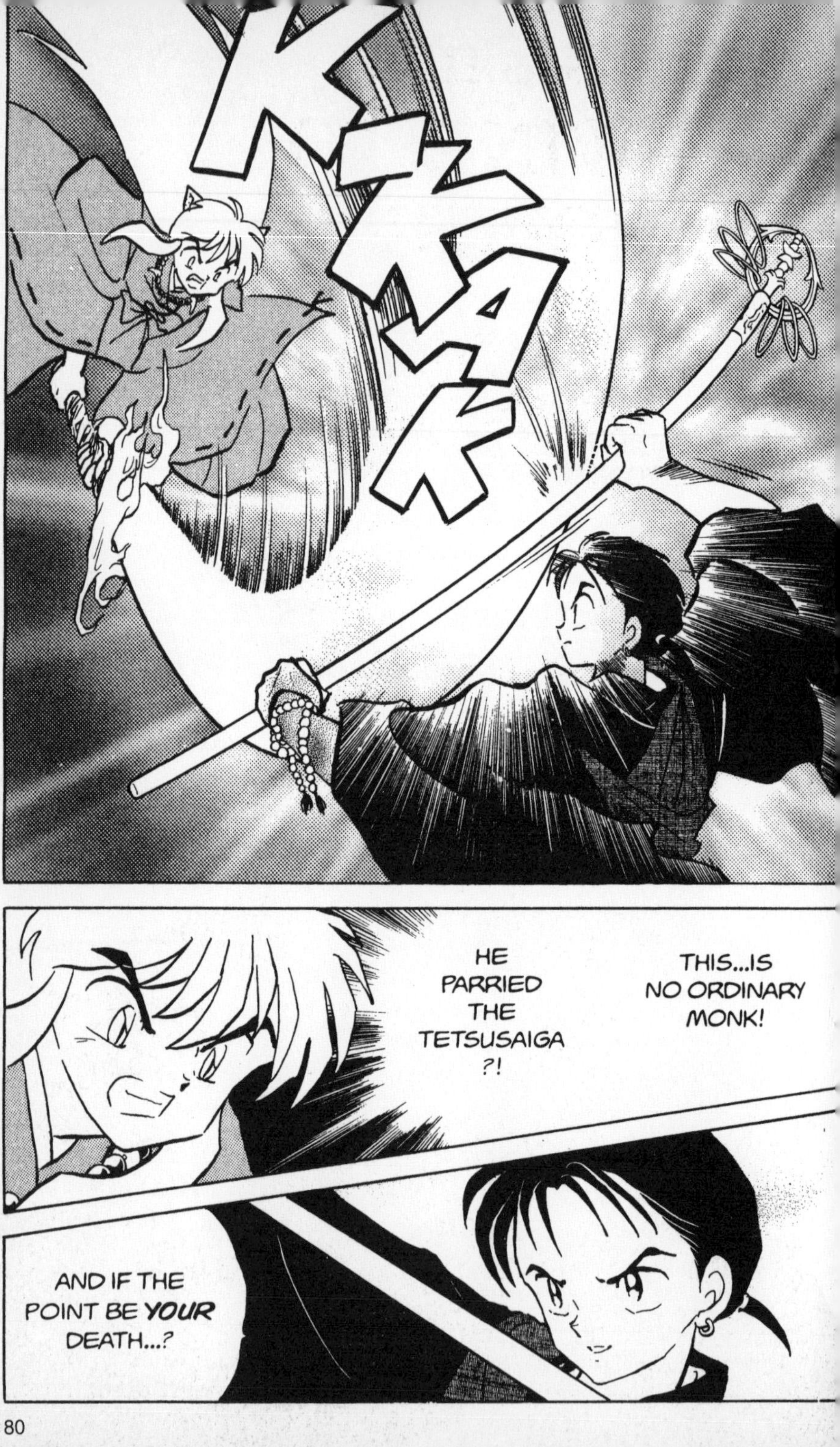
KKAK
HE PARRIED THE TETSUSAIGA ?!
THIS...IS NO ORDINARY MONK!
AND IF THE POINT BE YOUR DEATH...?

SCROLL FIVE

WIND TO NOWHERE

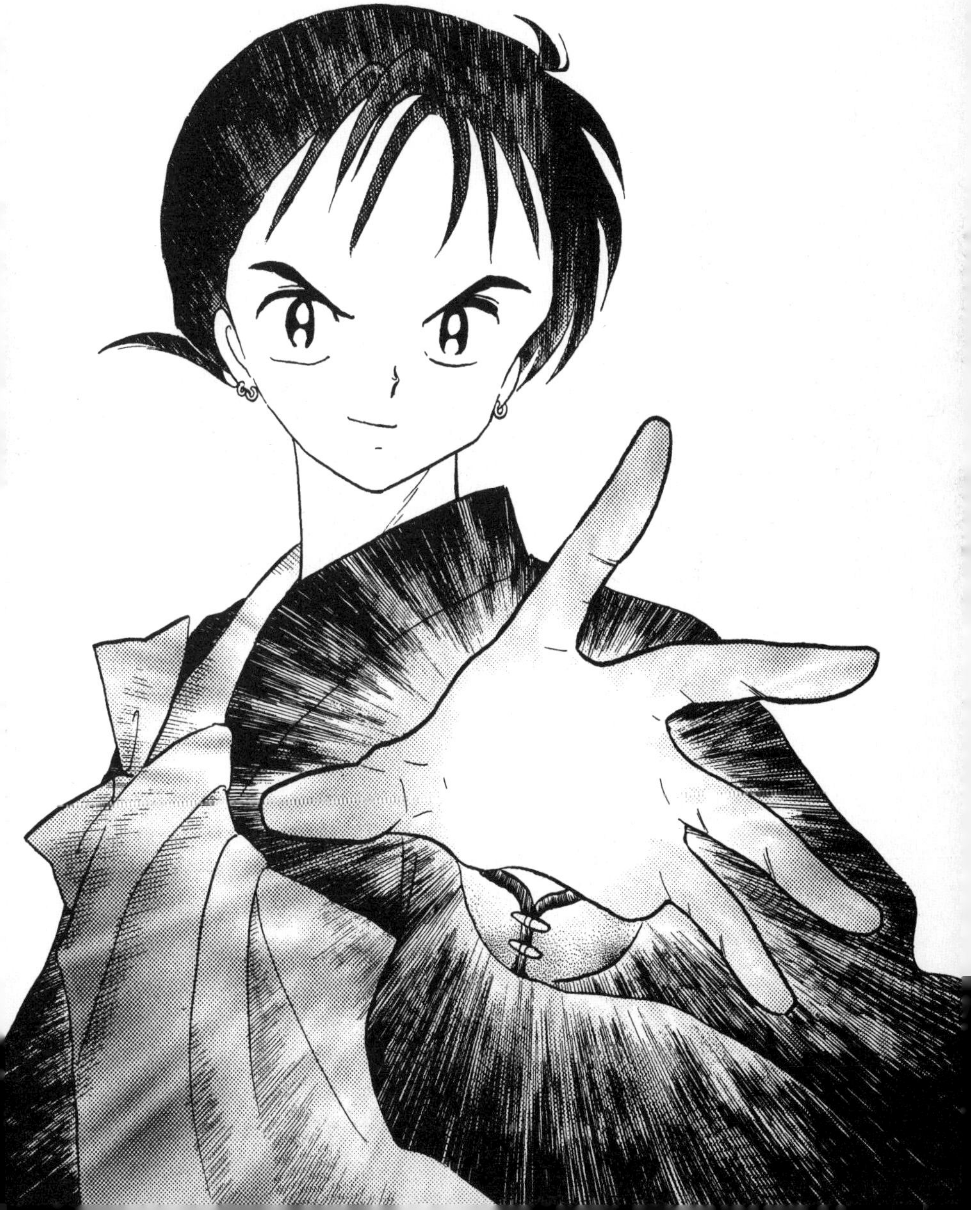

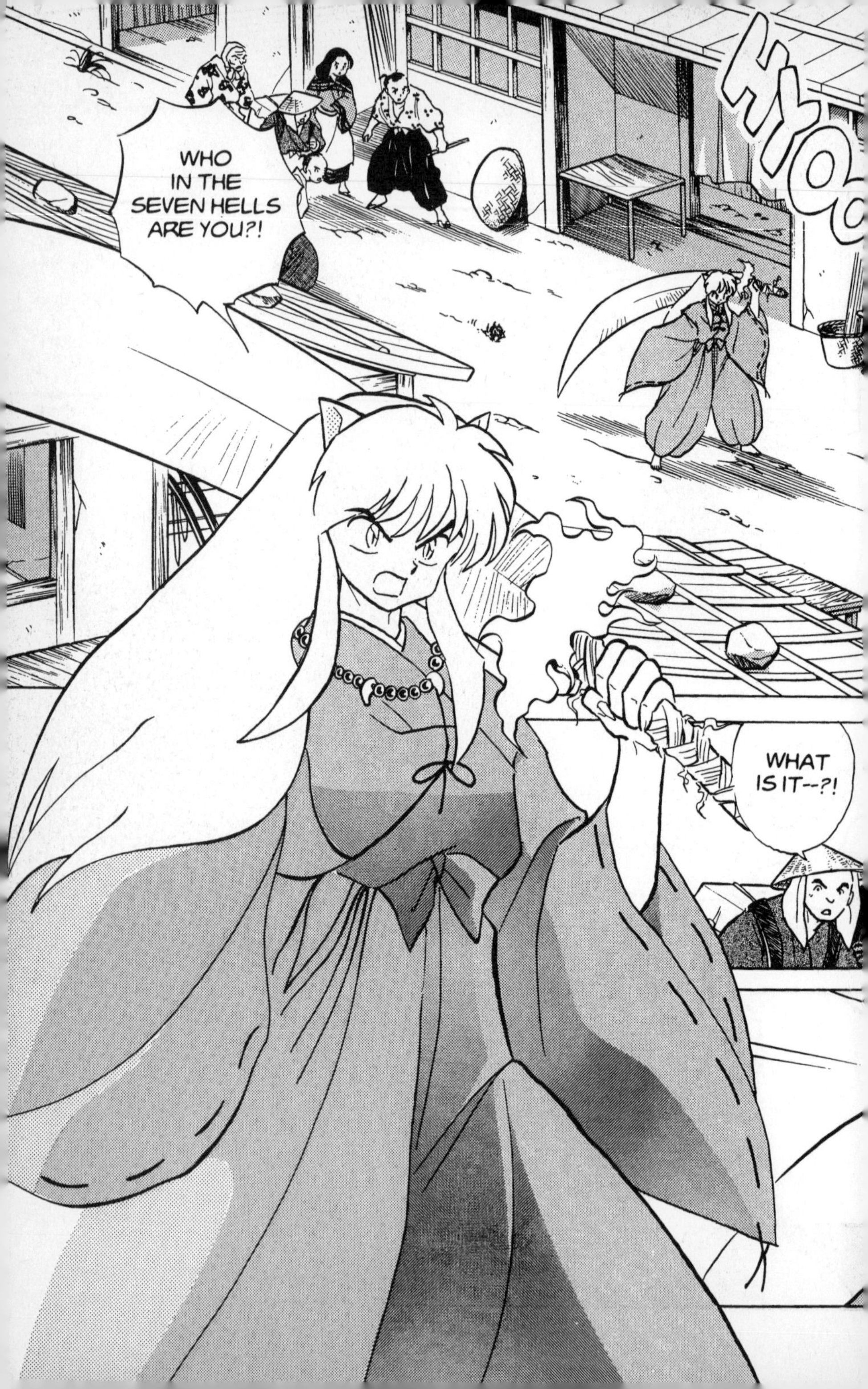
HYOO
WHO IN THE SEVEN HELLS ARE YOU?!
WHAT IS IT--?!

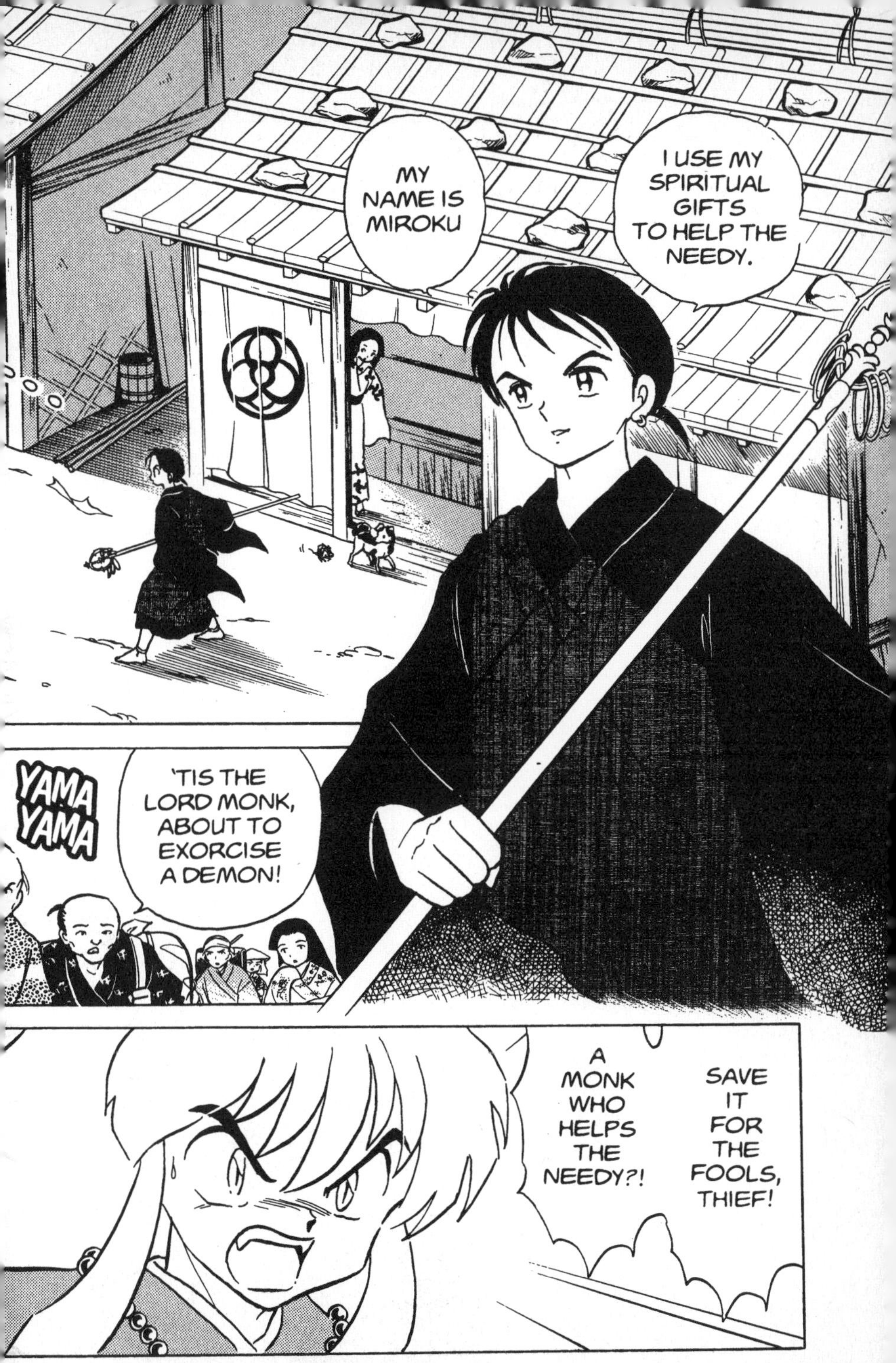
MY NAME IS MIROKU
I USE MY SPIRITUAL GIFTS TO HELP THE NEEDY.
YAMA YAMA
'TIS THE LORD MONK, ABOUT TO EXORCISE A DEMON!
A MONK WHO HELPS THE NEEDY?!
SAVE IT FOR THE FOOLS, THIEF!

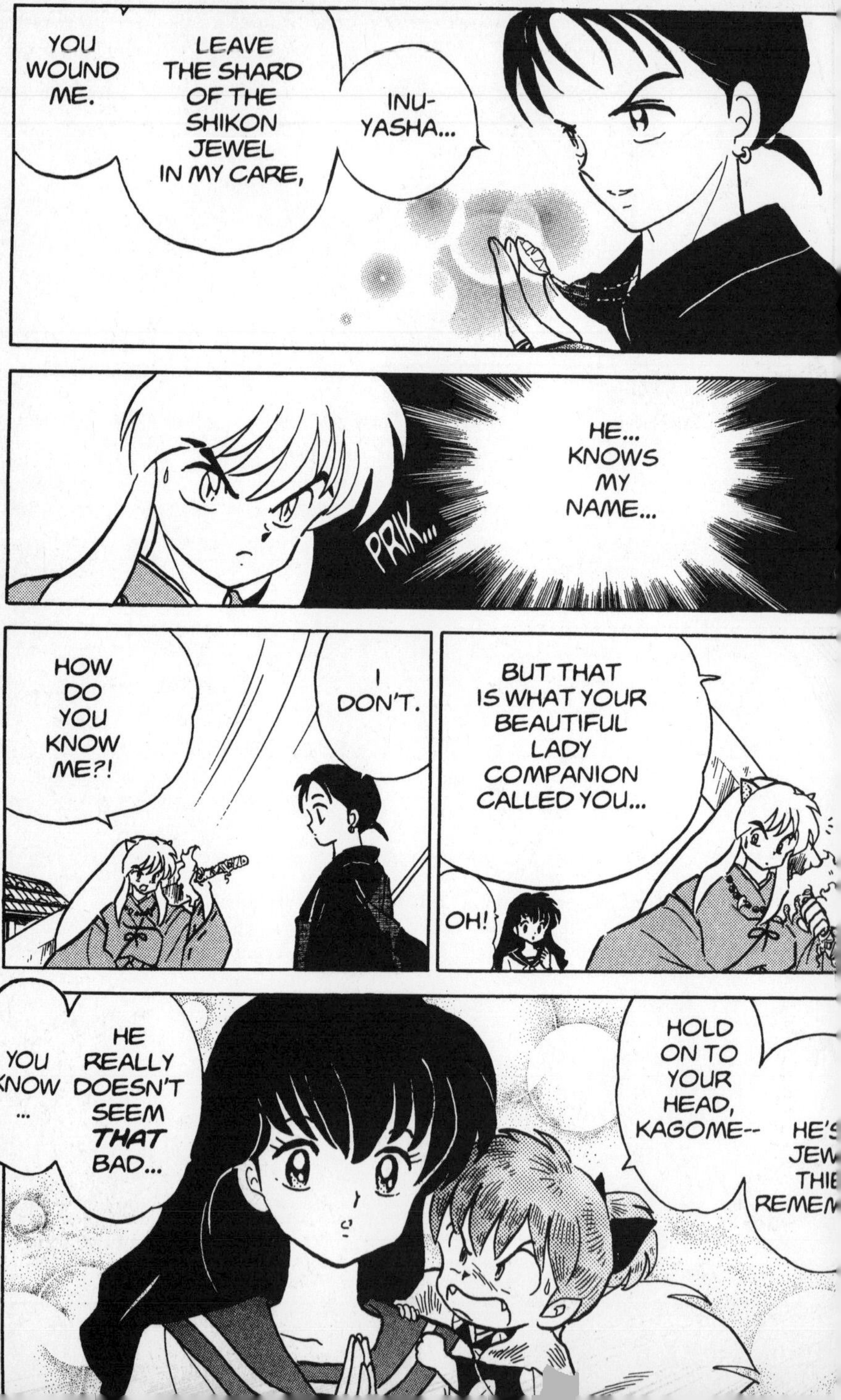
YOU WOUND ME.
LEAVE THE SHARD OF THE SHIKON JEWEL IN MY CARE,
INU-YASHA...
PRIK...
HE... KNOWS MY NAME...
HOW DO YOU KNOW ME?!
I DON'T.
BUT THAT IS WHAT YOUR BEAUTIFUL LADY COMPANION CALLED YOU...
OH!
YOU KNOW ...
HE REALLY DOESN'T SEEM ***THAT*** BAD...
HOLD ON TO YOUR HEAD, KAGOME--
HE'S JEW THIE REMEM

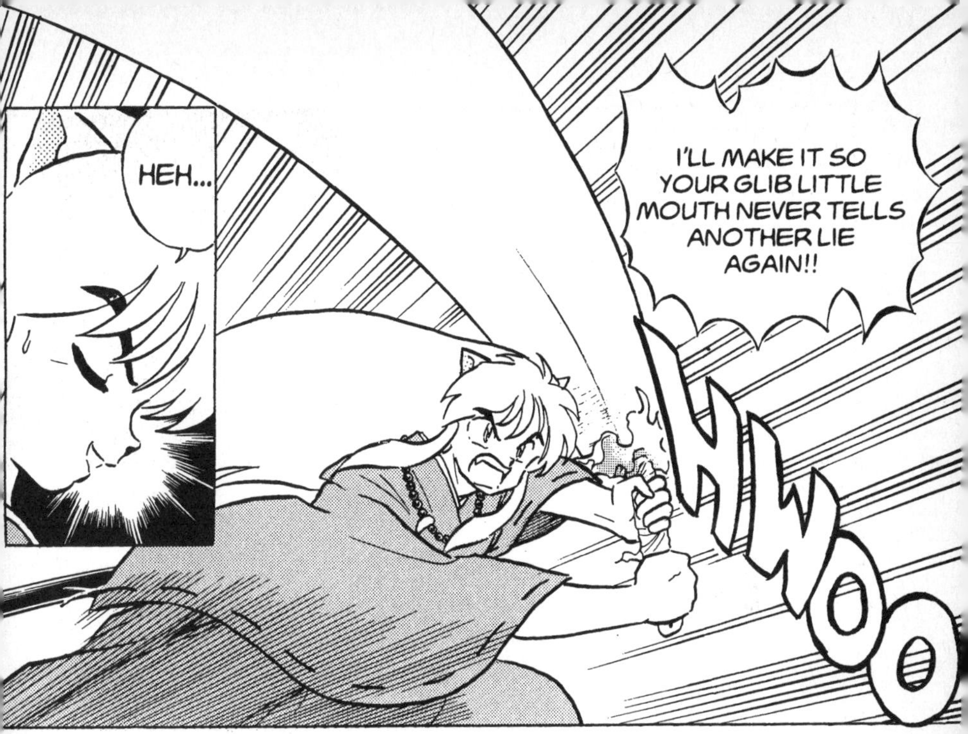
HEH...
I'LL MAKE IT SO YOUR GLIB LITTLE MOUTH NEVER TELLS ANOTHER LIE AGAIN!!
WHOOO
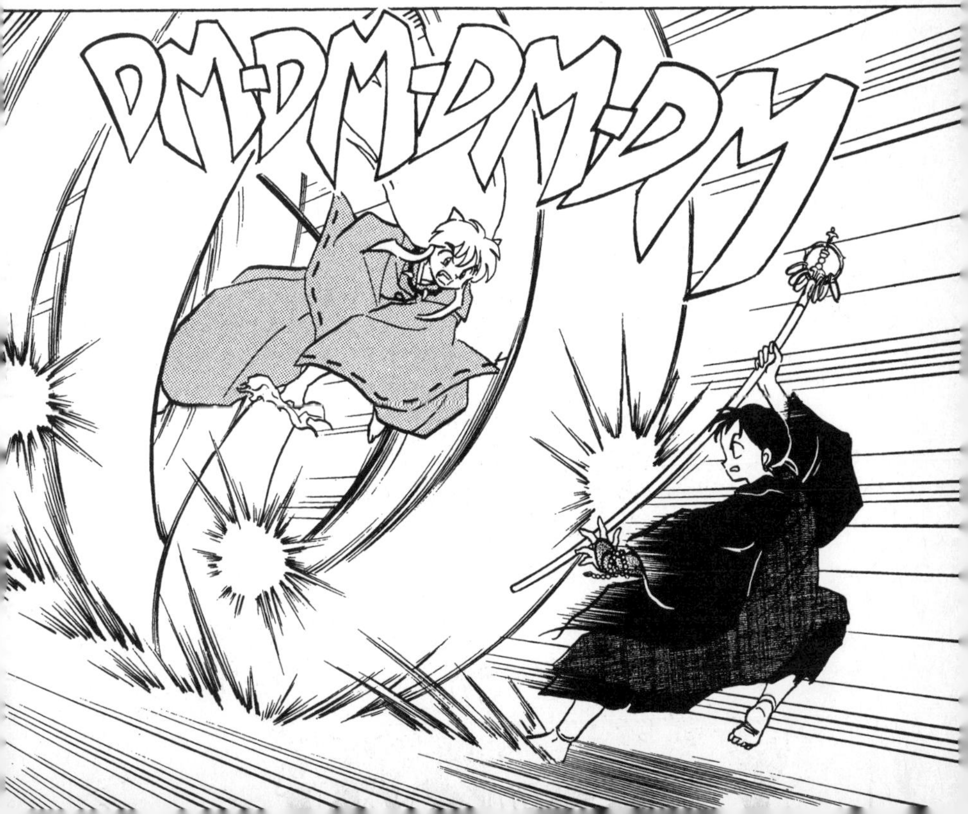
DM-DM-DM-DM-DM

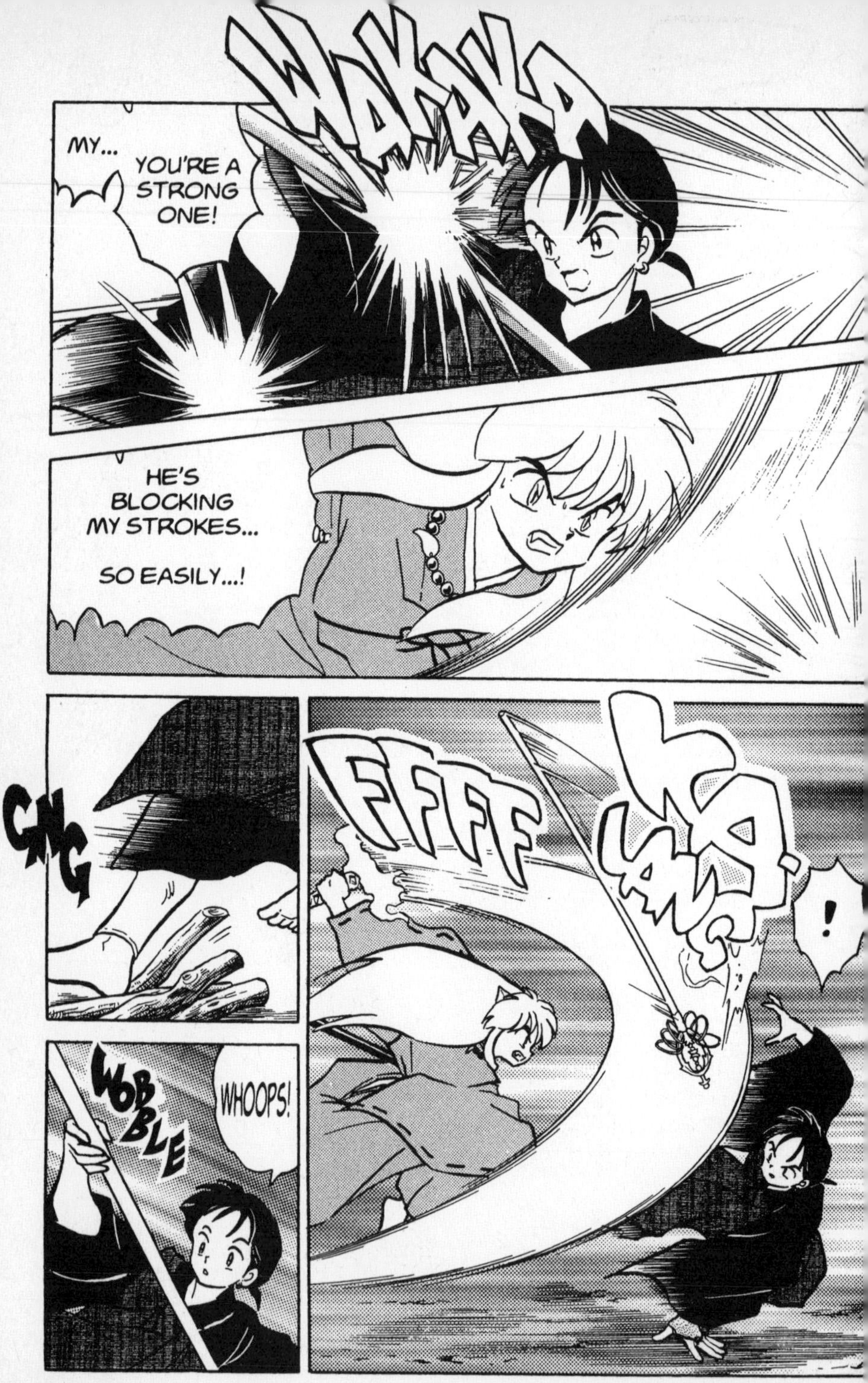
WAKAKA
MY...
YOU'RE A STRONG ONE!
HE'S BLOCKING MY STROKES...
SO EASILY...!
CNG
FFFF
KA LANG
!
WOBBLE
WHOOPS!

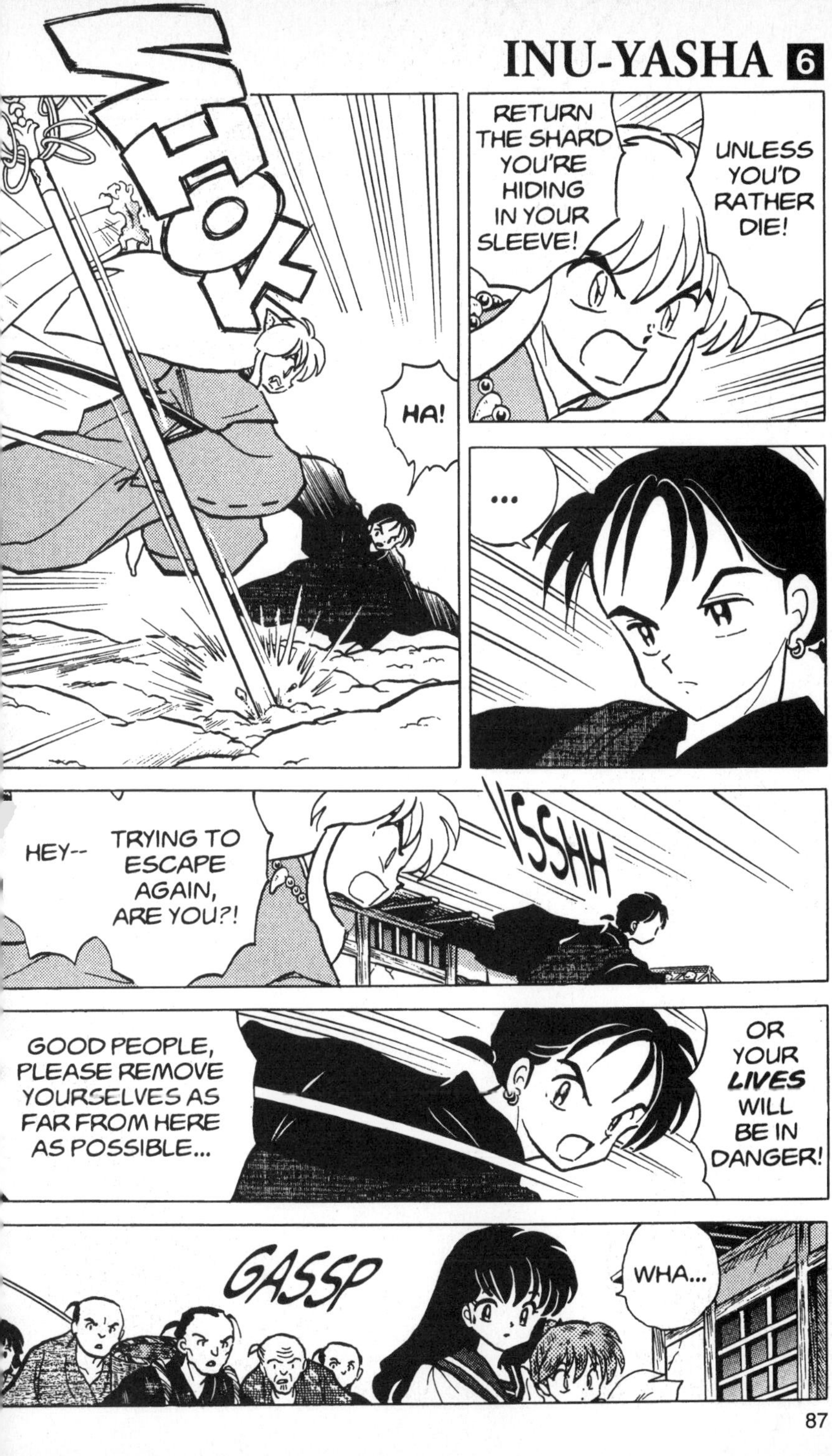
WHOK
HA!
RETURN THE SHARD YOU'RE HIDING IN YOUR SLEEVE!
UNLESS YOU'D RATHER DIE!
...
HEY--
TRYING TO ESCAPE AGAIN, ARE YOU?!
VSSHH
GOOD PEOPLE, PLEASE REMOVE YOURSELVES AS FAR FROM HERE AS POSSIBLE...
OR YOUR *LIVES* WILL BE IN DANGER!
GASSP
WHA...

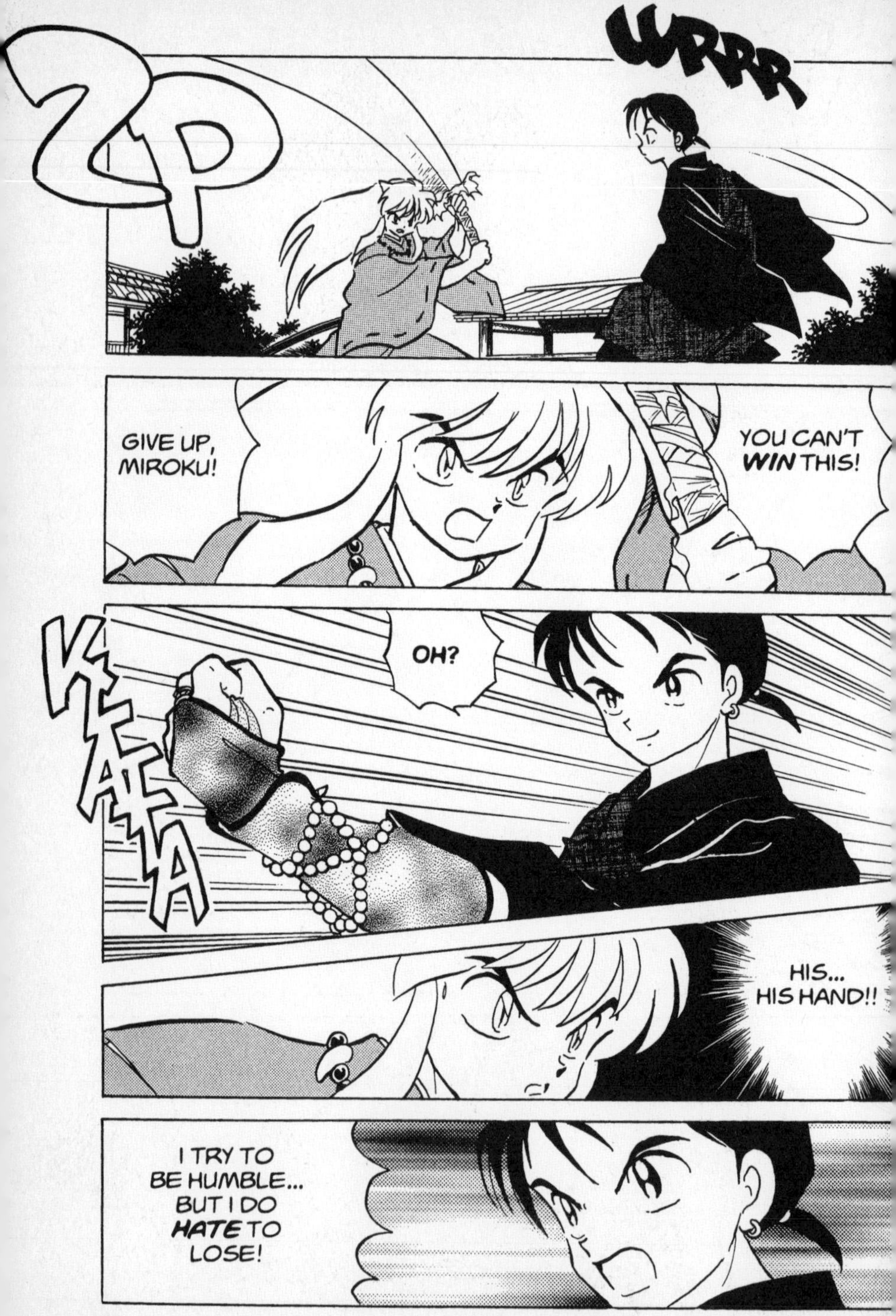

ZIP
WURRR
GIVE UP, MIROKU!
YOU CAN'T **WIN** THIS!
KLAKA
OH?
HIS... HIS HAND!!
I TRY TO BE HUMBLE... BUT I DO **HATE** TO LOSE!

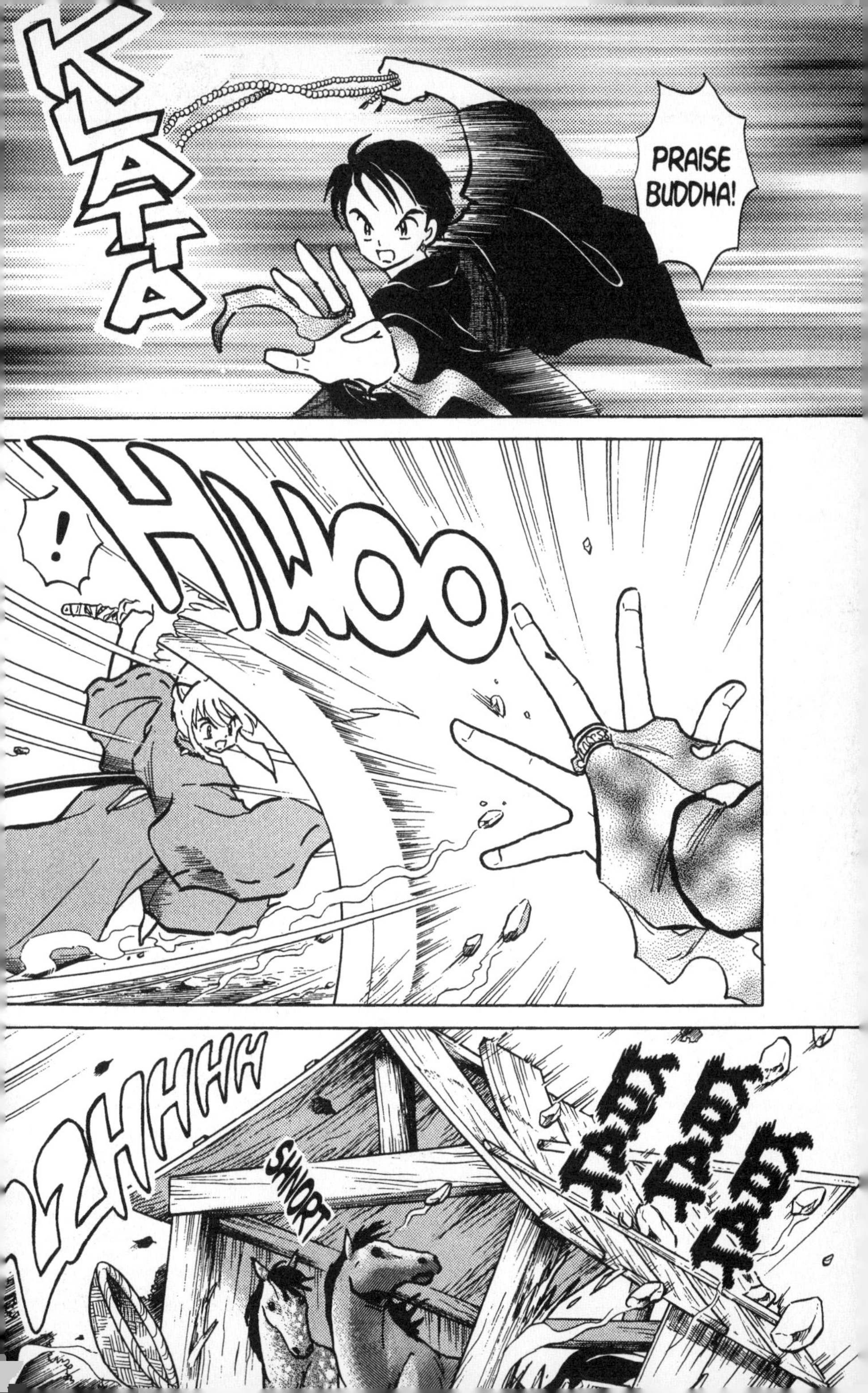
PRAISE BUDDHA!
KLATTA
!
HWOO
ZZHHHH
SNORT
TADAT TADAT TADAT

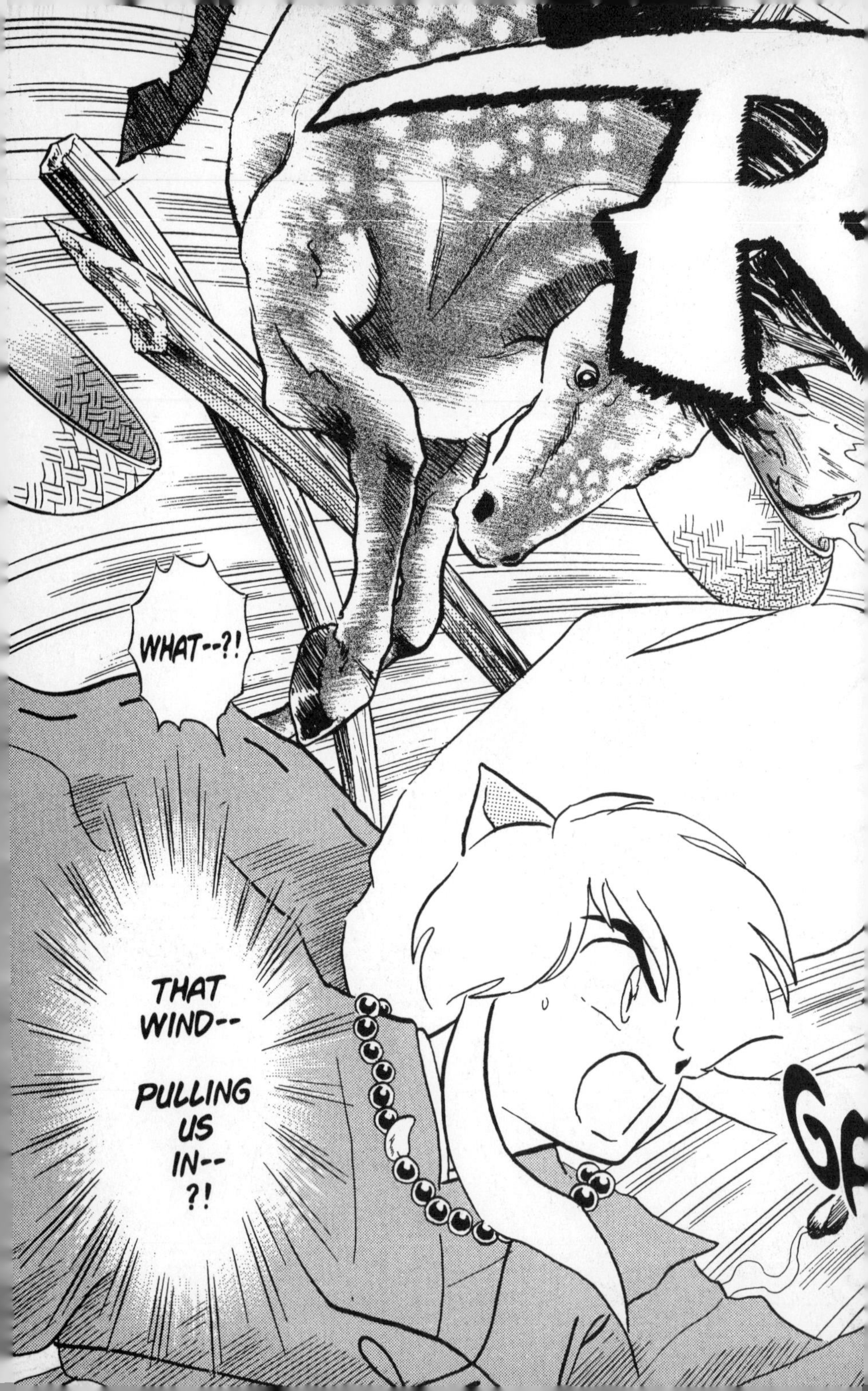
WHAT--?!
THAT WIND--
PULLING US IN--?!

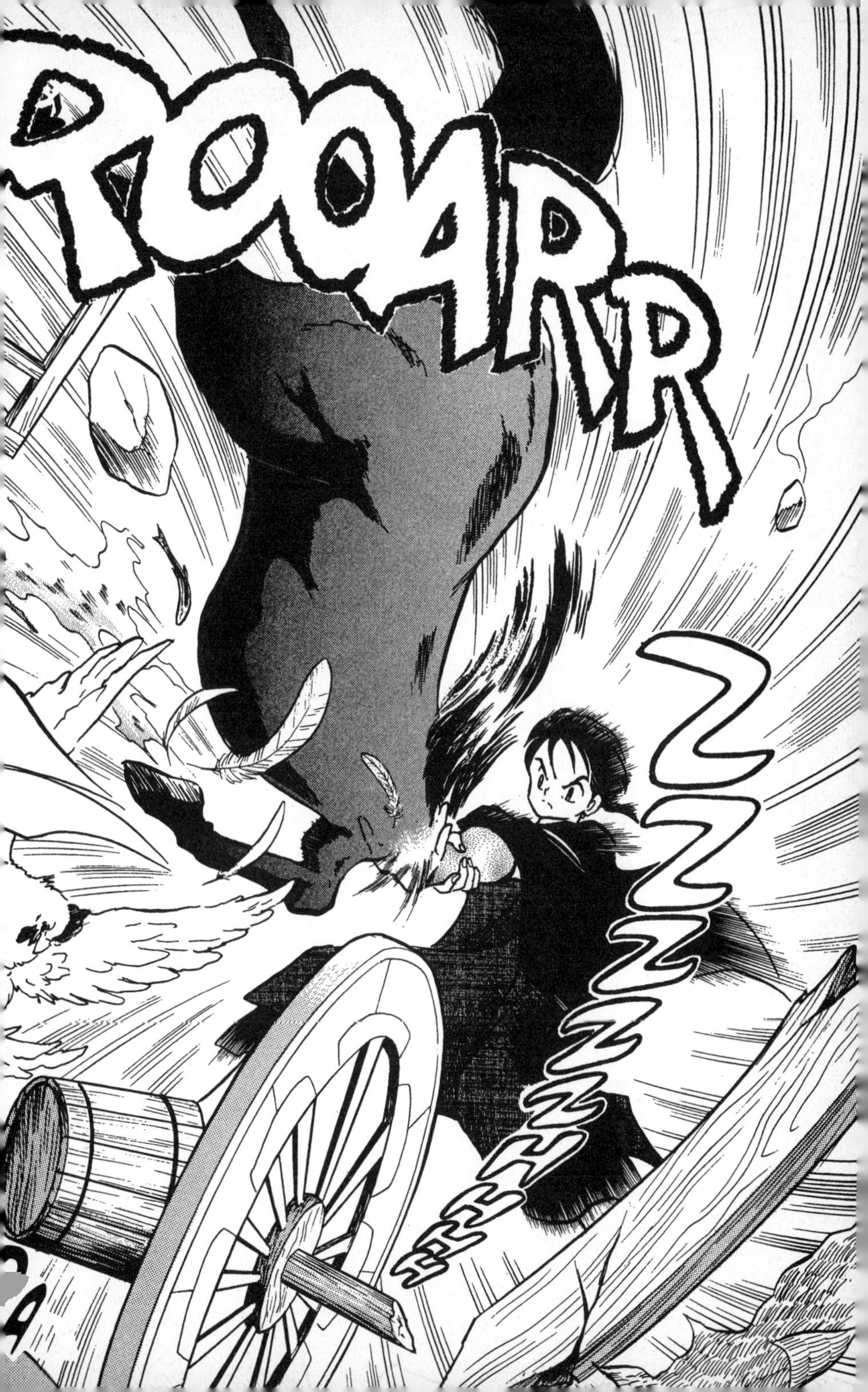

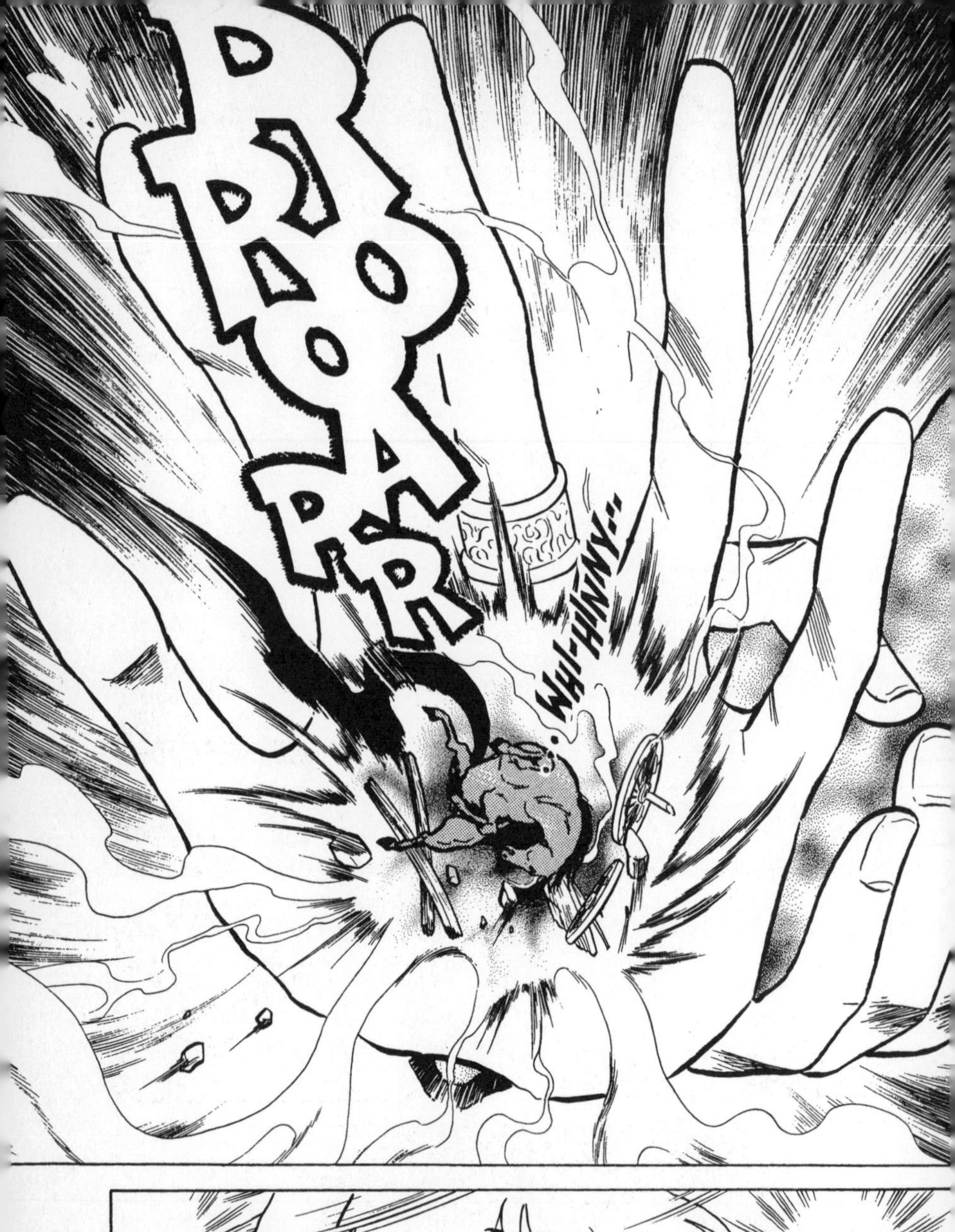
ROAR
WHI-HINNY!!

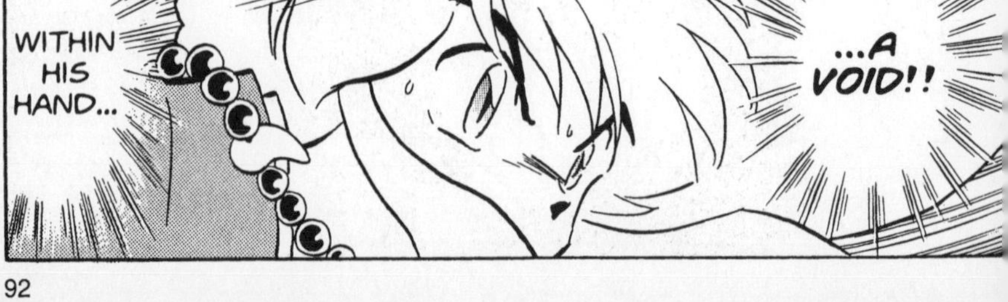
WITHIN HIS HAND...
...A VOID!!

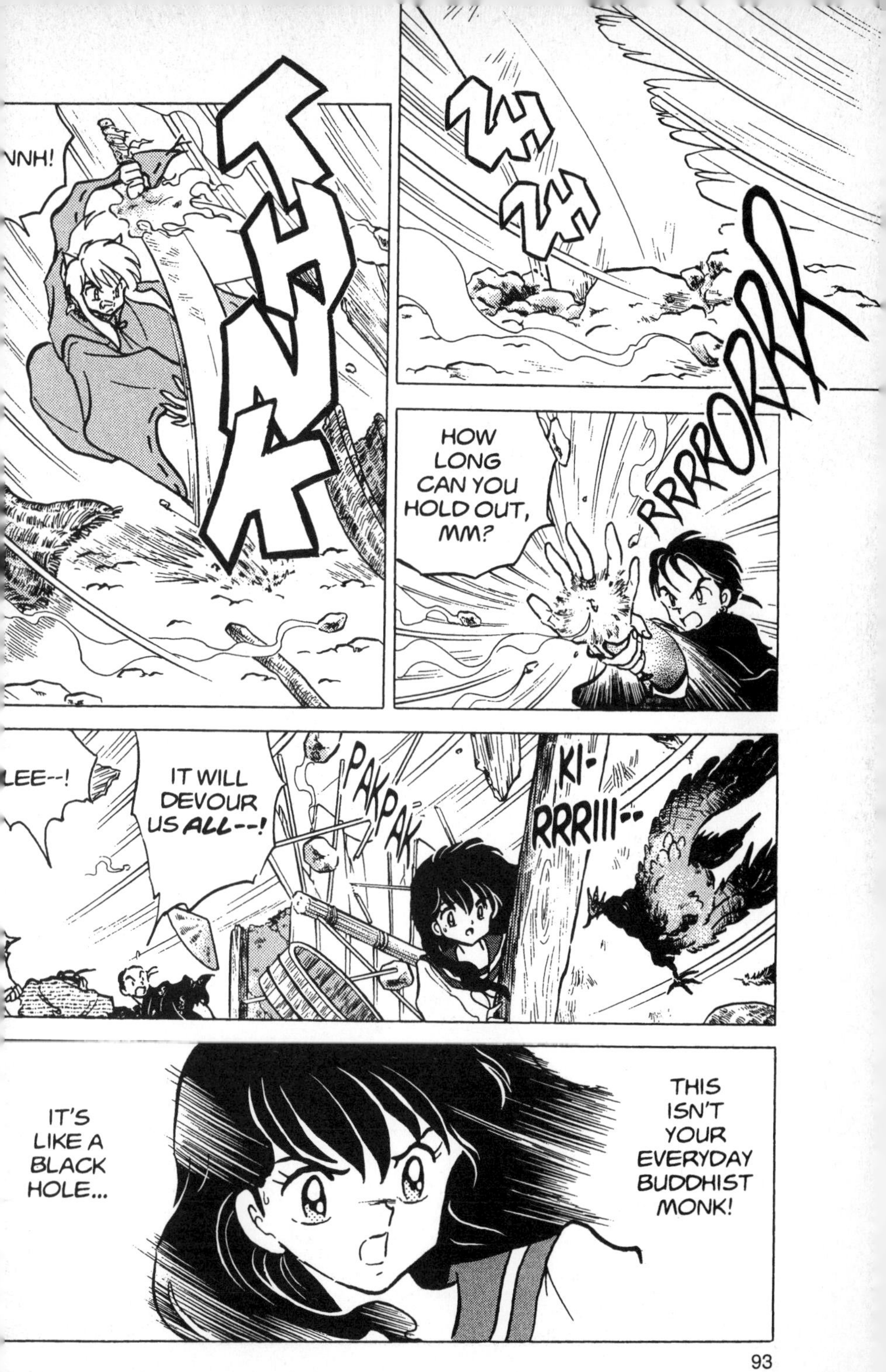
NNH!
THUNK
HOW LONG CAN YOU HOLD OUT, MM?
LEE--!
IT WILL DEVOUR US **ALL**--!
PAKPAK
KI-RRRIII--
IT'S LIKE A BLACK HOLE...
THIS ISN'T YOUR EVERYDAY BUDDHIST MONK!

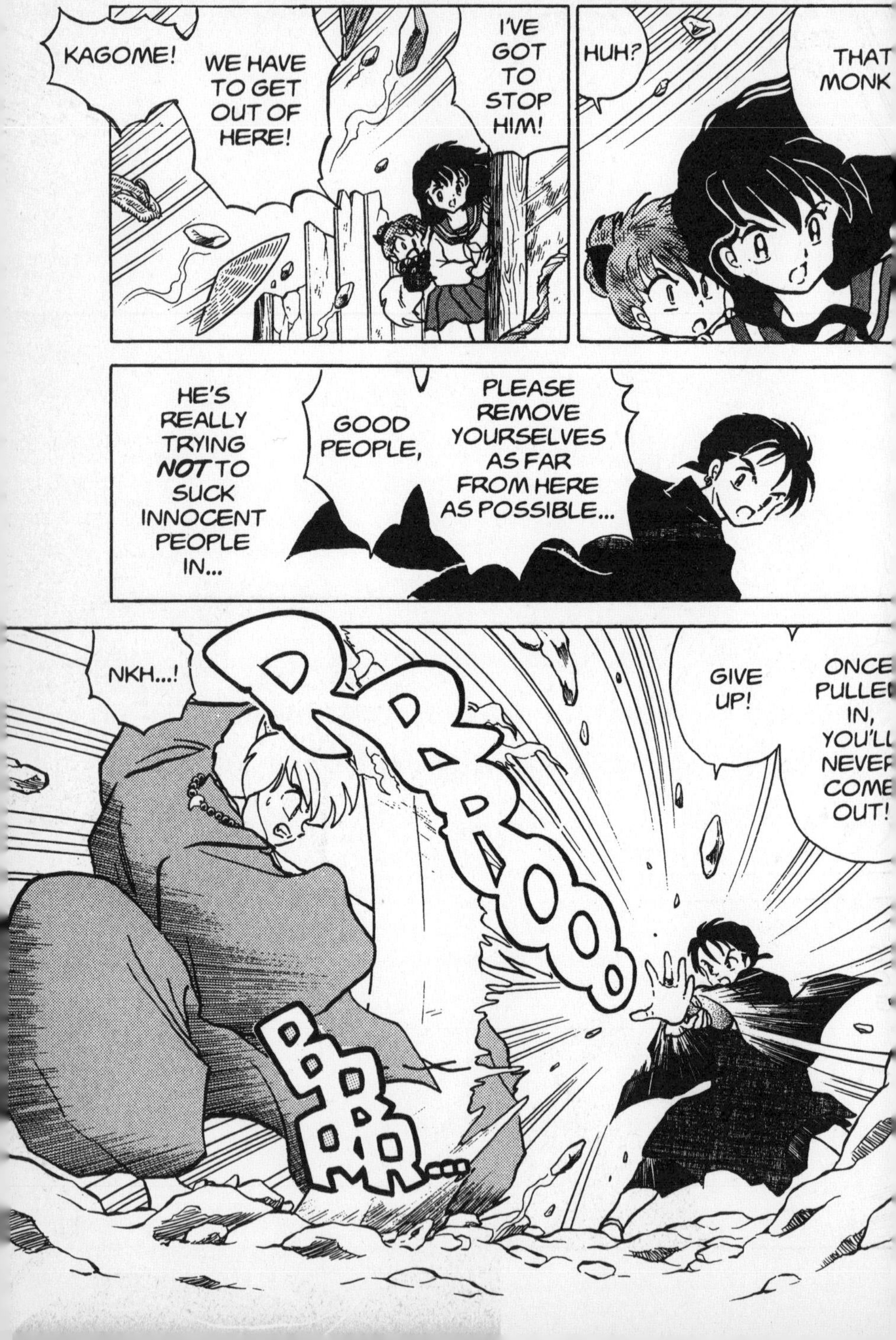
KAGOME!
WE HAVE TO GET OUT OF HERE!
I'VE GOT TO STOP HIM!
HUH?
THAT MONK
HE'S REALLY TRYING *NOT* TO SUCK INNOCENT PEOPLE IN...
GOOD PEOPLE,
PLEASE REMOVE YOURSELVES AS FAR FROM HERE AS POSSIBLE...
NKH...!
DOBOOO
GIVE UP!
ONCE PULLE IN, YOU'LL NEVER COME OUT!

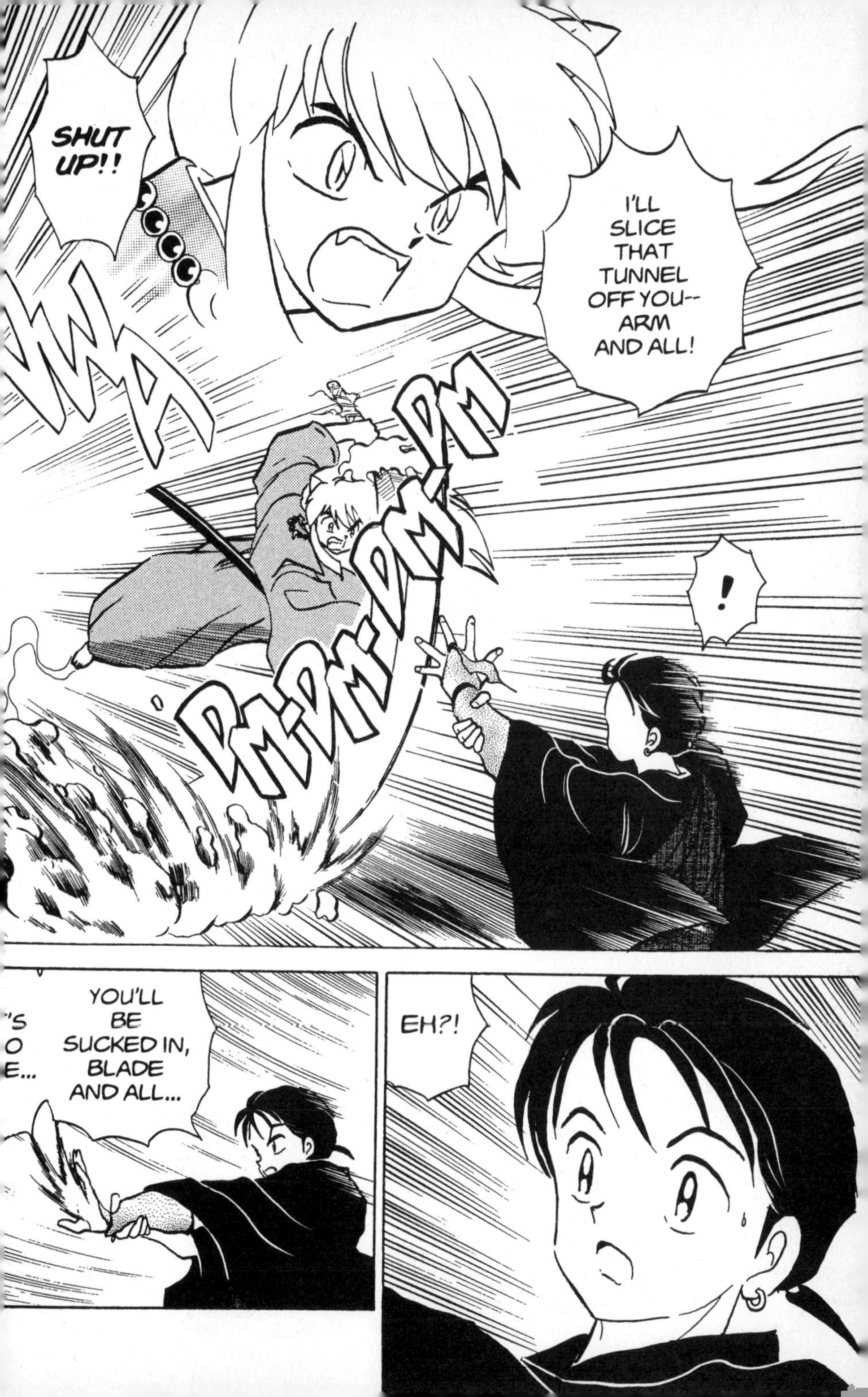
SHUT UP!!
I'LL SLICE THAT TUNNEL OFF YOU--ARM AND ALL!
!
'S O E...
YOU'LL BE SUCKED IN, BLADE AND ALL...
EH?!

FWOO

WHAT--?

KAGOME?!

KLATTA

GUHH!

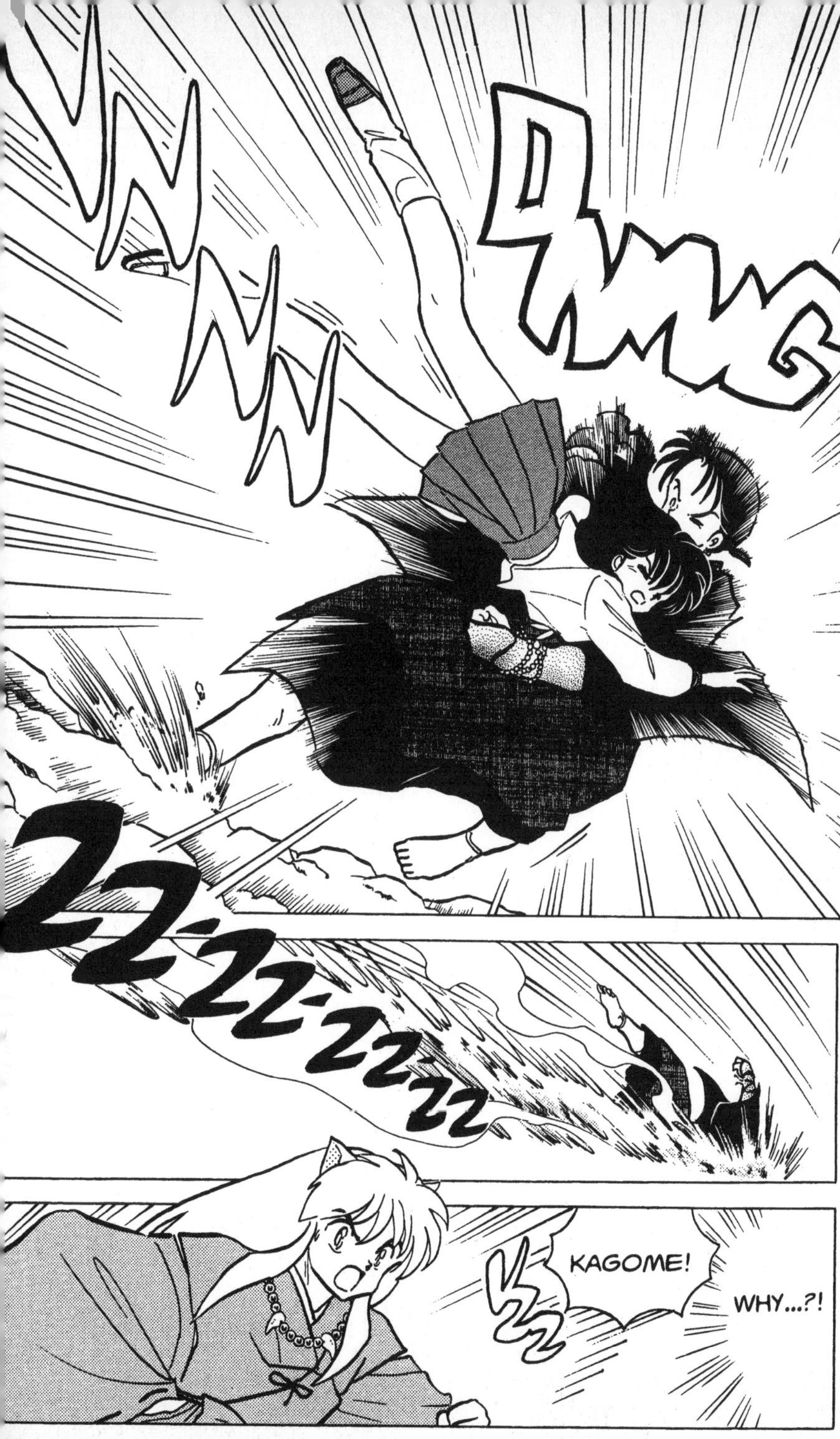
KAGOME!
WHY...?!

OMMM...

THIS ROSARY... IT PUTS A MYSTIC SEAL ON HIS HAND.

JUST LIKE I THOUGHT...

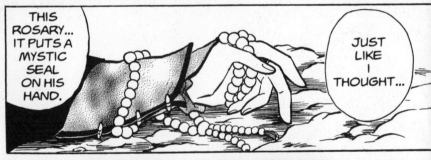

HE SEALED HIS HAND OF HIS OWN ACCORD...

HE REALLY *ISN'T* SO BAD, AFTER ALL!

SCROLL SIX

THE CURSED HAND

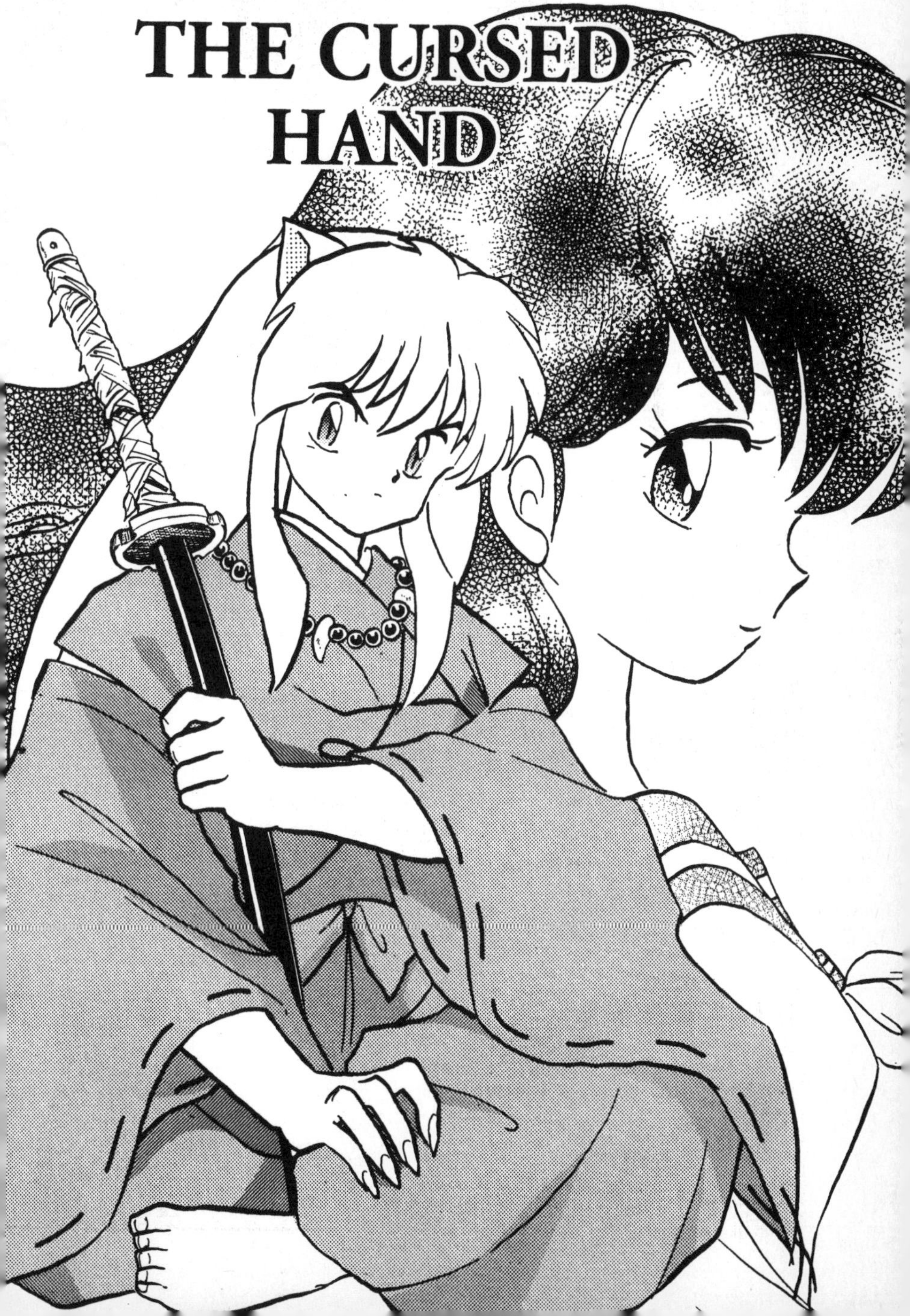

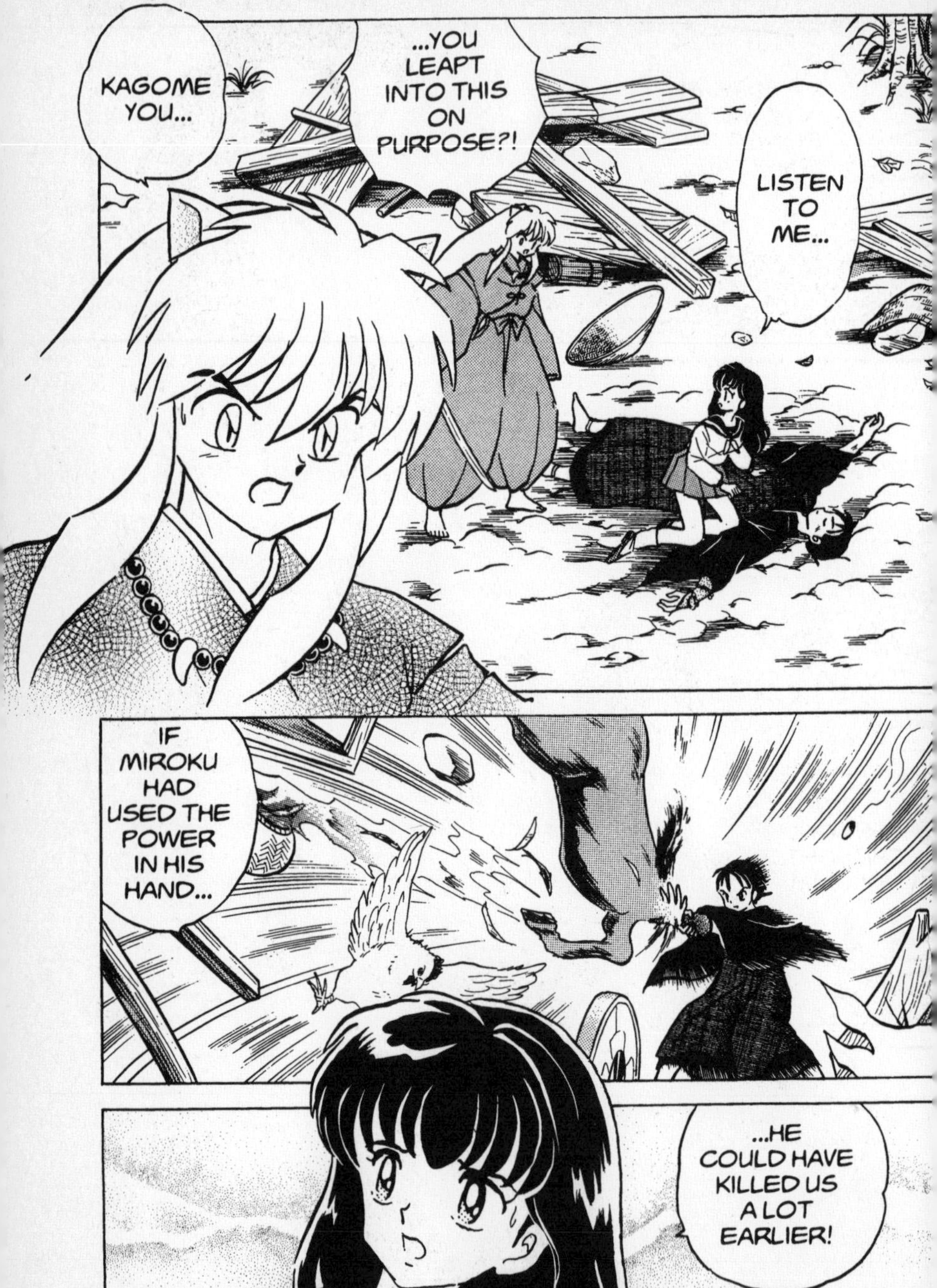
KAGOME YOU...
...YOU LEAPT INTO THIS ON PURPOSE?!
LISTEN TO ME...
IF MIROKU HAD USED THE POWER IN HIS HAND...
...HE COULD HAVE KILLED US A LOT EARLIER!

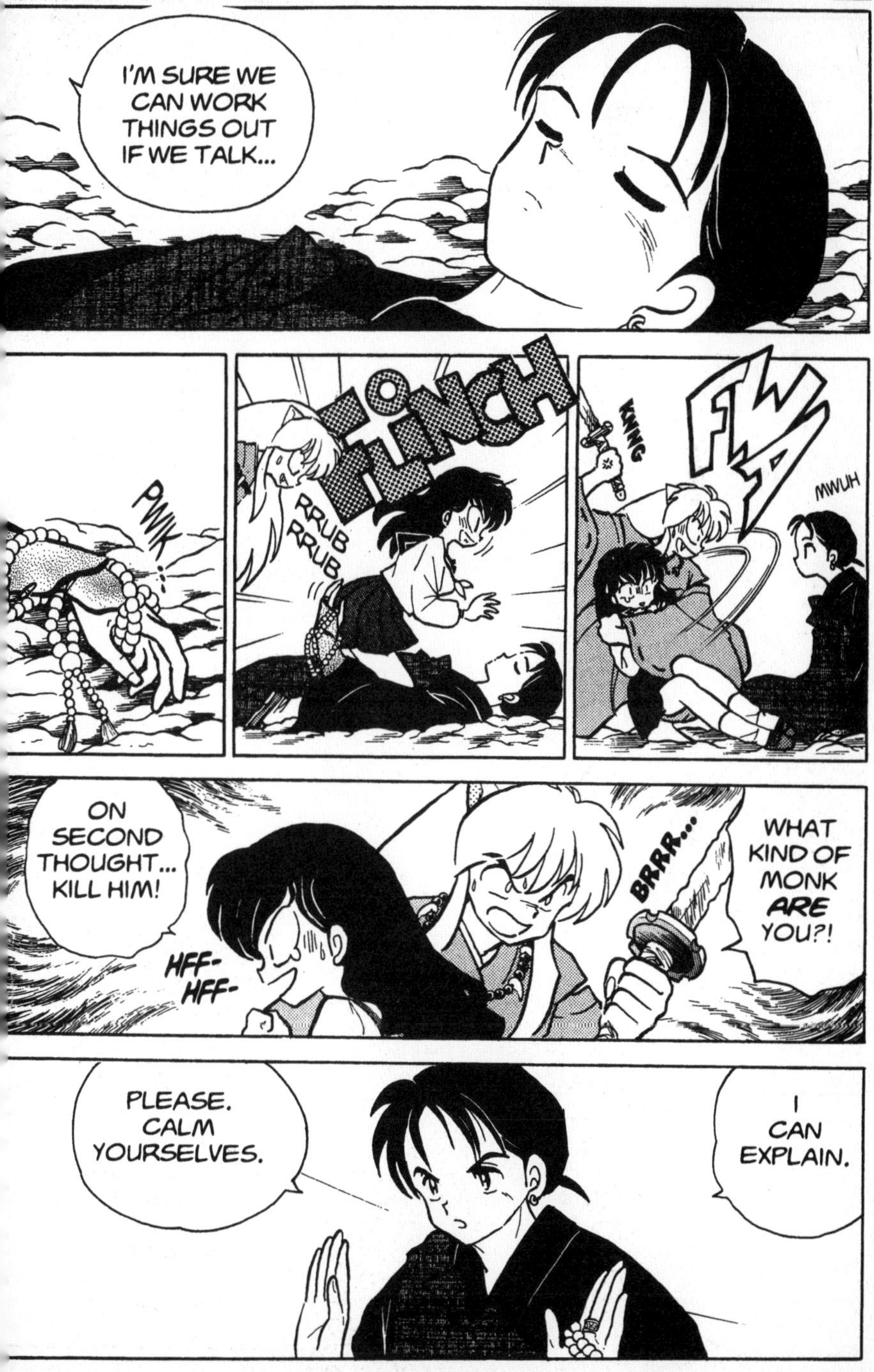
I'M SURE WE CAN WORK THINGS OUT IF WE TALK...
PWIK
FLINCH
RRUB RRUB
KWING
FWA
MWUH
ON SECOND THOUGHT... KILL HIM!
HFF- HFF-
BRRR...
WHAT KIND OF MONK ARE YOU?!
PLEASE. CALM YOURSELVES.
I CAN EXPLAIN.

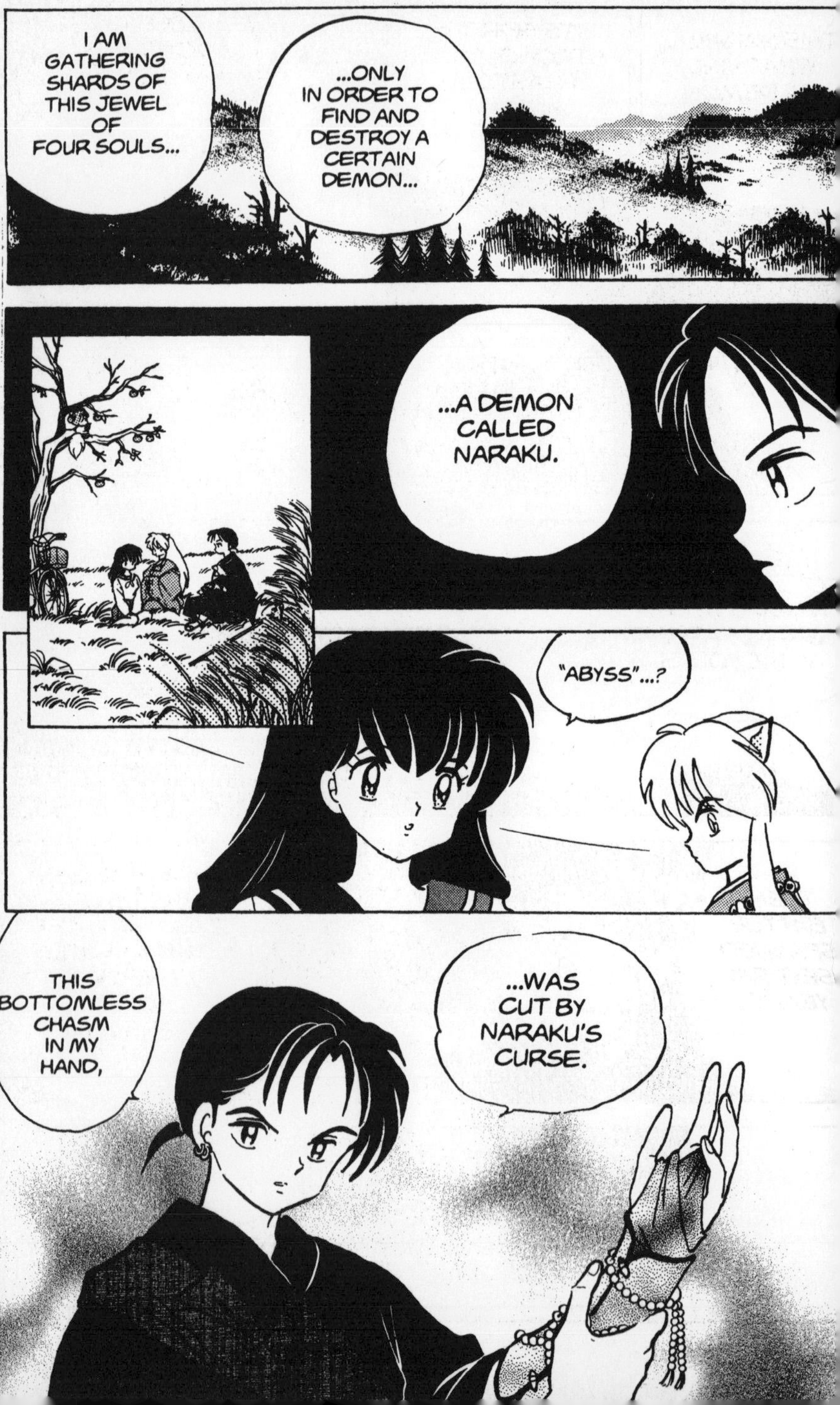
I AM GATHERING SHARDS OF THIS JEWEL OF FOUR SOULS...
...ONLY IN ORDER TO FIND AND DESTROY A CERTAIN DEMON...
...A DEMON CALLED NARAKU.
"ABYSS"...?
THIS BOTTOMLESS CHASM IN MY HAND,
...WAS CUT BY NARAKU'S CURSE.

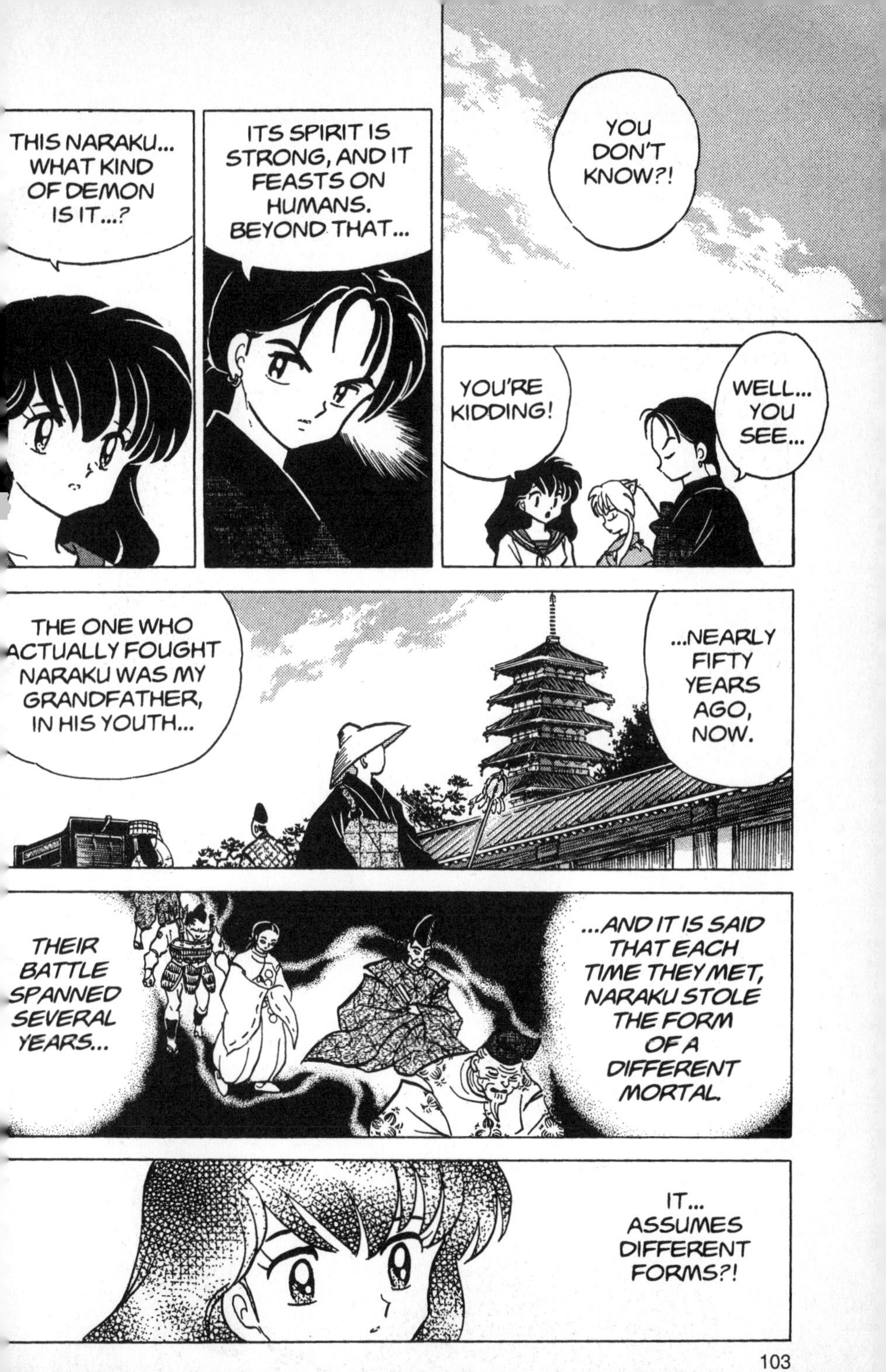
THIS NARAKU... WHAT KIND OF DEMON IS IT...?
ITS SPIRIT IS STRONG, AND IT FEASTS ON HUMANS. BEYOND THAT...
YOU DON'T KNOW?!
YOU'RE KIDDING!
WELL... YOU SEE...
THE ONE WHO ACTUALLY FOUGHT NARAKU WAS MY GRANDFATHER, IN HIS YOUTH...
...NEARLY FIFTY YEARS AGO, NOW.
THEIR BATTLE SPANNED SEVERAL YEARS...
...AND IT IS SAID THAT EACH TIME THEY MET, NARAKU STOLE THE FORM OF A DIFFERENT MORTAL.
IT... ASSUMES DIFFERENT FORMS?!

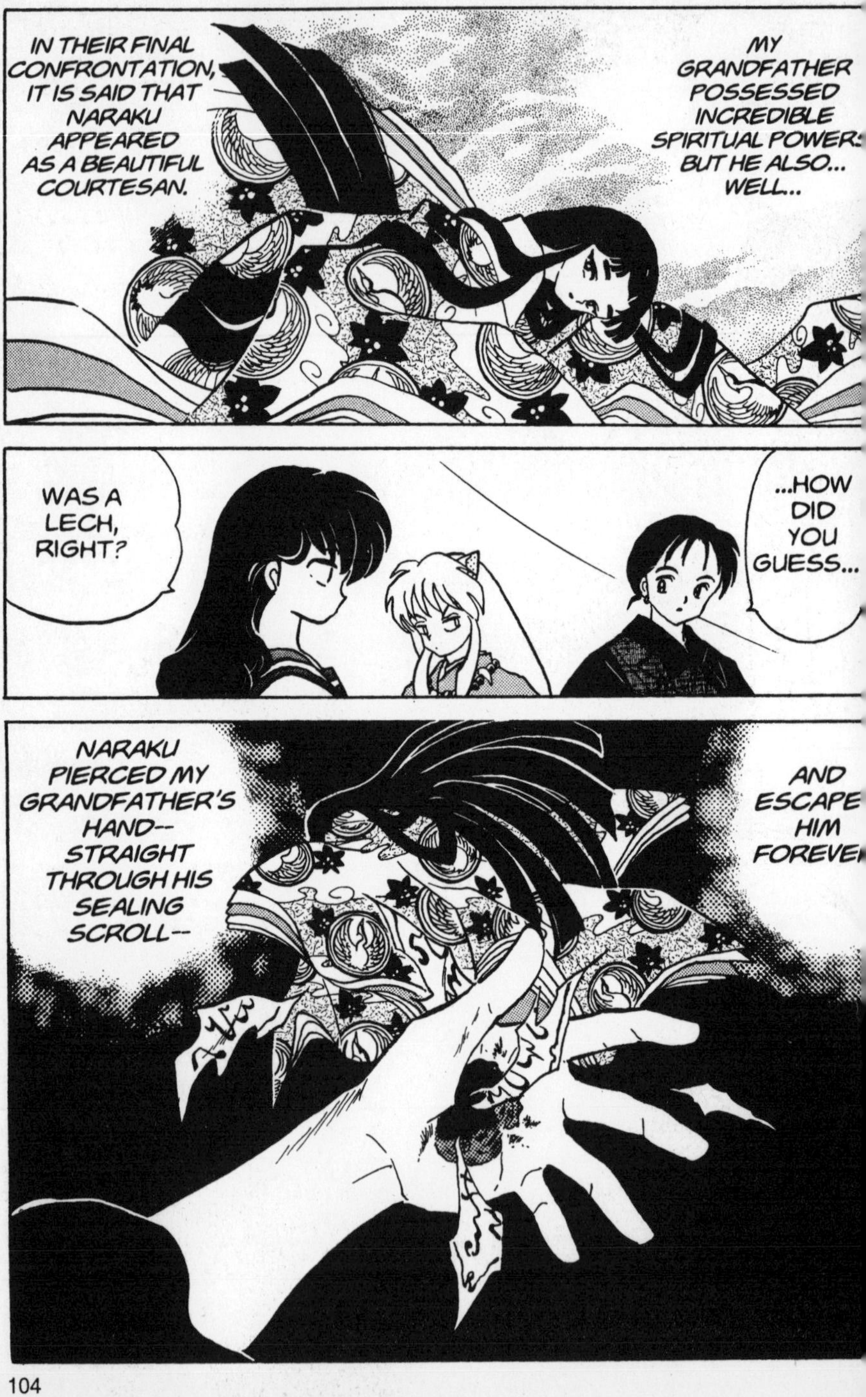
IN THEIR FINAL CONFRONTATION, IT IS SAID THAT NARAKU APPEARED AS A BEAUTIFUL COURTESAN.
MY GRANDFATHER POSSESSED INCREDIBLE SPIRITUAL POWER BUT HE ALSO... WELL...
WAS A LECH, RIGHT?
...HOW DID YOU GUESS...
NARAKU PIERCED MY GRANDFATHER'S HAND-- STRAIGHT THROUGH HIS SEALING SCROLL--
AND ESCAPE HIM FOREVE

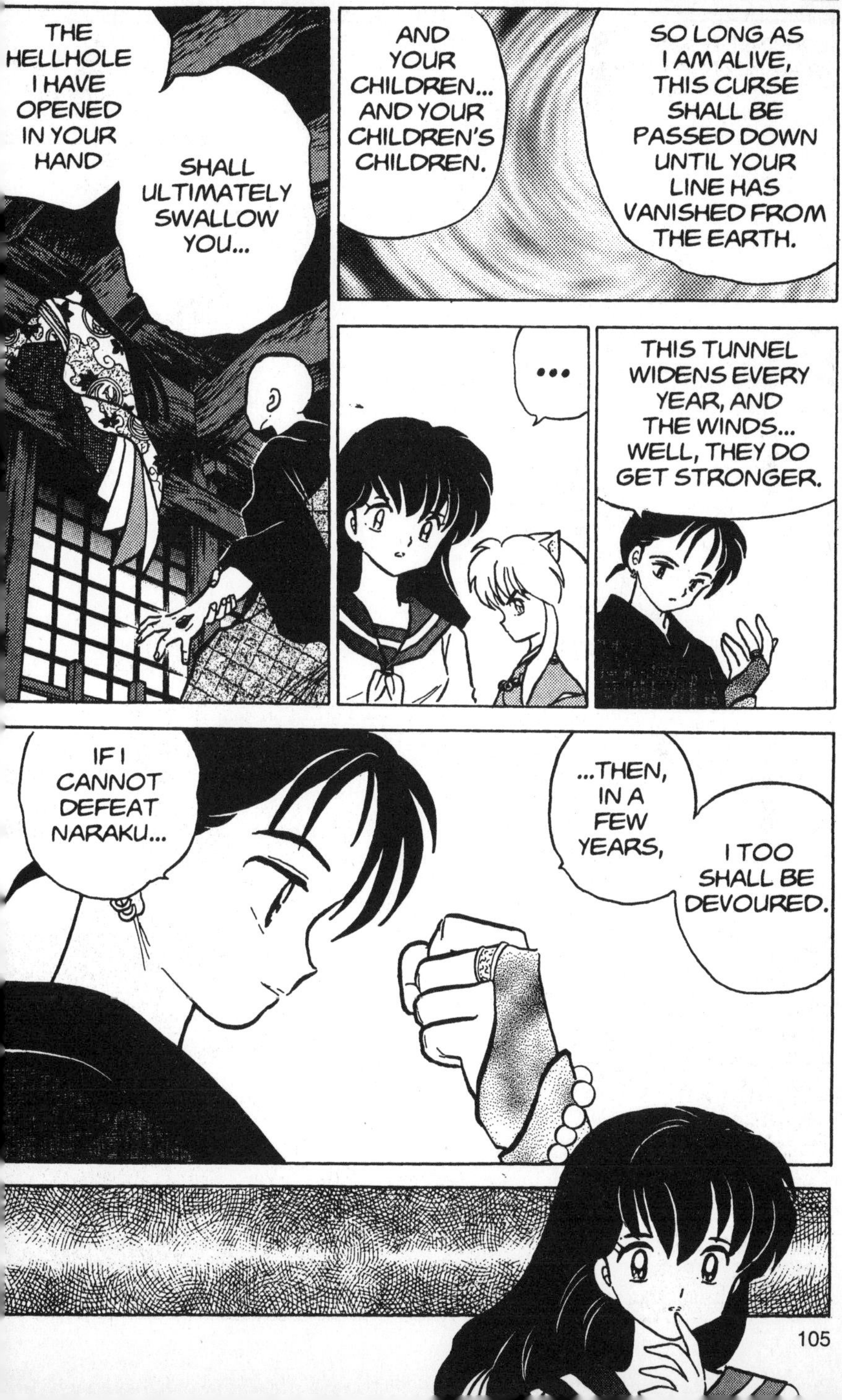
THE HELLHOLE I HAVE OPENED IN YOUR HAND
SHALL ULTIMATELY SWALLOW YOU...
AND YOUR CHILDREN... AND YOUR CHILDREN'S CHILDREN.
SO LONG AS I AM ALIVE, THIS CURSE SHALL BE PASSED DOWN UNTIL YOUR LINE HAS VANISHED FROM THE EARTH.
...
THIS TUNNEL WIDENS EVERY YEAR, AND THE WINDS... WELL, THEY DO GET STRONGER.
IF I CANNOT DEFEAT NARAKU...
...THEN, IN A FEW YEARS,
I TOO SHALL BE DEVOURED.

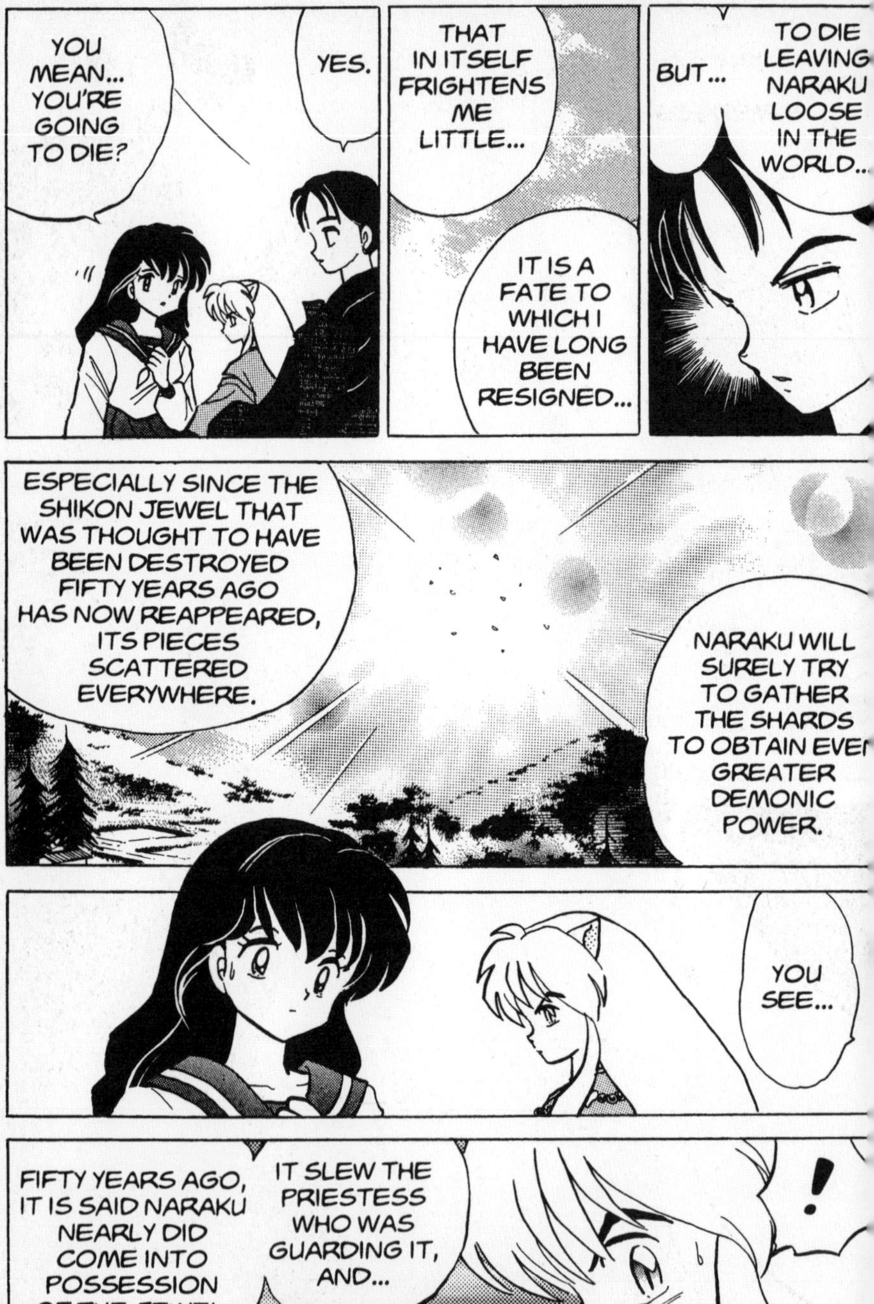
YOU MEAN... YOU'RE GOING TO DIE?
YES.
THAT IN ITSELF FRIGHTENS ME LITTLE...
IT IS A FATE TO WHICH I HAVE LONG BEEN RESIGNED...
BUT...
TO DIE LEAVING NARAKU LOOSE IN THE WORLD...
ESPECIALLY SINCE THE SHIKON JEWEL THAT WAS THOUGHT TO HAVE BEEN DESTROYED FIFTY YEARS AGO HAS NOW REAPPEARED, ITS PIECES SCATTERED EVERYWHERE.
NARAKU WILL SURELY TRY TO GATHER THE SHARDS TO OBTAIN EVEN GREATER DEMONIC POWER.
YOU SEE...
FIFTY YEARS AGO, IT IS SAID NARAKU NEARLY DID COME INTO POSSESSION OF THE JEWEL.
IT SLEW THE PRIESTESS WHO WAS GUARDING IT, AND...
!

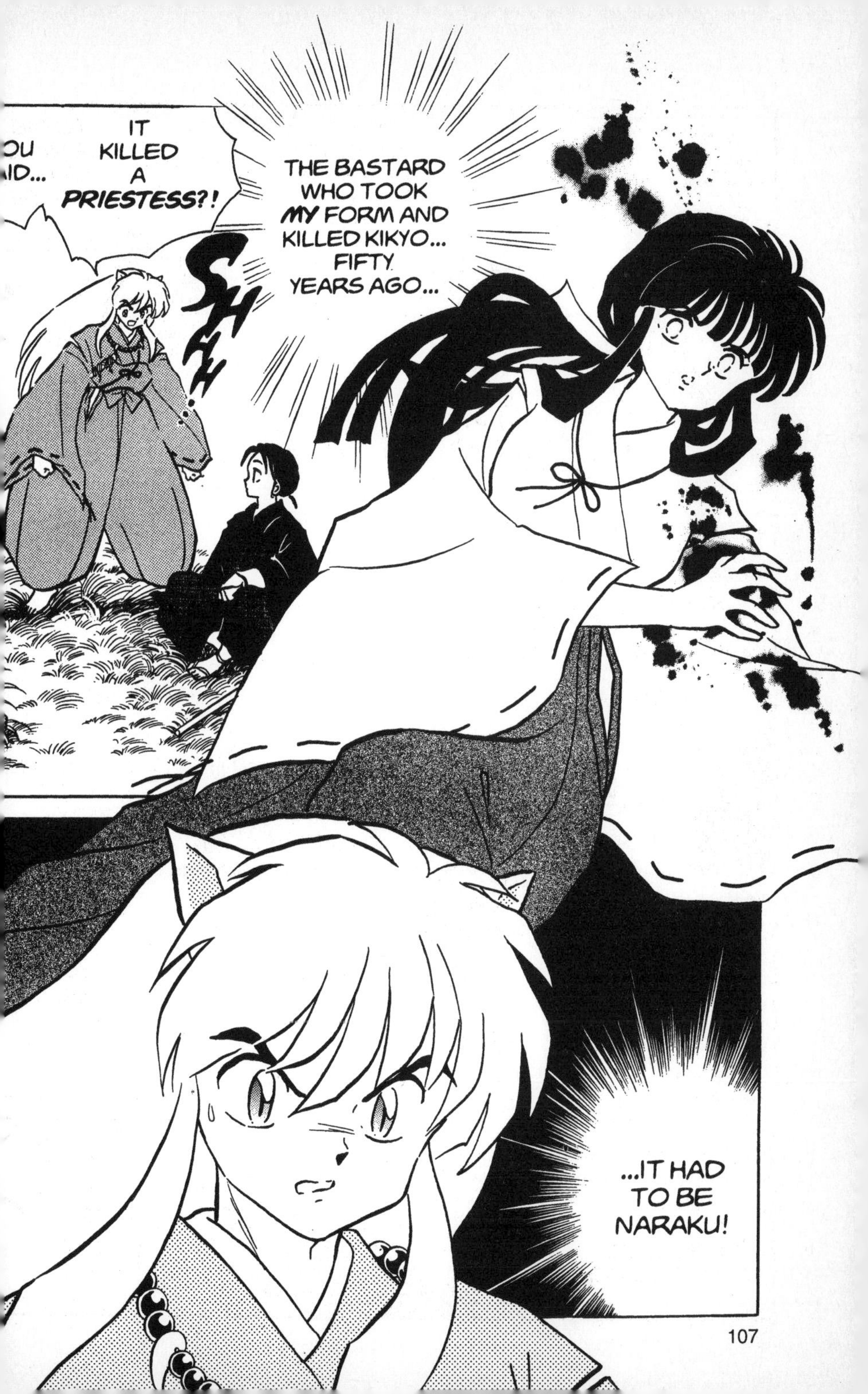

OU
ID...
IT KILLED A PRIESTESS?!
THE BASTARD WHO TOOK MY FORM AND KILLED KIKYO... FIFTY YEARS AGO...
SHHH
...IT HAD TO BE NARAKU!

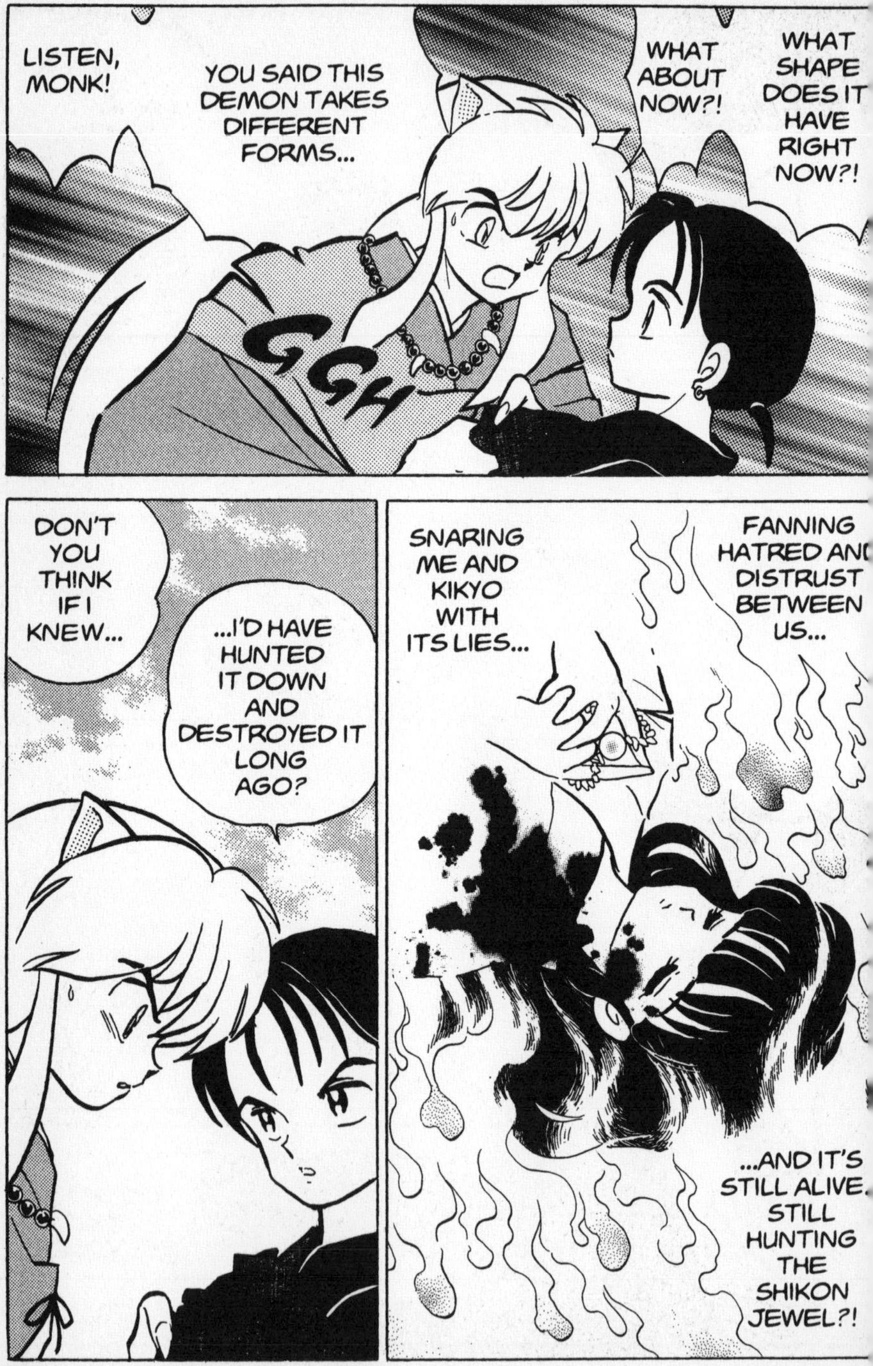

LISTEN, MONK!
YOU SAID THIS DEMON TAKES DIFFERENT FORMS...
GGH
WHAT ABOUT NOW?!
WHAT SHAPE DOES IT HAVE RIGHT NOW?!
DON'T YOU THINK IF I KNEW...
...I'D HAVE HUNTED IT DOWN AND DESTROYED IT LONG AGO?
SNARING ME AND KIKYO WITH ITS LIES...
FANNING HATRED AN DISTRUST BETWEEN US...
...AND IT'S STILL ALIVE. STILL HUNTING THE SHIKON JEWEL?!

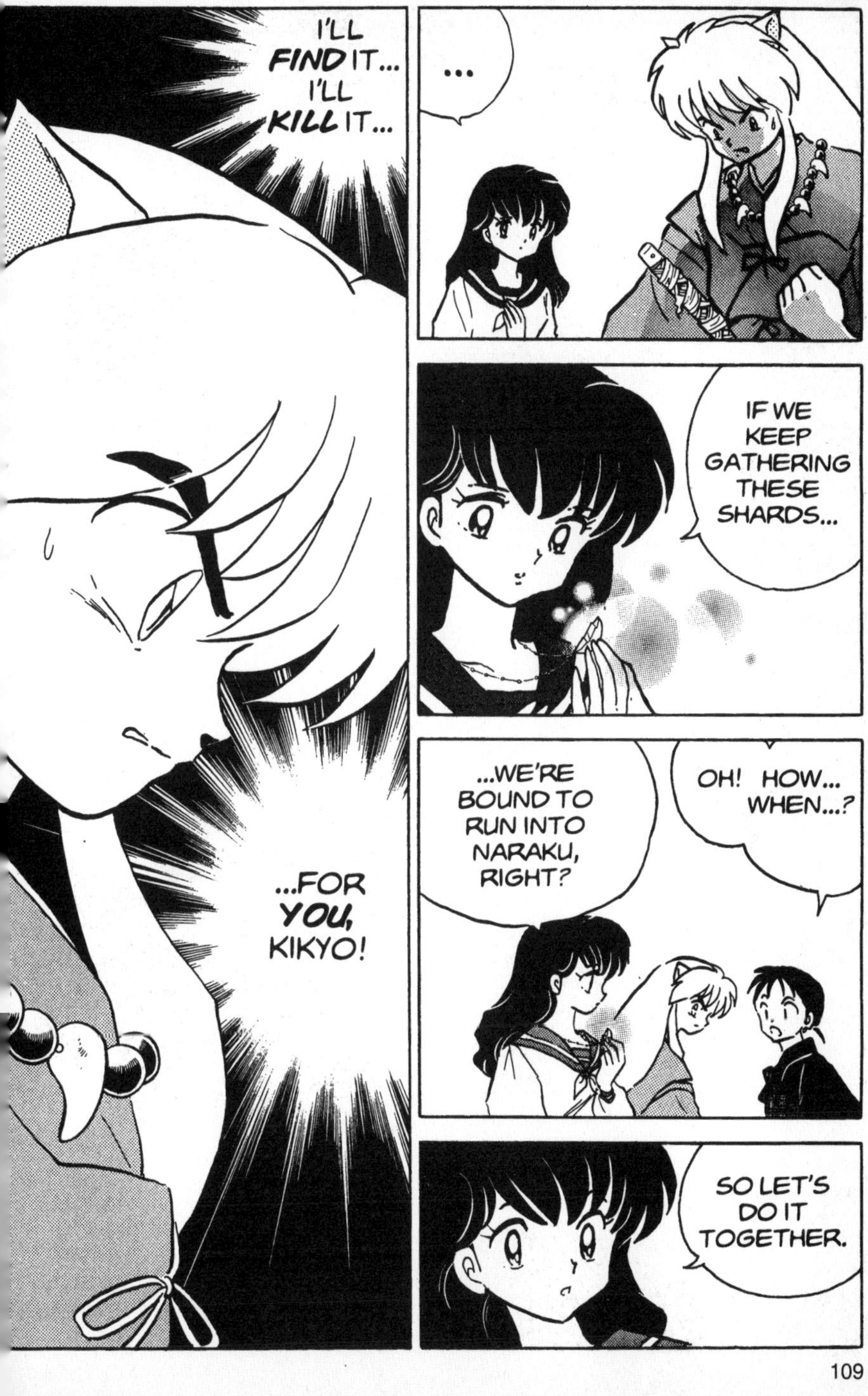
I'LL FIND IT... I'LL KILL IT...
...FOR YOU, KIKYO!
...
IF WE KEEP GATHERING THESE SHARDS...
...WE'RE BOUND TO RUN INTO NARAKU, RIGHT?
OH! HOW... WHEN...?
SO LET'S DO IT TOGETHER.

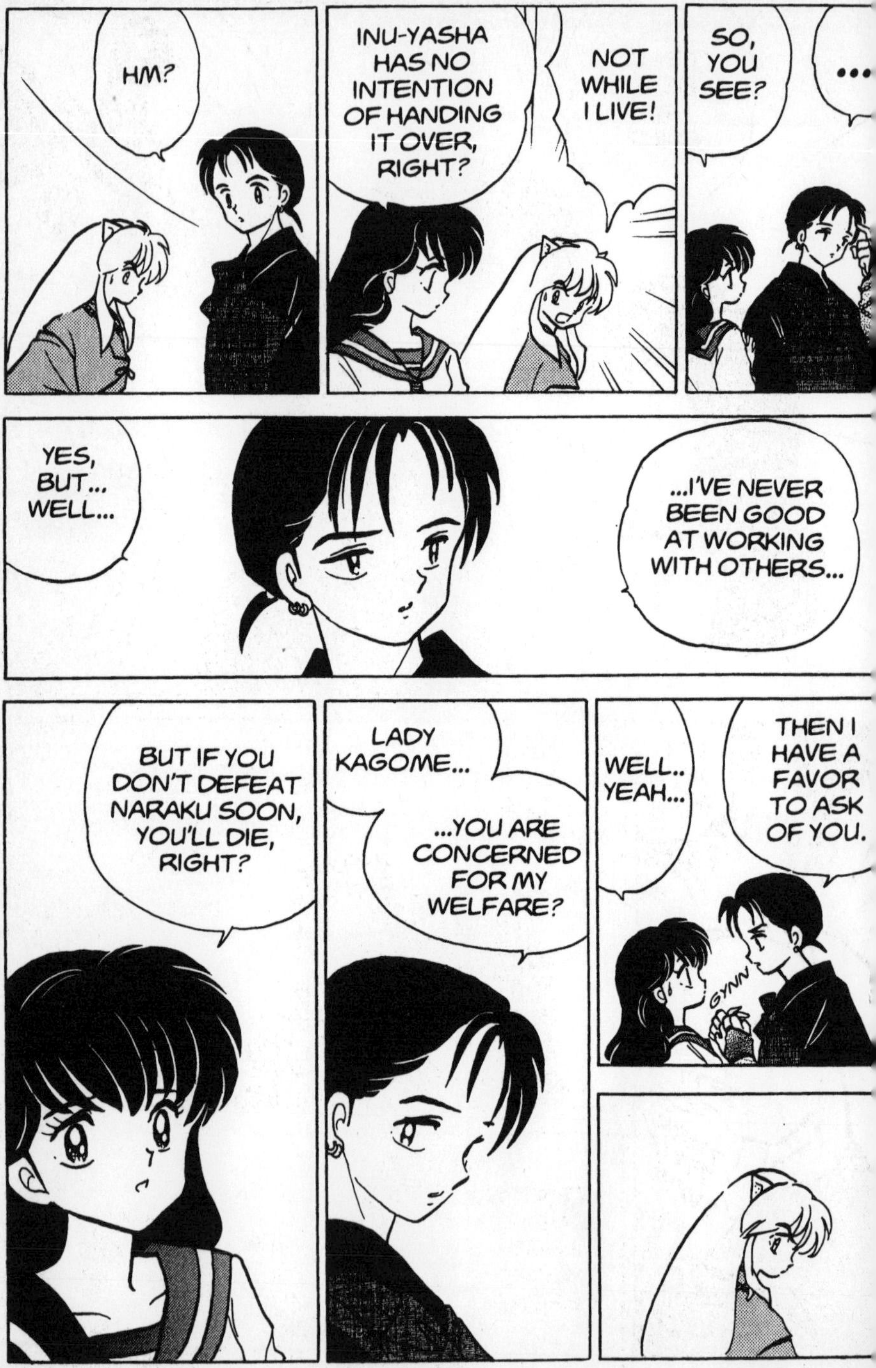
HM?
INU-YASHA HAS NO INTENTION OF HANDING IT OVER, RIGHT?
NOT WHILE I LIVE!
SO, YOU SEE?
...
YES, BUT... WELL...
...I'VE NEVER BEEN GOOD AT WORKING WITH OTHERS...
BUT IF YOU DON'T DEFEAT NARAKU SOON, YOU'LL DIE, RIGHT?
LADY KAGOME...
...YOU ARE CONCERNED FOR MY WELFARE?
WELL.. YEAH...
THEN I HAVE A FAVOR TO ASK OF YOU.
GYNN

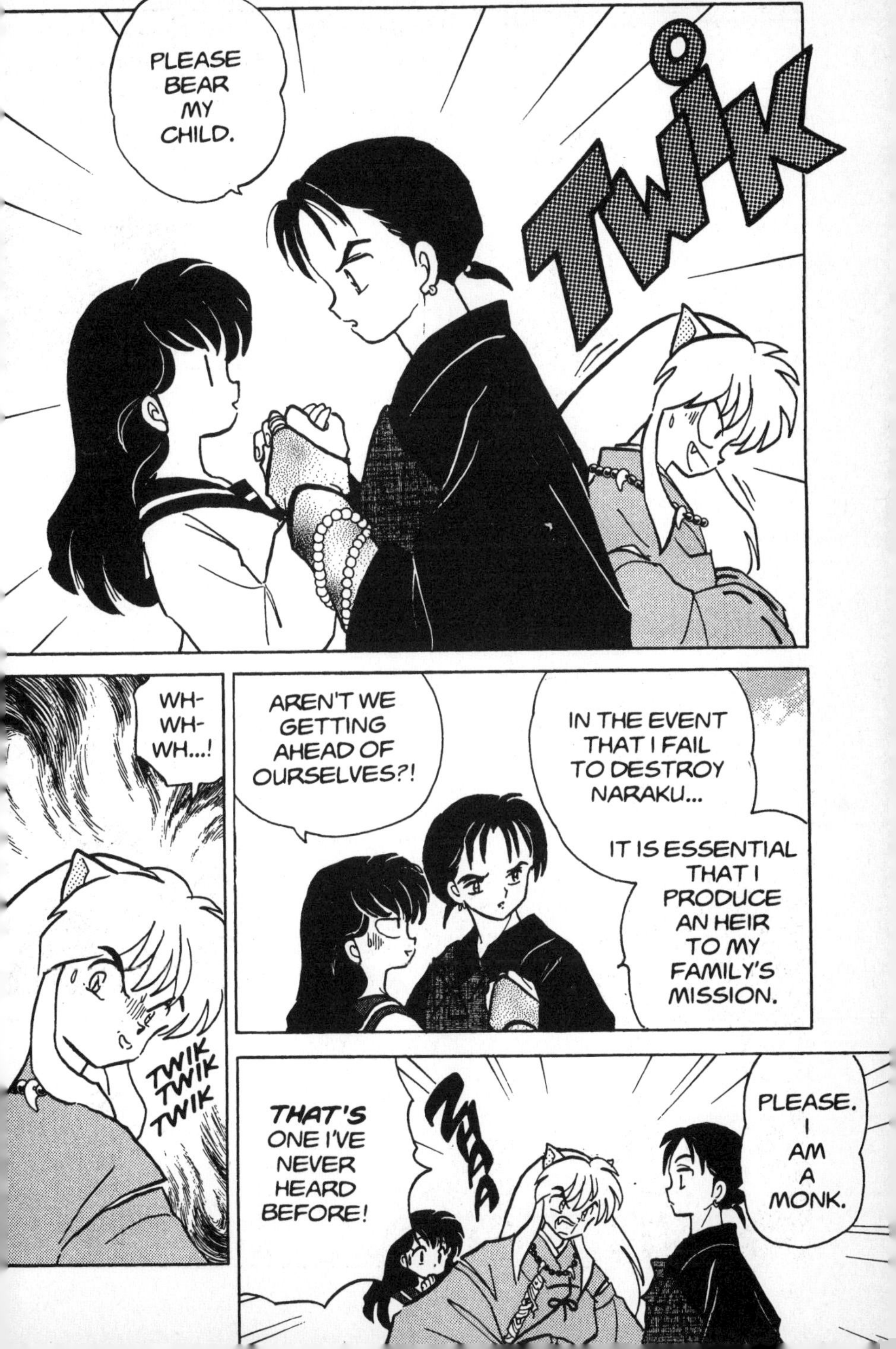
PLEASE BEAR MY CHILD.
TWIK
WH- WH- WH...!
TWIK TWIK TWIK
AREN'T WE GETTING AHEAD OF OURSELVES?!
IN THE EVENT THAT I FAIL TO DESTROY NARAKU...
IT IS ESSENTIAL THAT I PRODUCE AN HEIR TO MY FAMILY'S MISSION.
THAT'S ONE I'VE NEVER HEARD BEFORE!
PLEASE. I AM A MONK.

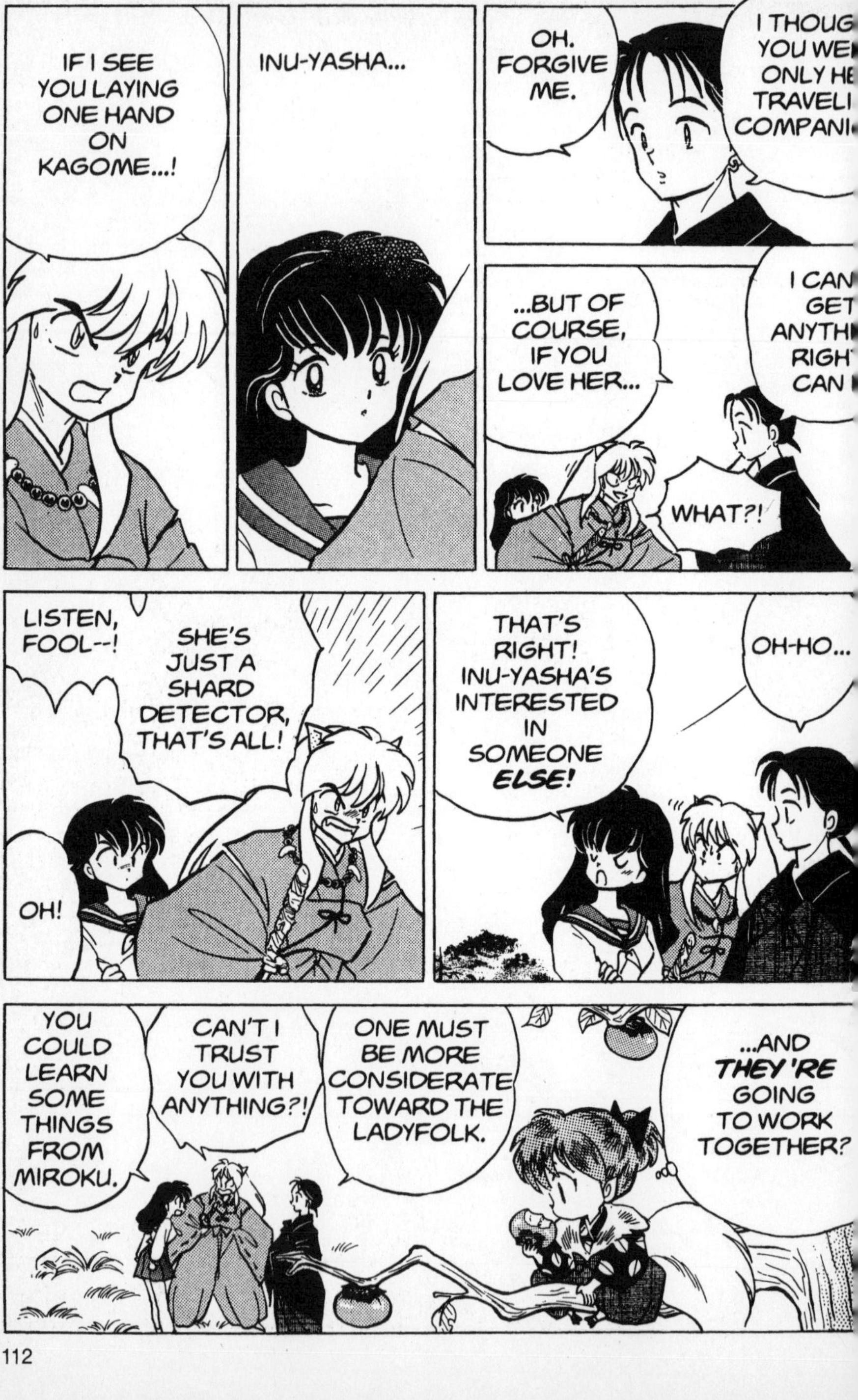
IF I SEE YOU LAYING ONE HAND ON KAGOME...!
INU-YASHA...
OH. FORGIVE ME.
I THOUG YOU WE ONLY HE TRAVELI COMPANI
...BUT OF COURSE, IF YOU LOVE HER...
I CAN GET ANYTH RIGHT CAN
WHAT?!
LISTEN, FOOL--!
SHE'S JUST A SHARD DETECTOR, THAT'S ALL!
OH!
THAT'S RIGHT! INU-YASHA'S INTERESTED IN SOMEONE ELSE!
OH-HO...
YOU COULD LEARN SOME THINGS FROM MIROKU.
CAN'T I TRUST YOU WITH ANYTHING?!
ONE MUST BE MORE CONSIDERATE TOWARD THE LADYFOLK.
...AND THEY'RE GOING TO WORK TOGETHER?

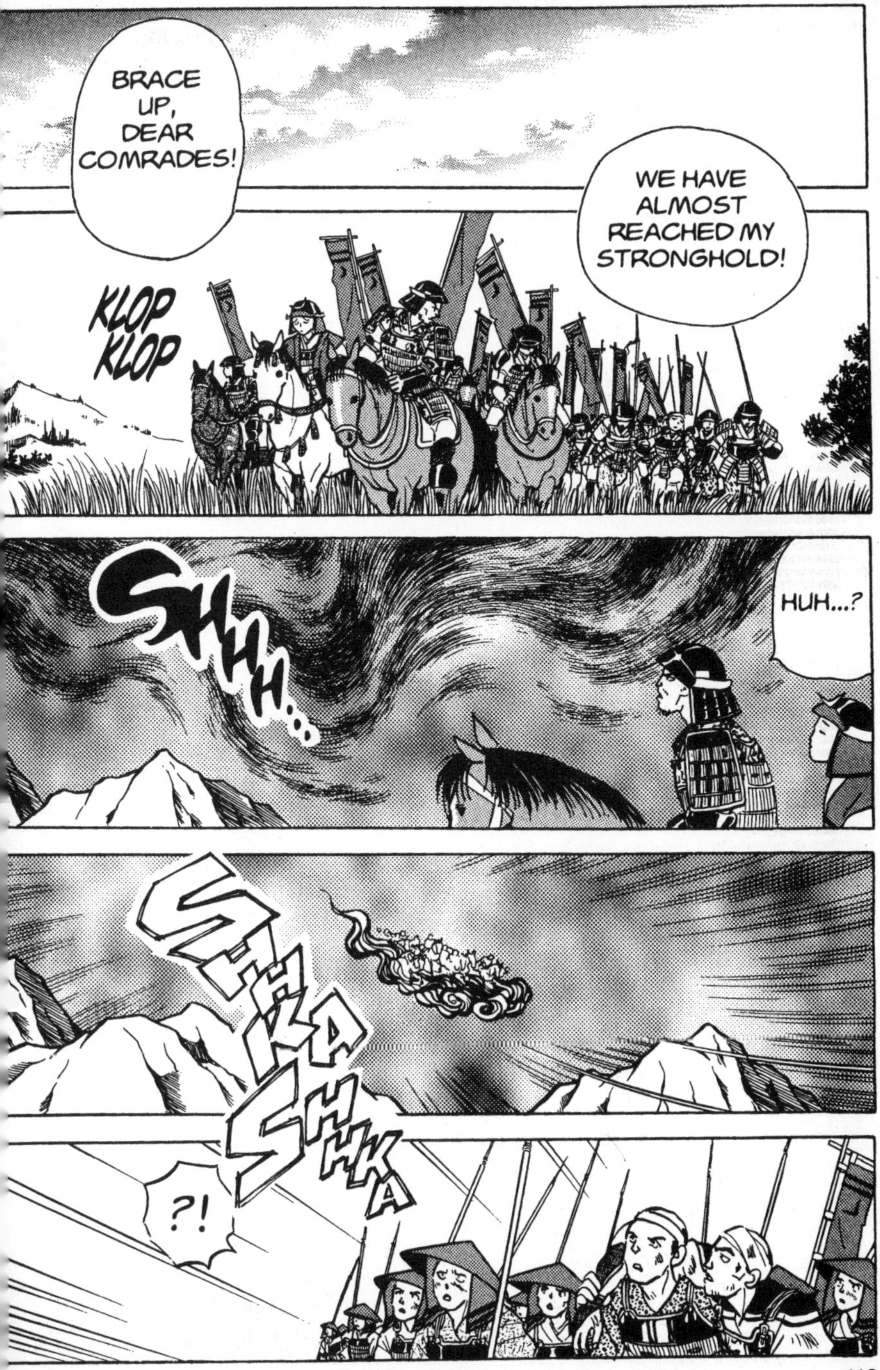
BRACE UP, DEAR COMRADES!
KLOP KLOP
WE HAVE ALMOST REACHED MY STRONGHOLD!
SHHHH...
HUH...?
SHHKA SHHKA
?!

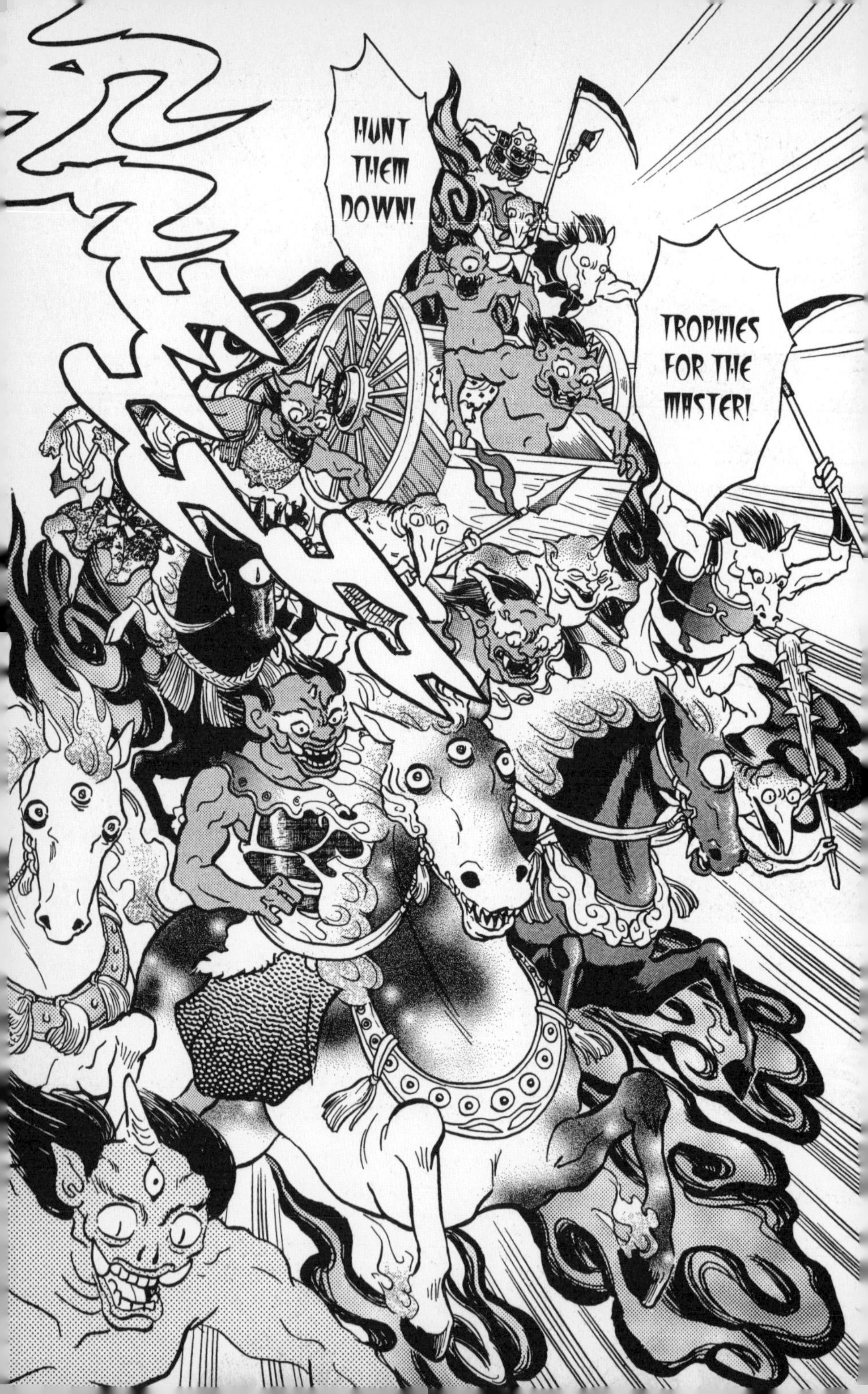
HUNT THEM DOWN!
TROPHIES FOR THE MASTER!

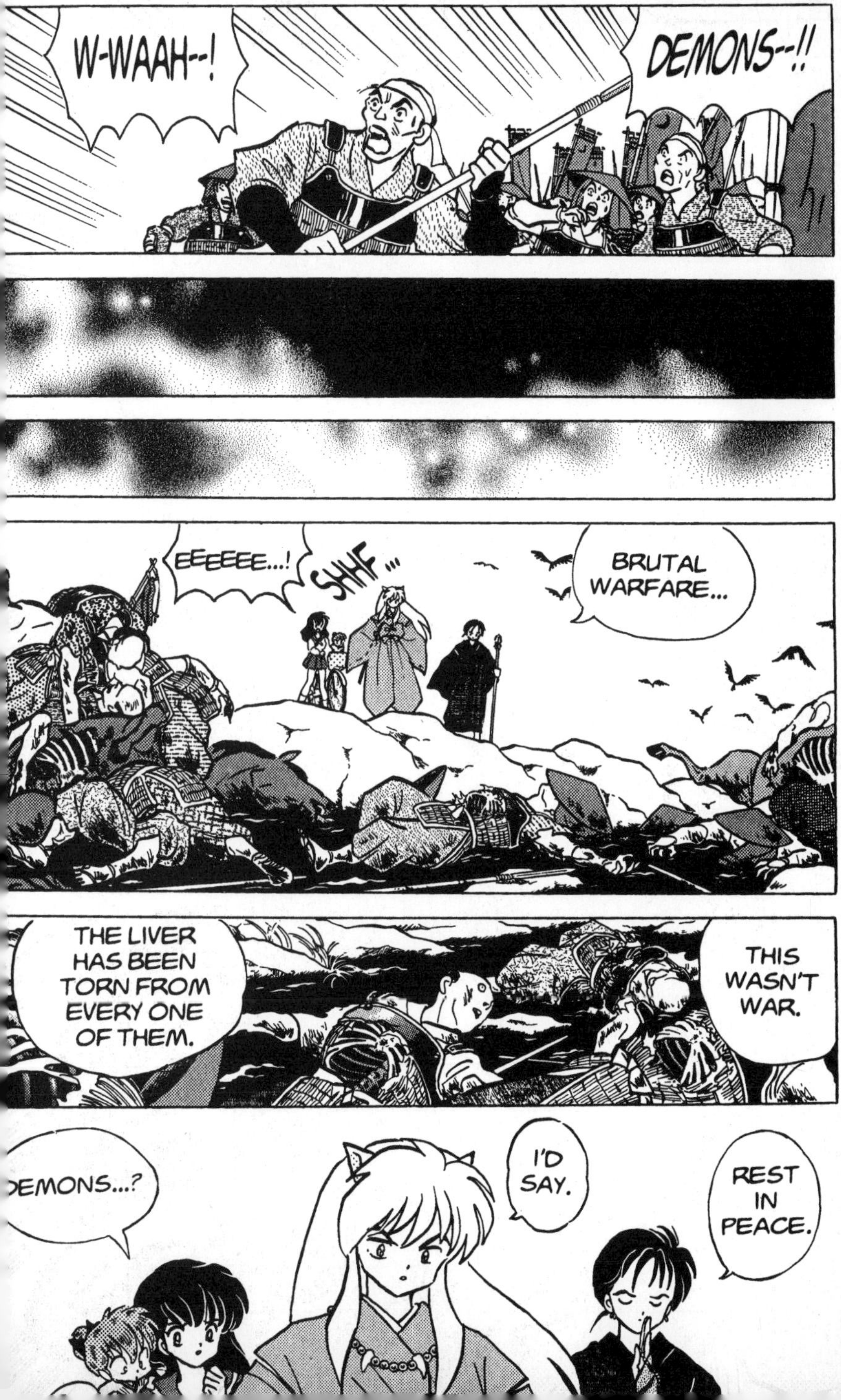
W-WAAH--!
DEMONS--!!
EEEEEE...!
SHHF...
BRUTAL WARFARE...
THE LIVER HAS BEEN TORN FROM EVERY ONE OF THEM.
THIS WASN'T WAR.
DEMONS...?
I'D SAY.
REST IN PEACE.

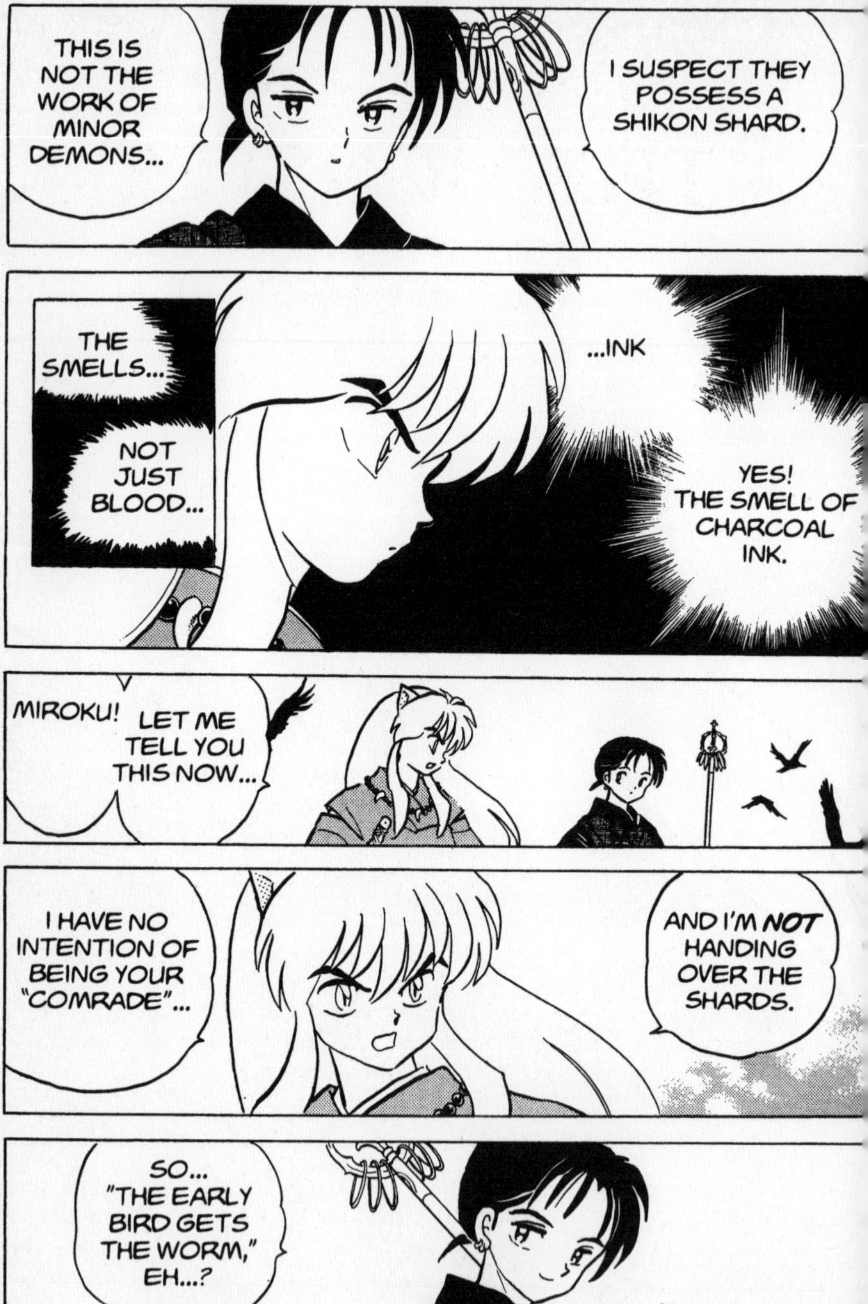

THIS IS NOT THE WORK OF MINOR DEMONS...
I SUSPECT THEY POSSESS A SHIKON SHARD.
THE SMELLS...
NOT JUST BLOOD...
...INK
YES! THE SMELL OF CHARCOAL INK.
MIROKU!
LET ME TELL YOU THIS NOW...
I HAVE NO INTENTION OF BEING YOUR "COMRADE"...
AND I'M **NOT** HANDING OVER THE SHARDS.
SO... "THE EARLY BIRD GETS THE WORM," EH...?

SCROLL SEVEN

THE MONSTER WITHIN

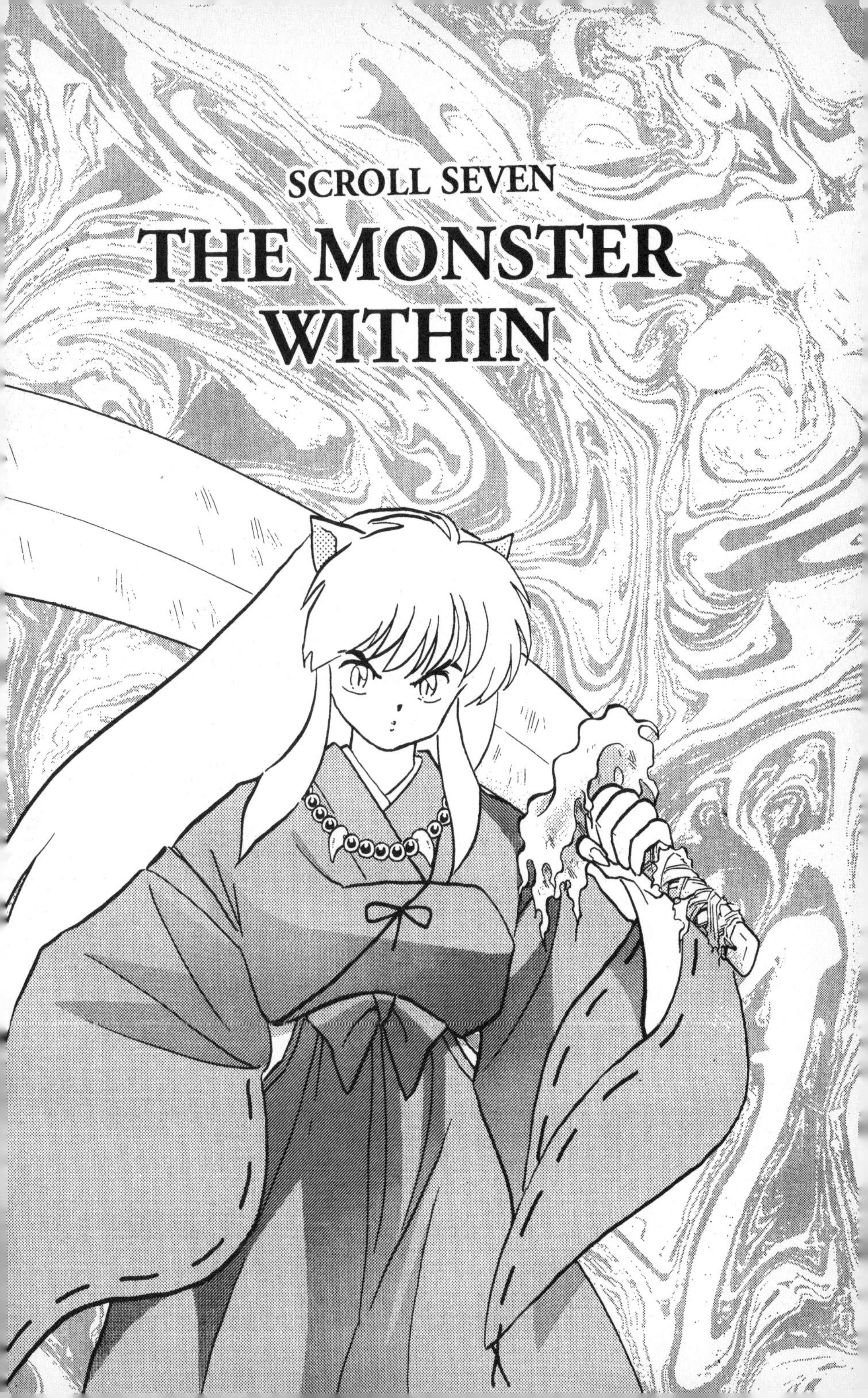

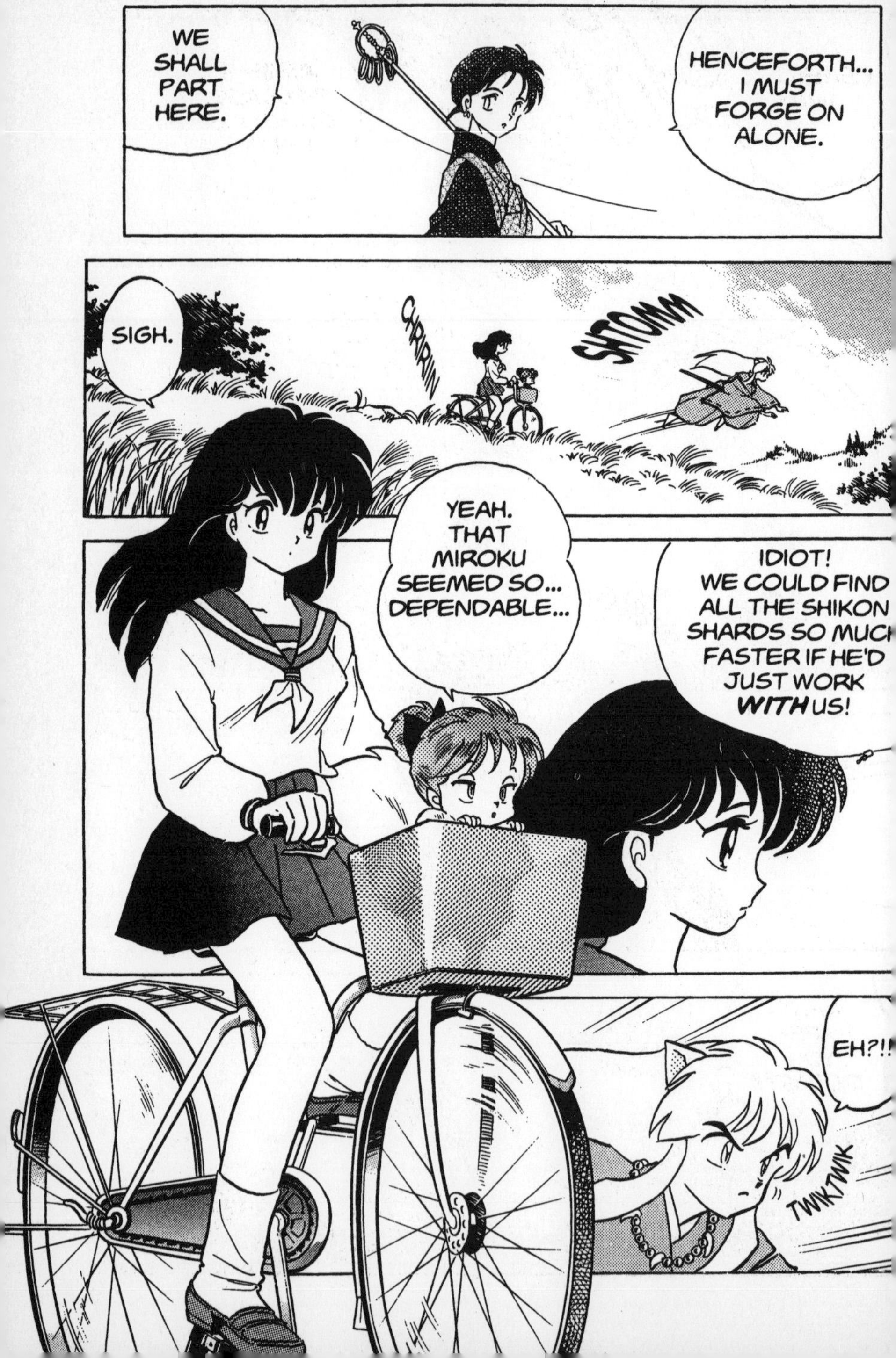
WE SHALL PART HERE.
HENCEFORTH... I MUST FORGE ON ALONE.
SIGH.
CHIRIRIN
SHTOMM
YEAH. THAT MIROKU SEEMED SO... DEPENDABLE...
IDIOT! WE COULD FIND ALL THE SHIKON SHARDS SO MUCH FASTER IF HE'D JUST WORK **WITH** US!
EH?!!
TWIKTWIK

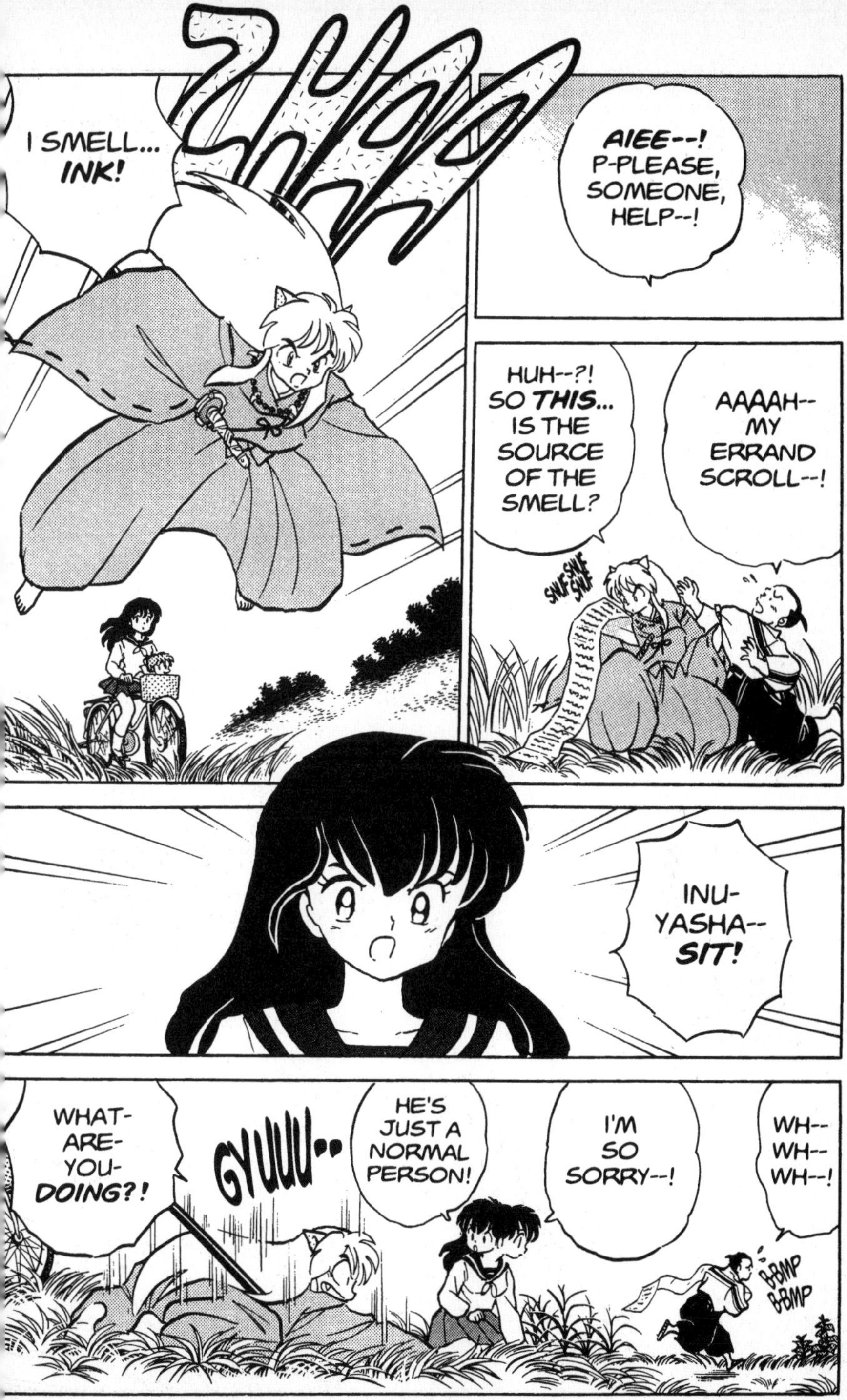

I SMELL... **INK!**
AIEE--! P-PLEASE, SOMEONE, HELP--!
HUH--?! SO **THIS**... IS THE SOURCE OF THE SMELL?
AAAAH-- MY ERRAND SCROLL--!
SNIF SNIF
INU-YASHA-- **SIT!**
WHAT-ARE-YOU-**DOING?!**
GYUUU..
HE'S JUST A NORMAL PERSON!
I'M SO SORRY--!
WH-- WH-- WH--!
BBMP BBMP

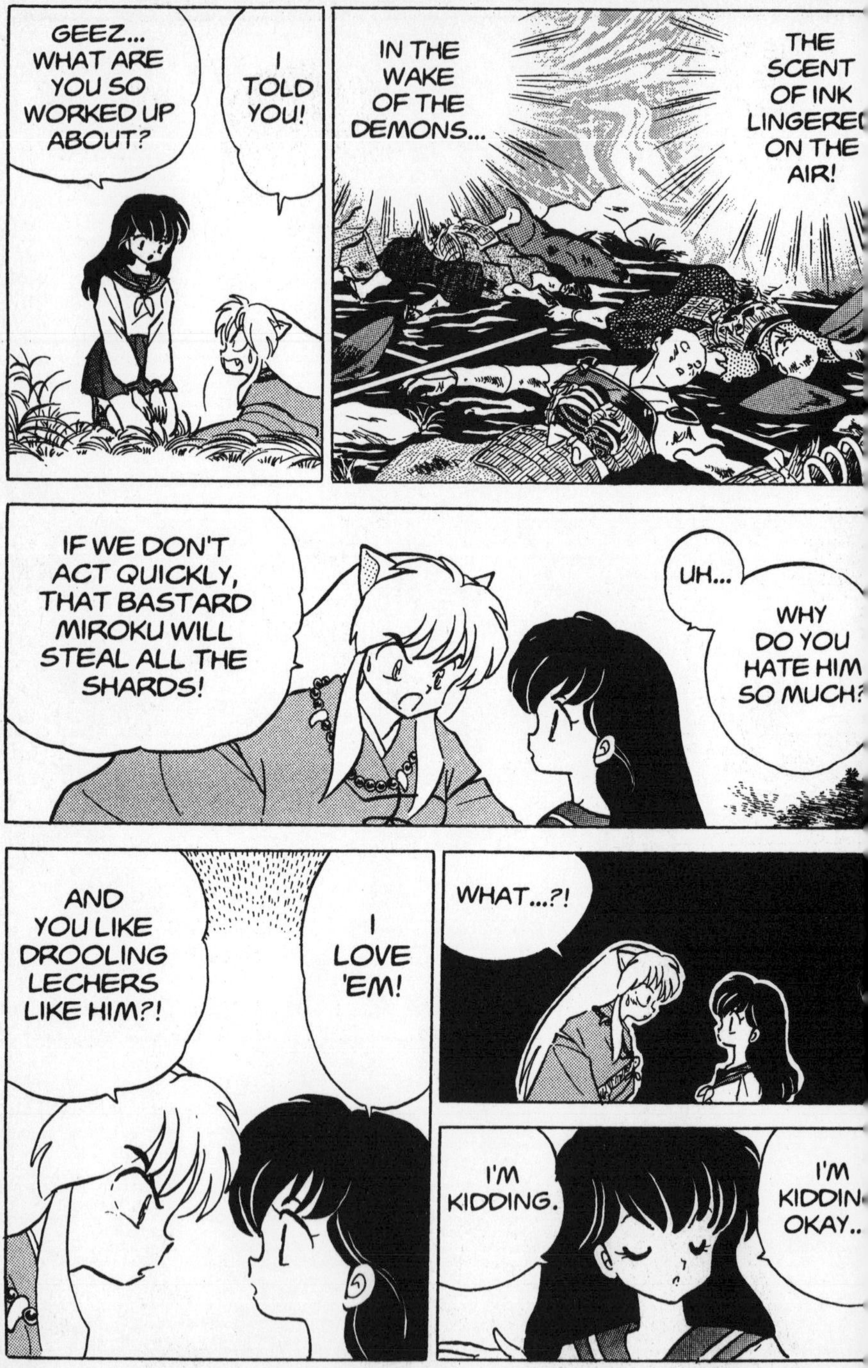
GEEZ... WHAT ARE YOU SO WORKED UP ABOUT?
I TOLD YOU!
IN THE WAKE OF THE DEMONS...
THE SCENT OF INK LINGERED ON THE AIR!
IF WE DON'T ACT QUICKLY, THAT BASTARD MIROKU WILL STEAL ALL THE SHARDS!
UH...
WHY DO YOU HATE HIM SO MUCH?
AND YOU LIKE DROOLING LECHERS LIKE HIM?!
I LOVE 'EM!
WHAT...?!
I'M KIDDING.

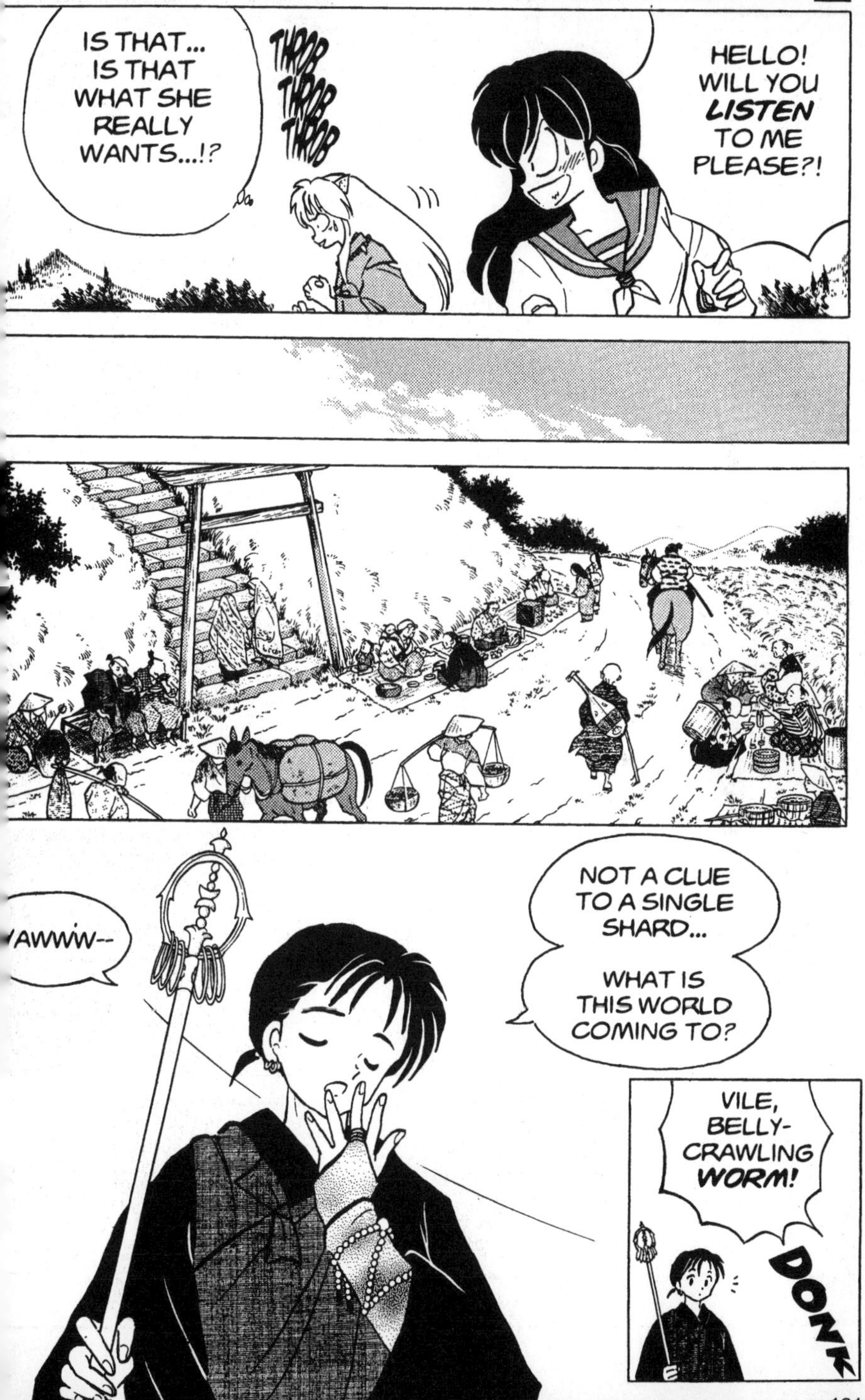
IS THAT... IS THAT WHAT SHE REALLY WANTS...!?
THROB THROB THROB
HELLO! WILL YOU LISTEN TO ME PLEASE?!
AWWW--
NOT A CLUE TO A SINGLE SHARD...
WHAT IS THIS WORLD COMING TO?
VILE, BELLY-CRAWLING WORM!
DONK

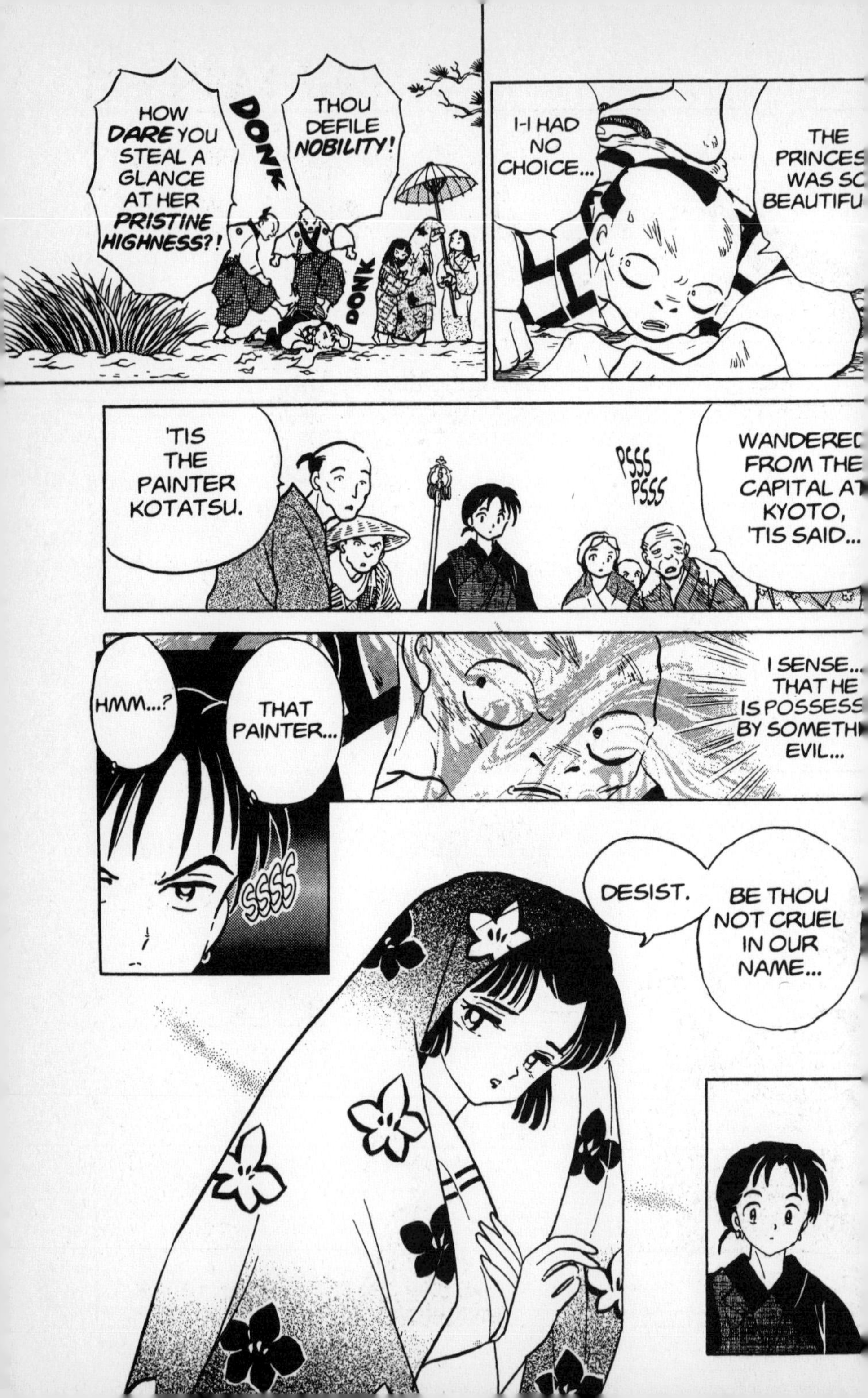
HOW DARE YOU STEAL A GLANCE AT HER PRISTINE HIGHNESS?!
DONK
THOU DEFILE NOBILITY!
DONK
I-I HAD NO CHOICE...
THE PRINCES WAS S BEAUTIFU
'TIS THE PAINTER KOTATSU.
PSSS PSSS
WANDERE FROM THE CAPITAL A KYOTO, 'TIS SAID...
HMM...?
THAT PAINTER...
I SENSE... THAT HE IS POSSESS BY SOMETH EVIL...
SSSS
DESIST.
BE THOU NOT CRUEL IN OUR NAME...

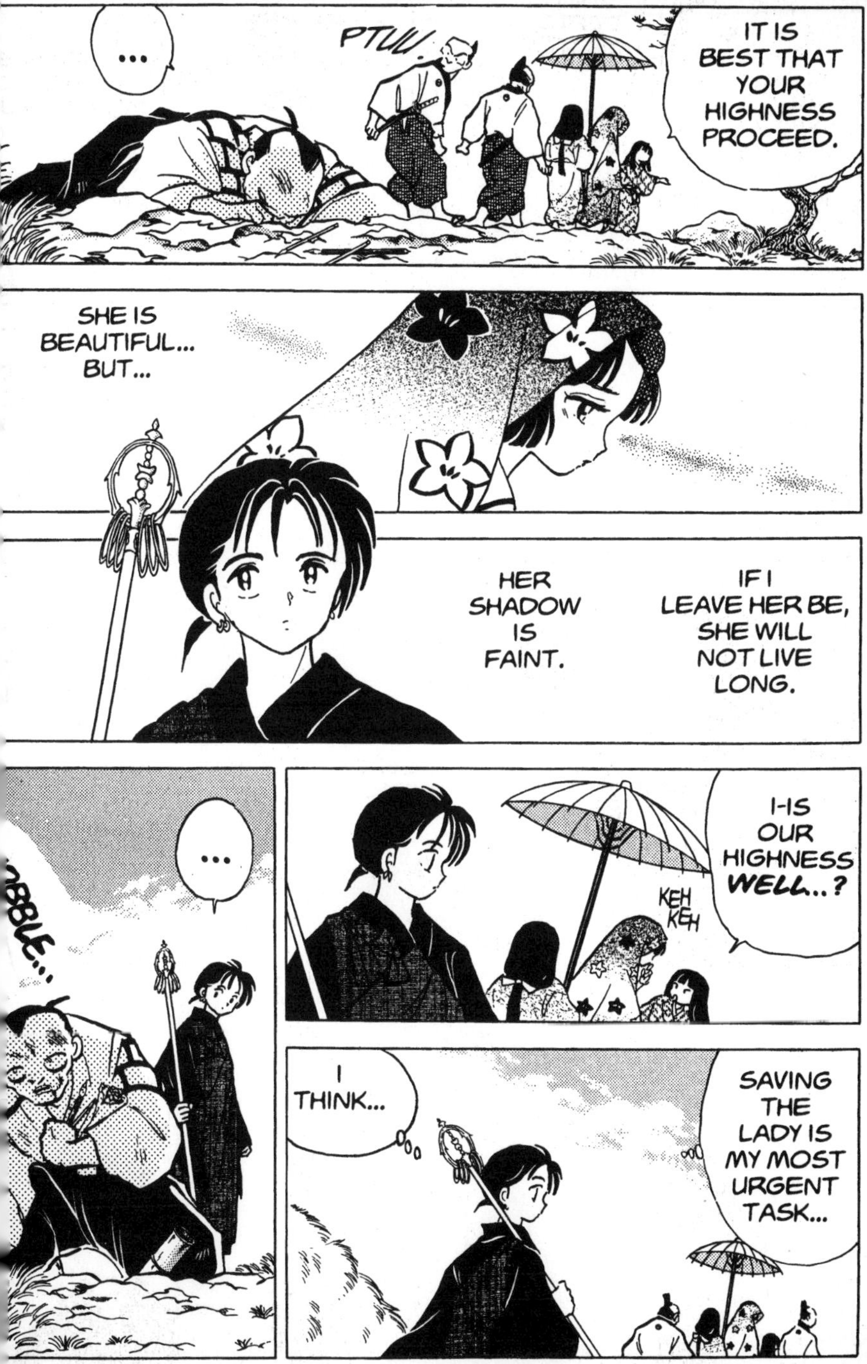
...
PTUU
IT IS BEST THAT YOUR HIGHNESS PROCEED.
SHE IS BEAUTIFUL... BUT...
HER SHADOW IS FAINT.
IF I LEAVE HER BE, SHE WILL NOT LIVE LONG.
...
I-IS OUR HIGHNESS WELL...?
KEH KEH
I THINK...
SAVING THE LADY IS MY MOST URGENT TASK...

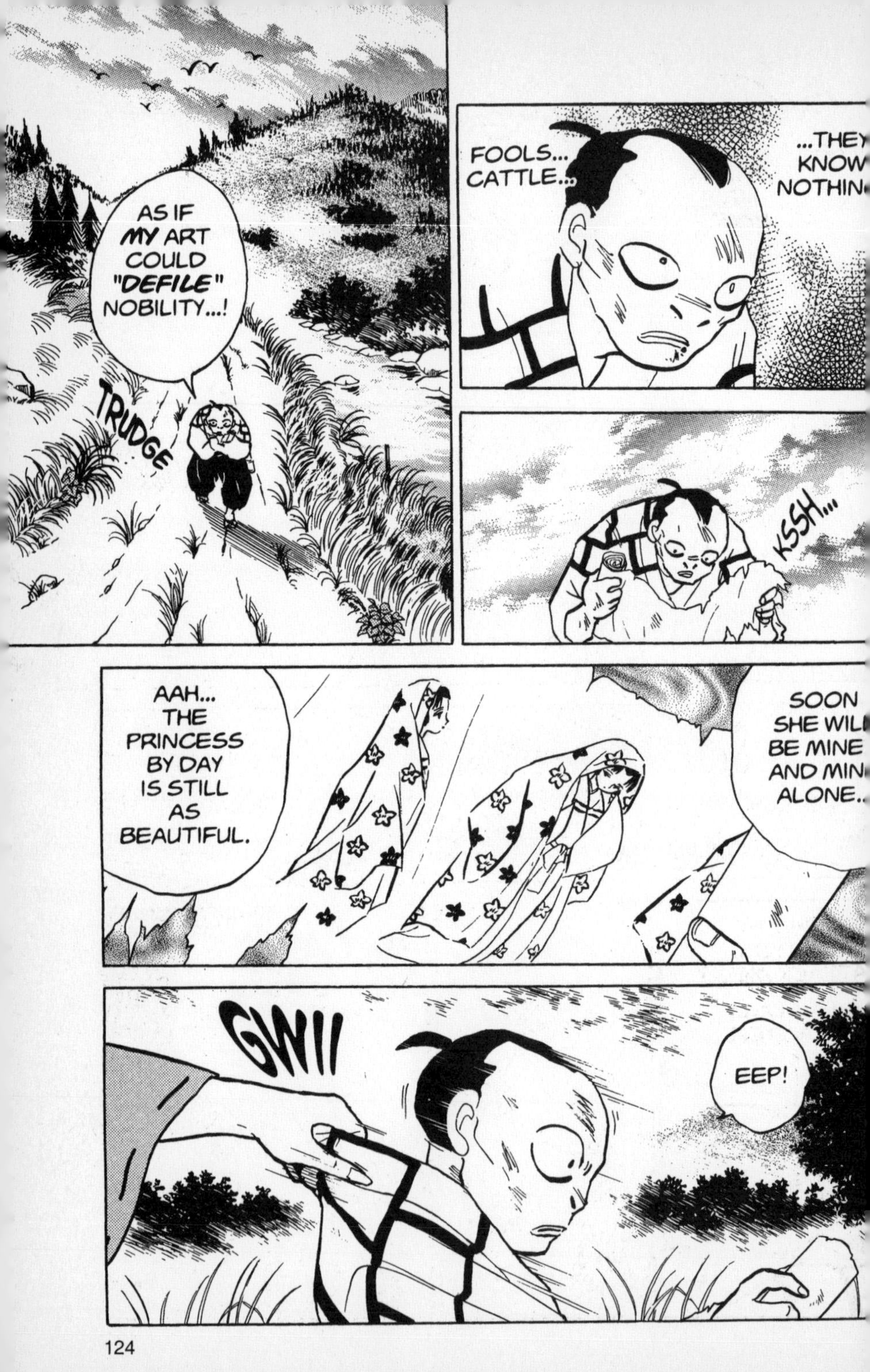
AS IF *MY* ART COULD "*DEFILE*" NOBILITY...!
TRUDGE
FOOLS... CATTLE...
...THEY KNOW NOTHIN
KSSH...
AAH... THE PRINCESS BY DAY IS STILL AS BEAUTIFUL.
SOON SHE WIL BE MINE AND MIN ALONE..
GWII
EEP!

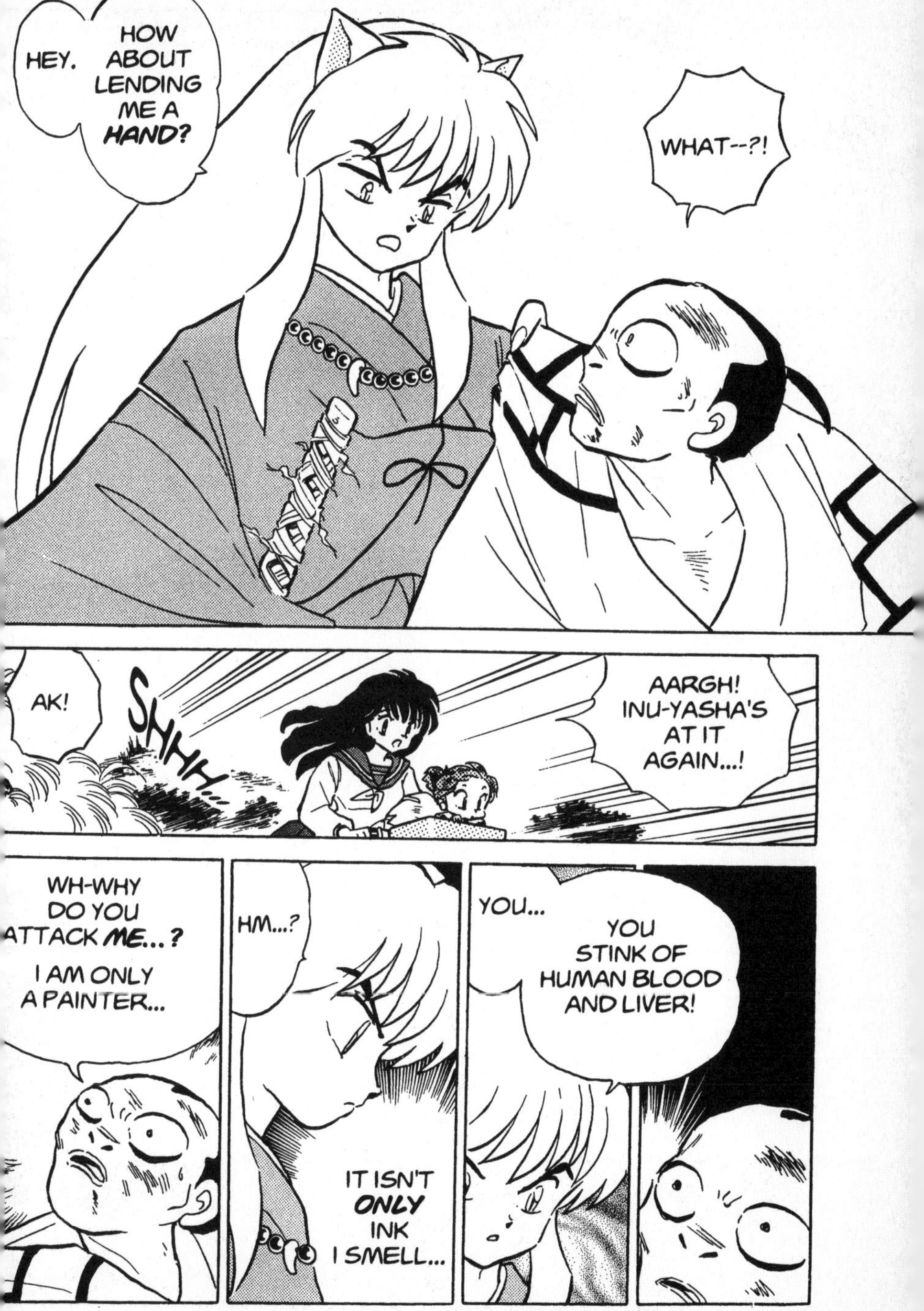
HEY.
HOW ABOUT LENDING ME A *HAND?*
WHAT--?!
AK!
SHHH...
AARGH! INU-YASHA'S AT IT AGAIN...!
WH-WHY DO YOU ATTACK *ME*...?
I AM ONLY A PAINTER...
HM...?
IT ISN'T *ONLY* INK I SMELL...
YOU...
YOU STINK OF HUMAN BLOOD AND LIVER!

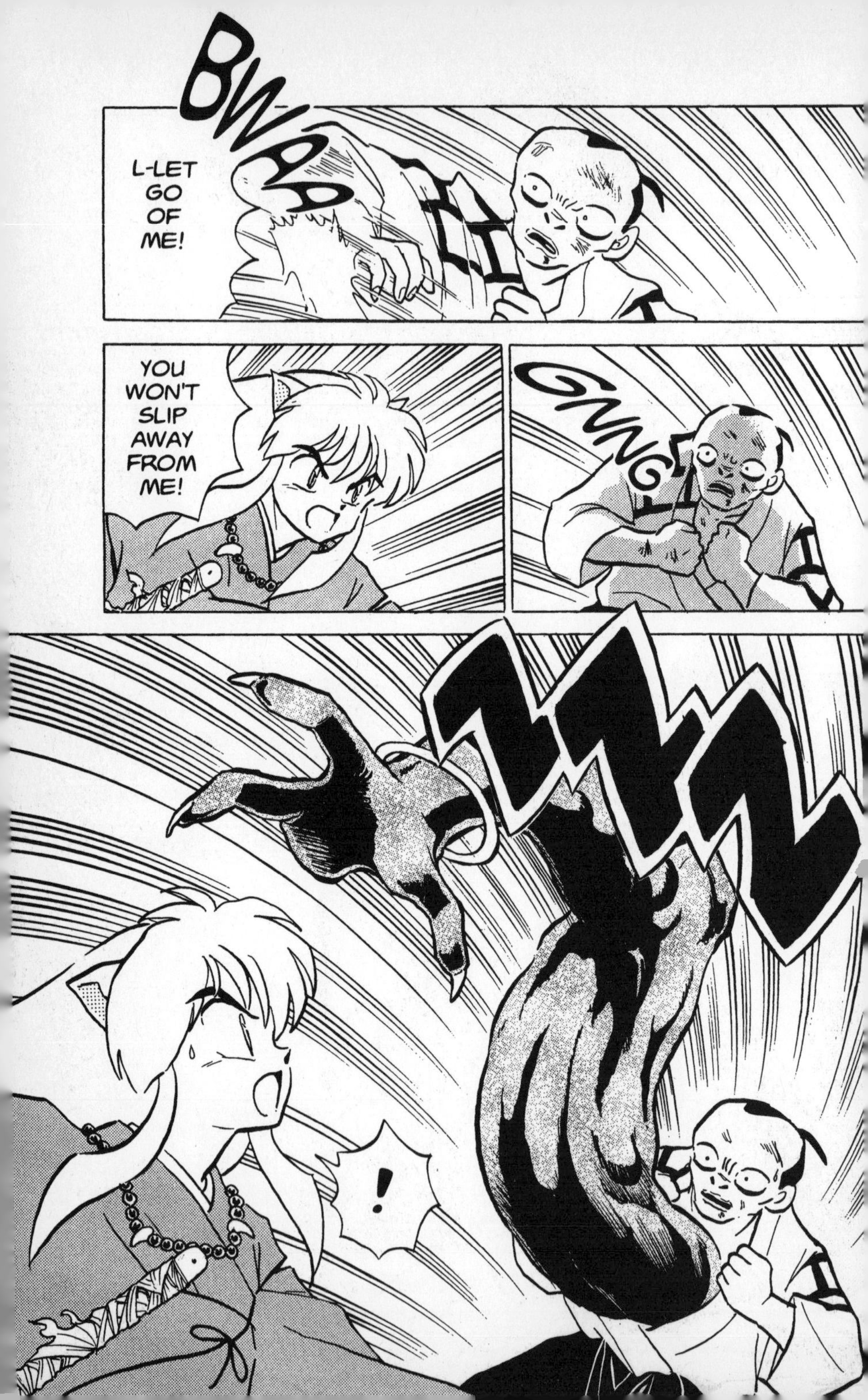
BWAAH
L-LET GO OF ME!
YOU WON'T SLIP AWAY FROM ME!
GNNG
ZZZ
!

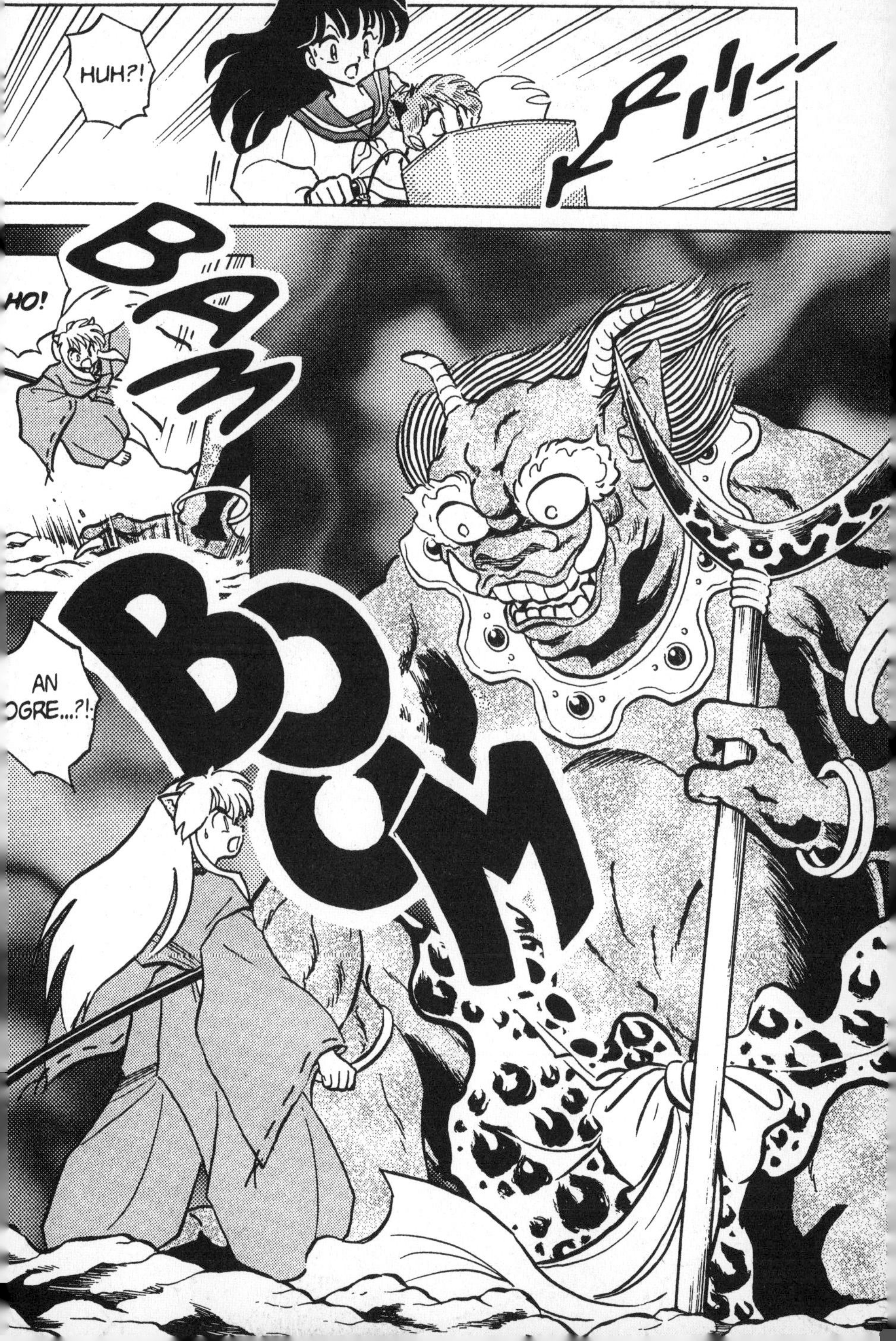
HUH?!
KRIII...
BAM
HO!
BOOM
AN OGRE...?!

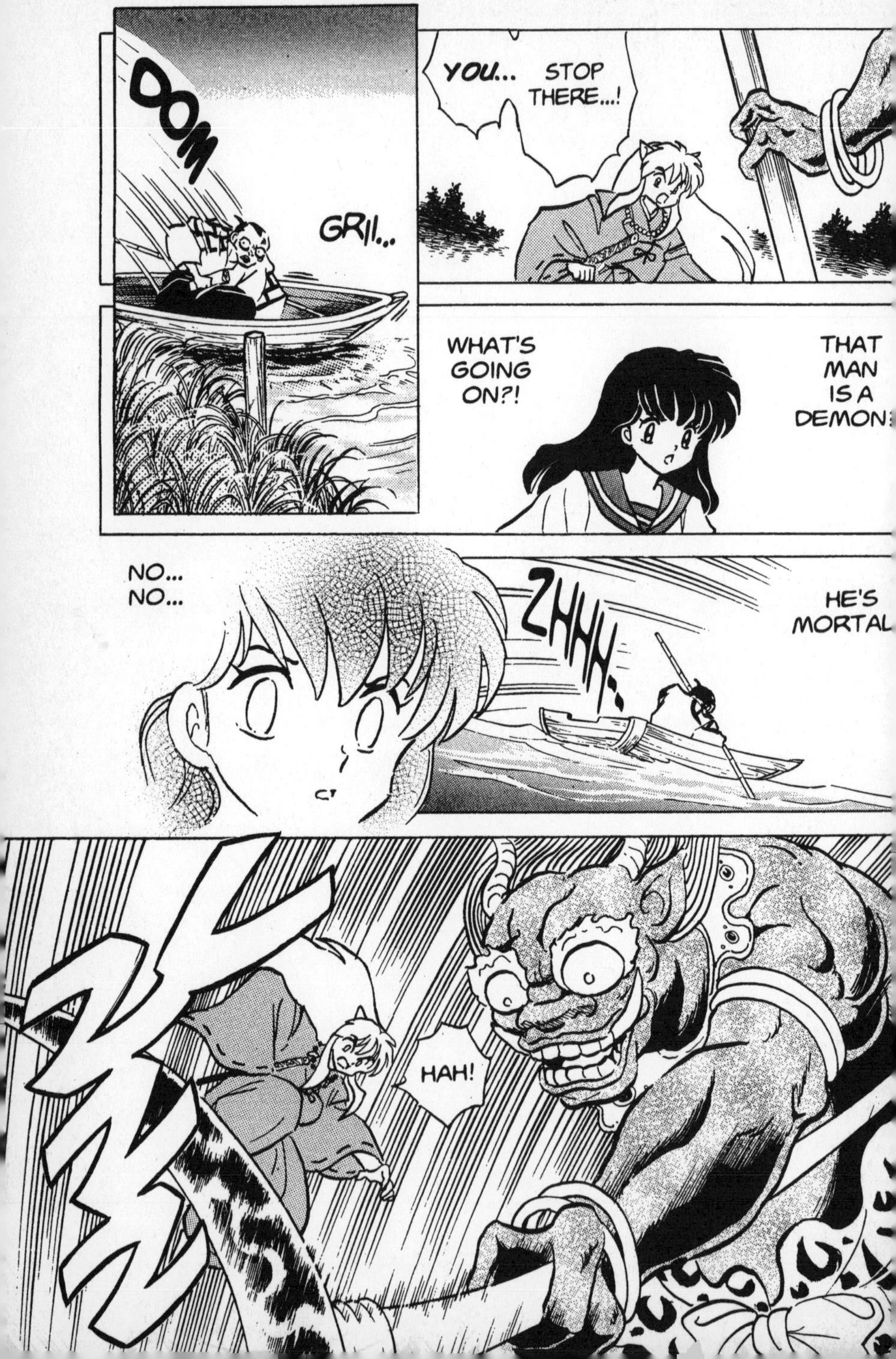
DOM
GRII...
YOU... STOP THERE...!
WHAT'S GOING ON?!
THAT MAN IS A DEMON
NO... NO...
ZHHH..
HE'S MORTAL
HAH!

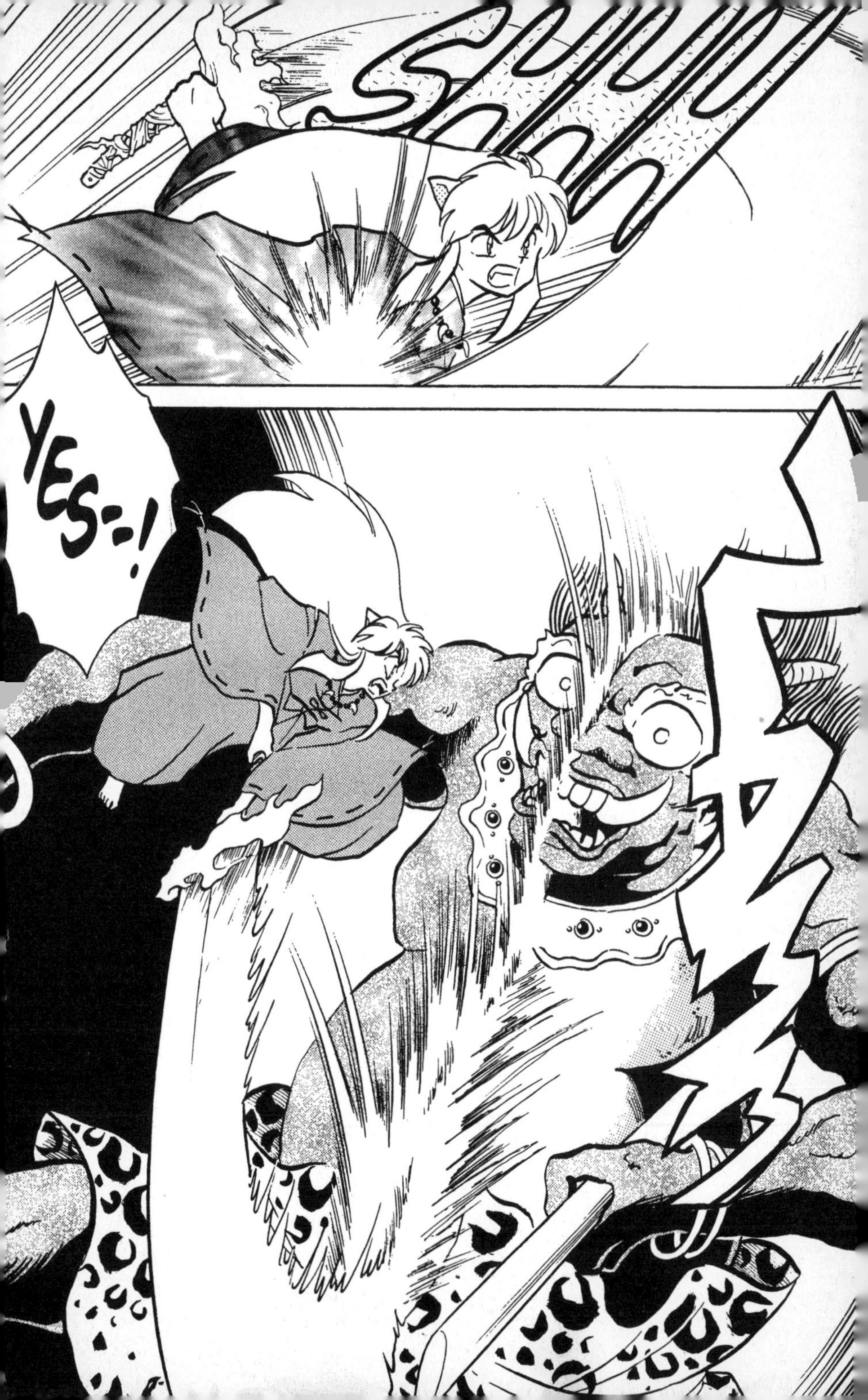
YES—!

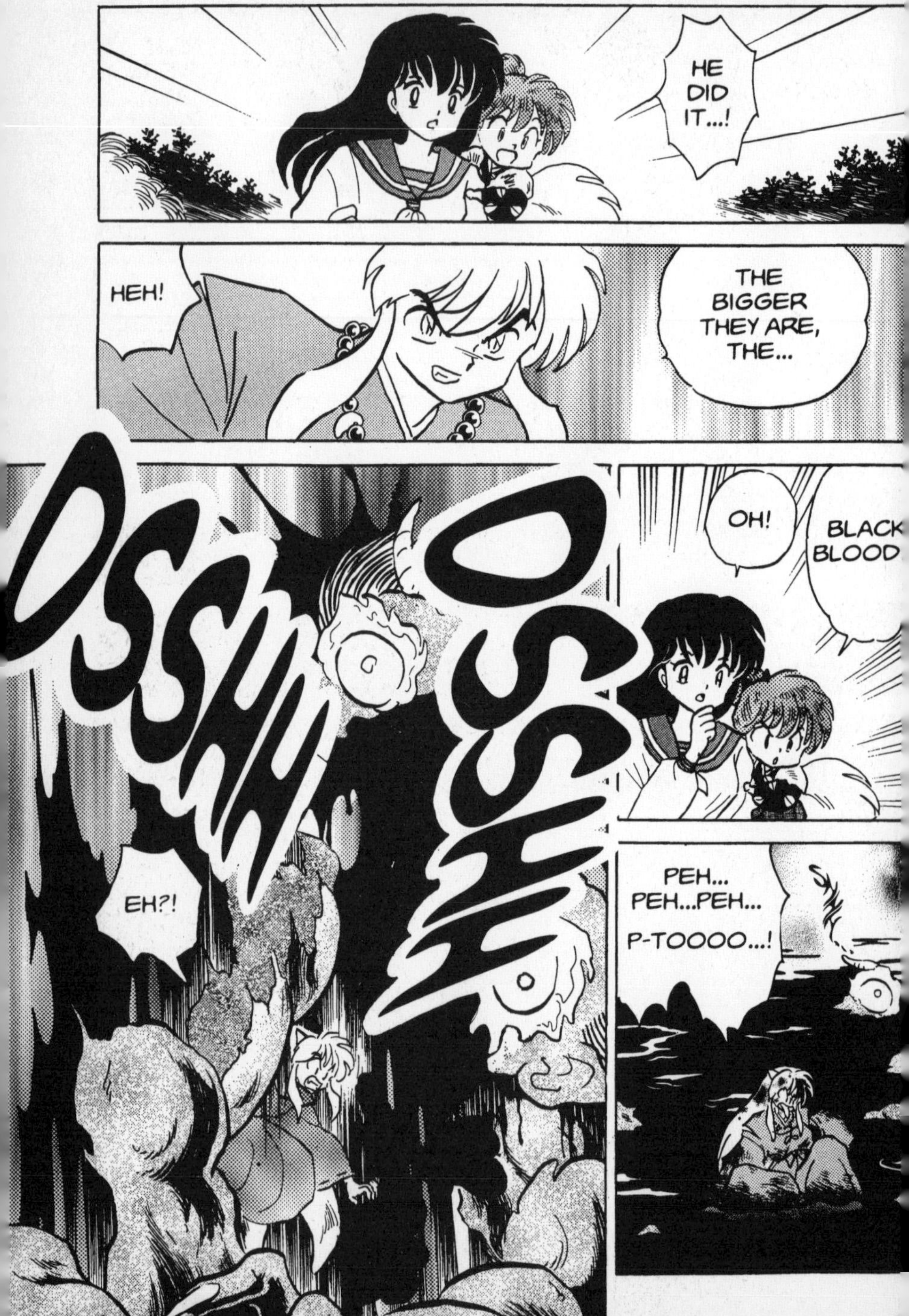

HE DID IT...!
HEH!
THE BIGGER THEY ARE, THE...
DOSSHH
DOSSHH
EH?!
OH!
BLACK BLOOD
PEH... PEH...PEH...
P-TOOOO...!

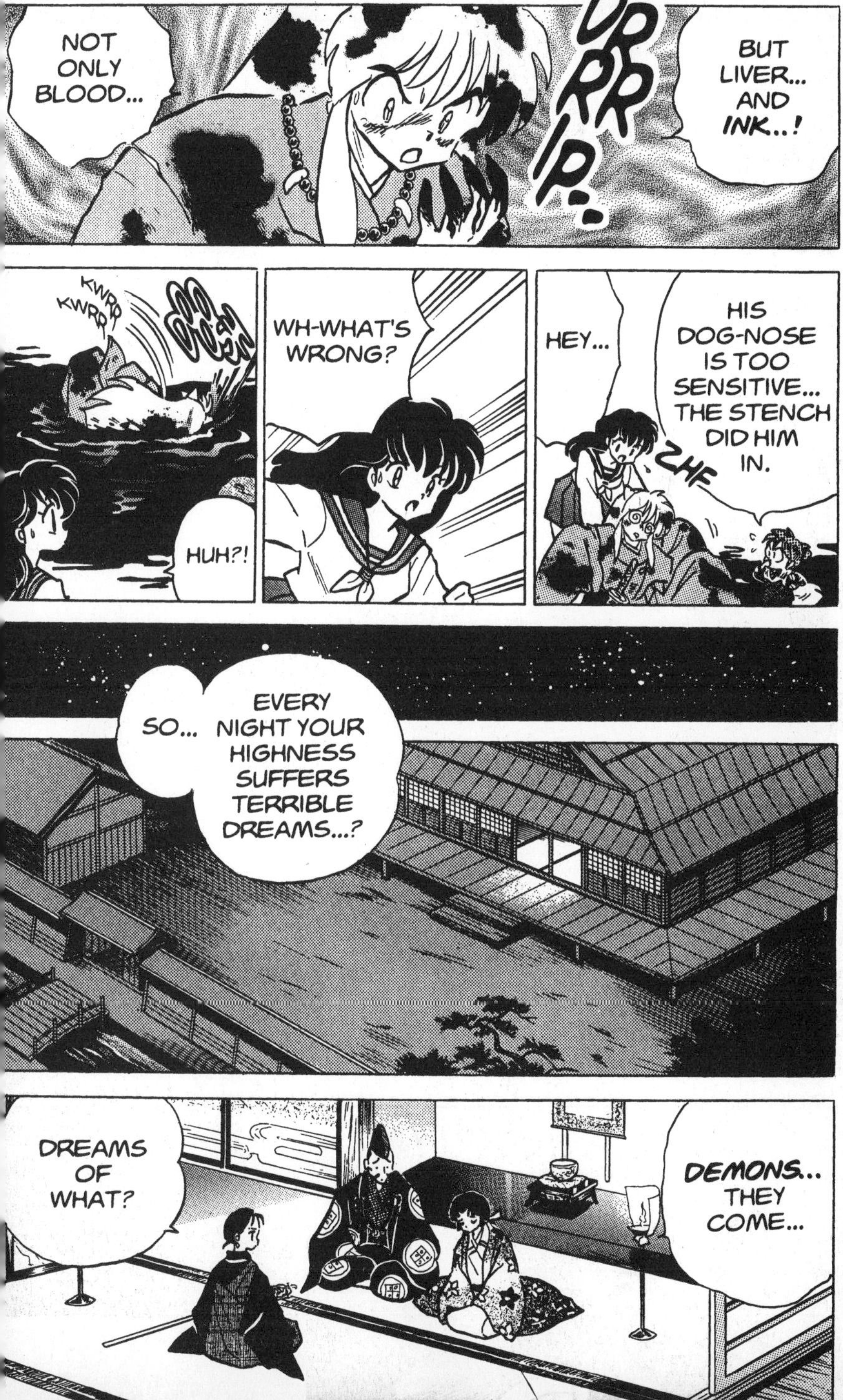
NOT ONLY BLOOD...
DRRRIP...
BUT LIVER... AND INK..!
KWRP KWRP
HUH?!
WH-WHAT'S WRONG?
HEY...
HIS DOG-NOSE IS TOO SENSITIVE... THE STENCH DID HIM IN.
ZHF
SO...
EVERY NIGHT YOUR HIGHNESS SUFFERS TERRIBLE DREAMS...?
DREAMS OF WHAT?
DEMONS... THEY COME...

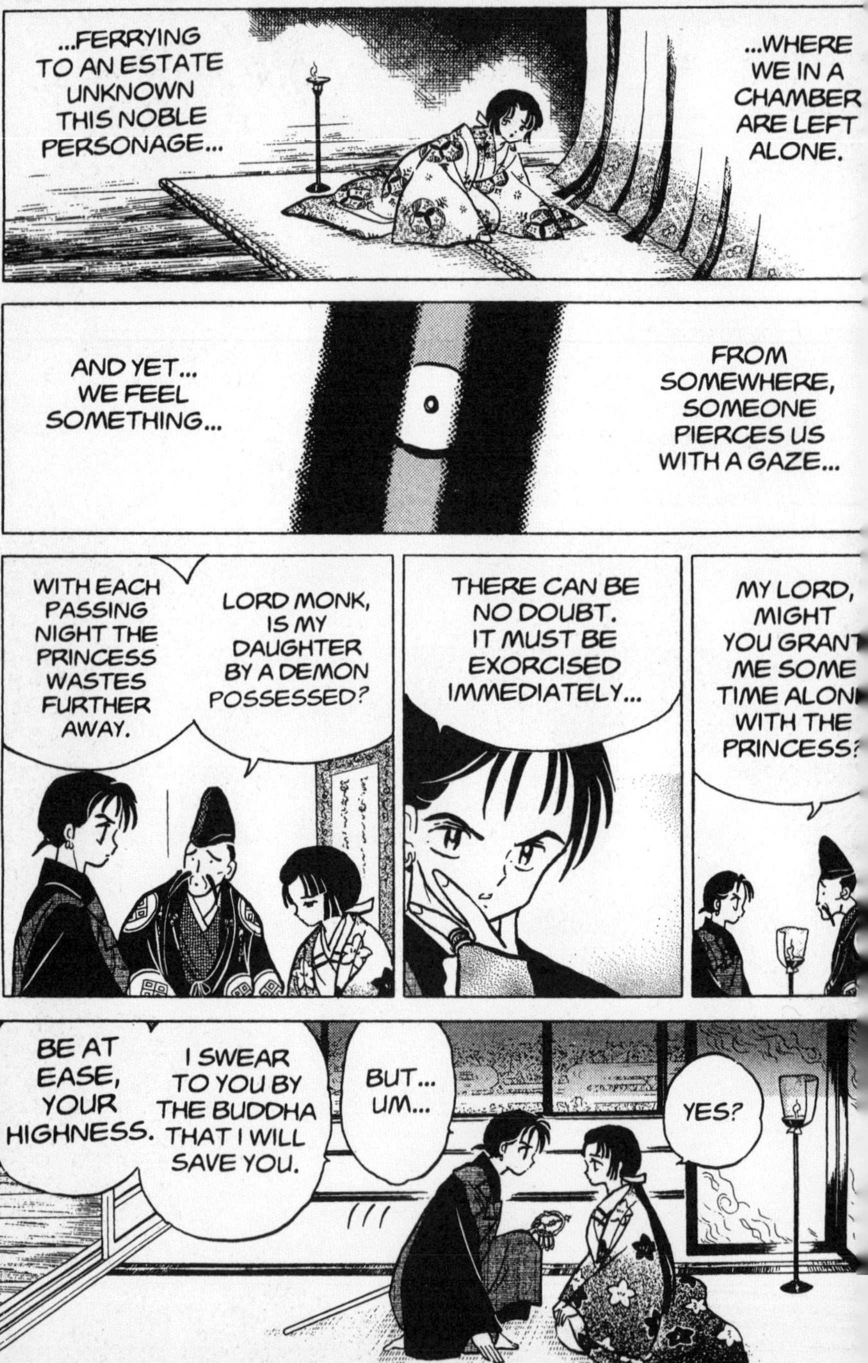
...FERRYING TO AN ESTATE UNKNOWN THIS NOBLE PERSONAGE...
...WHERE WE IN A CHAMBER ARE LEFT ALONE.
AND YET... WE FEEL SOMETHING...
FROM SOMEWHERE, SOMEONE PIERCES US WITH A GAZE...
WITH EACH PASSING NIGHT THE PRINCESS WASTES FURTHER AWAY.
LORD MONK, IS MY DAUGHTER BY A DEMON POSSESSED?
THERE CAN BE NO DOUBT. IT MUST BE EXORCISED IMMEDIATELY...
MY LORD, MIGHT YOU GRANT ME SOME TIME ALONE WITH THE PRINCESS?
BE AT EASE, YOUR HIGHNESS.
I SWEAR TO YOU BY THE BUDDHA THAT I WILL SAVE YOU.
BUT... UM...
YES?

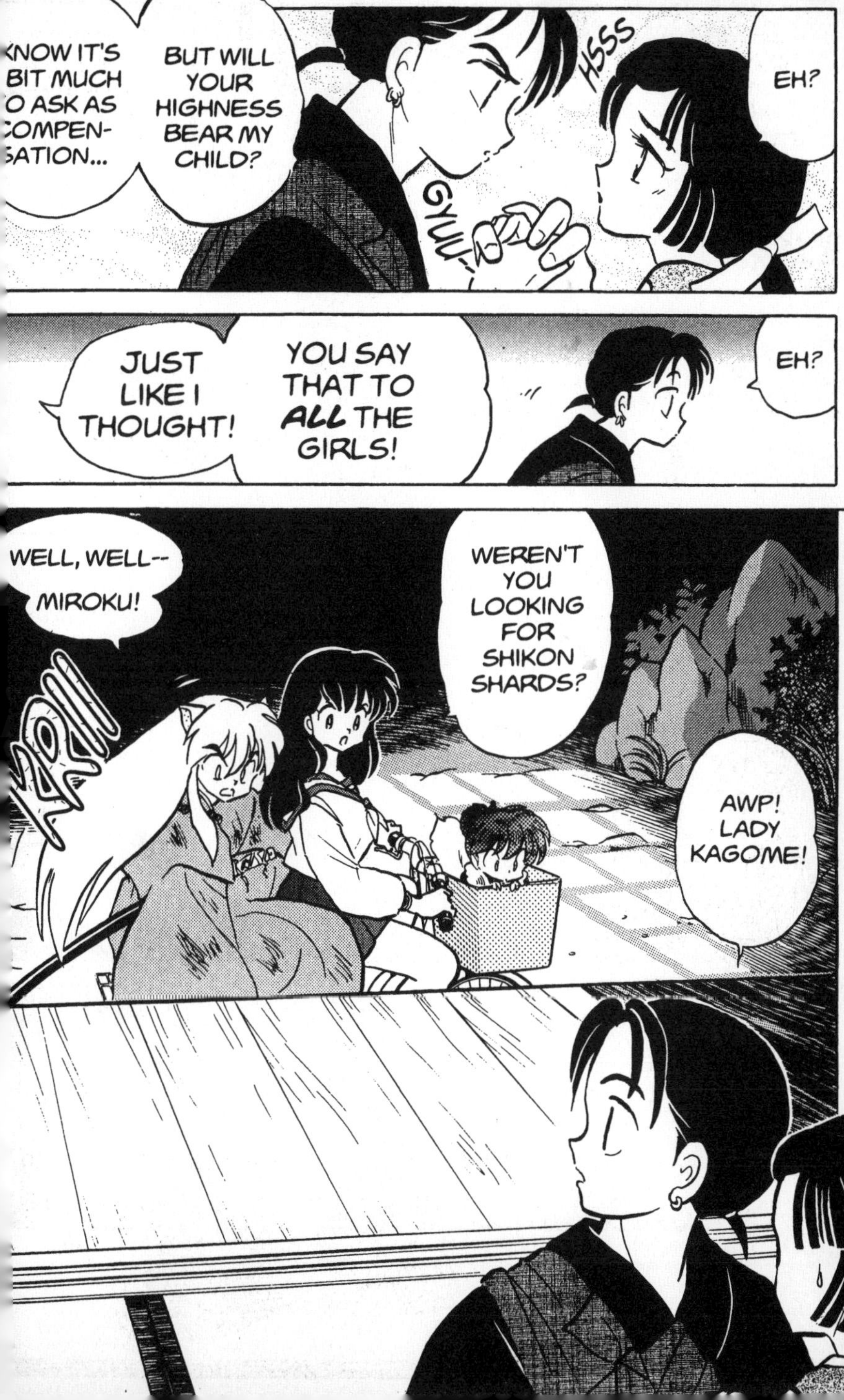
KNOW IT'S BIT MUCH O ASK AS COMPEN-SATION...
BUT WILL YOUR HIGHNESS BEAR MY CHILD?
HSSS
GYUU--
EH?
JUST LIKE I THOUGHT!
YOU SAY THAT TO ALL THE GIRLS!
EH?
WELL, WELL-- MIROKU!
WERE'NT YOU LOOKING FOR SHIKON SHARDS?
AWP! LADY KAGOME!

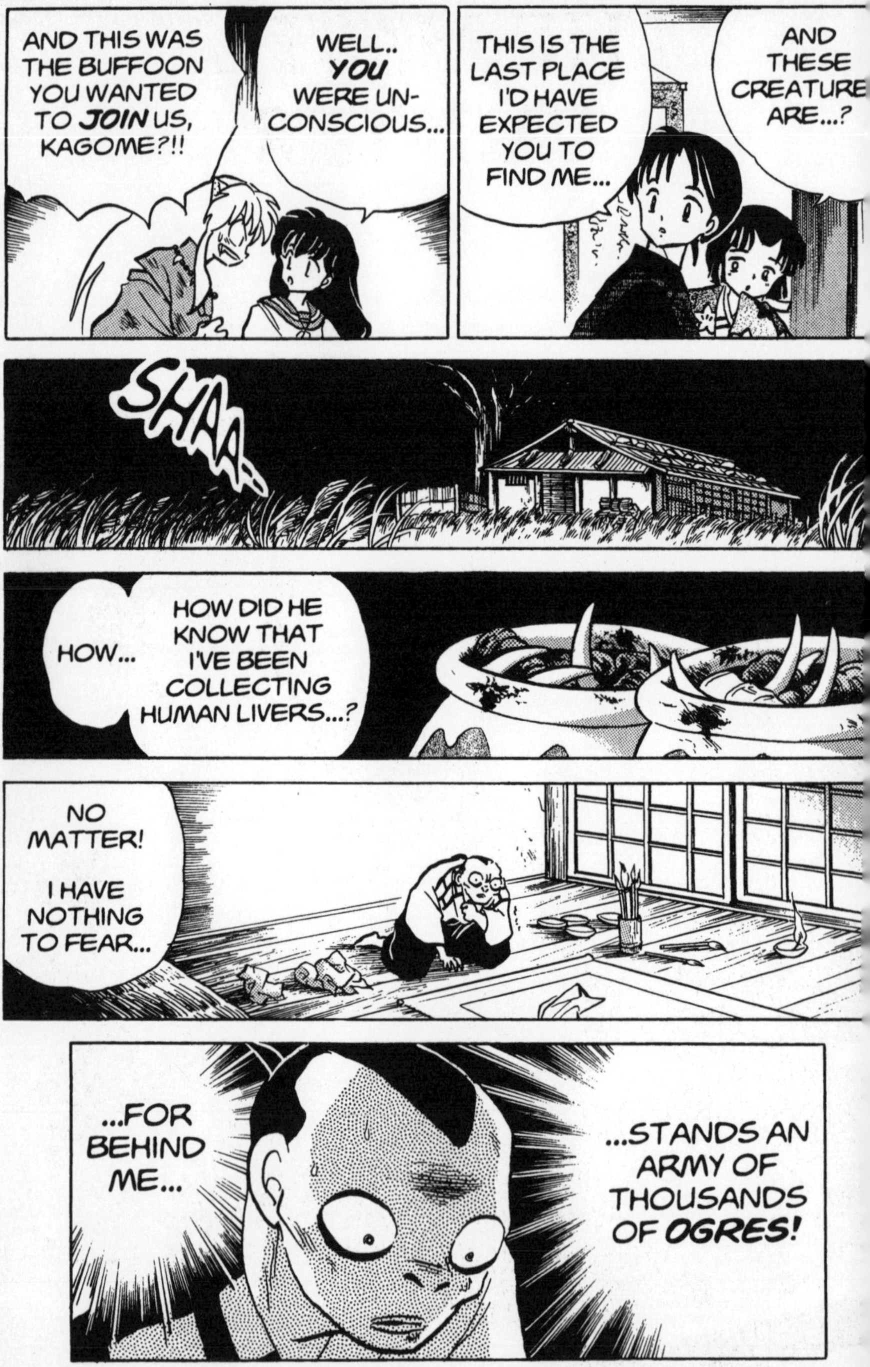
AND THIS WAS THE BUFFOON YOU WANTED TO JOIN US, KAGOME?!!
WELL.. YOU WERE UN-CONSCIOUS...
THIS IS THE LAST PLACE I'D HAVE EXPECTED YOU TO FIND ME...
AND THESE CREATURE ARE...?
SHAA
HOW...
HOW DID HE KNOW THAT I'VE BEEN COLLECTING HUMAN LIVERS...?
NO MATTER!
I HAVE NOTHING TO FEAR...
...FOR BEHIND ME...
...STANDS AN ARMY OF THOUSANDS OF OGRES!

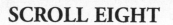

SCROLL EIGHT

THE MASTER PAINTER

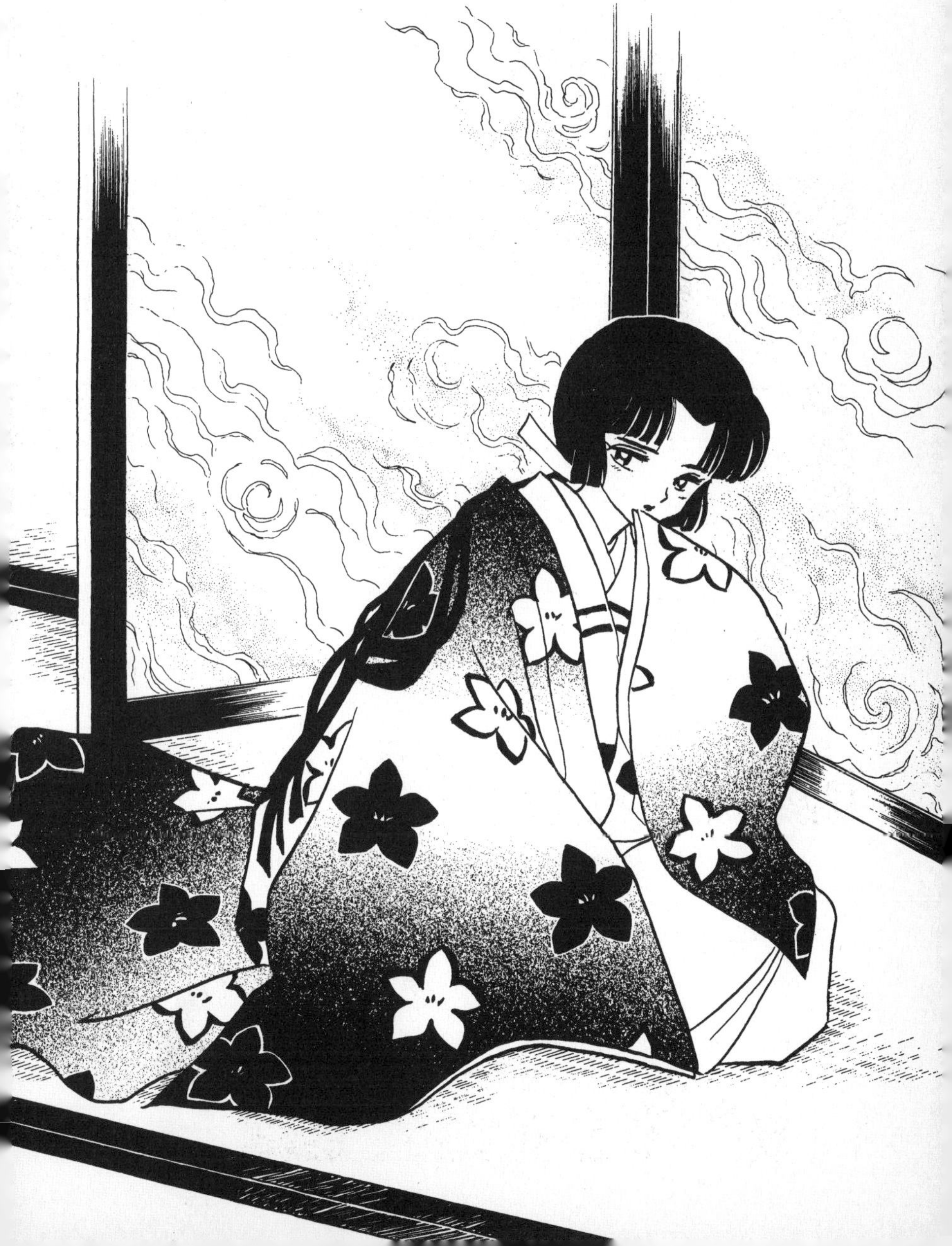

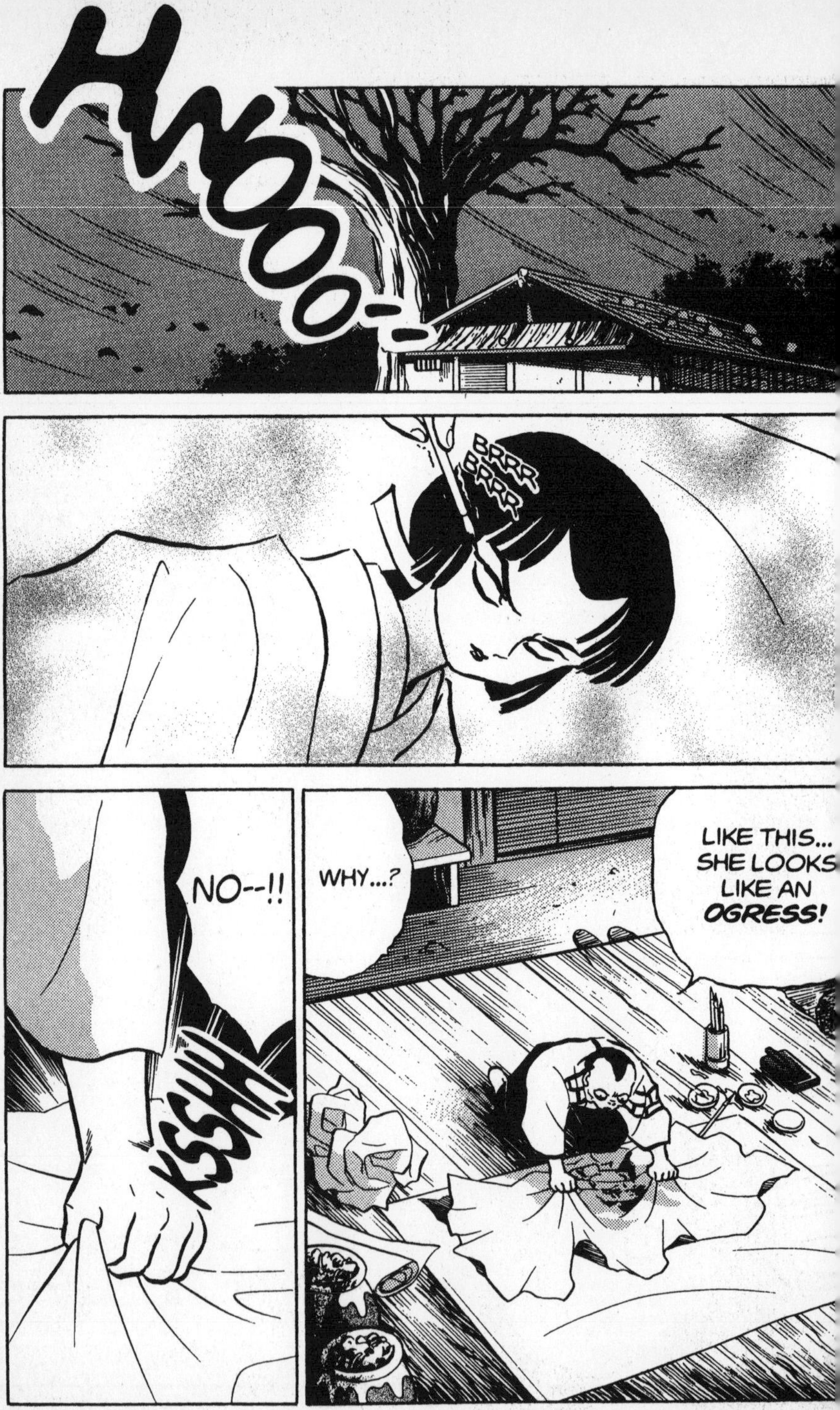
HWOOO--
BRRRR
BRRRR
NO--!!
KSSHH
WHY...?
LIKE THIS... SHE LOOKS LIKE AN OGRESS!

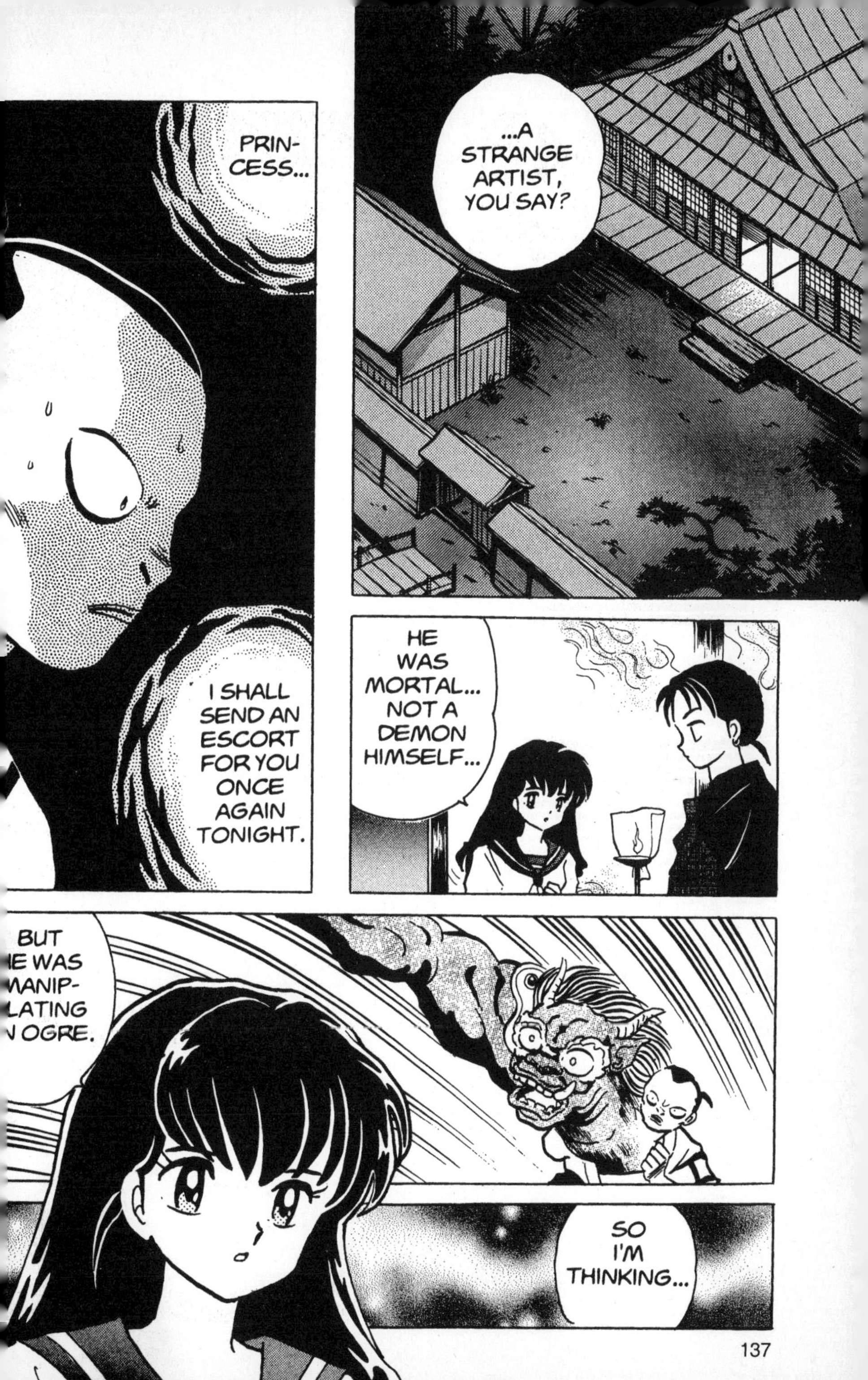
PRIN-CESS...
I SHALL SEND AN ESCORT FOR YOU ONCE AGAIN TONIGHT.
...A STRANGE ARTIST, YOU SAY?
HE WAS MORTAL... NOT A DEMON HIMSELF...
BUT E WAS MANIP-LATING N OGRE.
SO I'M THINKING...

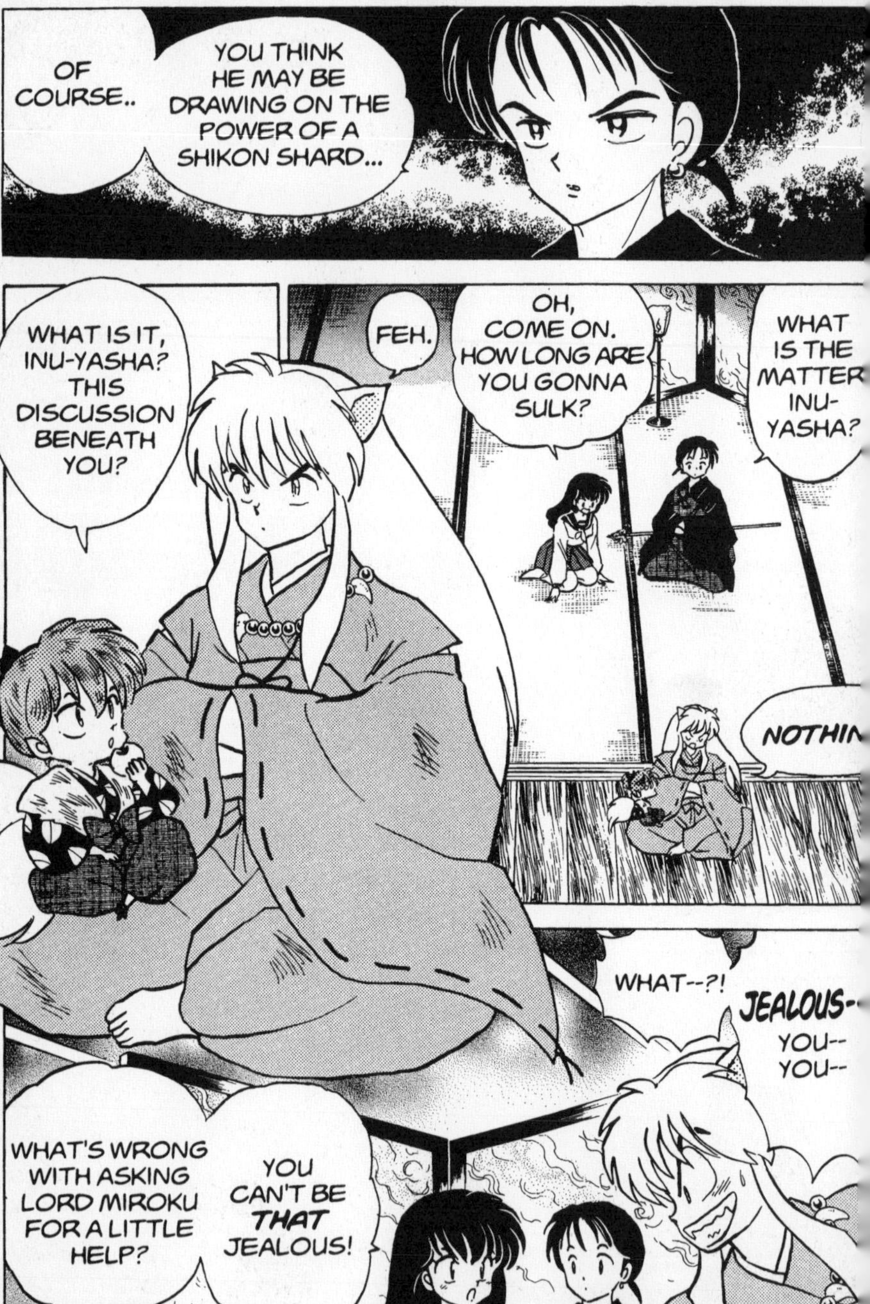

OF COURSE..
YOU THINK HE MAY BE DRAWING ON THE POWER OF A SHIKON SHARD...
WHAT IS IT, INU-YASHA? THIS DISCUSSION BENEATH YOU?
FEH.
OH, COME ON. HOW LONG ARE YOU GONNA SULK?
WHAT IS THE MATTER INU-YASHA?
NOTHIN
WHAT'S WRONG WITH ASKING LORD MIROKU FOR A LITTLE HELP?
YOU CAN'T BE *THAT* JEALOUS!
WHAT--?!
JEALOUS--
YOU-- YOU--

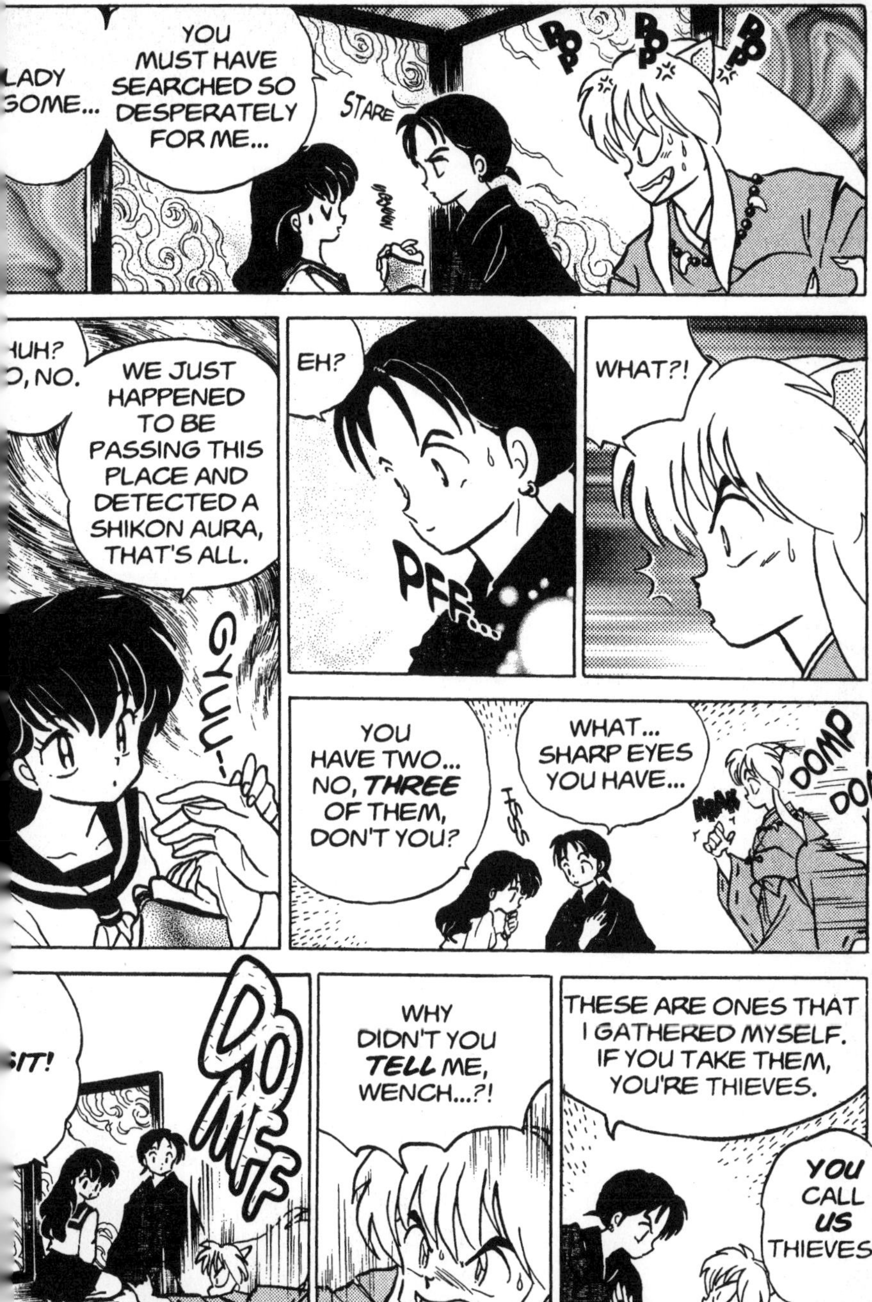

LADY
SOME...
YOU MUST HAVE SEARCHED SO DESPERATELY FOR ME...
STARE
BOP
BOP
BOP
HUH?
O, NO.
WE JUST HAPPENED TO BE PASSING THIS PLACE AND DETECTED A SHIKON AURA, THAT'S ALL.
GYUU-
EH?
PFF...
WHAT?!
YOU HAVE TWO... NO, THREE OF THEM, DON'T YOU?
WHAT... SHARP EYES YOU HAVE...
DOMP
DOMP
SIT!
DOMF
WHY DIDN'T YOU TELL ME, WENCH...?!
THESE ARE ONES THAT I GATHERED MYSELF. IF YOU TAKE THEM, YOU'RE THIEVES.
YOU CALL US THIEVES?!

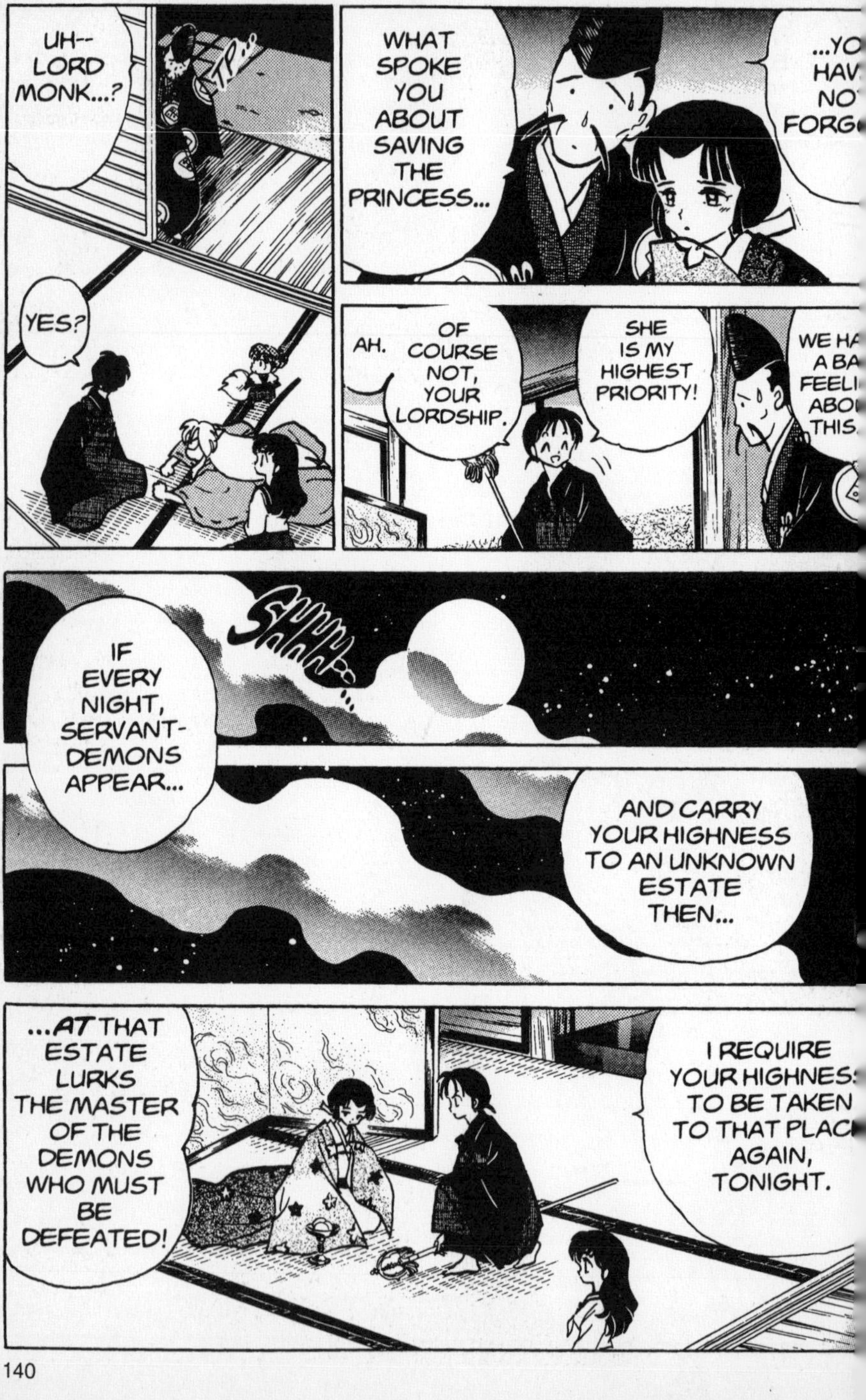
UH-- LORD MONK...?
YES?
WHAT SPOKE YOU ABOUT SAVING THE PRINCESS...
...YO HAV NO FORG
AH.
OF COURSE NOT, YOUR LORDSHIP.
SHE IS MY HIGHEST PRIORITY!
WE HA A BA FEELI ABO THIS.
SHHHH...
IF EVERY NIGHT, SERVANT-DEMONS APPEAR...
AND CARRY YOUR HIGHNESS TO AN UNKNOWN ESTATE THEN...
...AT THAT ESTATE LURKS THE MASTER OF THE DEMONS WHO MUST BE DEFEATED!
I REQUIRE YOUR HIGHNES TO BE TAKEN TO THAT PLAC AGAIN, TONIGHT.

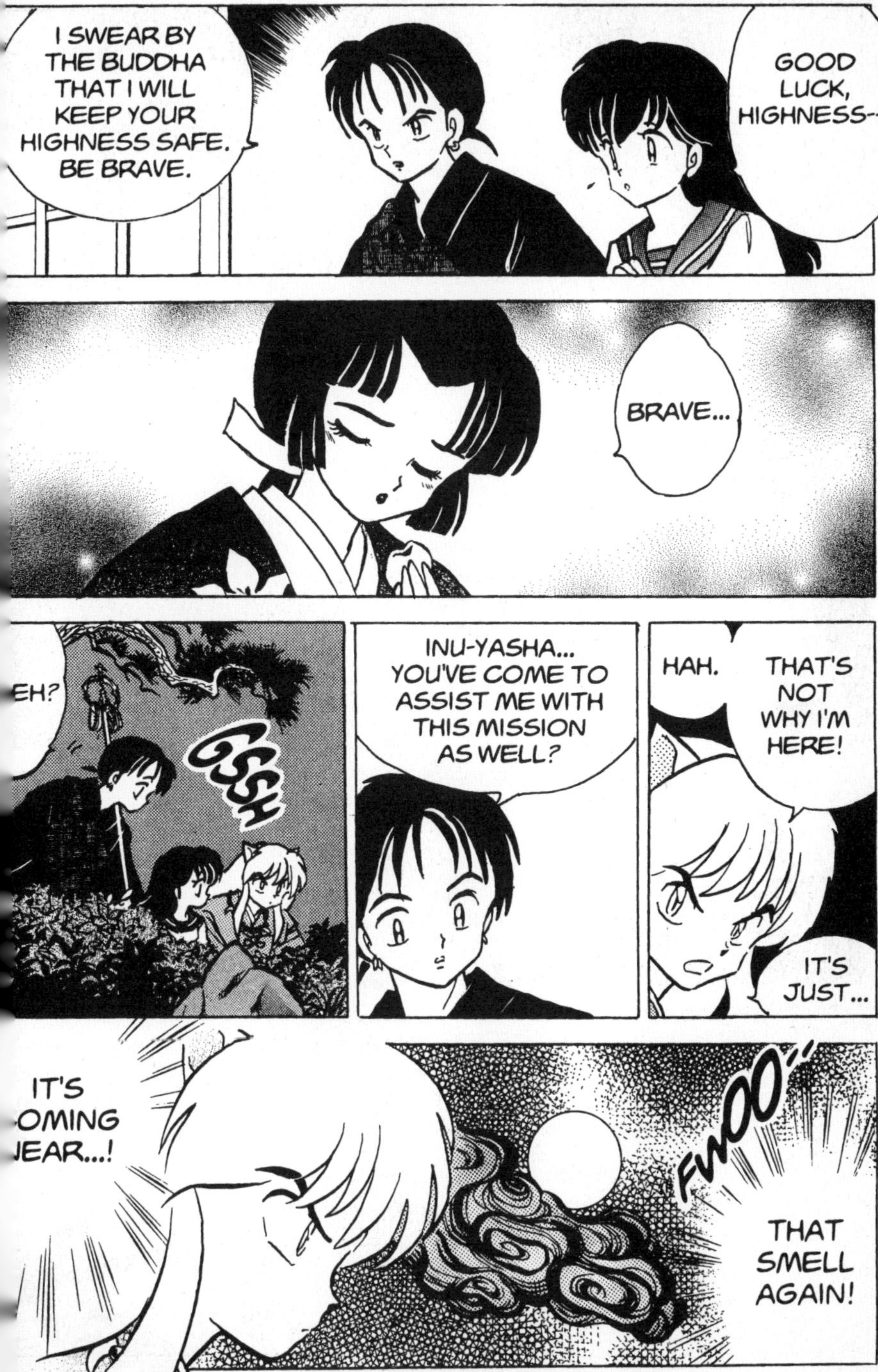
I SWEAR BY THE BUDDHA THAT I WILL KEEP YOUR HIGHNESS SAFE. BE BRAVE.
GOOD LUCK, HIGHNESS--!
BRAVE...
EH?
GSSH
INU-YASHA... YOU'VE COME TO ASSIST ME WITH THIS MISSION AS WELL?
HAH.
THAT'S NOT WHY I'M HERE!
IT'S JUST...
IT'S OMING NEAR...!
FWOO
THAT SMELL AGAIN!

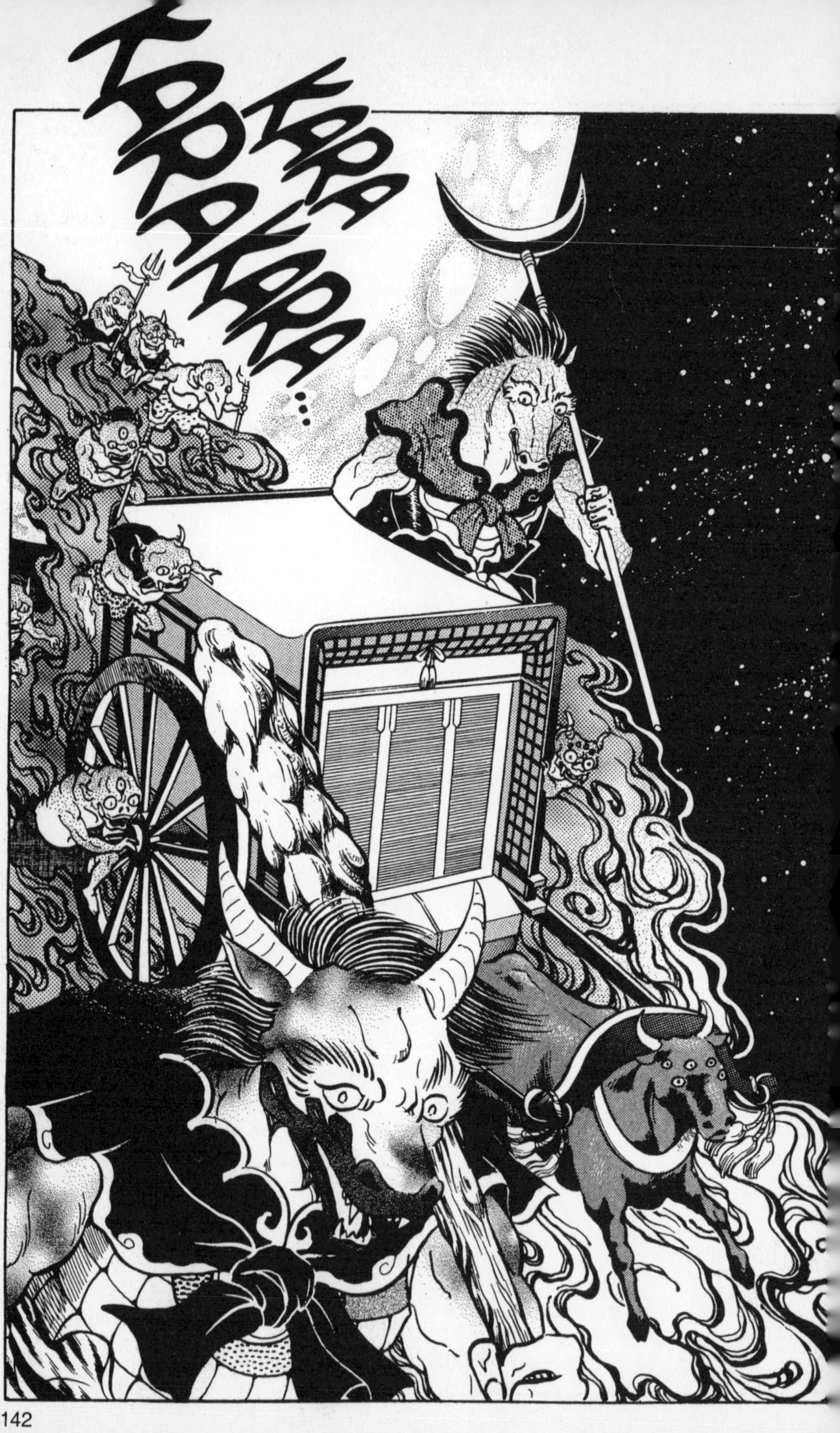
KARA KARA KARA...

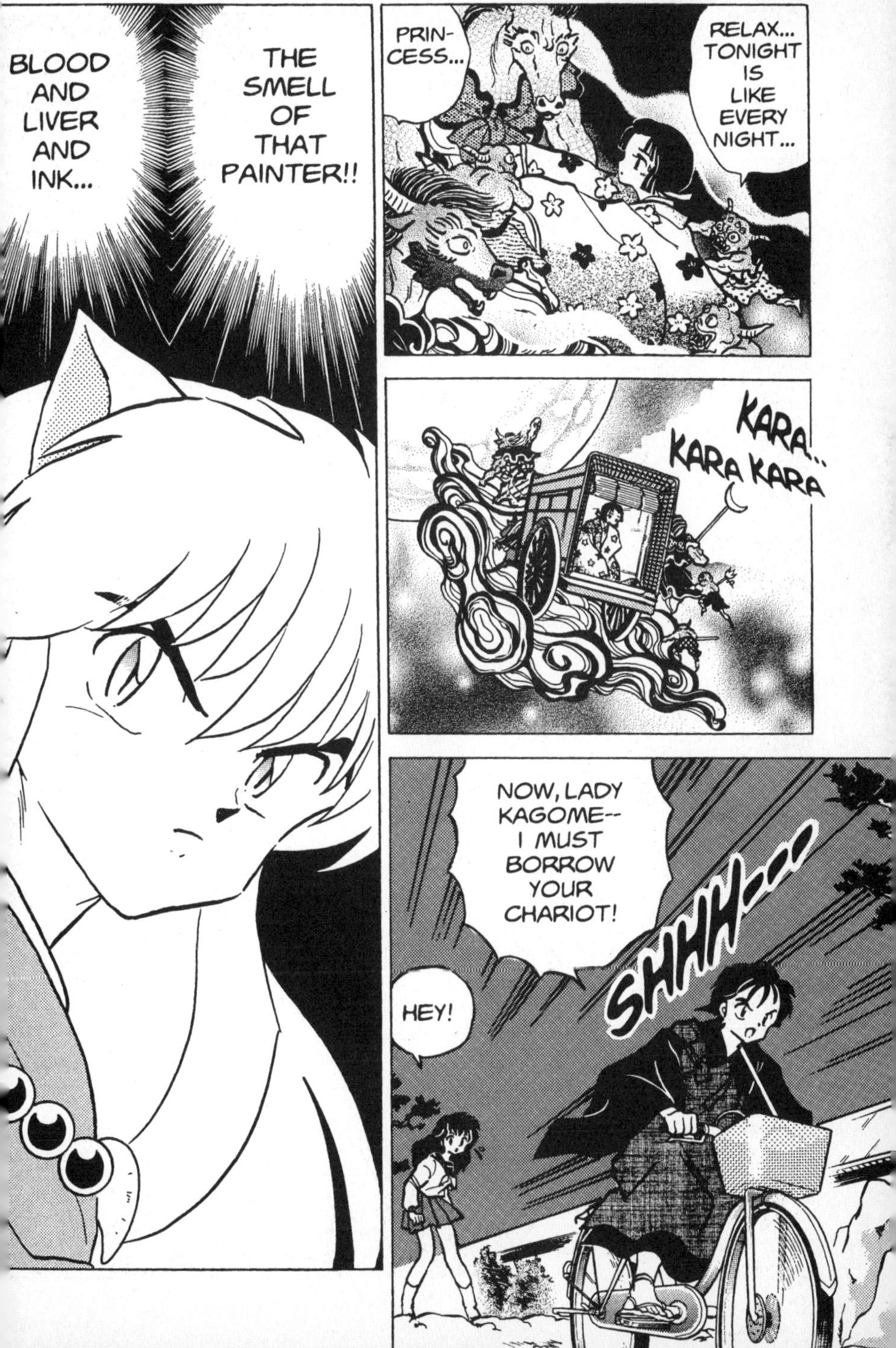
BLOOD AND LIVER AND INK...
THE SMELL OF THAT PAINTER!!
PRIN-CESS...
RELAX... TONIGHT IS LIKE EVERY NIGHT...
KARA... KARA KARA
NOW, LADY KAGOME-- I MUST BORROW YOUR CHARIOT!
HEY!
SHHH---

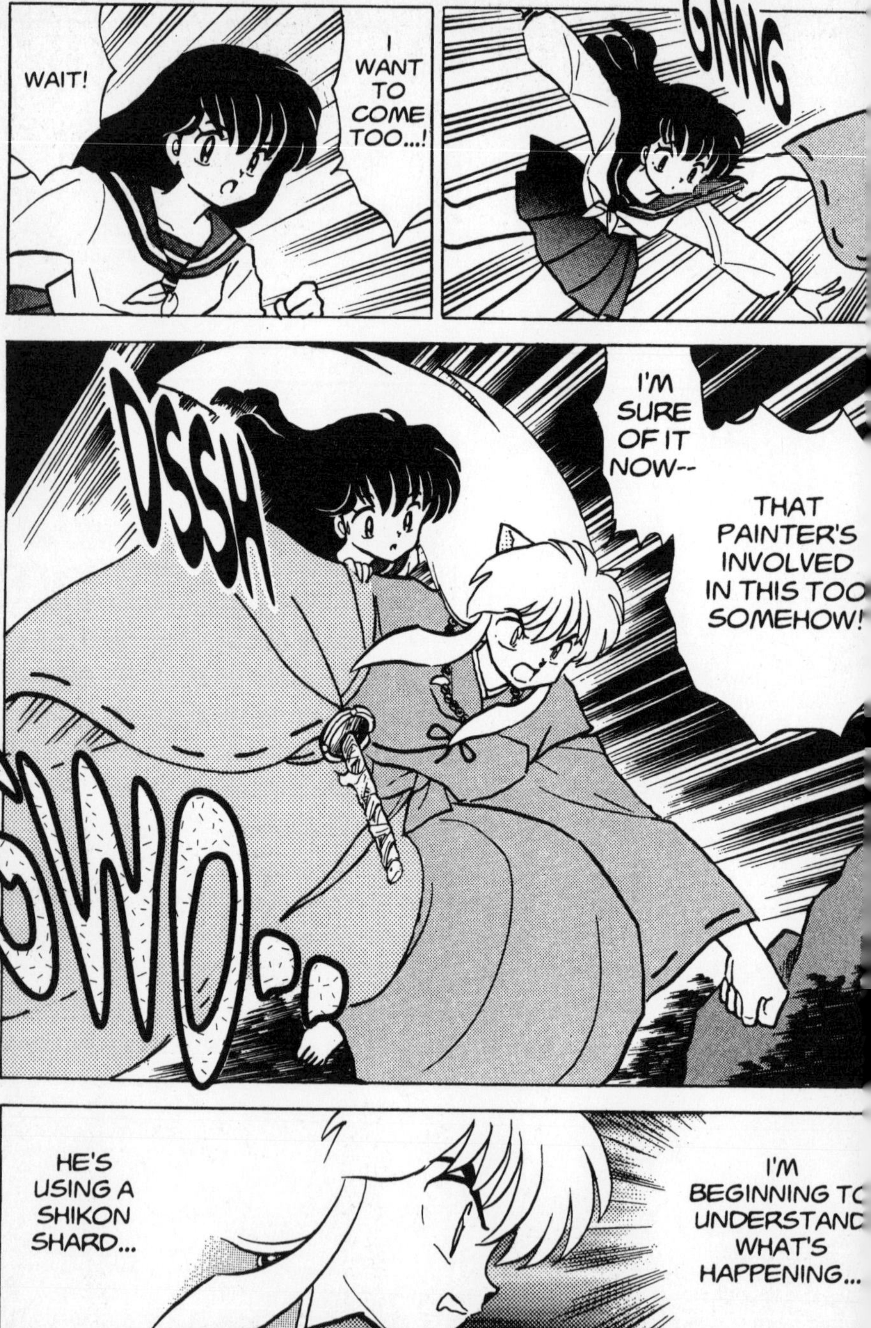
WAIT!
I WANT TO COME TOO...!
GNNG
DSSH
GWO..
I'M SURE OF IT NOW--
THAT PAINTER'S INVOLVED IN THIS TOO SOMEHOW!
HE'S USING A SHIKON SHARD...
I'M BEGINNING TO UNDERSTAND WHAT'S HAPPENING...

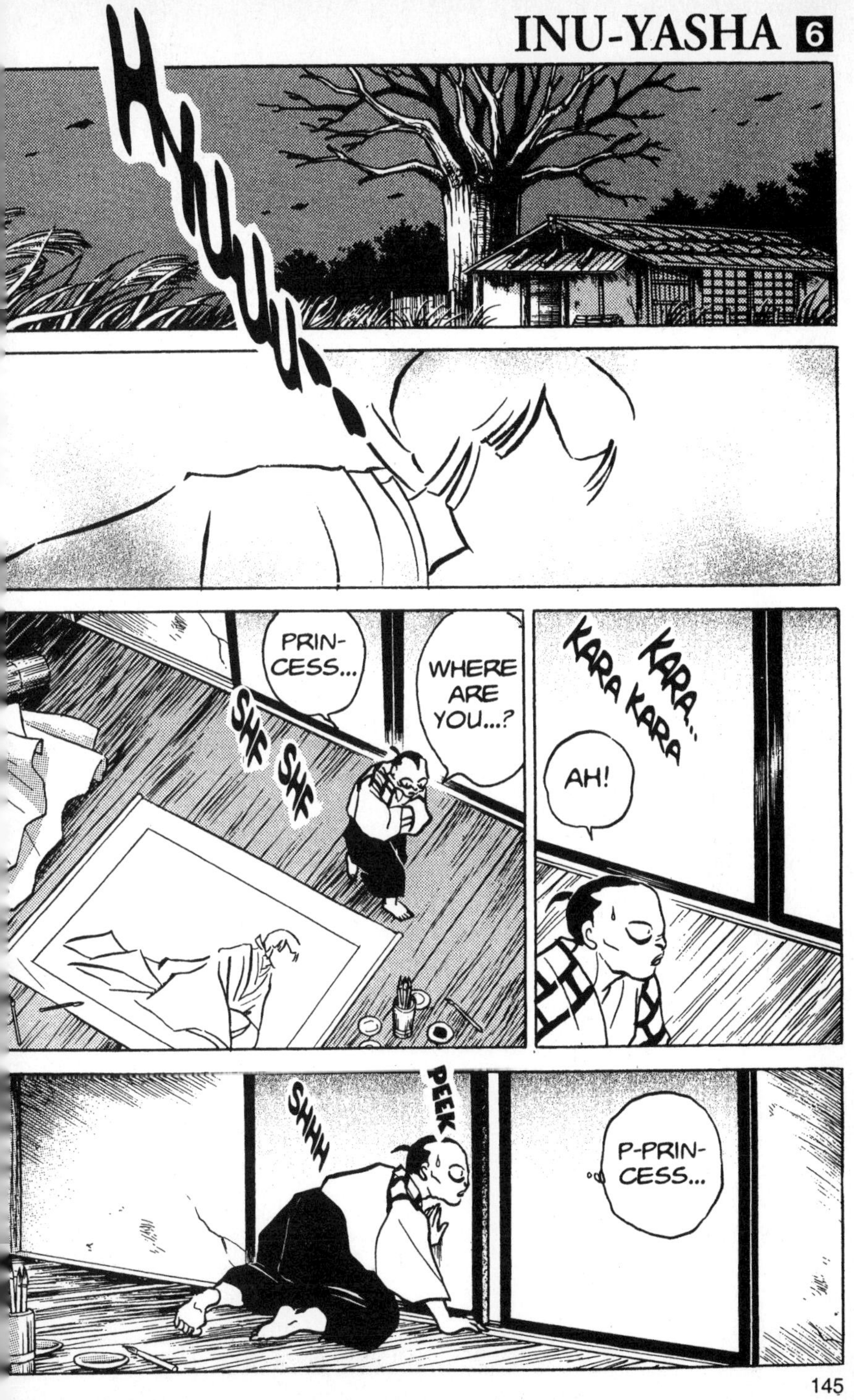
HUUUU...
SHF SHF
PRIN-CESS...
WHERE ARE YOU...?
KARA... KARA KARA
AH!
SHHH
PEEK
P-PRIN-CESS...

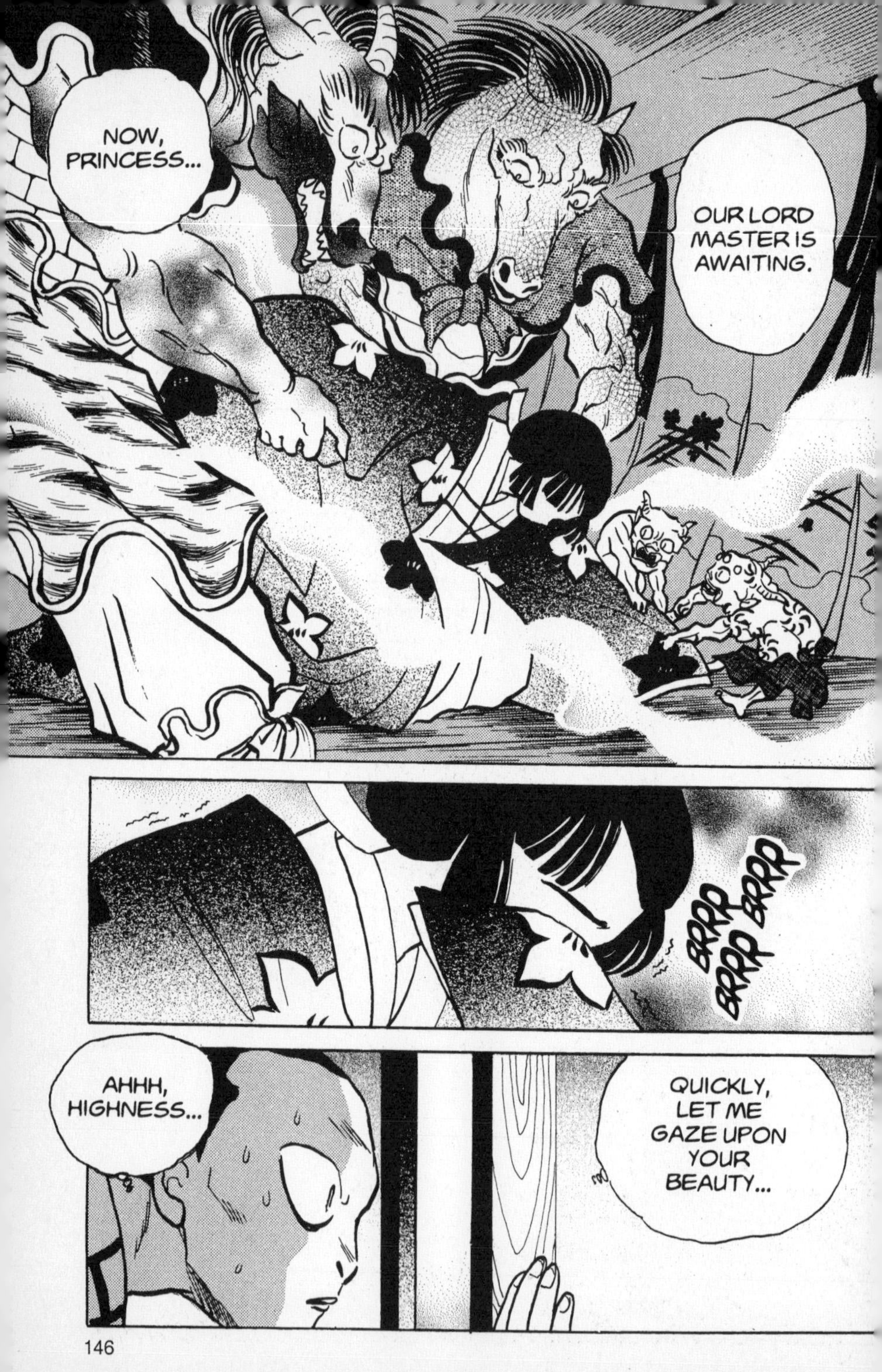
NOW, PRINCESS...
OUR LORD MASTER IS AWAITING.
BRRR BRRRR BRRRR BRRRR
AHHH, HIGHNESS...
QUICKLY, LET ME GAZE UPON YOUR BEAUTY...

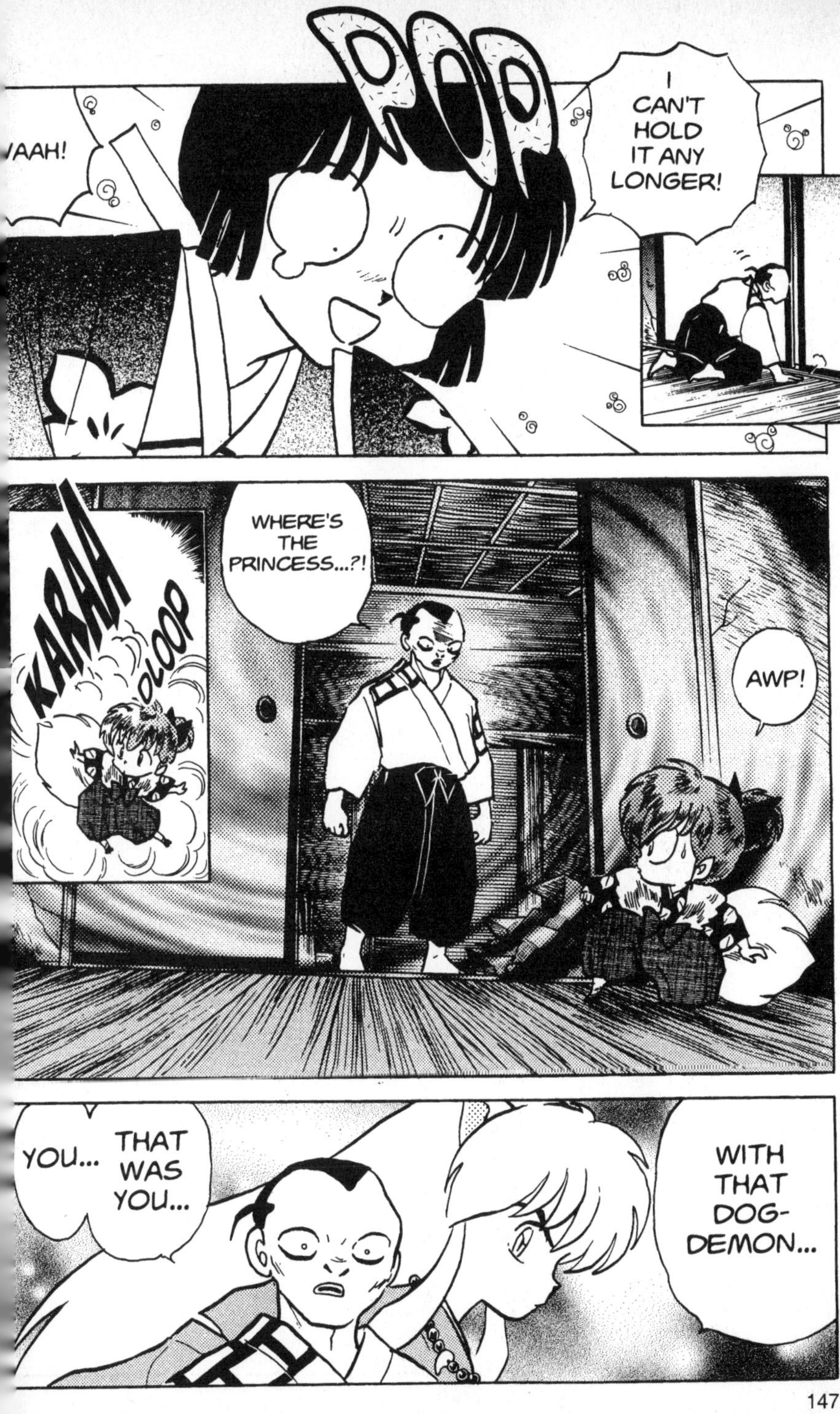
AAH!
POP
I CAN'T HOLD IT ANY LONGER!
KARAH
DLOOP
WHERE'S THE PRINCESS...?!
AWP!
YOU... THAT WAS YOU...
WITH THAT DOG-DEMON...

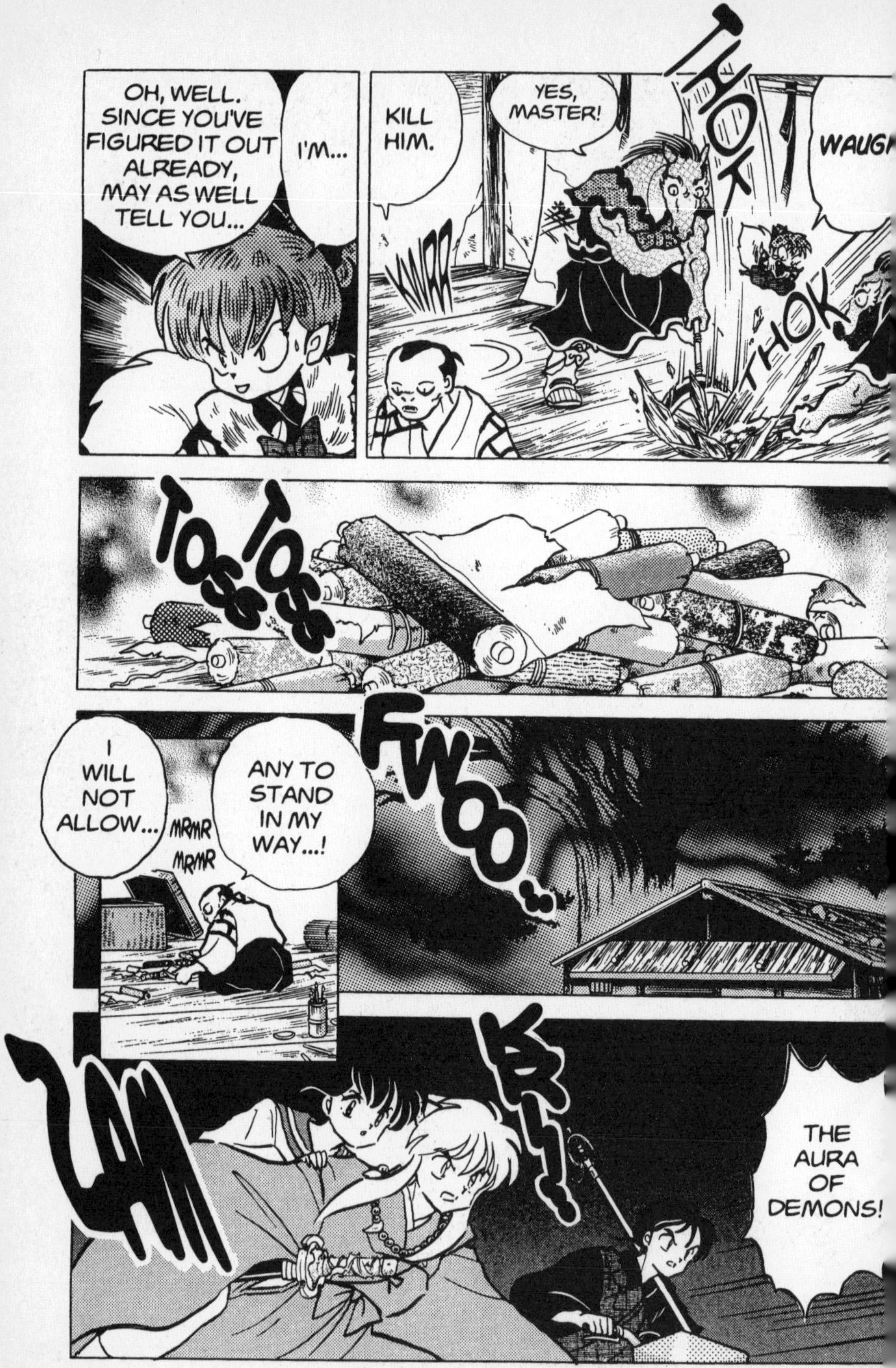
OH, WELL. SINCE YOU'VE FIGURED IT OUT ALREADY, MAY AS WELL TELL YOU...
I'M...
KILL HIM.
YES, MASTER!
KWRR
THOK
WAUG
THOK
TOSS
TOSS
I WILL NOT ALLOW...
MRMR MRMR
ANY TO STAND IN MY WAY...!
FWOO...
THE AURA OF DEMONS!

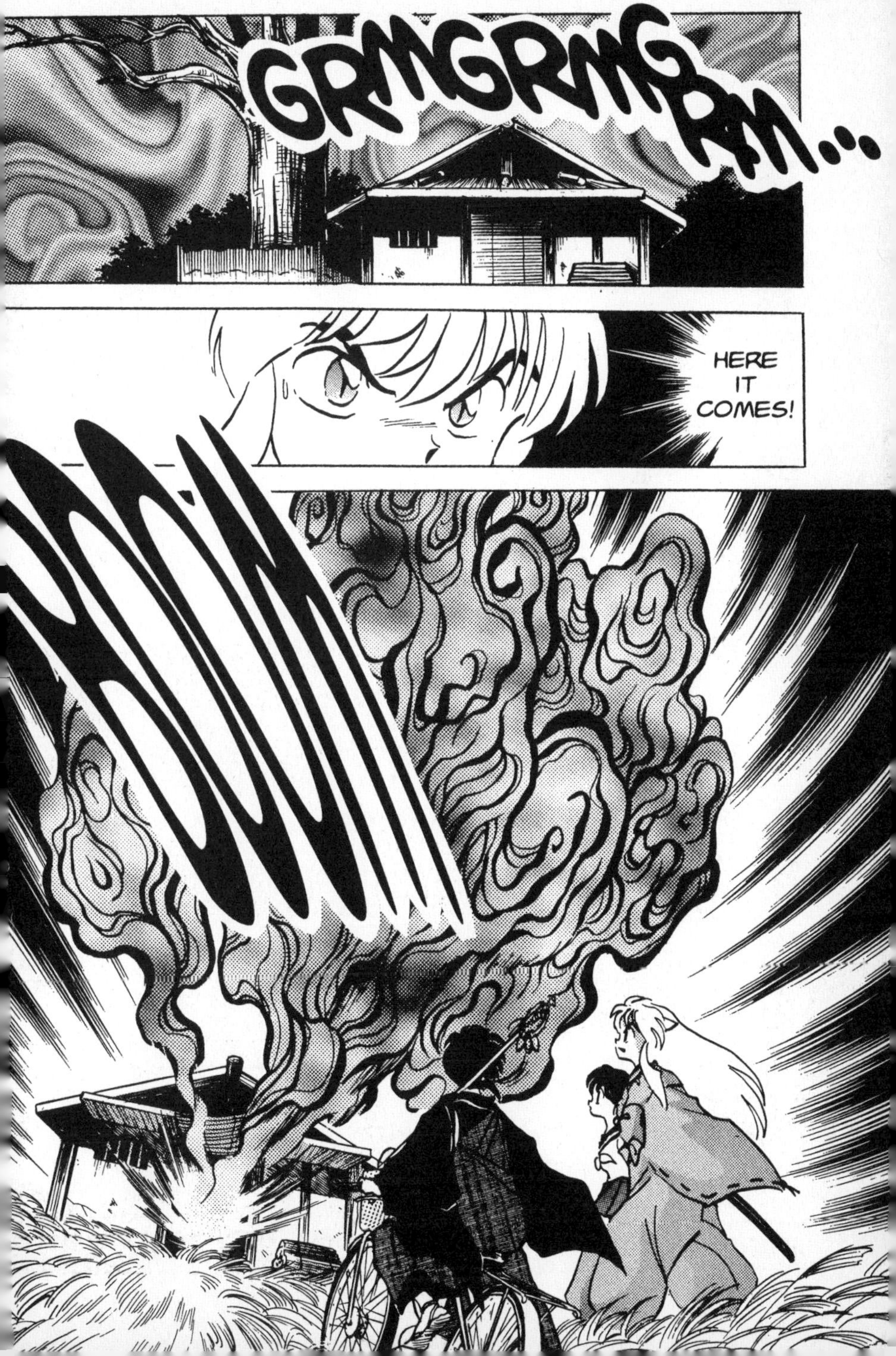
GRMGRMGRM...
HERE IT COMES!

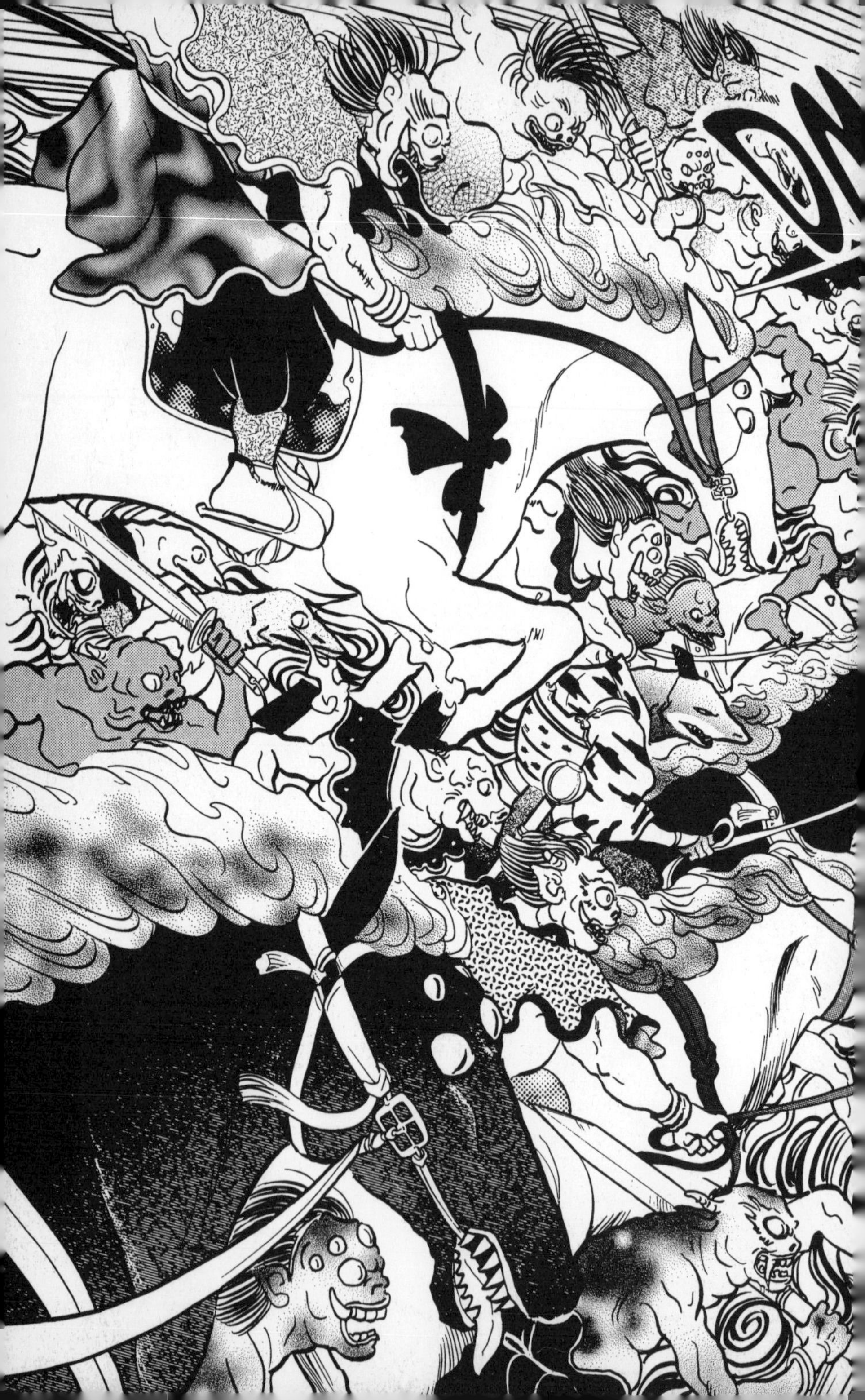

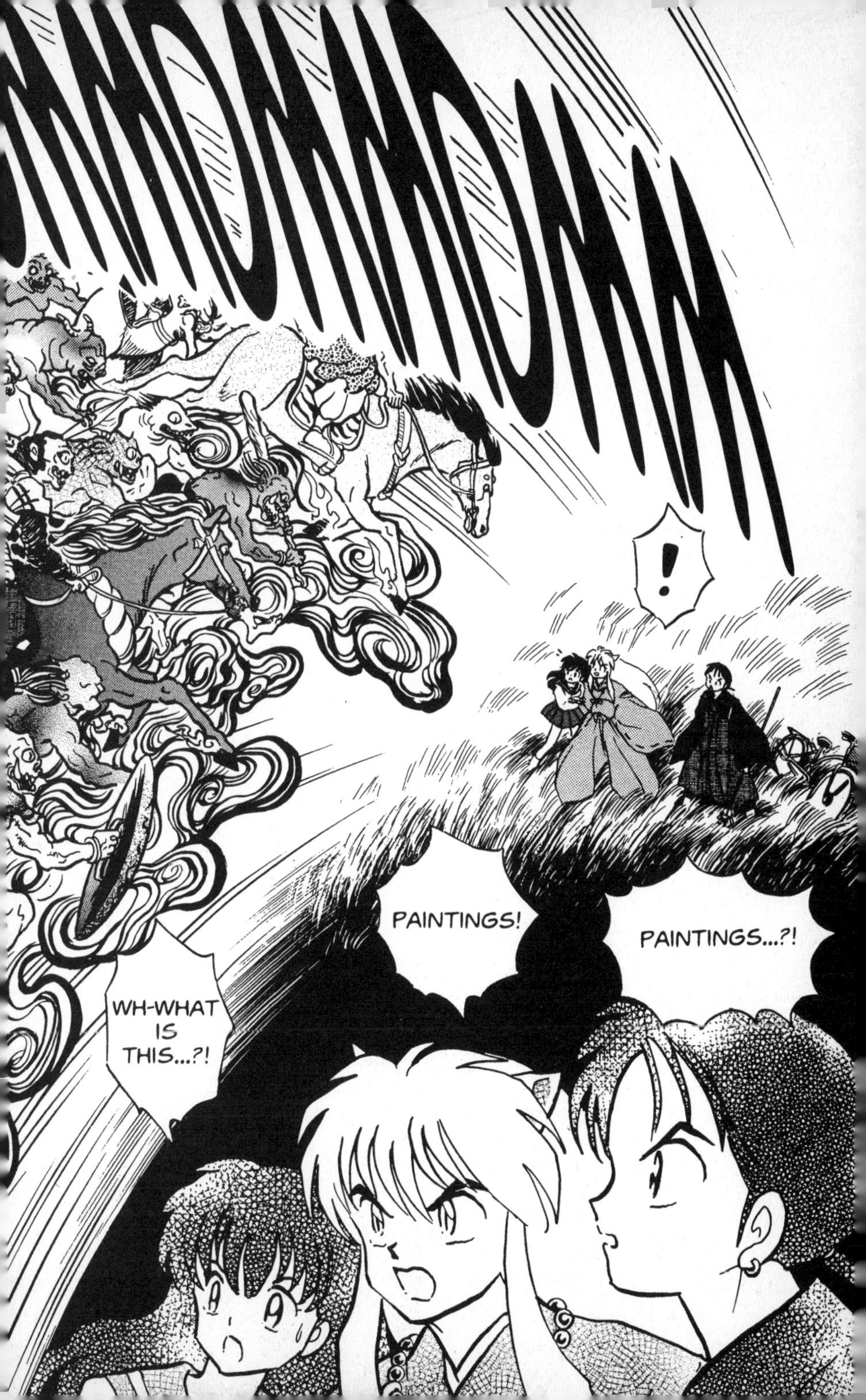
!
WH-WHAT IS THIS...?!
PAINTINGS!
PAINTINGS...?!

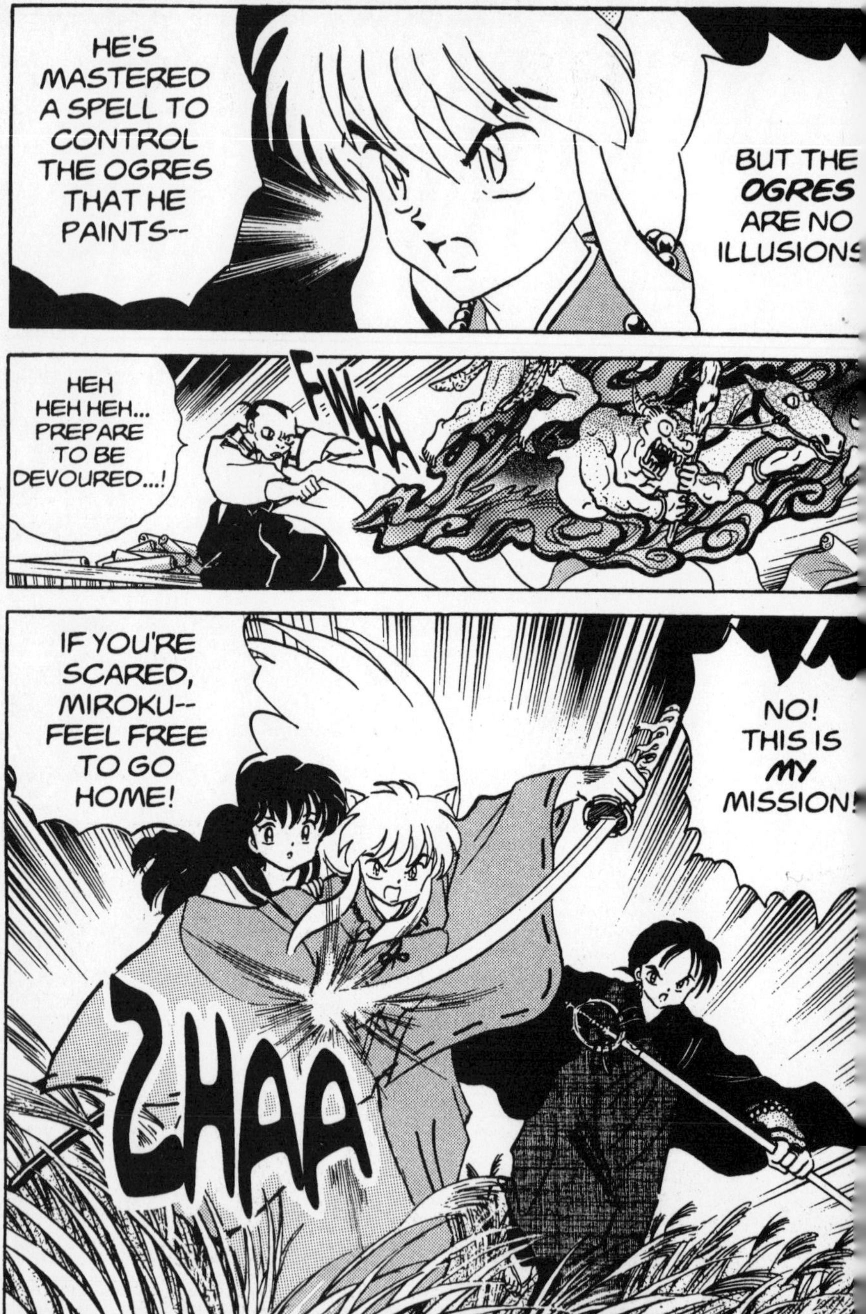
HE'S MASTERED A SPELL TO CONTROL THE OGRES THAT HE PAINTS--
BUT THE *OGRES* ARE NO ILLUSIONS
HEH HEH HEH... PREPARE TO BE DEVOURED...!
FWOOAA
IF YOU'RE SCARED, MIROKU-- FEEL FREE TO GO HOME!
NO! THIS IS *MY* MISSION!
ZHAA

SCROLL NINE

THE ARTIST'S DREAM

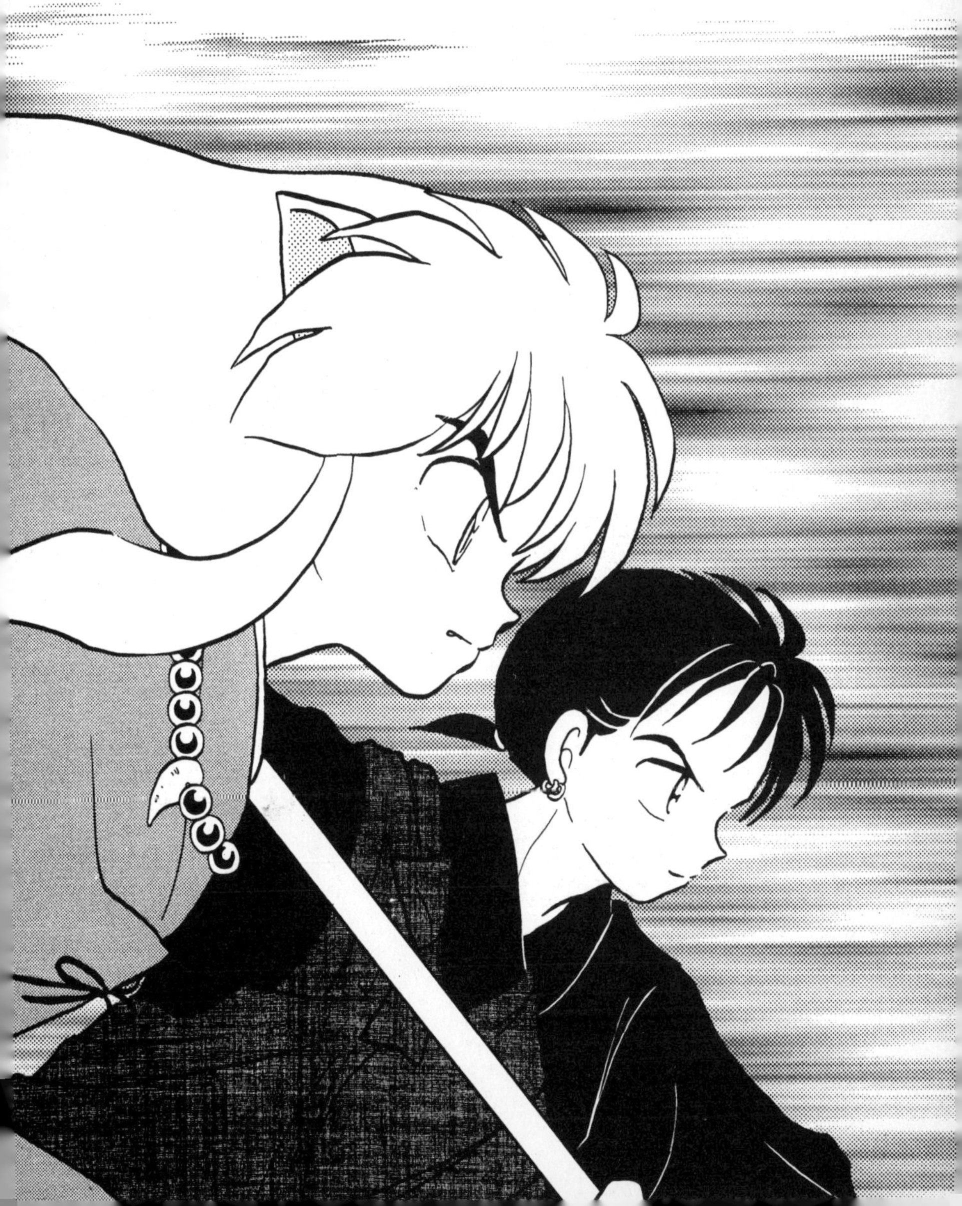

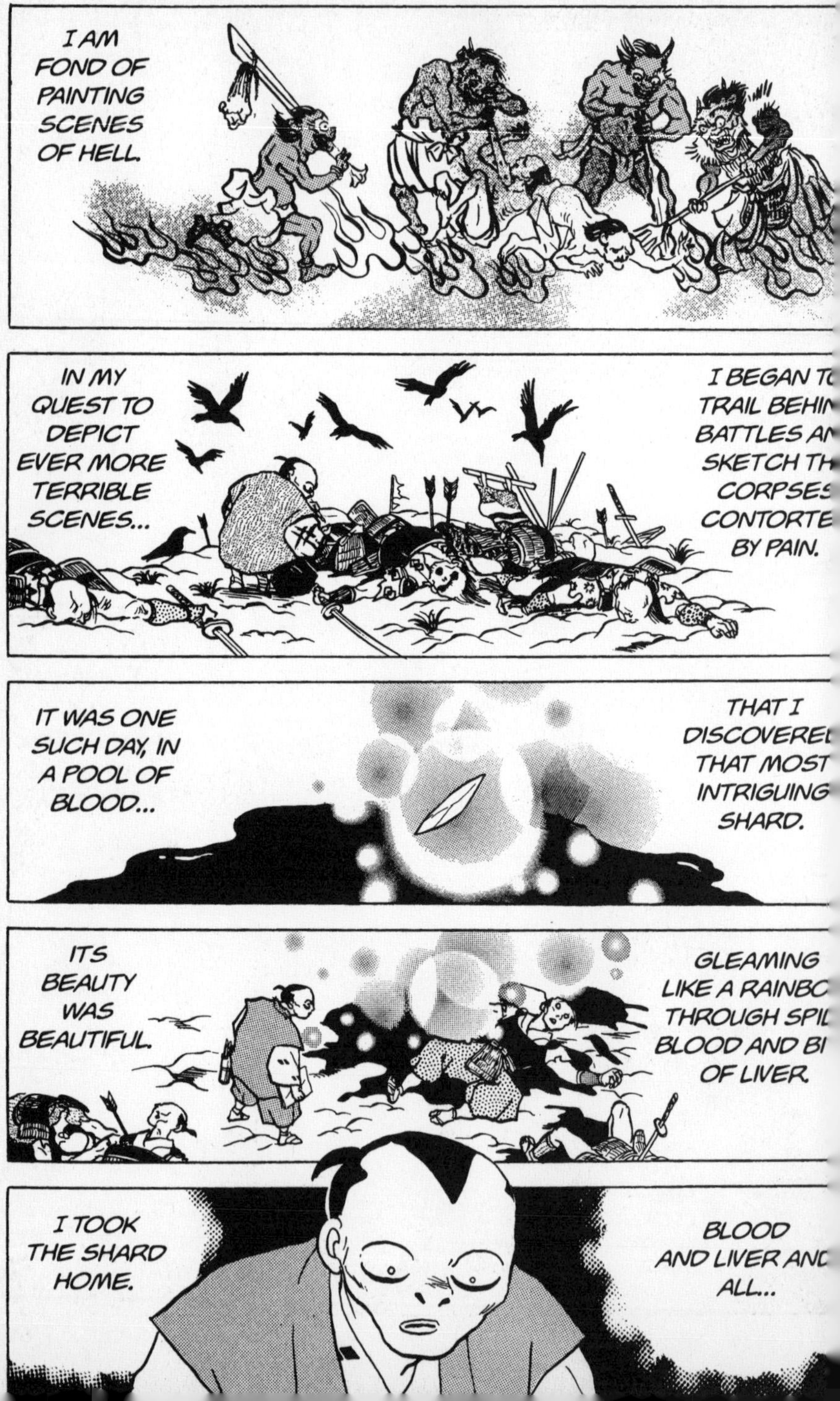
I AM FOND OF PAINTING SCENES OF HELL.
IN MY QUEST TO DEPICT EVER MORE TERRIBLE SCENES...
I BEGAN T TRAIL BEHIN BATTLES AN SKETCH TH CORPSES CONTORTE BY PAIN.
IT WAS ONE SUCH DAY, IN A POOL OF BLOOD...
THAT I DISCOVERE THAT MOST INTRIGUING SHARD.
ITS BEAUTY WAS BEAUTIFUL.
GLEAMING LIKE A RAINBO THROUGH SPIL BLOOD AND BI OF LIVER.
I TOOK THE SHARD HOME.
BLOOD AND LIVER AN ALL...

I DISSOLVED IT IN THE INK, AND PAINTED AN OGRE.

BLUP...

THEN, BY A MIRACLE, MY OGRE CAME TO LIFE.

MORE...

MORE BLOOD... MORE LIVER...

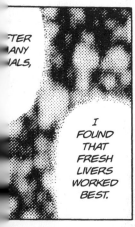

...FTER MANY ...IALS,

I FOUND THAT FRESH LIVERS WORKED BEST.

AT FIRST, I MERELY USED MY ASSISTANTS.

LATER, I WAS FORCED TO AMBUSH PASSERSBY.

BUT I KILLED A LITTLE TOO OFTEN...

AND I COULD STAY IN THE CITY NO LONGER.

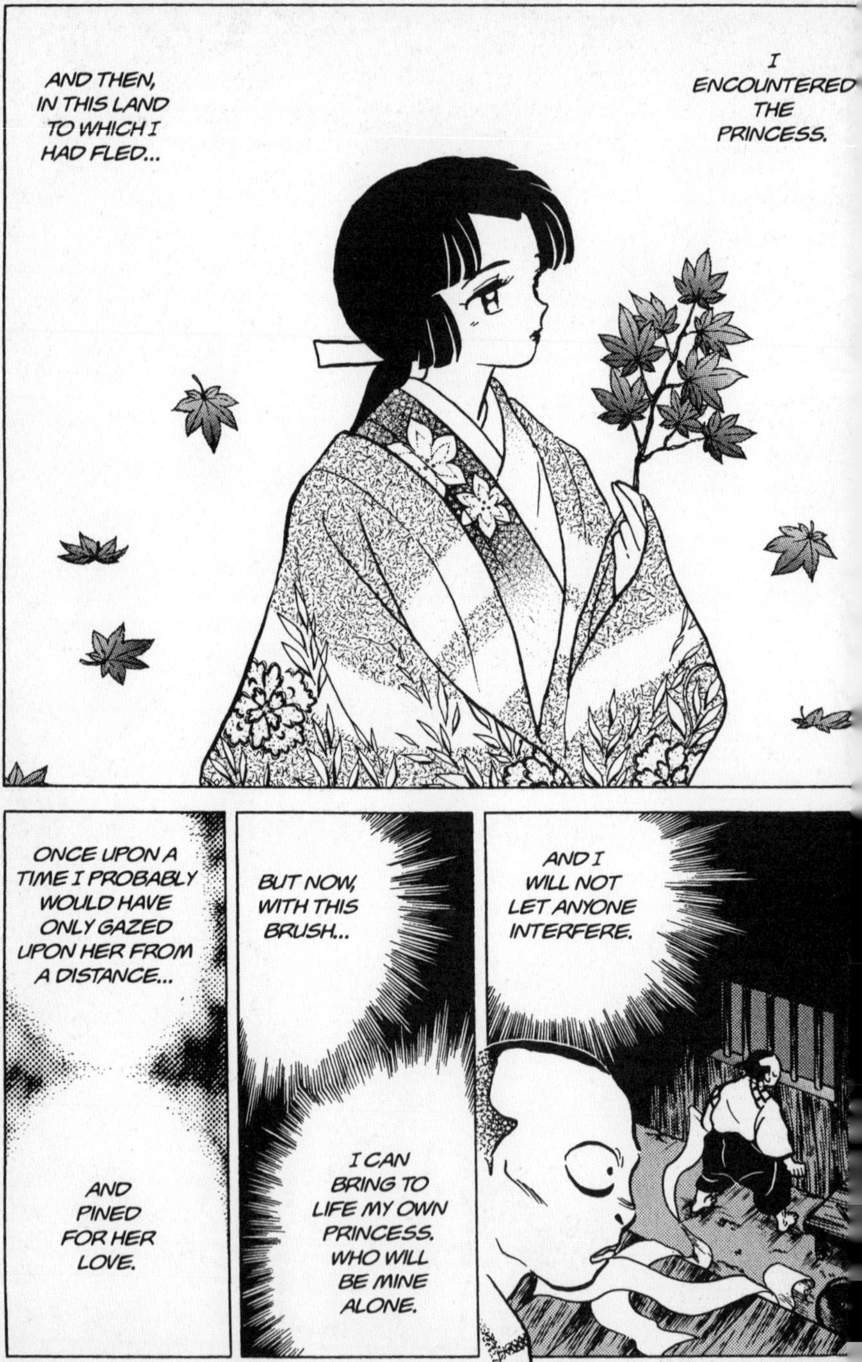
AND THEN, IN THIS LAND TO WHICH I HAD FLED...
I ENCOUNTERED THE PRINCESS.
ONCE UPON A TIME I PROBABLY WOULD HAVE ONLY GAZED UPON HER FROM A DISTANCE...
AND PINED FOR HER LOVE.
BUT NOW, WITH THIS BRUSH...
I CAN BRING TO LIFE MY OWN PRINCESS. WHO WILL BE MINE ALONE.
AND I WILL NOT LET ANYONE INTERFERE.

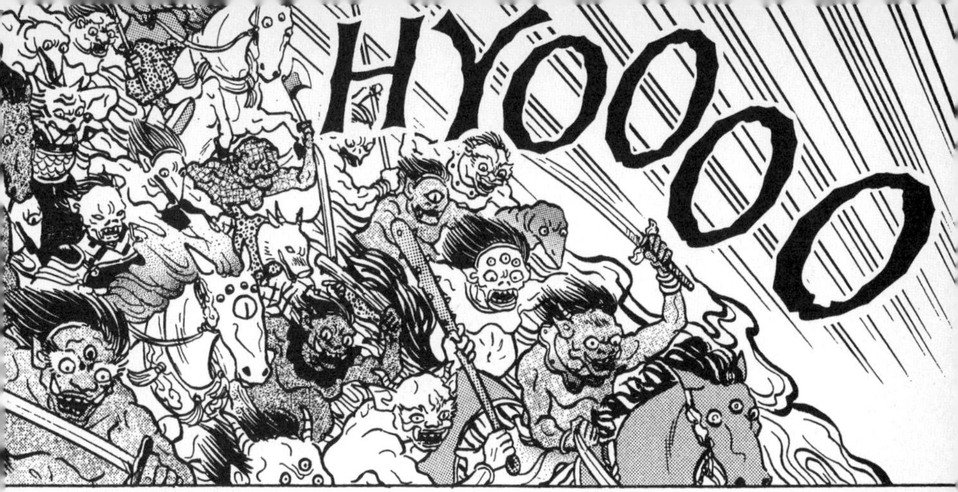
HYOOOO

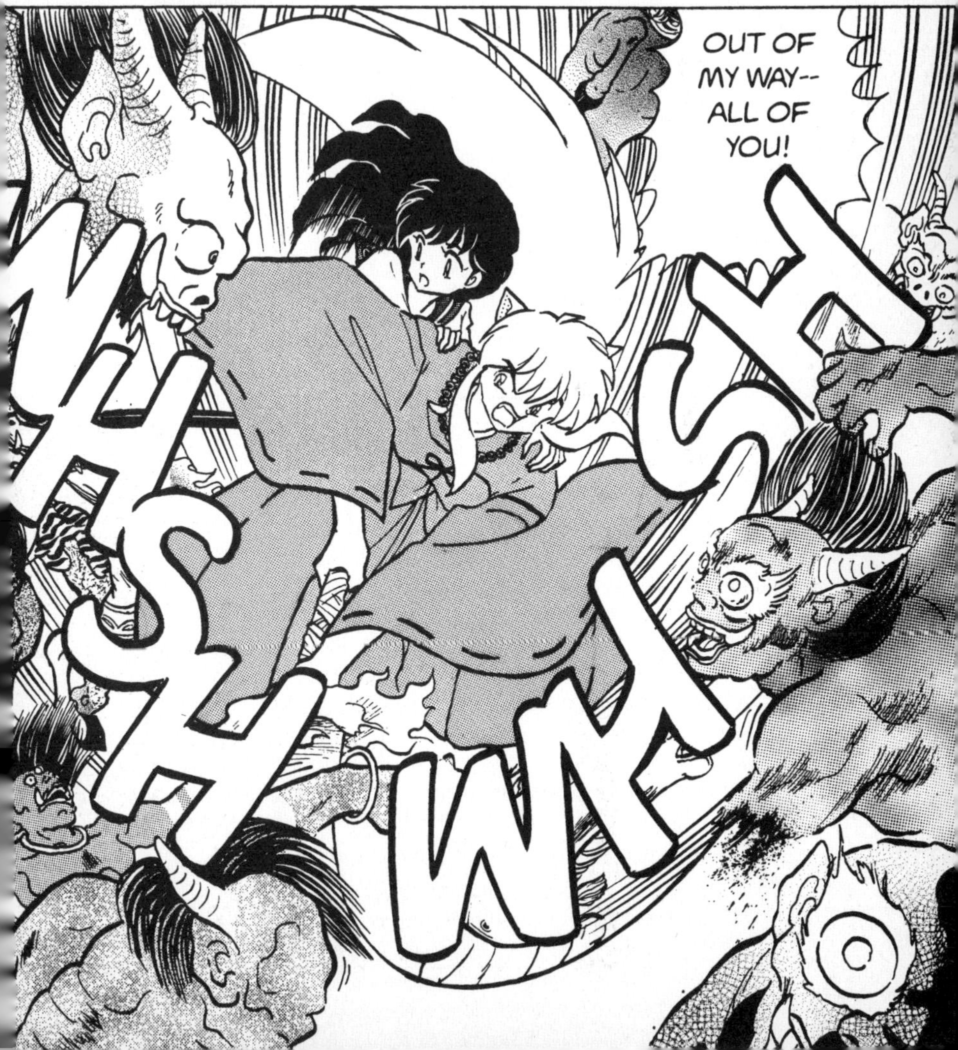
OUT OF MY WAY-- ALL OF YOU!
SHWISH
SHWISH

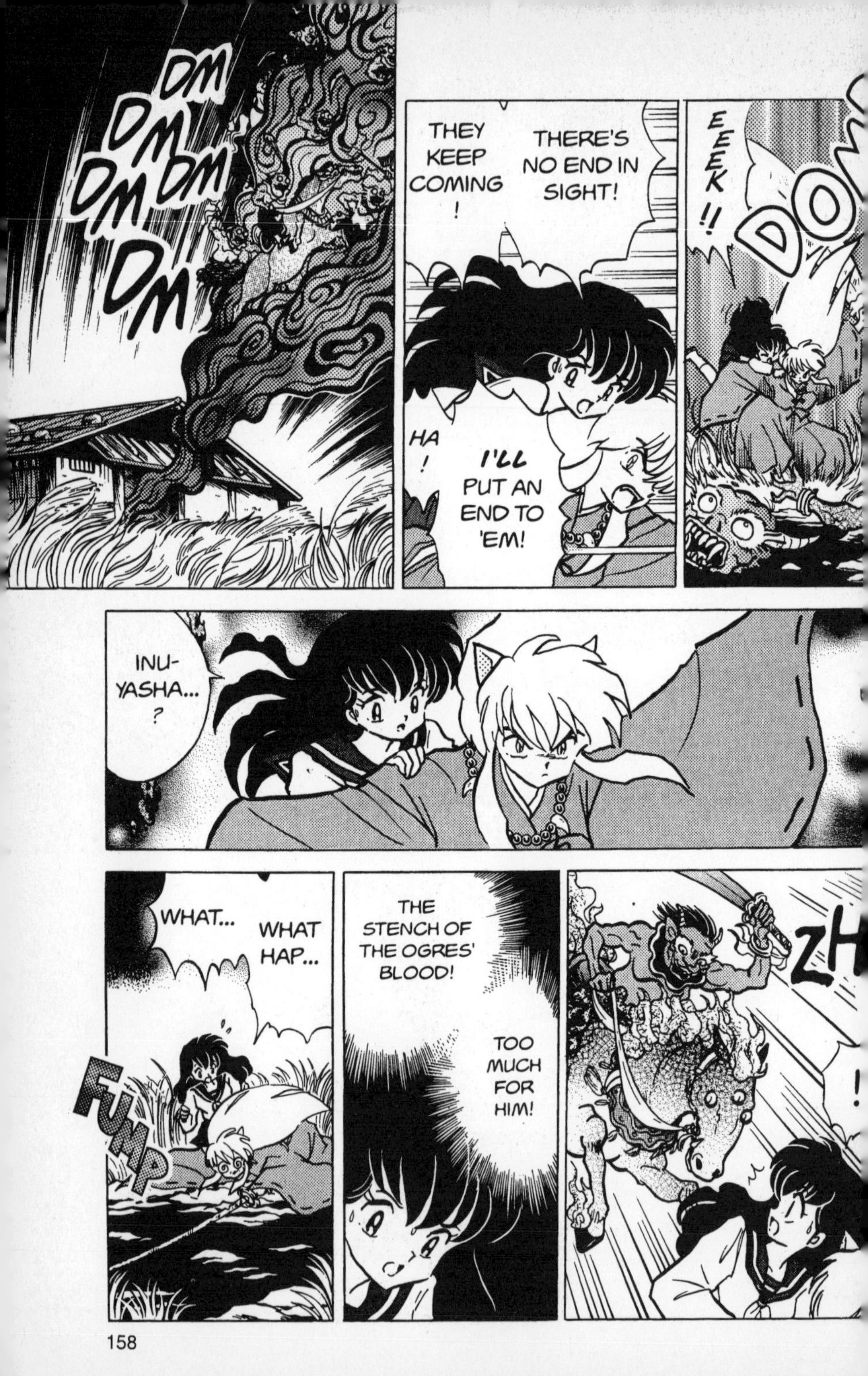
DM DM DM DM DM DM
THEY KEEP COMING!
THERE'S NO END IN SIGHT!
HA!
I'LL PUT AN END TO 'EM!
EEEK!!
DOM
INU-YASHA...?
WHAT...
WHAT HAP...
FUMP
THE STENCH OF THE OGRES' BLOOD!
TOO MUCH FOR HIM!
ZH
!

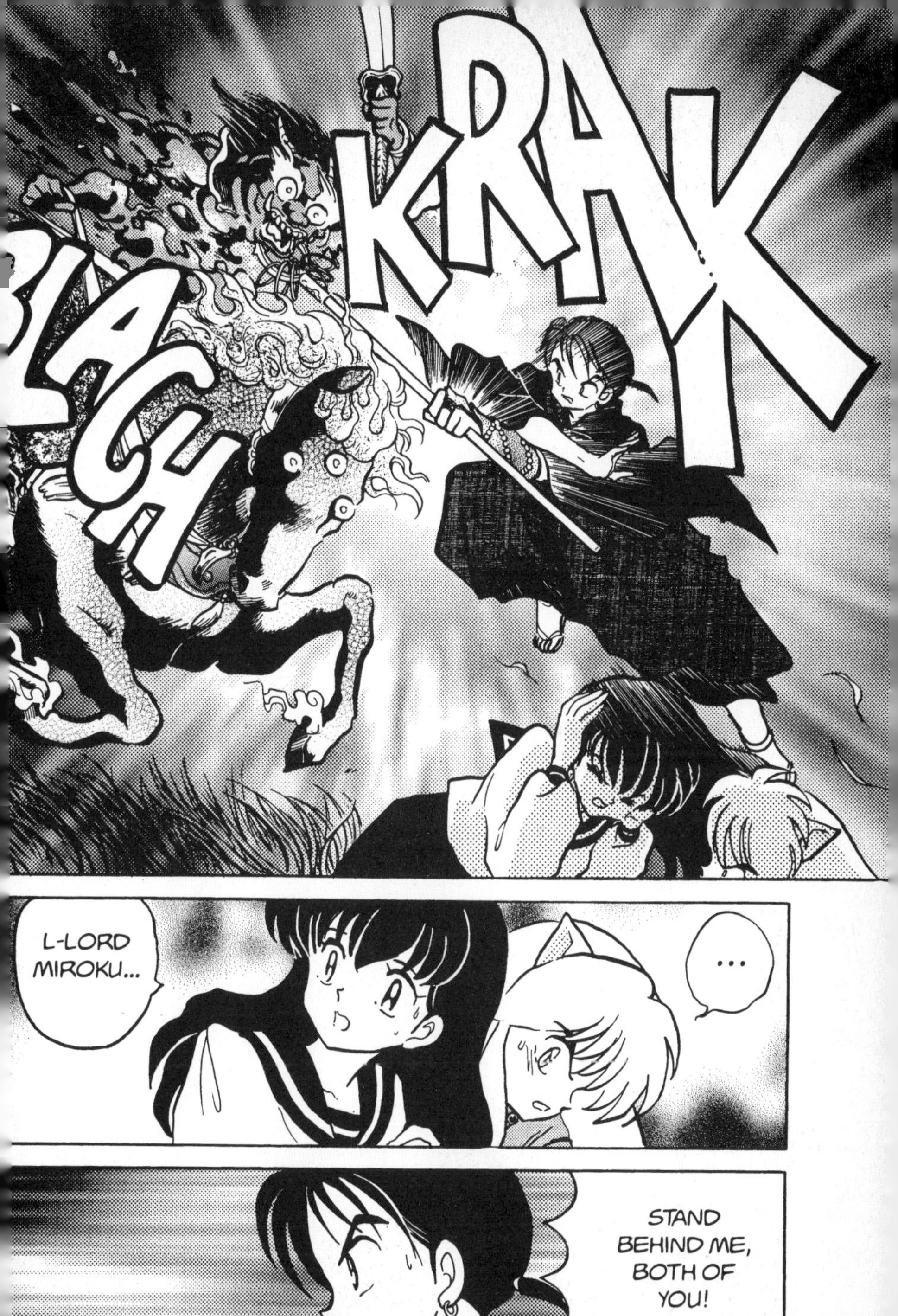
KRAK
BLAGH
L-LORD MIROKU...
...
STAND BEHIND ME, BOTH OF YOU!

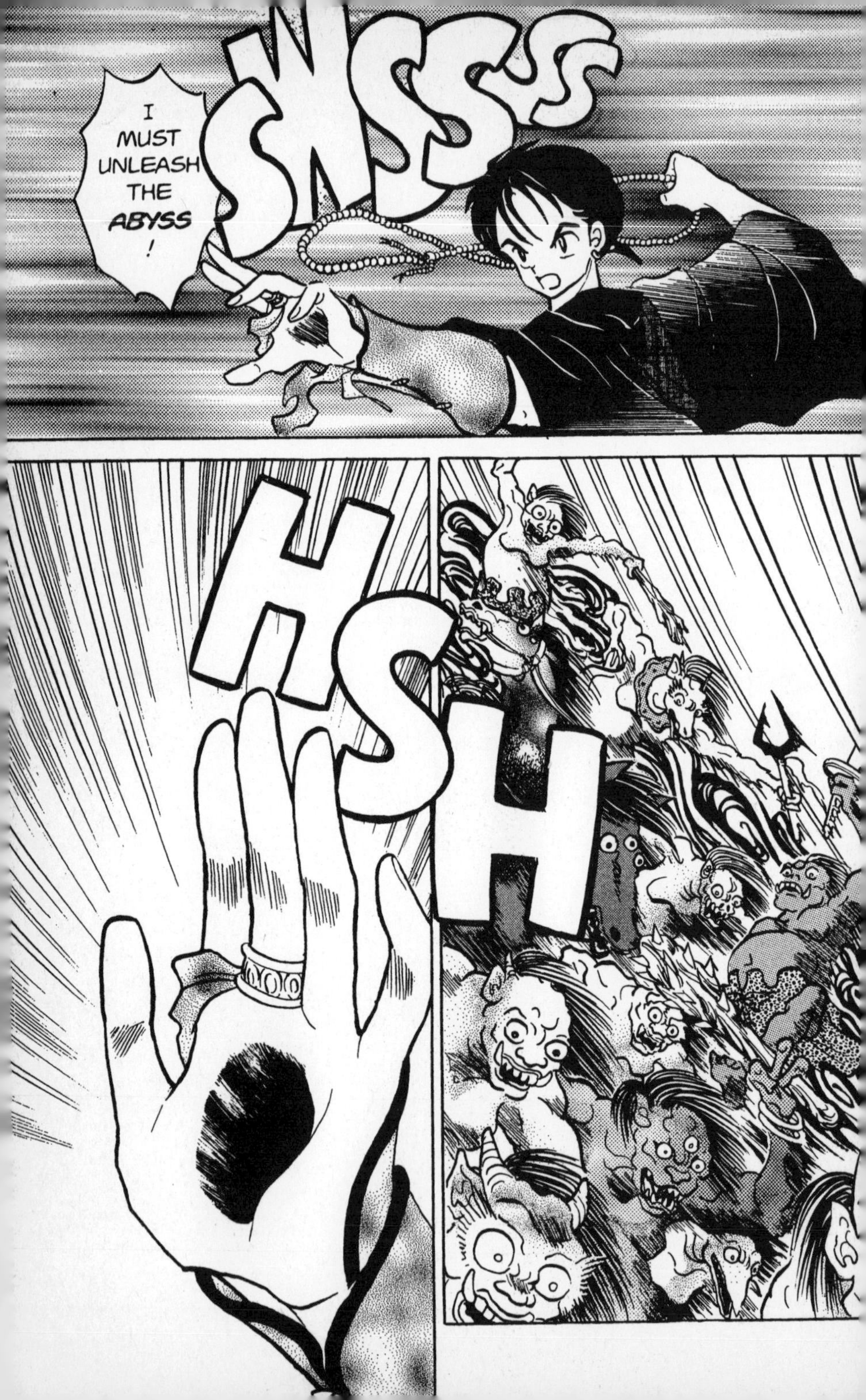
I MUST UNLEASH THE ABYSS!
SWSS
HSSH

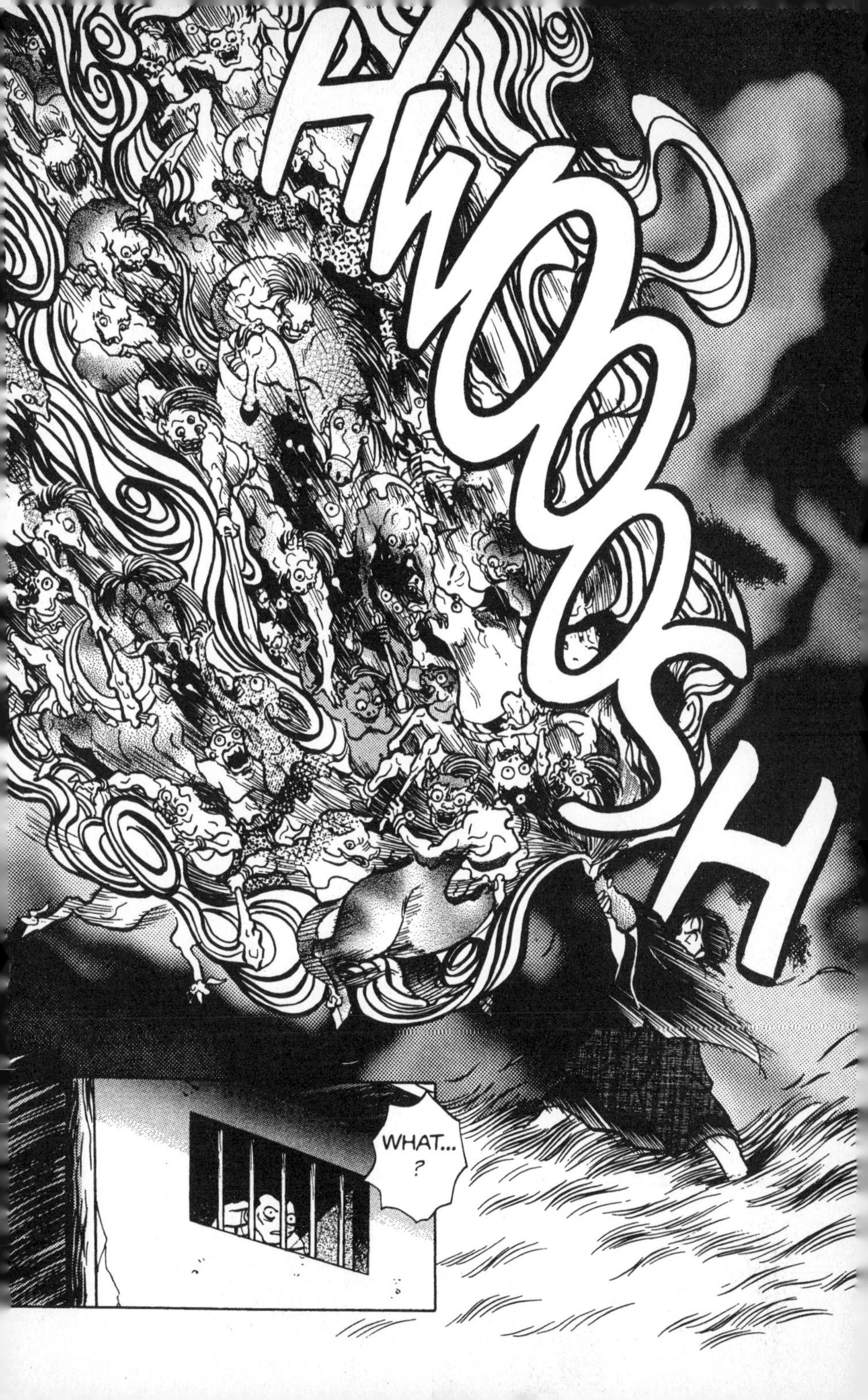
HWOOOOSH
WHAT... ?

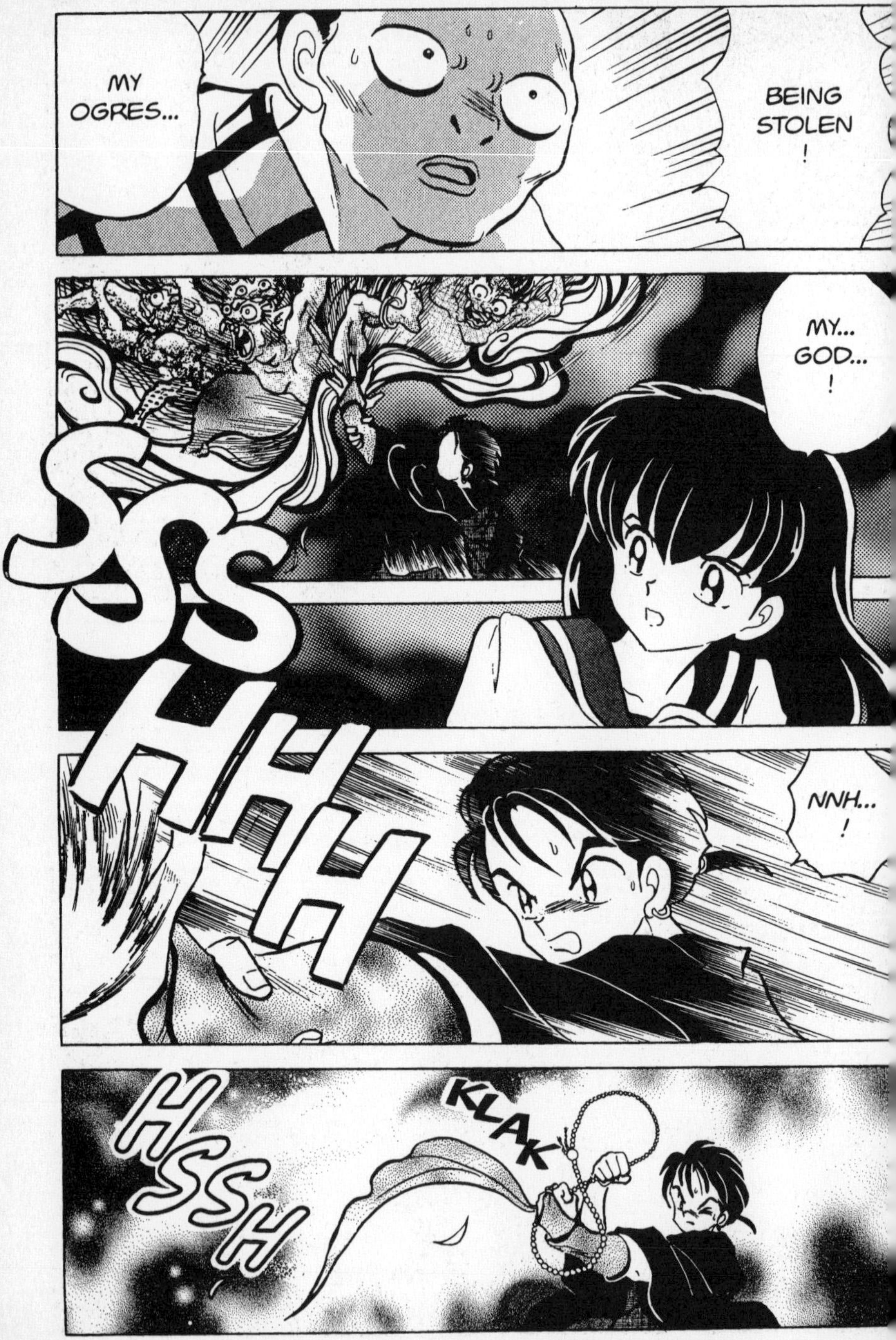
MY OGRES...
BEING STOLEN
!
SSS
MY... GOD...
!
HHH
NNH...
!
HSSH
KLAK

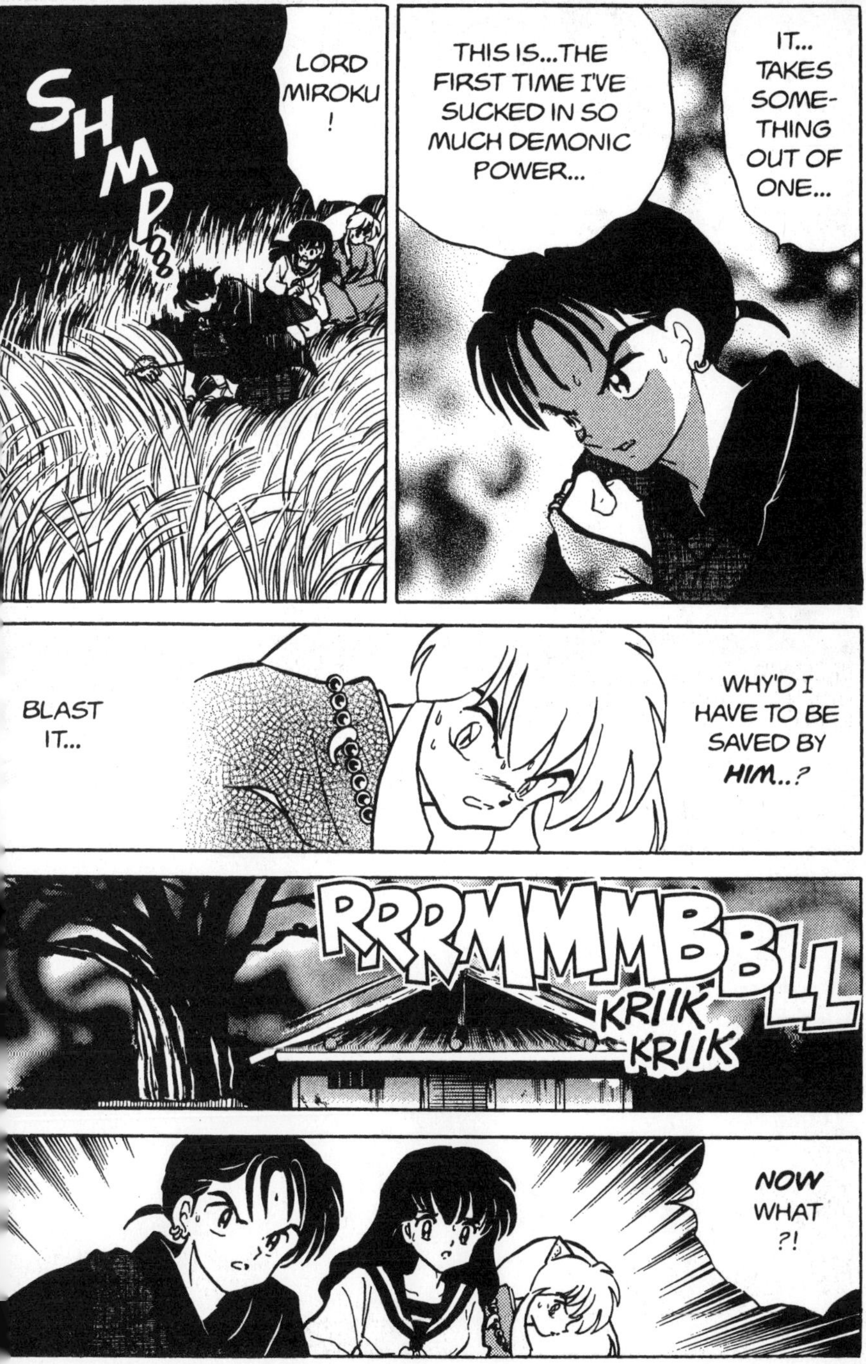
SHMPOOO
LORD MIROKU!
THIS IS...THE FIRST TIME I'VE SUCKED IN SO MUCH DEMONIC POWER...
IT... TAKES SOMETHING OUT OF ONE...
BLAST IT...
WHY'D I HAVE TO BE SAVED BY ***HIM***...?
RRRMMMMBBLL
KRIIK KRIIK
NOW WHAT?!

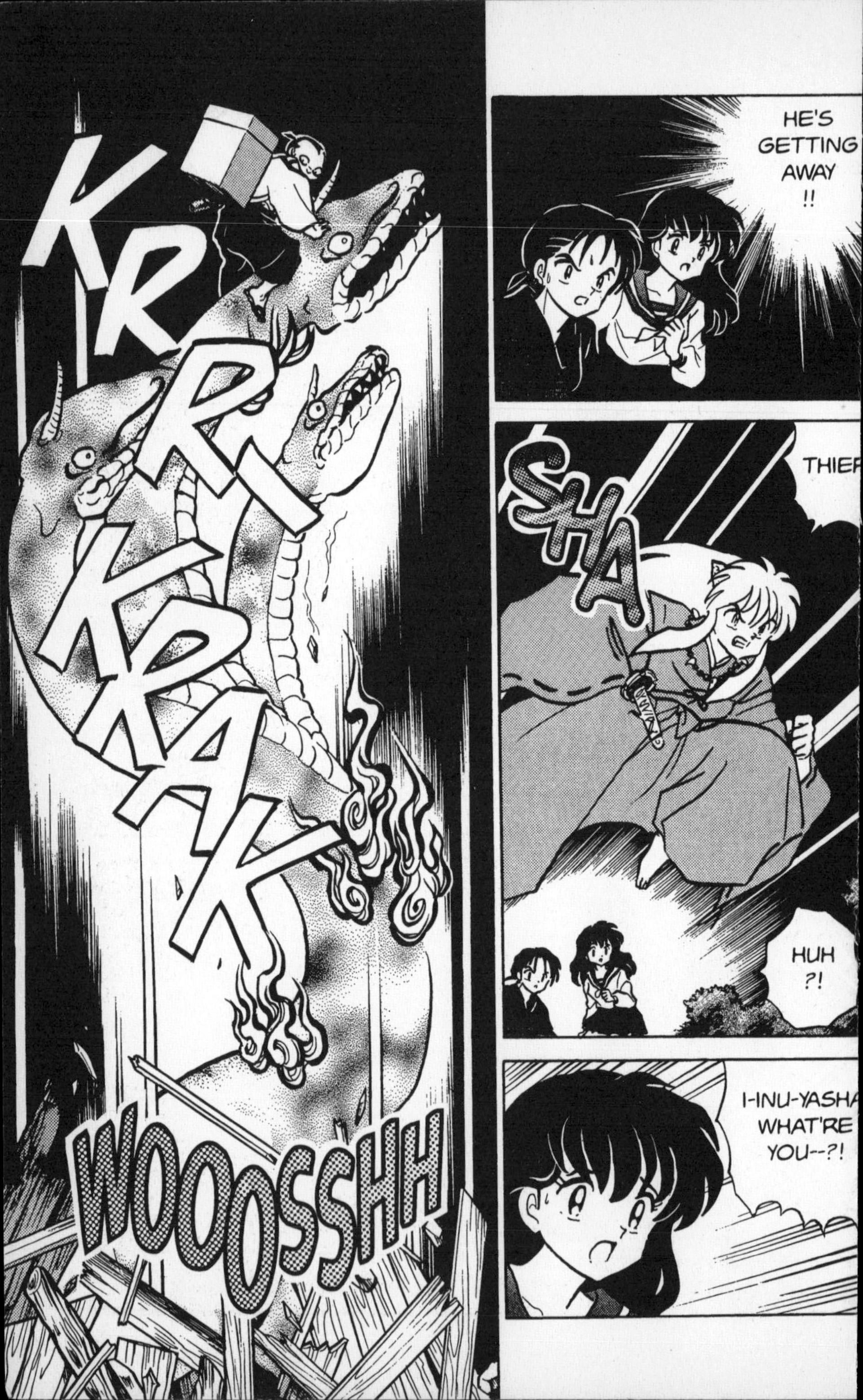
KRRIKRAK
WOOOSSHH
HE'S GETTING AWAY !!
SHA
THIEF
HUH ?!
I-INU-YASHA WHAT'RE YOU--?!

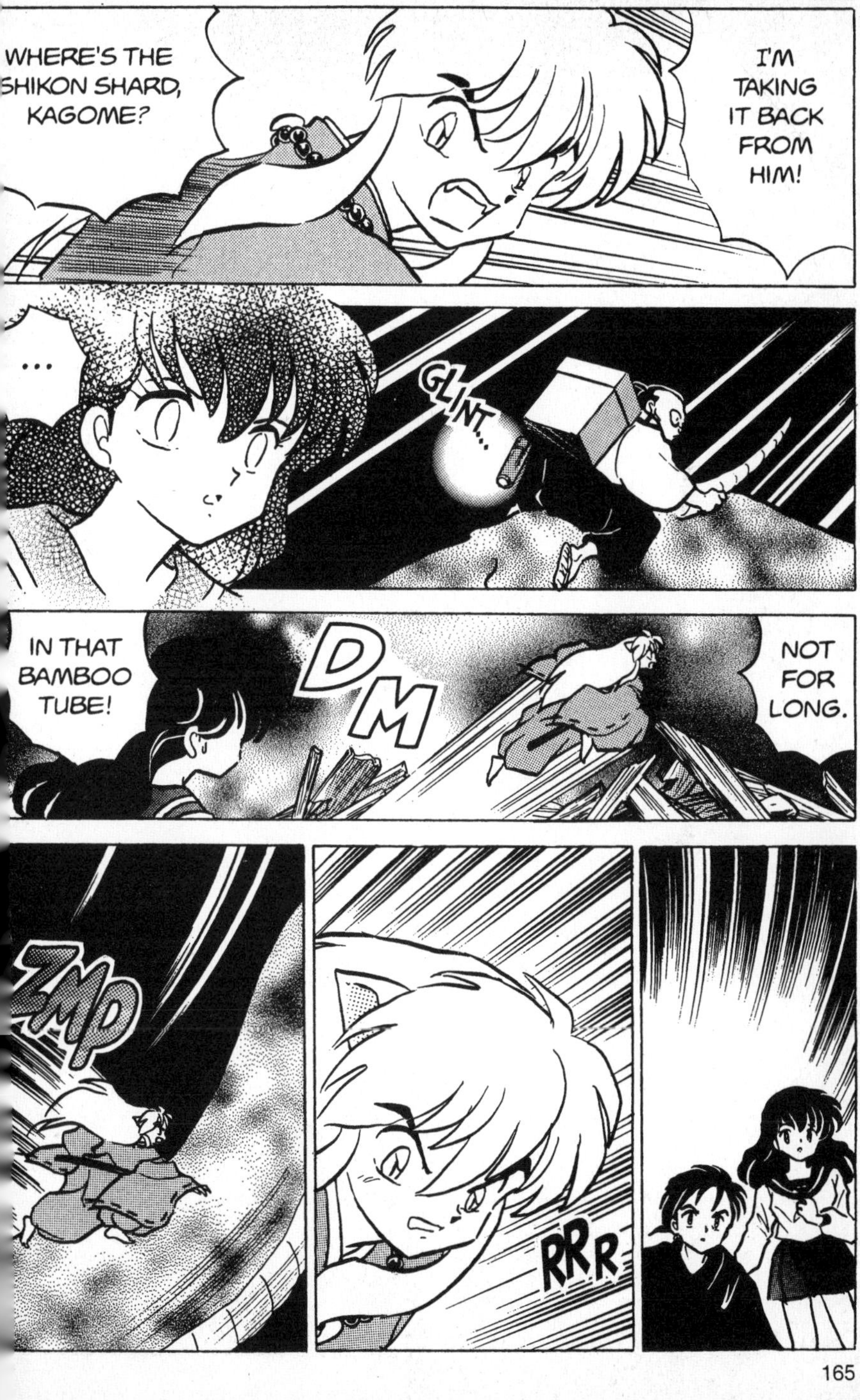
WHERE'S THE SHIKON SHARD, KAGOME?
I'M TAKING IT BACK FROM HIM!
...
GLINT...
IN THAT BAMBOO TUBE!
DM
NOT FOR LONG.
ZMP
RRR

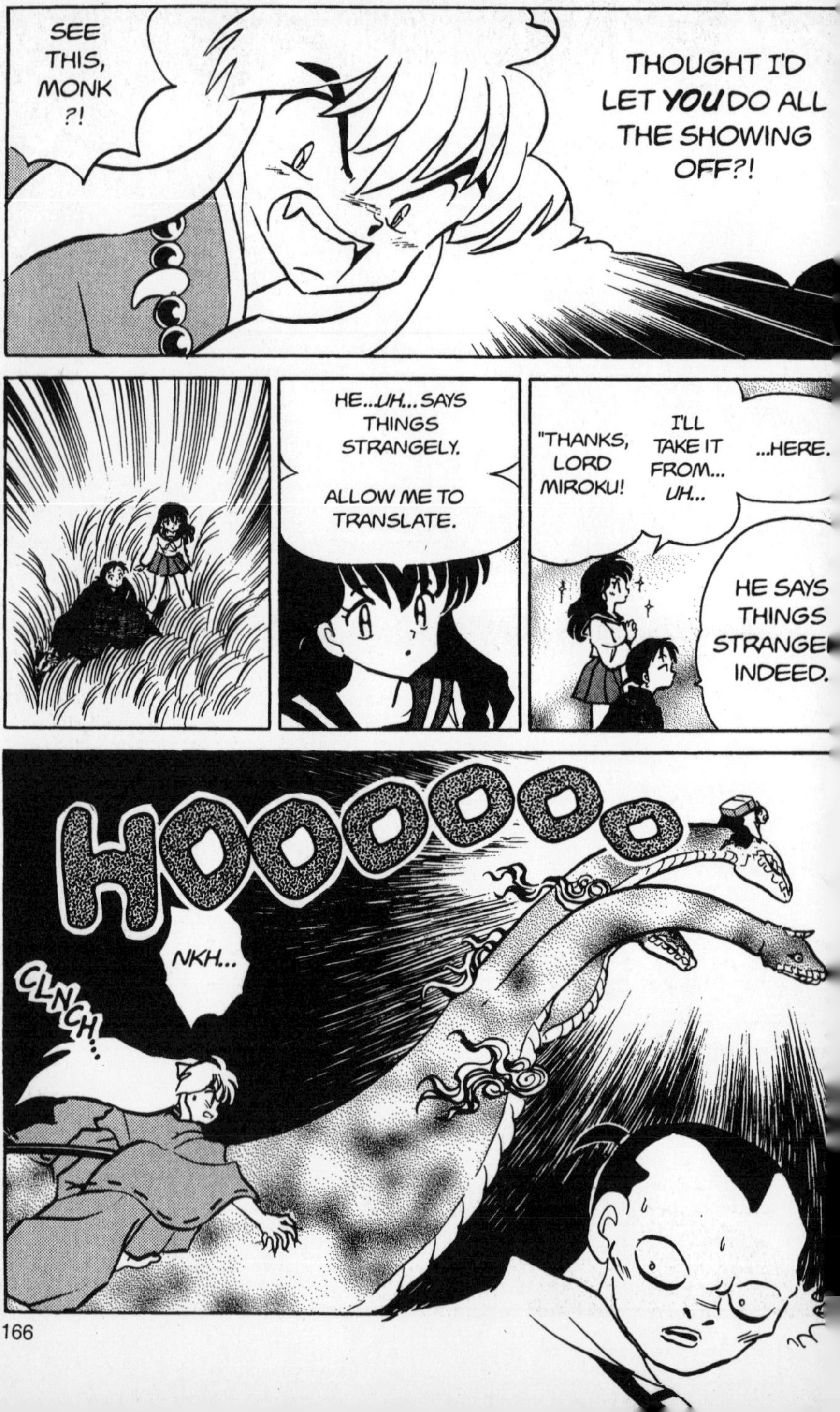
SEE THIS, MONK ?!
THOUGHT I'D LET YOU DO ALL THE SHOWING OFF?!
HE...UH... SAYS THINGS STRANGELY.
ALLOW ME TO TRANSLATE.
"THANKS, LORD MIROKU!
I'LL TAKE IT FROM... UH...
...HERE.
HE SAYS THINGS STRANGE INDEED.
HOOOOOO
NKH...
CLNCH...

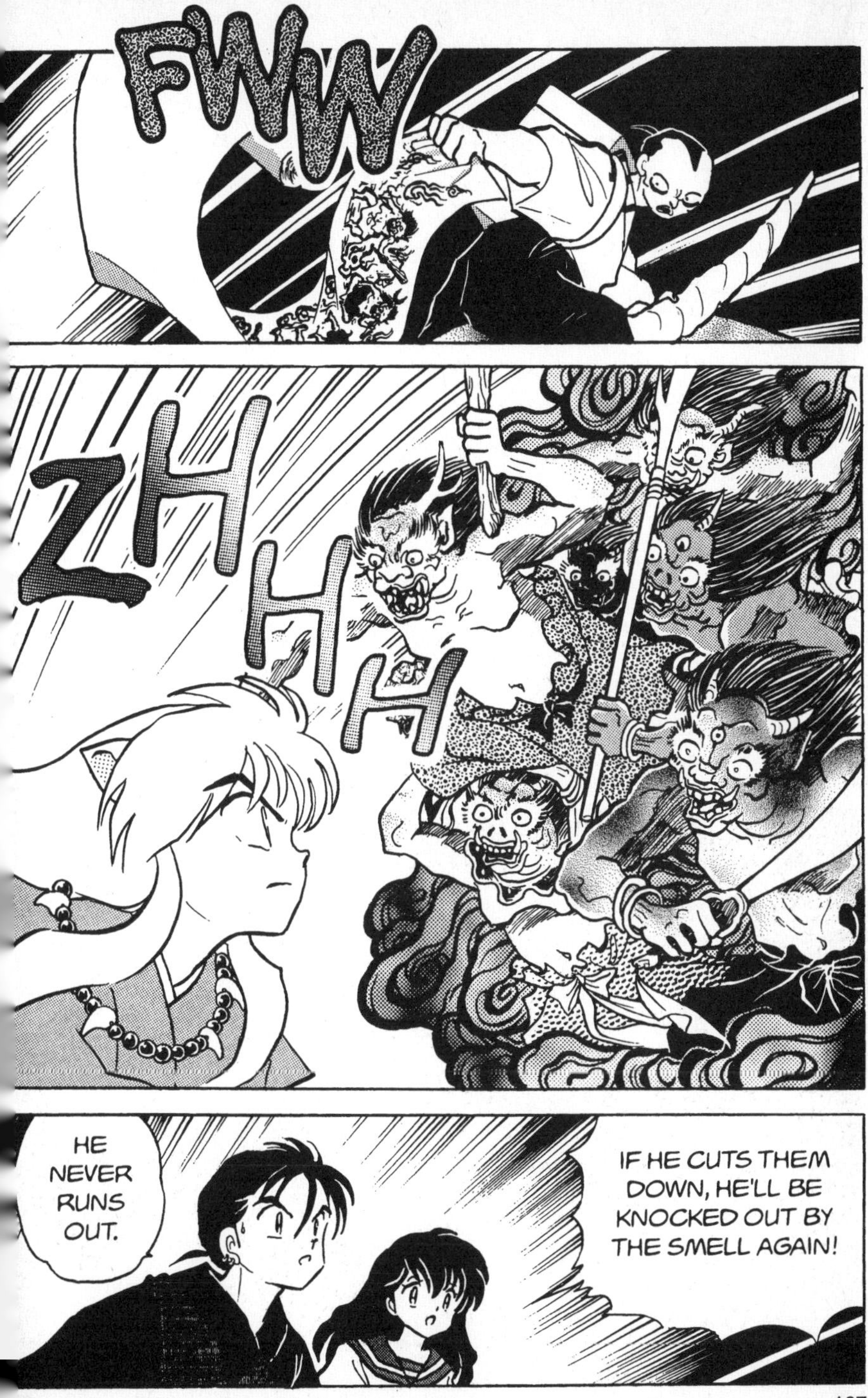
FWW
ZHHH
HE NEVER RUNS OUT.
IF HE CUTS THEM DOWN, HE'LL BE KNOCKED OUT BY THE SMELL AGAIN!

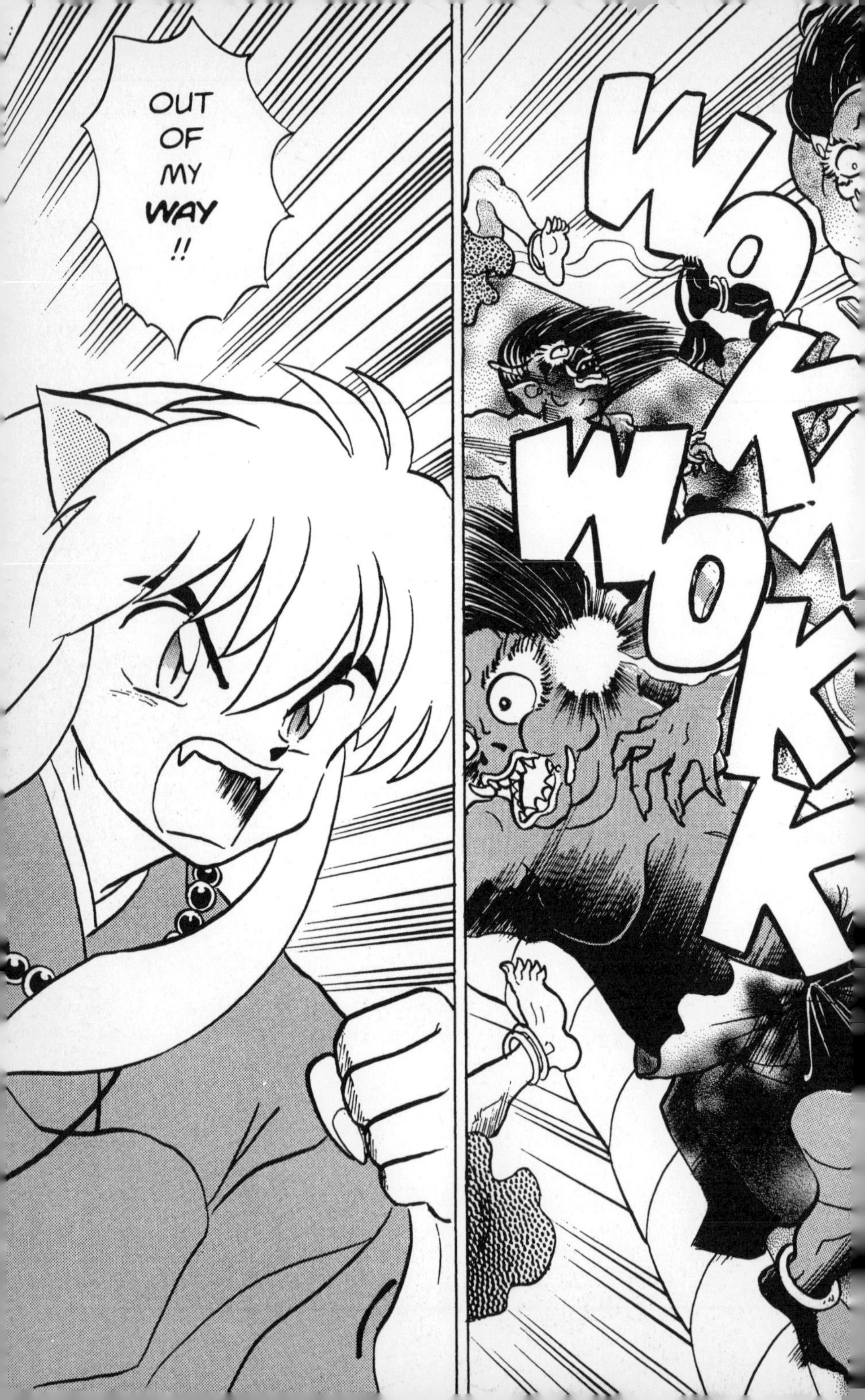
OUT OF MY WAY !!
WA WA WA

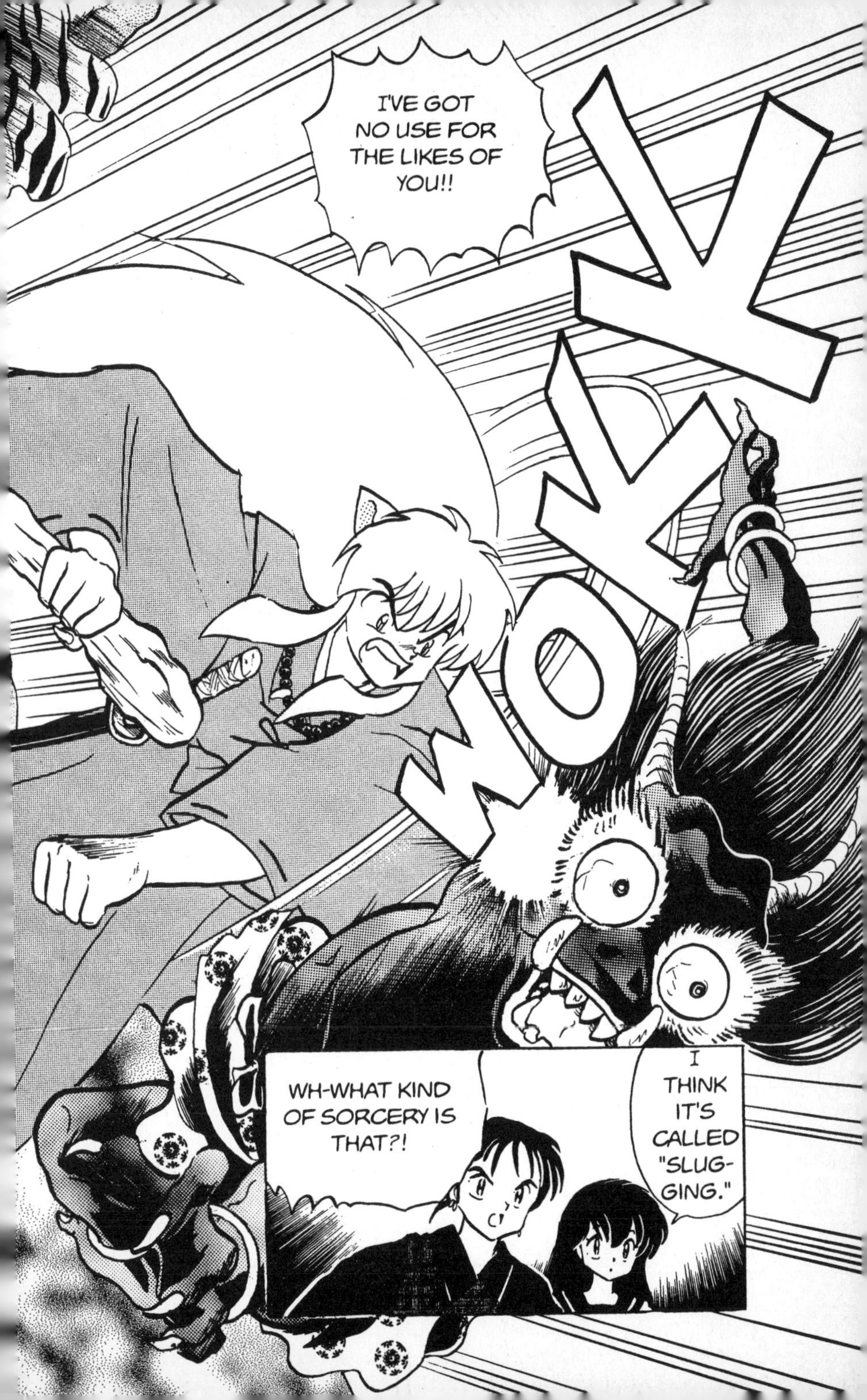
I'VE GOT NO USE FOR THE LIKES OF YOU!!
WOK
WH-WHAT KIND OF SORCERY IS THAT?!
I THINK IT'S CALLED "SLUG-GING."

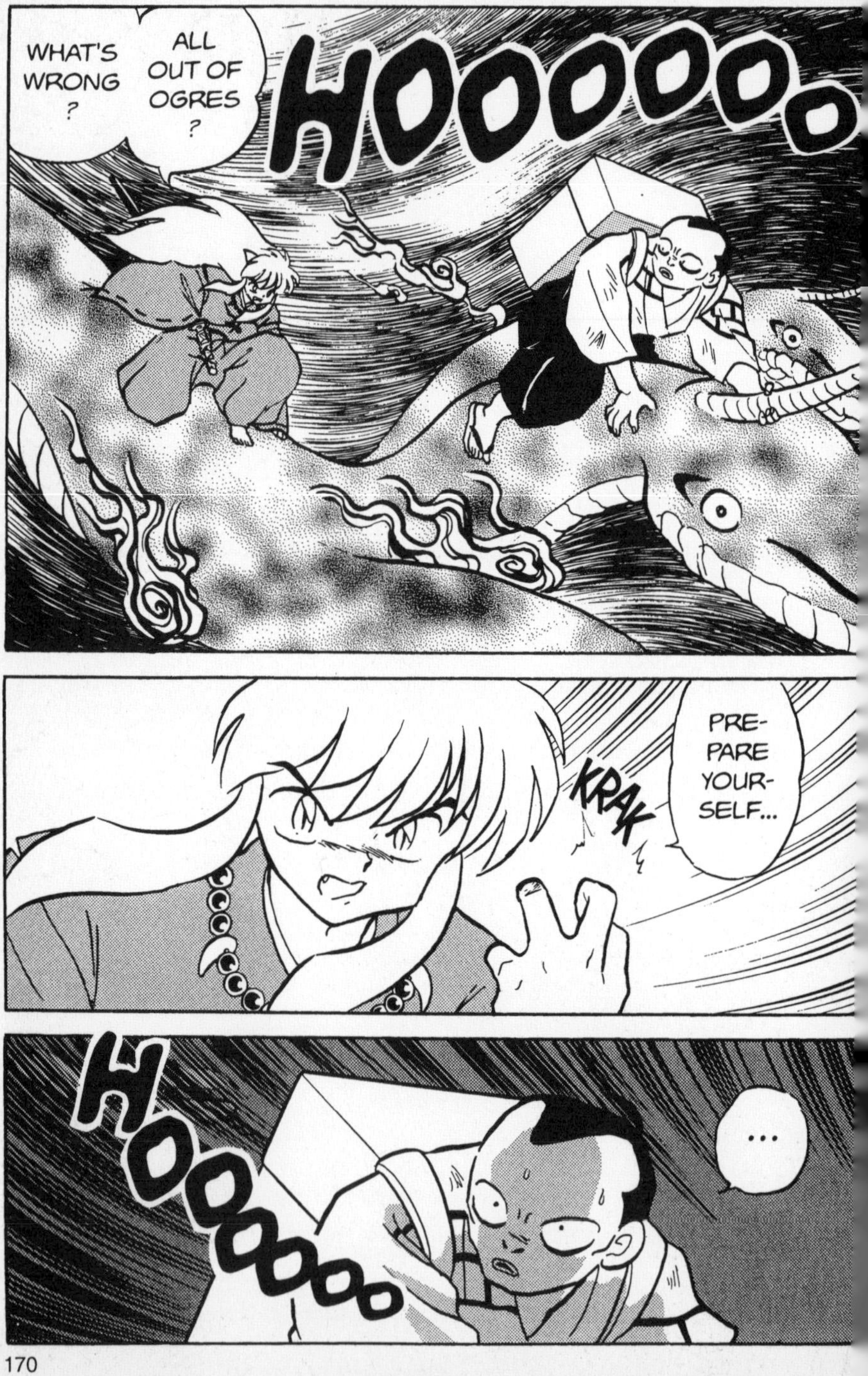
WHAT'S WRONG ?
ALL OUT OF OGRES ?
HOOOOOO
KRAK
PRE-PARE YOUR-SELF...
HOOOOOOO
...

SCROLL TEN
TAINTED INK

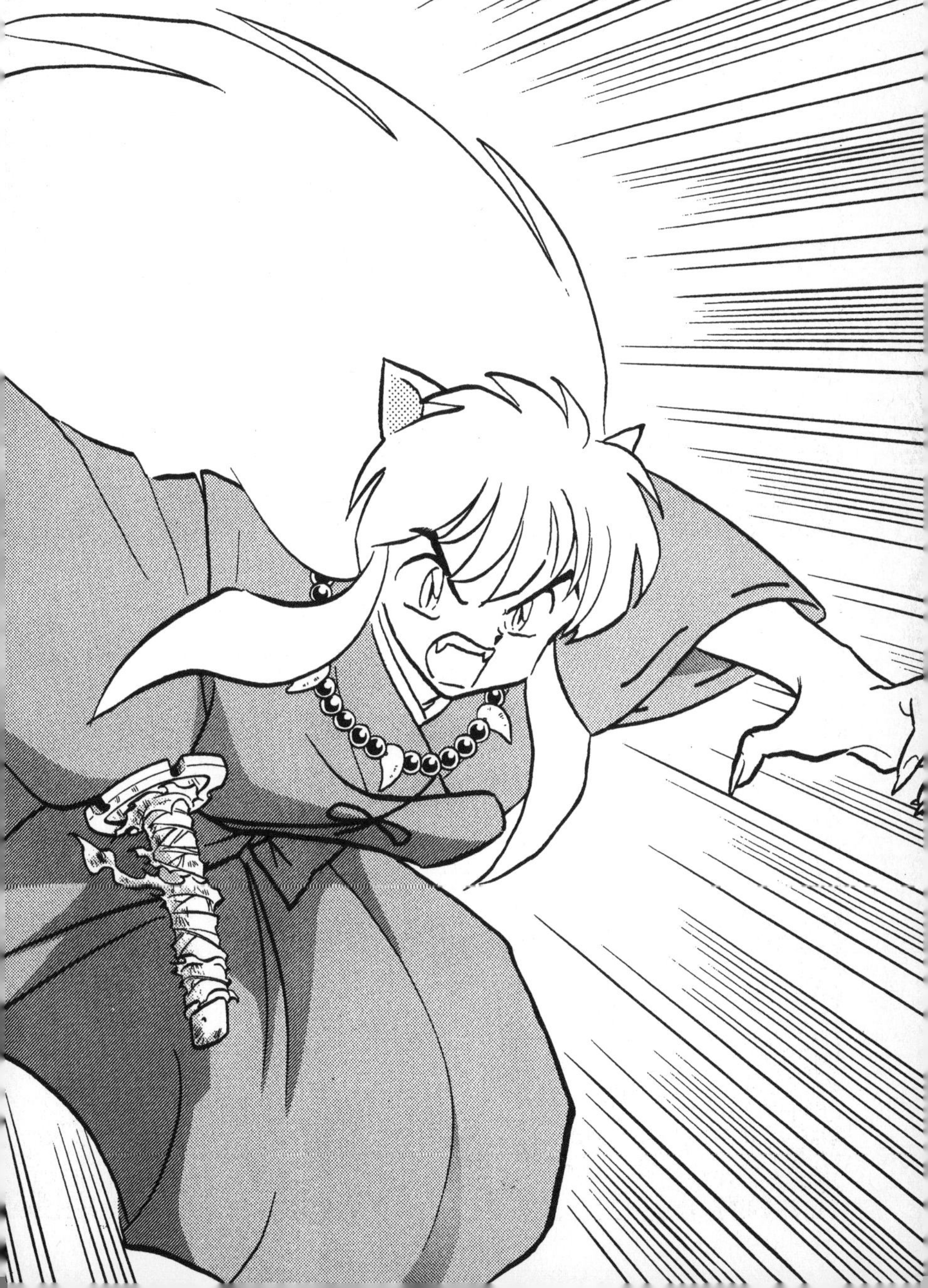

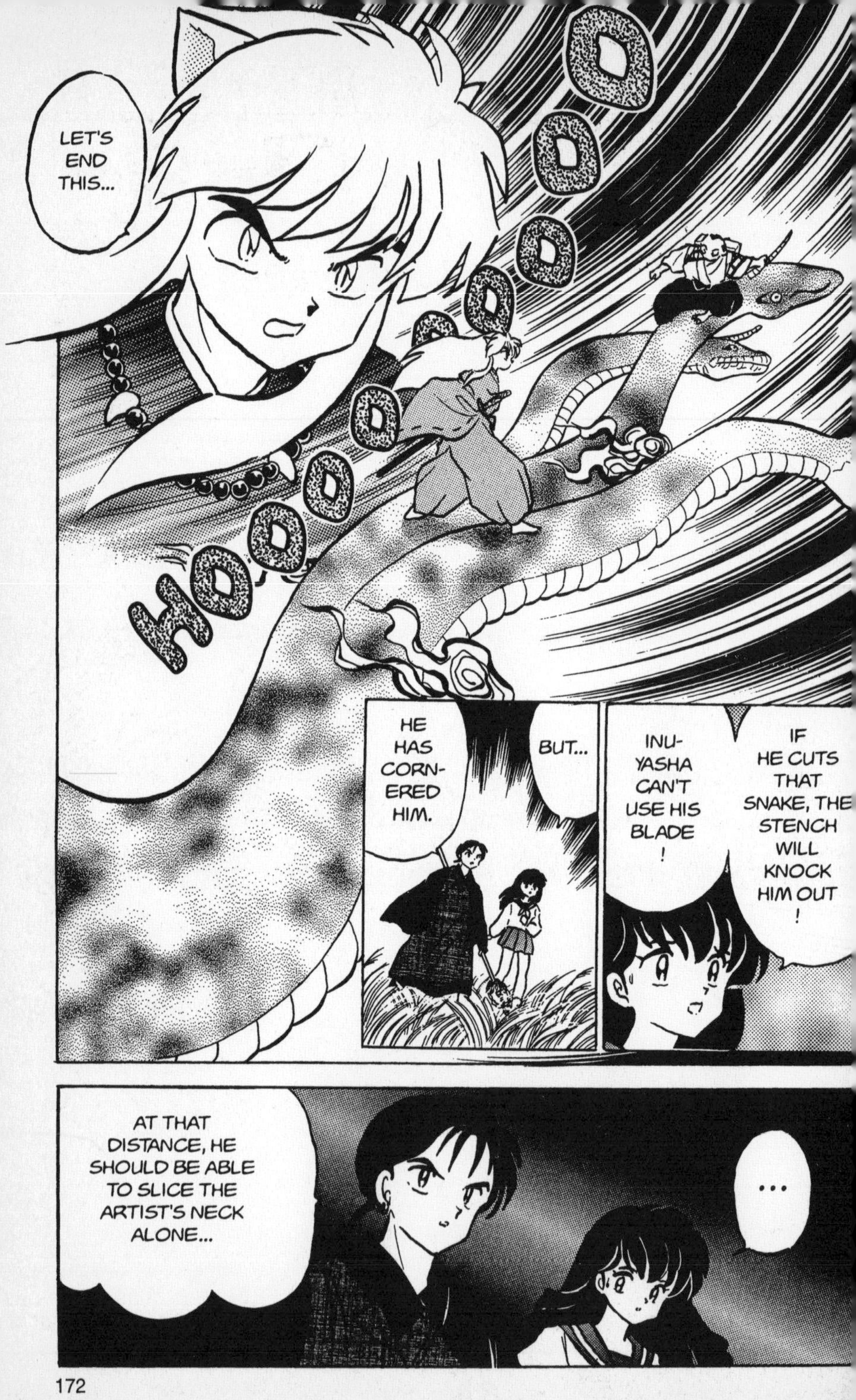
LET'S END THIS...
HOOOOOOOOO
HE HAS CORN-ERED HIM.
BUT...
INU-YASHA CAN'T USE HIS BLADE!
IF HE CUTS THAT SNAKE, THE STENCH WILL KNOCK HIM OUT!
AT THAT DISTANCE, HE SHOULD BE ABLE TO SLICE THE ARTIST'S NECK ALONE...
...

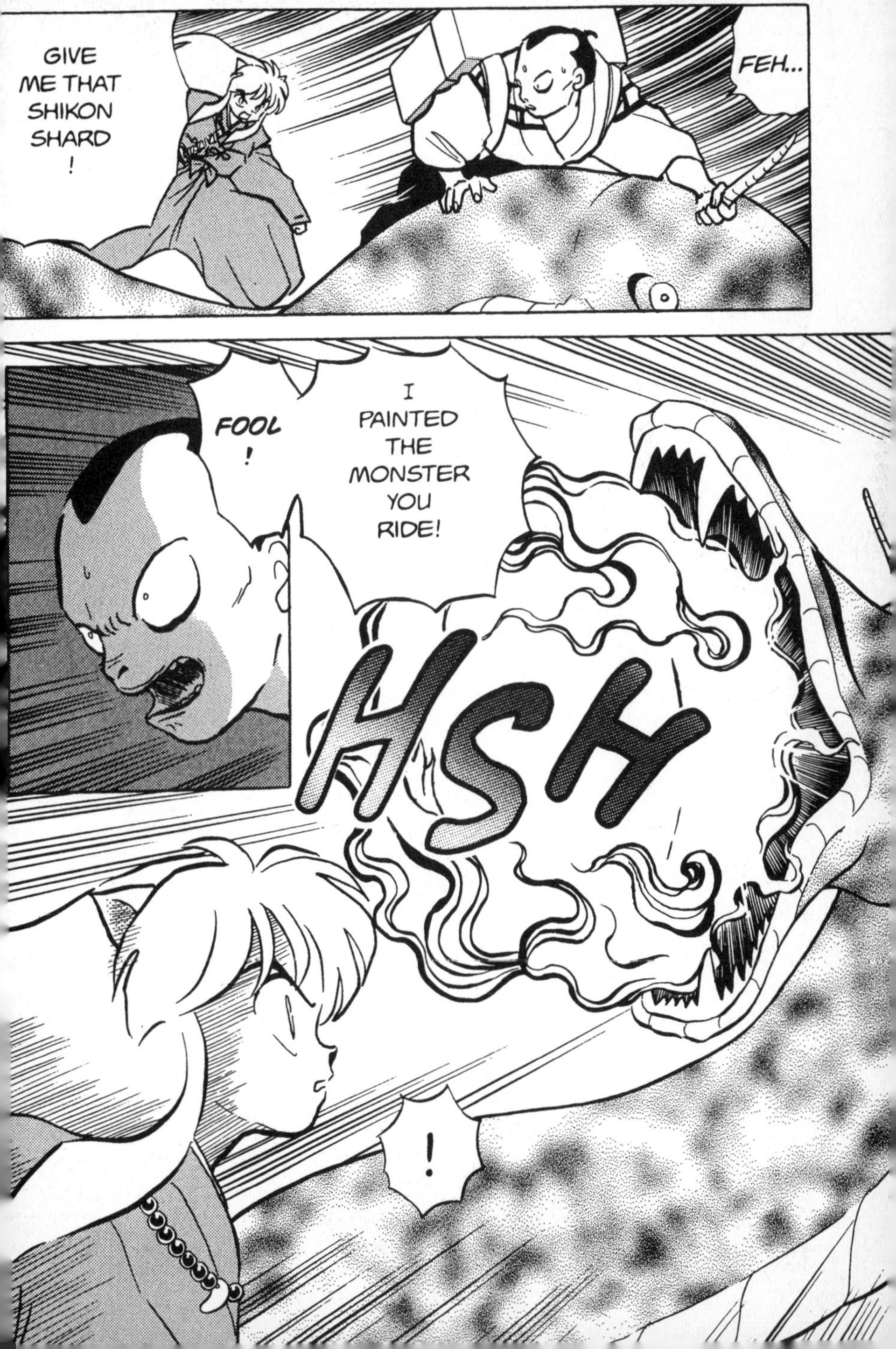
GIVE ME THAT SHIKON SHARD!
FEH...
FOOL!
I PAINTED THE MONSTER YOU RIDE!
HSH
!

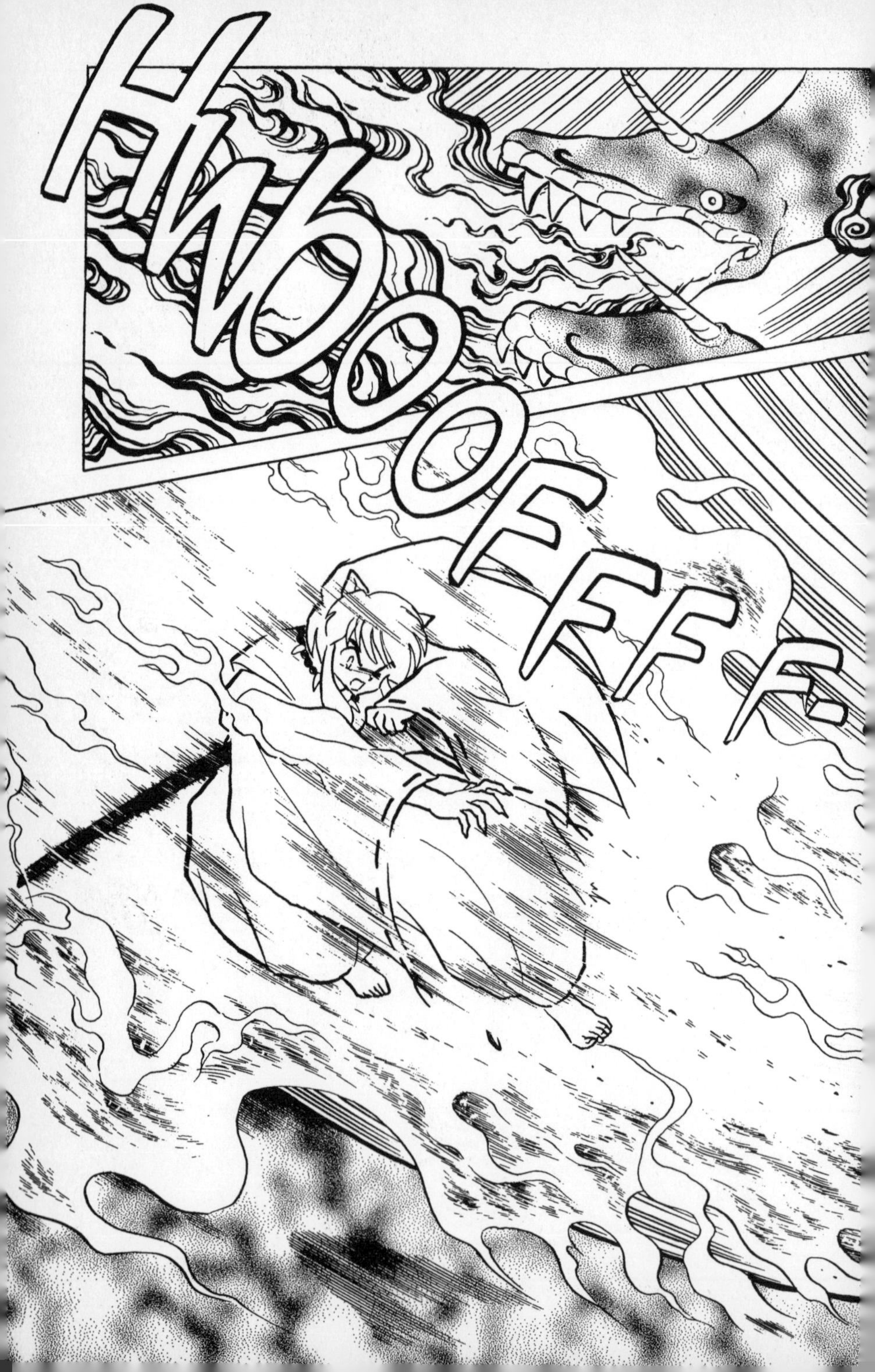
HWOOOOFFFF

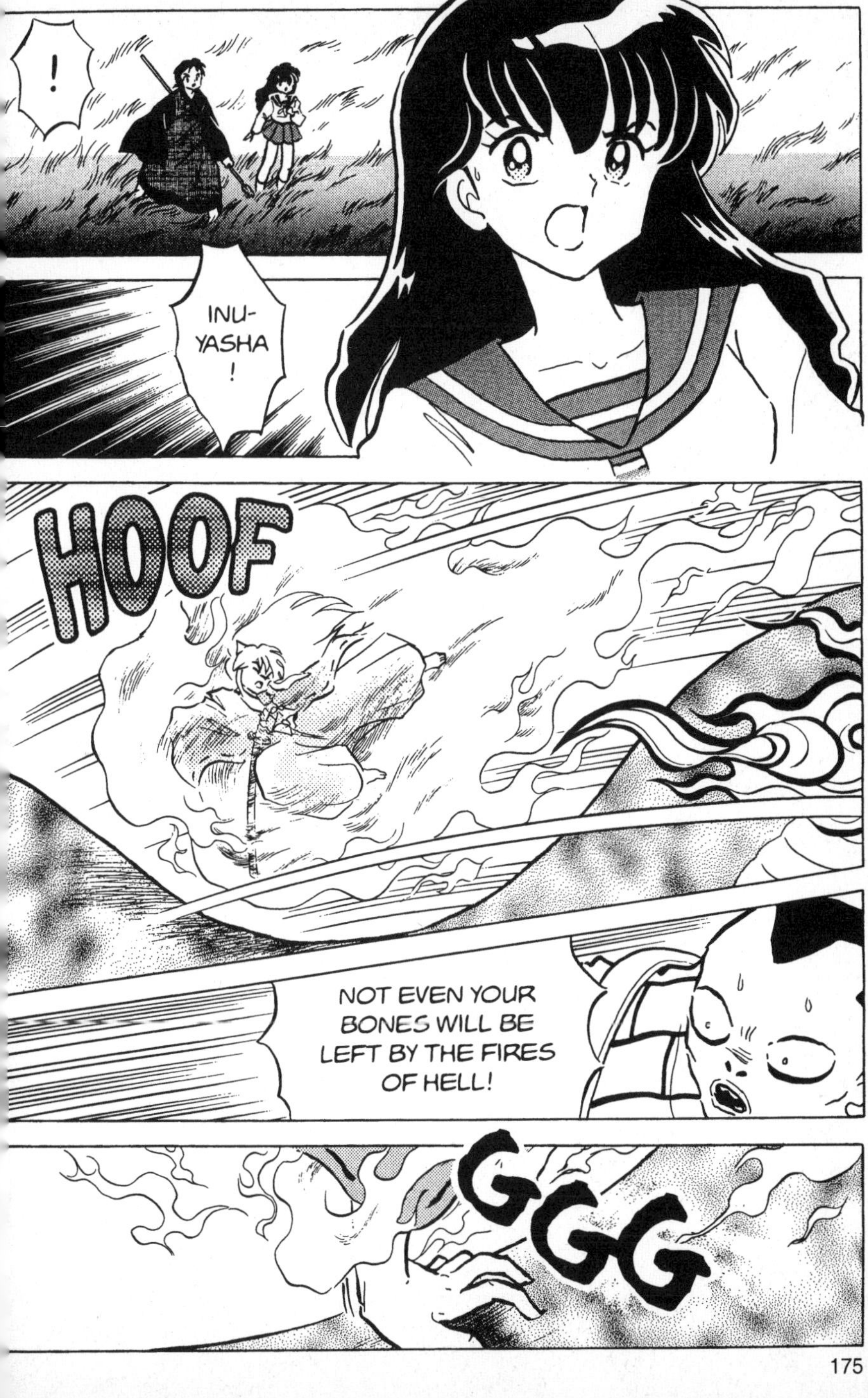
!
INU-YASHA!
HOOF
NOT EVEN YOUR BONES WILL BE LEFT BY THE FIRES OF HELL!
GGG

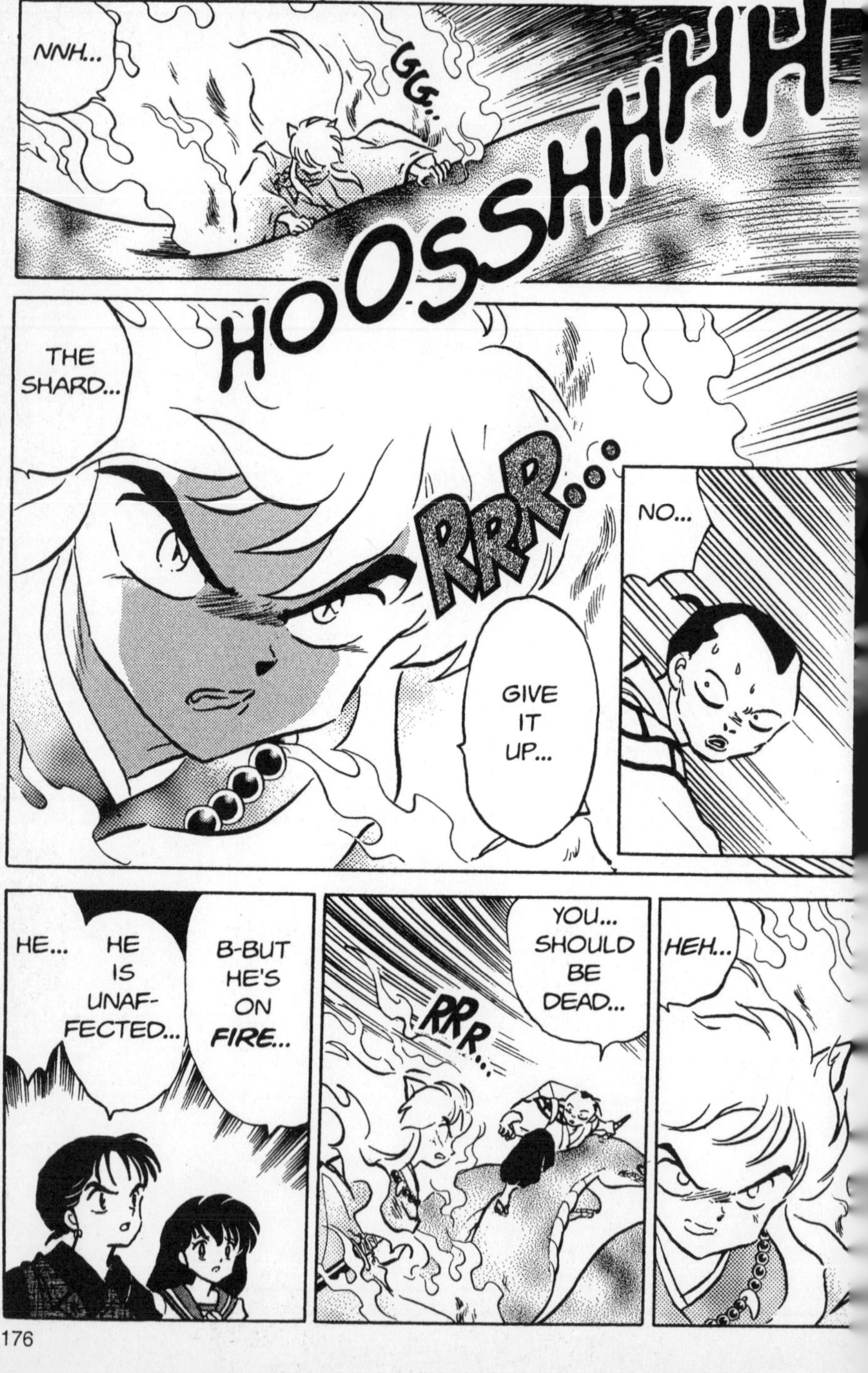
NNH...
GG..
HOOSSHHHHH
THE SHARD...
RRR...
GIVE IT UP...
NO...
HE...
HE IS UNAF-FECTED...
B-BUT HE'S ON *FIRE*...
RRR...
YOU... SHOULD BE DEAD...
HEH...

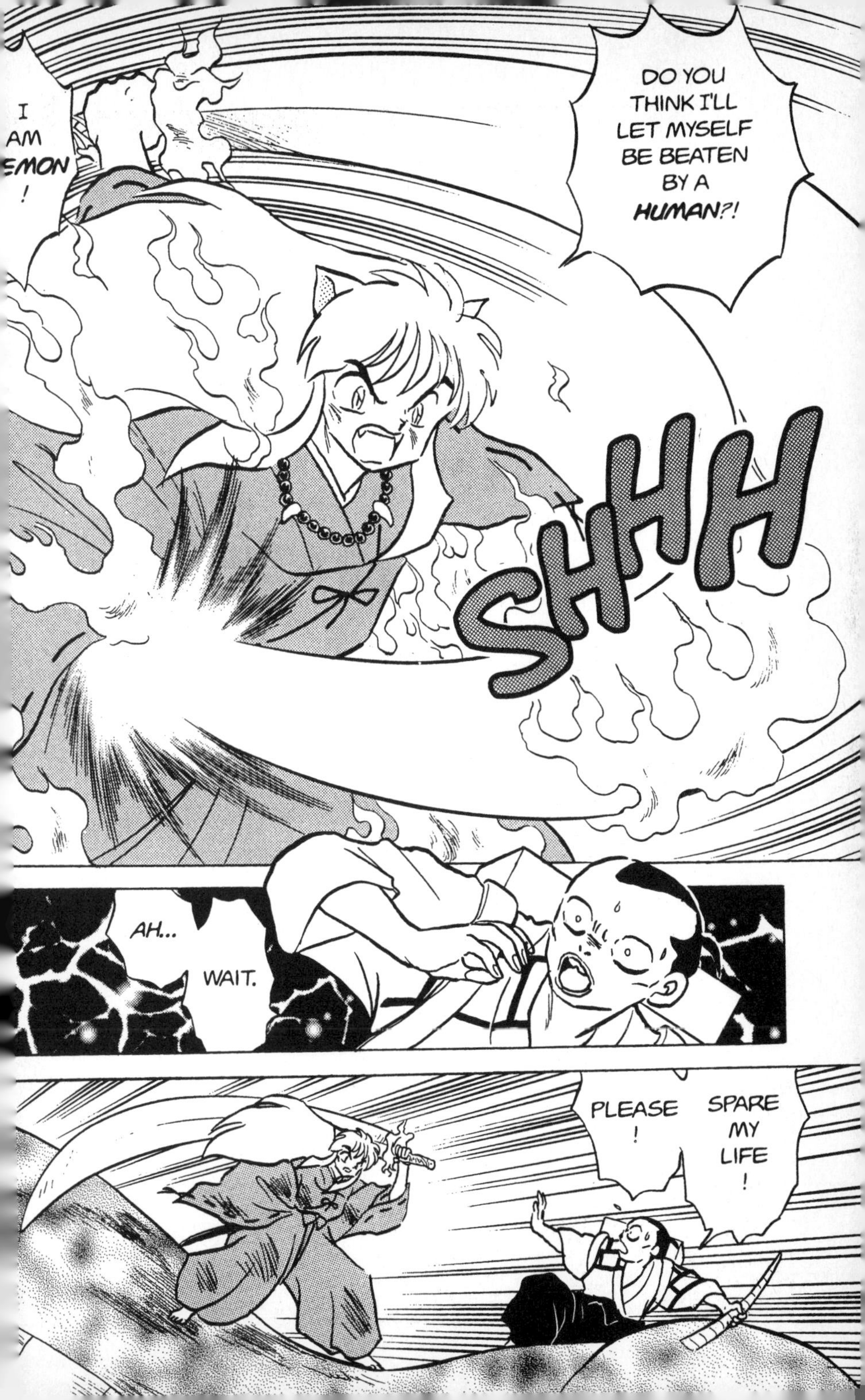
I AM EMON!
DO YOU THINK I'LL LET MYSELF BE BEATEN BY A HUMAN?!
SHHH
AH...
WAIT.
PLEASE!
SPARE MY LIFE!

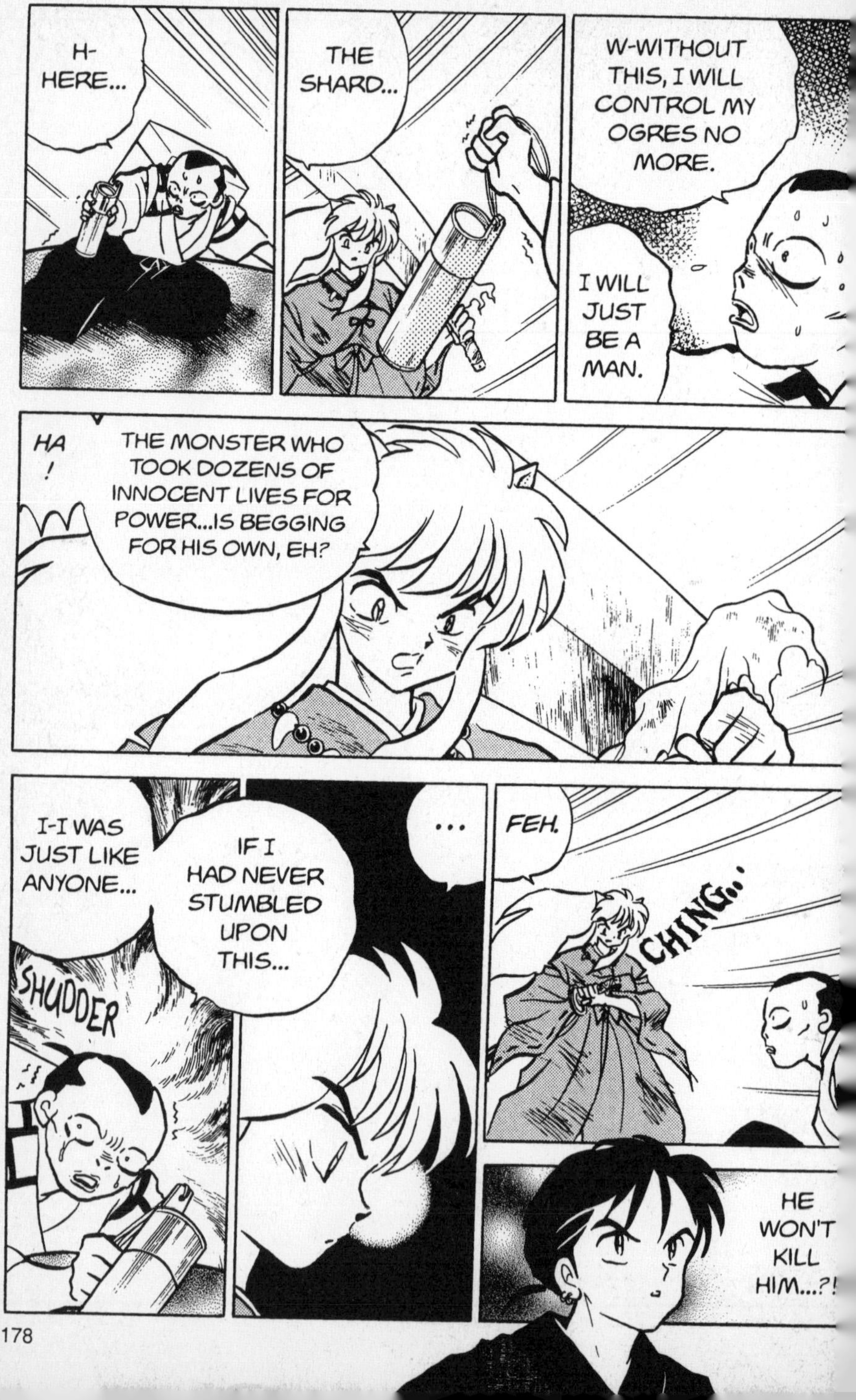
H-HERE...
THE SHARD...
W-WITHOUT THIS, I WILL CONTROL MY OGRES NO MORE.
I WILL JUST BE A MAN.
HA!
THE MONSTER WHO TOOK DOZENS OF INNOCENT LIVES FOR POWER...IS BEGGING FOR HIS OWN, EH?
I-I WAS JUST LIKE ANYONE...
IF I HAD NEVER STUMBLED UPON THIS...
SHUDDER
...
FEH.
CHING...
HE WON'T KILL HIM...?!

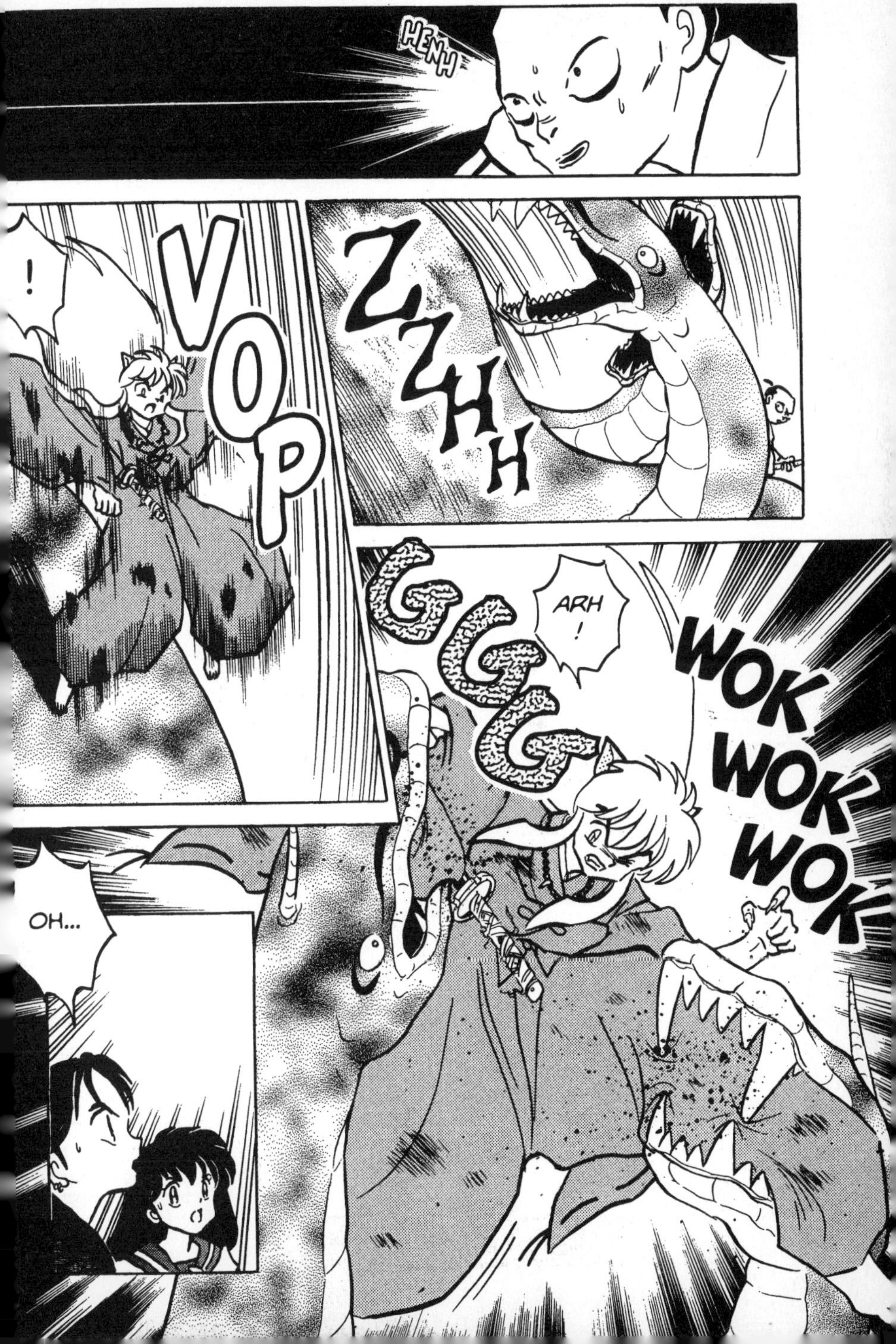
HENH
!
VOP
ZZZHHH
GGGG
ARH !
WOK WOK WOK WOK
OH...

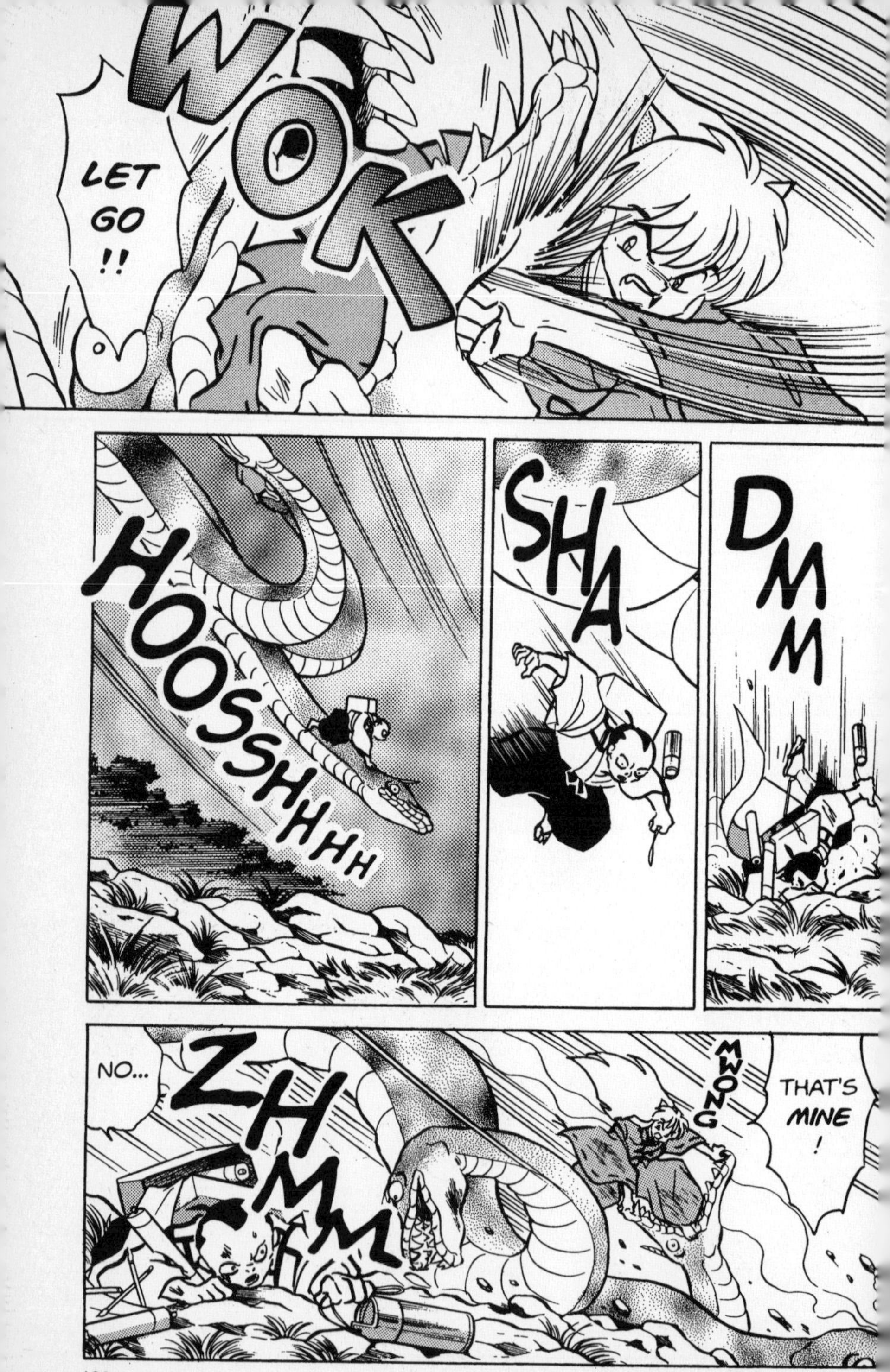
WOK
LET GO !!
HOOSSHHHHH
SHA
DMM
NO...
ZHMM
MWONG
THAT'S MINE !

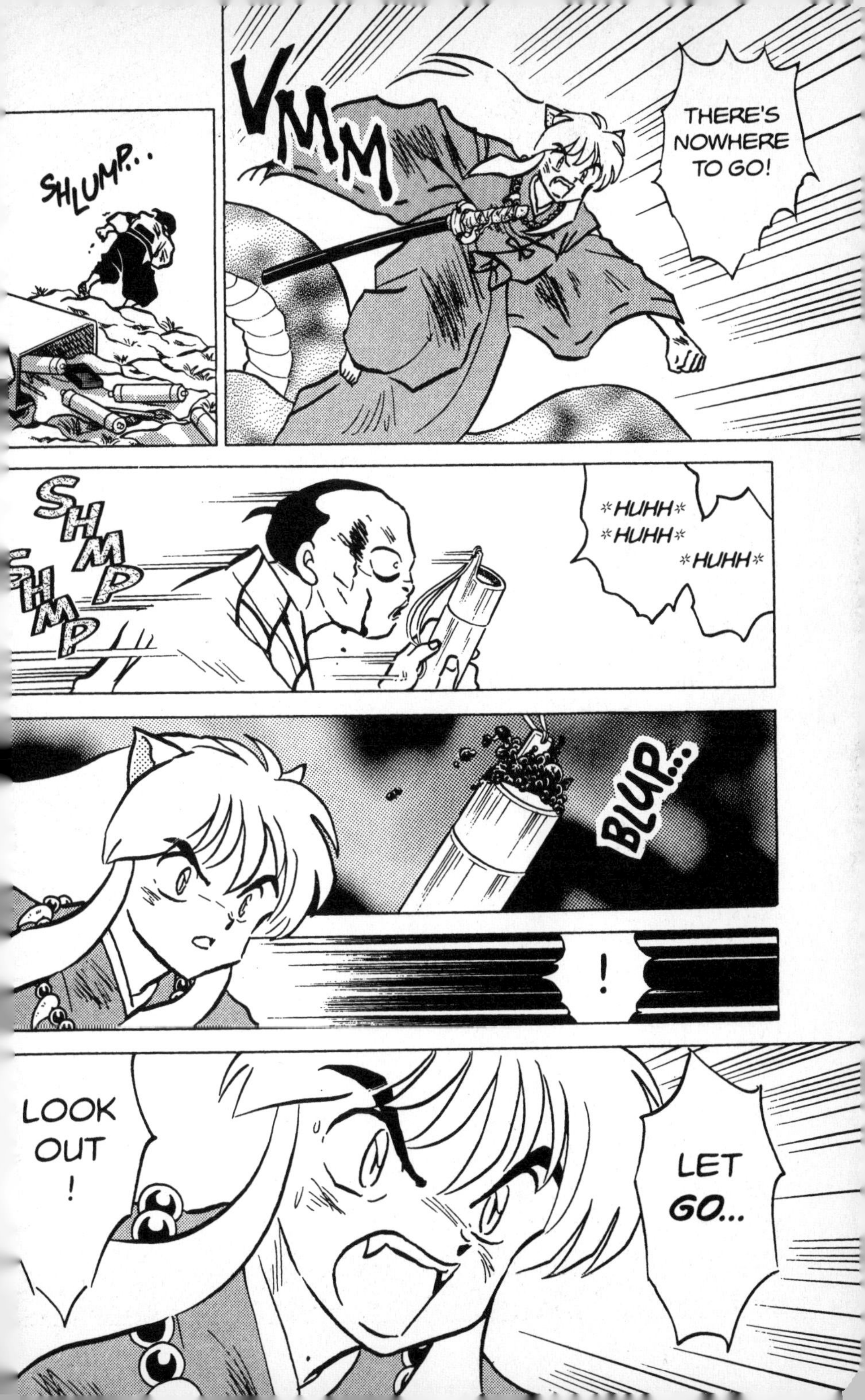
SHLUMP...
VMM
THERE'S NOWHERE TO GO!
SHMP SHMP
HUHH *HUHH* *HUHH*
BLUP...
!
LOOK OUT !
LET GO...

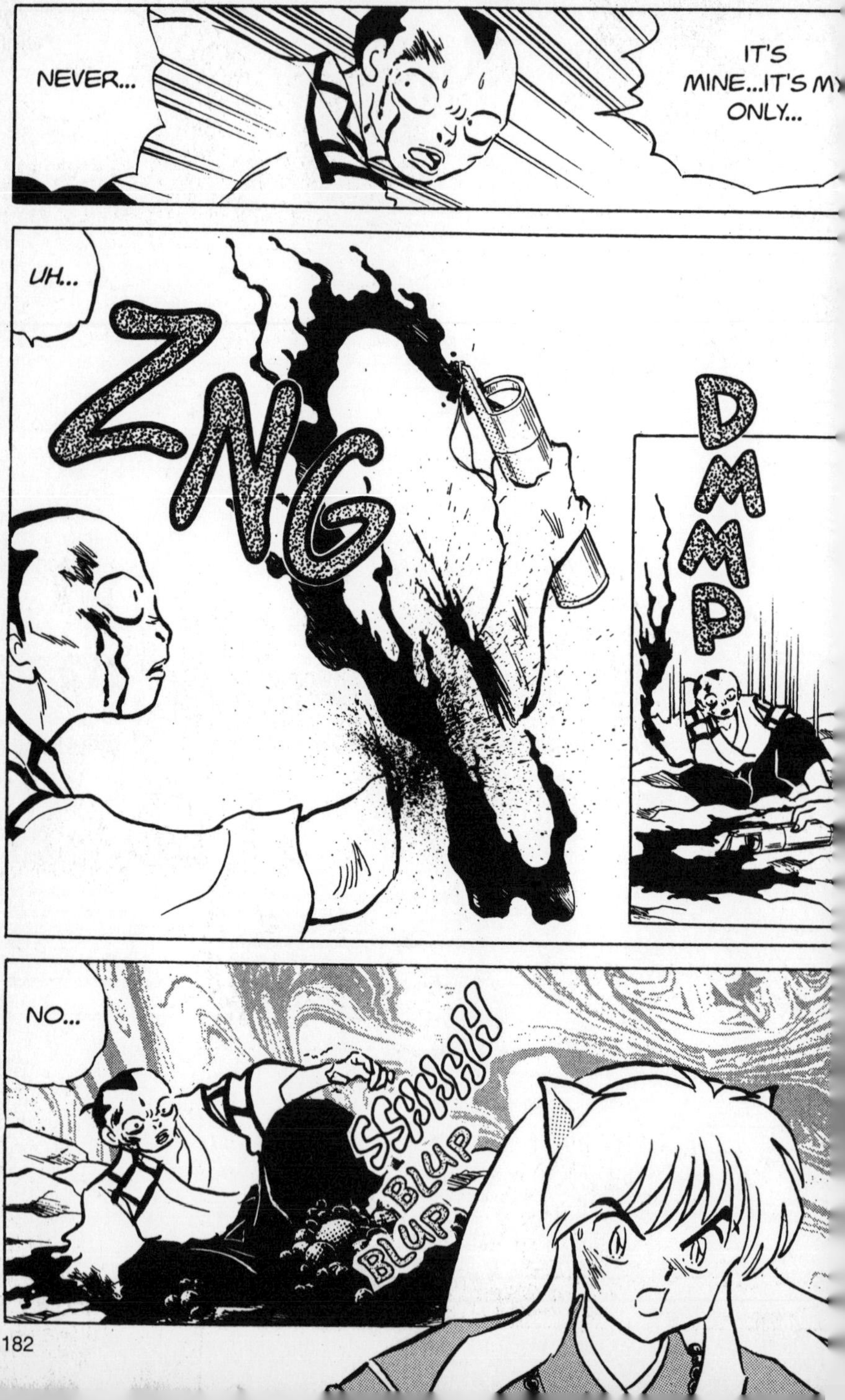
NEVER...
IT'S MINE...IT'S MY ONLY...
UH...
ZNG
DMMP
NO...
SSHHHHH
BLUP
BLUP

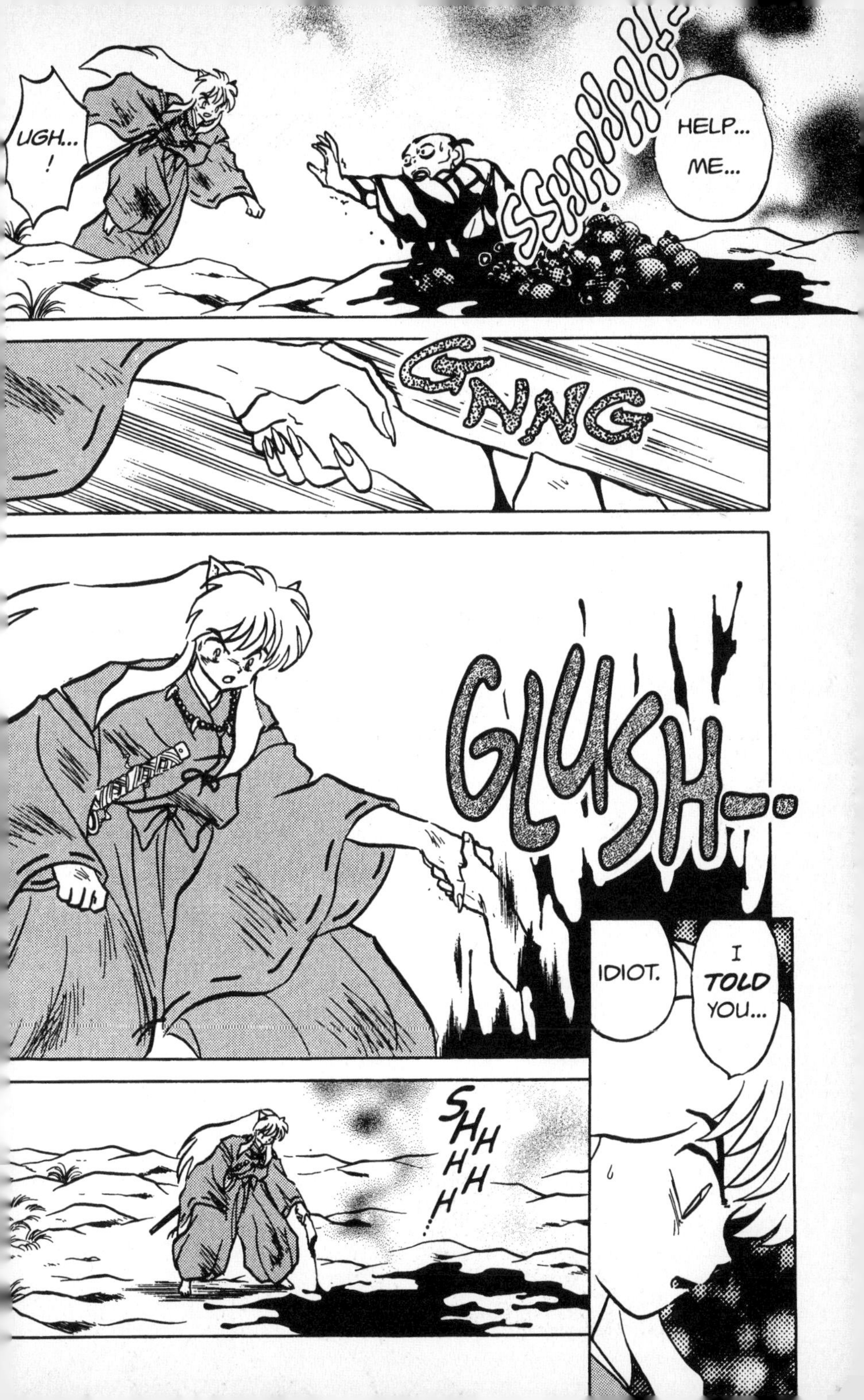

UGH...!
SSSHHHHHHHH...
HELP... ME...
GNNG
GLUSH...
SHHHHH...!
IDIOT.
I TOLD YOU...

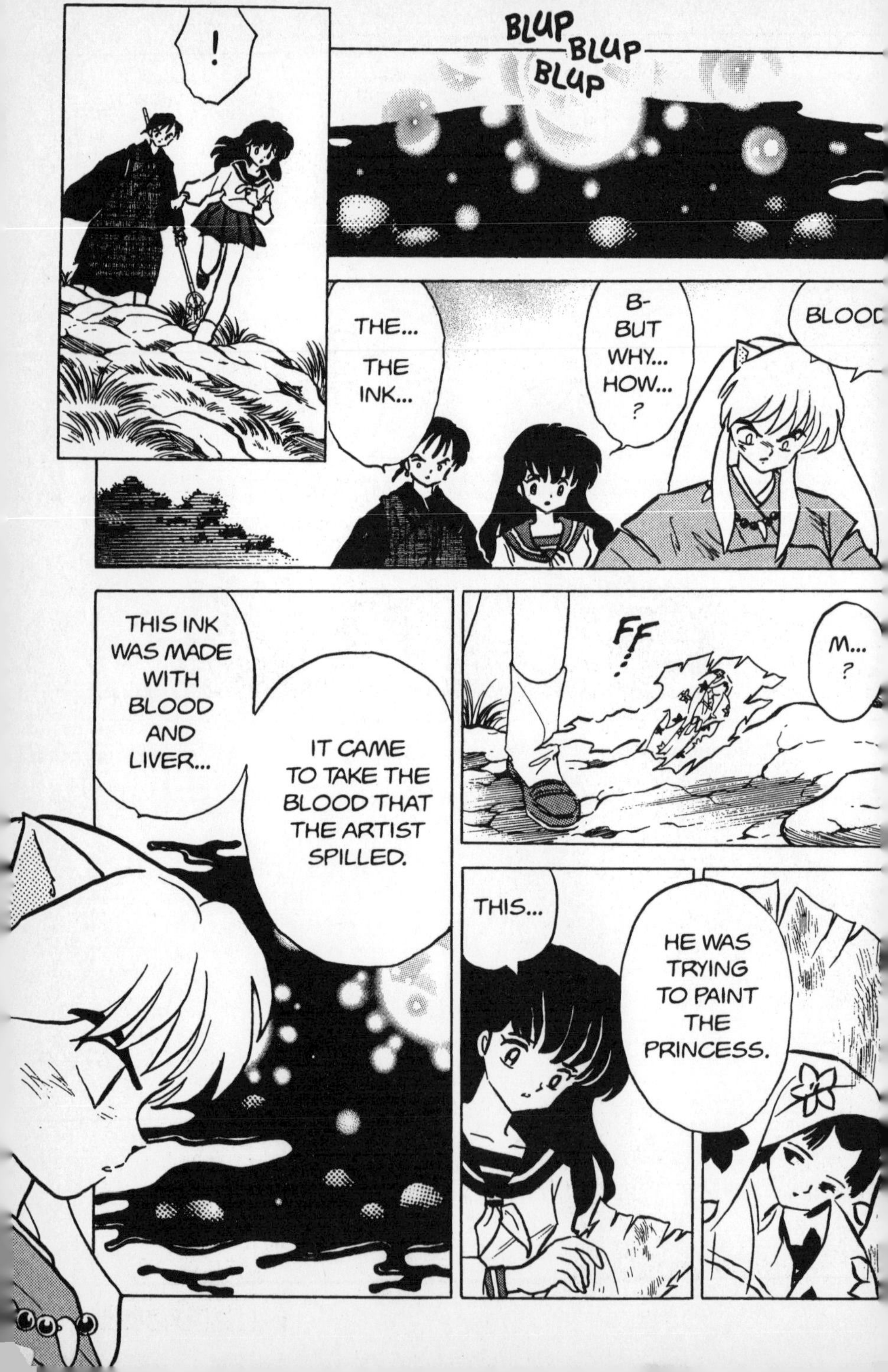
!
BLUP BLUP BLUP
THE... THE INK...
B- BUT WHY... HOW... ?
BLOOD
THIS INK WAS MADE WITH BLOOD AND LIVER...
IT CAME TO TAKE THE BLOOD THAT THE ARTIST SPILLED.
FF
M... ?
THIS...
HE WAS TRYING TO PAINT THE PRINCESS.

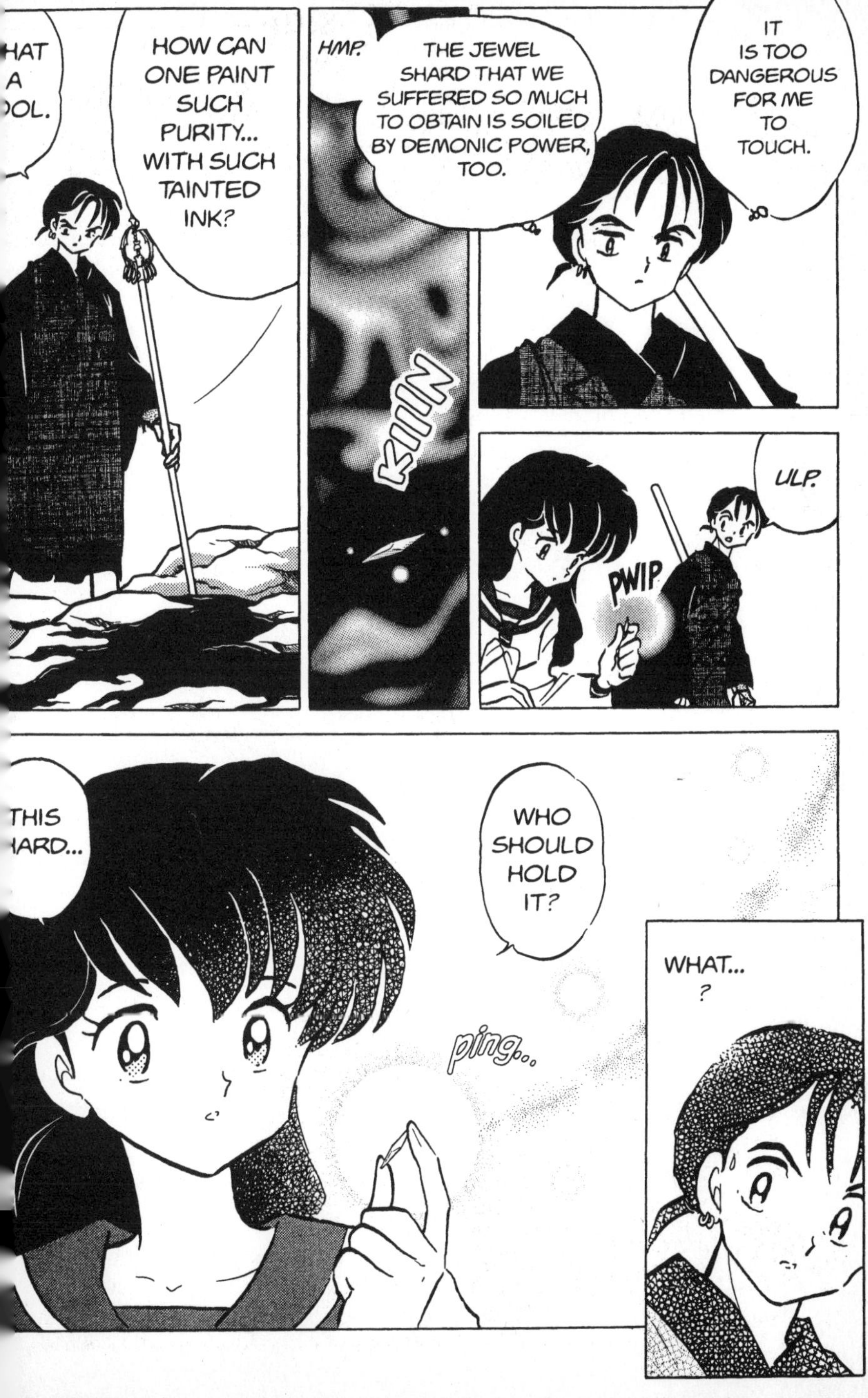
HAT A OOL.
HOW CAN ONE PAINT SUCH PURITY... WITH SUCH TAINTED INK?
HMP.
THE JEWEL SHARD THAT WE SUFFERED SO MUCH TO OBTAIN IS SOILED BY DEMONIC POWER, TOO.
KIIIN
IT IS TOO DANGEROUS FOR ME TO TOUCH.
PWIP
ULP.
THIS HARD...
WHO SHOULD HOLD IT?
ping..
WHAT...?

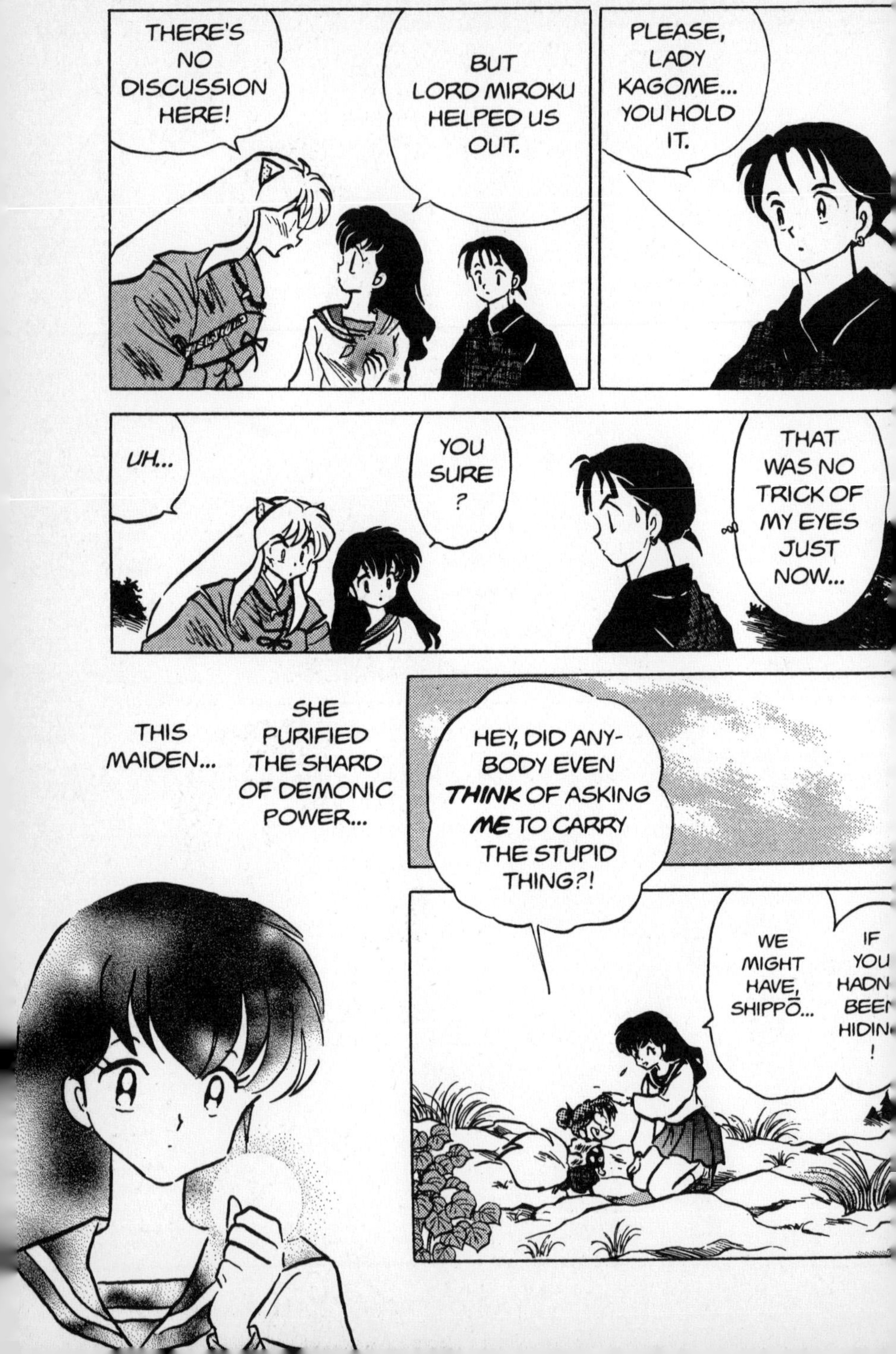

THERE'S NO DISCUSSION HERE!
BUT LORD MIROKU HELPED US OUT.
PLEASE, LADY KAGOME... YOU HOLD IT.
UH...
YOU SURE?
THAT WAS NO TRICK OF MY EYES JUST NOW...
THIS MAIDEN...
SHE PURIFIED THE SHARD OF DEMONIC POWER...
HEY, DID ANYBODY EVEN *THINK* OF ASKING *ME* TO CARRY THE STUPID THING?!
WE MIGHT HAVE, SHIPPŌ...
IF YOU HADN BEEN HIDIN !

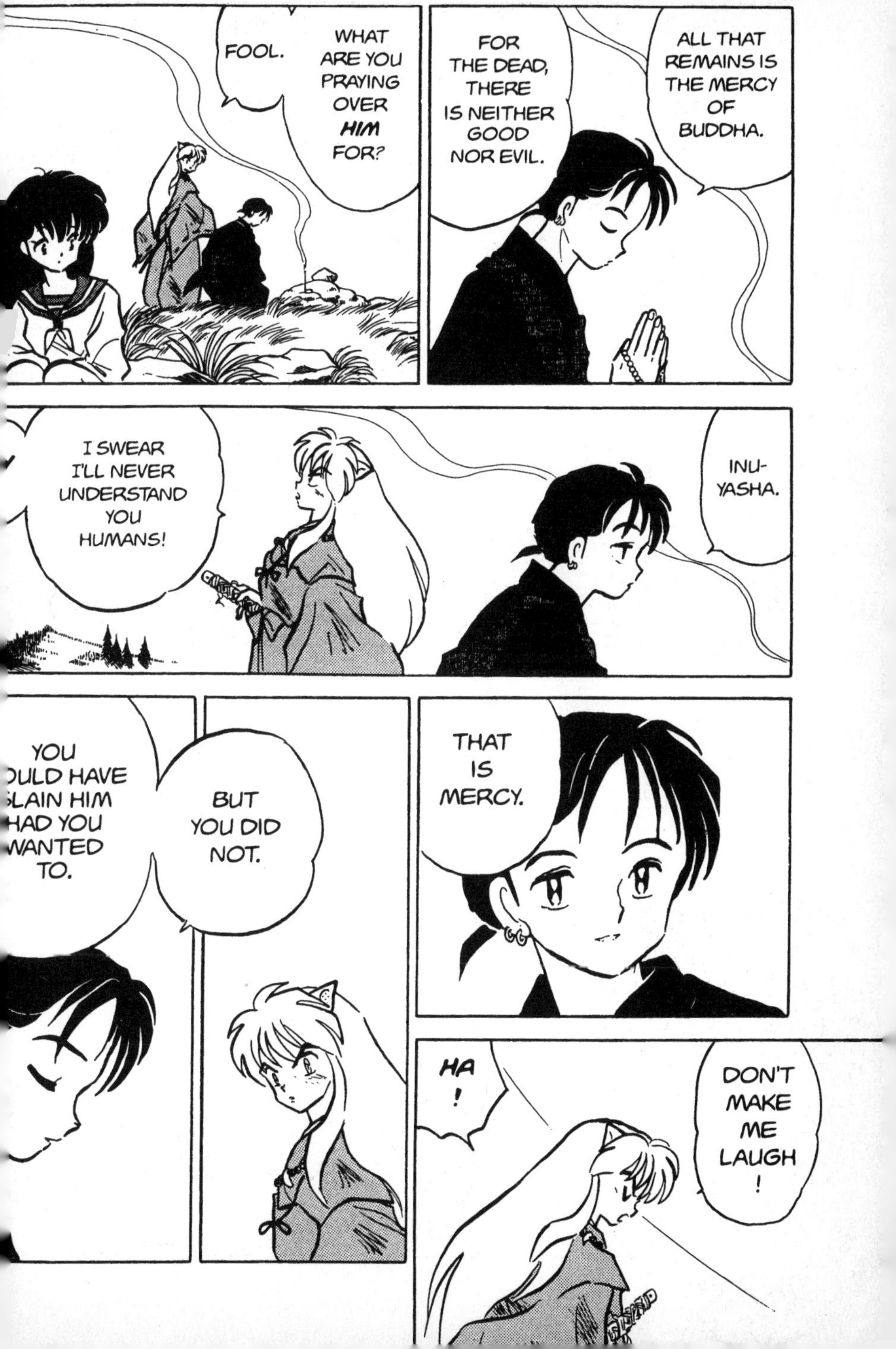
FOOL.
WHAT ARE YOU PRAYING OVER *HIM* FOR?
FOR THE DEAD, THERE IS NEITHER GOOD NOR EVIL.
ALL THAT REMAINS IS THE MERCY OF BUDDHA.
I SWEAR I'LL NEVER UNDERSTAND YOU HUMANS!
INU-YASHA.
YOU OULD HAVE LAIN HIM HAD YOU WANTED TO.
BUT YOU DID NOT.
THAT IS MERCY.
HA !
DON'T MAKE ME LAUGH !

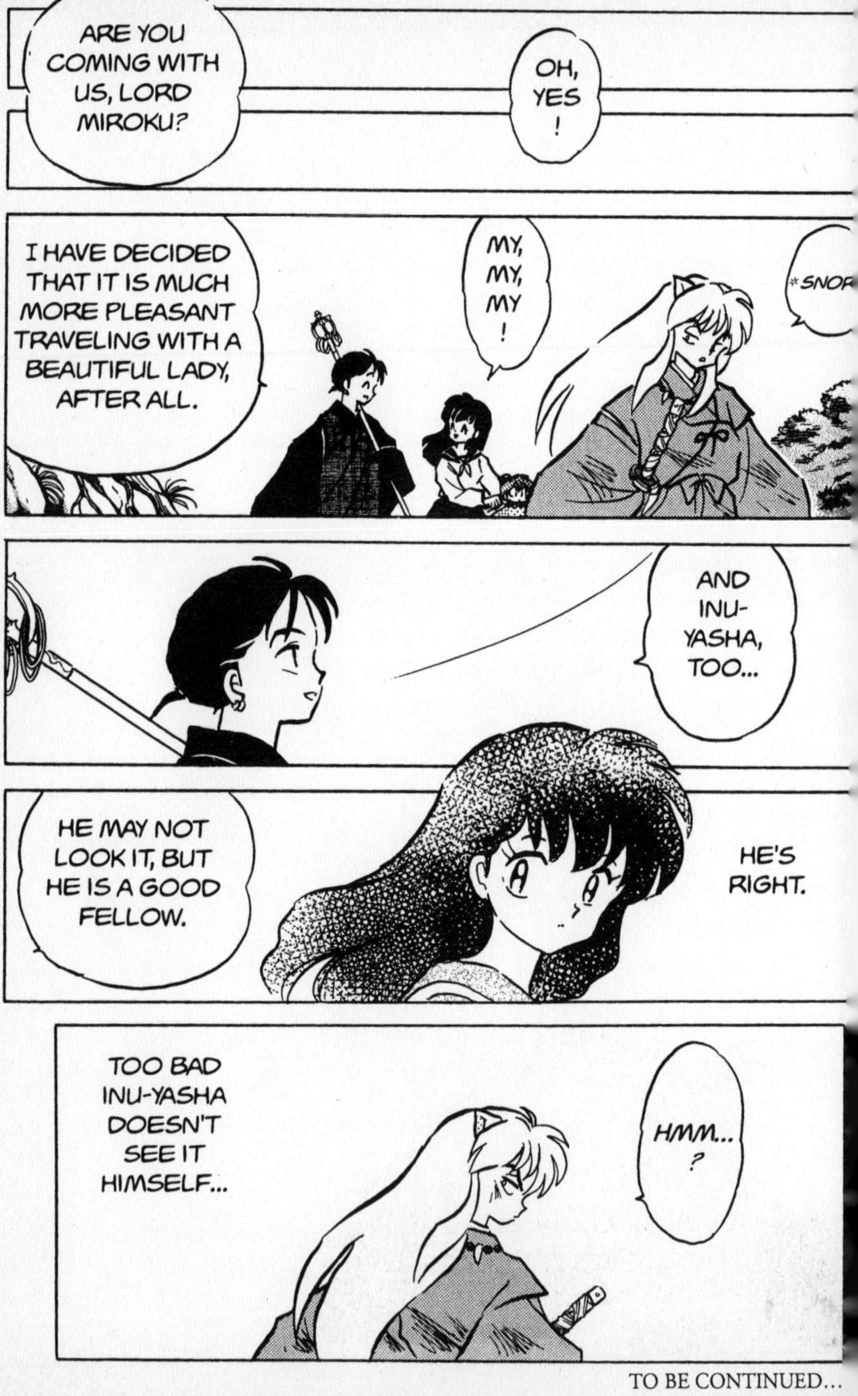
ARE YOU COMING WITH US, LORD MIROKU?
OH, YES!
I HAVE DECIDED THAT IT IS MUCH MORE PLEASANT TRAVELING WITH A BEAUTIFUL LADY, AFTER ALL.
MY, MY, MY!
*SNOR
AND INU-YASHA, TOO...
HE MAY NOT LOOK IT, BUT HE IS A GOOD FELLOW.
HE'S RIGHT.
TOO BAD INU-YASHA DOESN'T SEE IT HIMSELF...
HMM...?

TO BE CONTINUED...

Rumiko Takahashi

Rumiko Takahashi was born in 1957 in Niigata, Japan. She attended women's college in Tokyo, where she began studying comics with Kazuo Koike, author of *Crying Freeman*. In 1978, she won a prize in Shogakukan's annual "New Comic Artist Contest," and in that same year her boy-meets-alien comedy series *Lum*Urusei Yatsura* began appearing in the weekly manga magazine *Shônen Sunday*. This phenomenally successful series ran for nine years and sold over 22 million copies. Takahashi's later *Ranma 1/2* series enjoyed even greater popularity.

Takahashi is considered by many to be one of the world's most popular manga artists. With the publication of Volume 34 of her *Ranma 1/2* series in Japan, Takahashi's total sales passed one hundred million copies of her compiled works.

Takahashi's serial titles include *Lum*Urusei Yatsura, Ranma 1/2, One-Pound Gospel, Maison Ikkoku* and *Inu-Yasha*. Additionally, Takahashi has drawn many short stories which have been published in America under the title "Rumic Theater," and several installments of a saga known as her "Mermaid" series. Most of Takahashi's major stories have also been animated, and are widely available in translation worldwide. *Inu-Yasha* is her most recent serial story, first published in *Shônen Sunday* in 1996.